Dear Readers:

I grew up in the heart of urban New York City, so it was always a treat to spend summers in Maine. When I was a very small child, my parents and I rented houses, but after a while we bought a plot of land and had a full tent village. It was true luxury camping.

But there wasn't a lot to do in rural Maine, so I soon discovered the local library—a tiny place only open three days a week. I would take out ten books at a time, read them all before the library reopened, then exchange them for more. This was how I discovered a life-long love for romantic suspense with a paranormal twist.

Our land was right on the water, so most of my reading was done on a large rock on the beach. In those days, as soon as the tide went down, there would be harbor seals on all the exposed rocks. None of them ever came close enough to touch, but they were there, nonetheless.

So when I decided to start writing in the genre I had always loved, where better to set my story than in Maine? I have also always been drawn to the legends of the selkies. And when I learned that 400 grey seals—the breed that gives rise to most of those legends—live off the coast of Maine, a story was born.

For what if that group of seals was really more than it seemed? And what if magic did lurk on the fringes of our world? I can only hope you enjoy learning the answer as much as I loved creating it.

—Kate Brallier

SEAL ISLAND

KATE BRALLIER

tor romance

A TOM DOHERTY ASSOCIATES BOOK
NEW YORK

This is a work of fiction. All the characters and events portrayed in this book are either products of the author's imagination or are used fictitiously.

SEAL ISLAND

Copyright © 2005 by Kate Brallier

Edited by Anna Genoese

A Tor Book
Published by Tom Doherty Associates, LLC
175 Fifth Avenue
New York, NY 10010

www.tor.com

Tor® is a registered trademark of Tom Doherty Associates, LLC.

ISBN 0-765-34892-6
EAN 978-0765-34892-0

First edition: March 2005

Printed in the United States of America

0 9 8 7 6 5 4 3 2 1

This book is dedicated in loving memory
to my uncle, Ted—who, among so
many other things, gave me Maine.

I only wish I could have told you how much that
meant to me, and how much I still miss you.

Thanks go to the following:

To my stalwart agent, Kay McCauley, for having faith through the dark times.

To my Editress Extraordinaire, Anna Genoese—she of the boundless enthusiasm and energy—for strengthening the book in innumerable ways.

To my parents, for endless encouragement—and for following my uncle's lead and carting me up to Maine every summer since I was two and a half.

To the extraordinary real place in Maine that served as the genesis for Seal Island. I'm naming no names, for fear of drawing still more summer folks up, but those of you in the know might well recognize it, though I've played a bit fast and loose with geography . . .

To my aunt, Joan Weaver, for always being an impeccable hostess during my adult visits to said place, and for giving me insights into what life is like for those who live there year-round, or close to it—and the community that they can build.

And last, but certainly not least, to my own amazing author husband, David Keck, for adding his own brand of magic to my life. You are my joy and inspiration—and make my life better just by being in it. So thanks for taking the leap of faith and uprooting your life for me. It means the world.

1

SOMETIMES ALL IT TAKES to change your life is a single instant; no one knows that better than I. But the last thing I had expected, in early June of what some people might call the new millennium, was to find myself flying to Bangor, Maine, with my stable old life behind me, the bulk of my possessions packed into storage, two suitcases of assorted clothes and mementos between myself and the world, and an unknown future stretching out before me. But that was exactly where I found myself—for reasons I still couldn't quite comprehend or credit.

Aunt Allegra—not even a proper aunt, just my mother's younger cousin—had possessed little impact on my life beyond two brief visits in my youth and a bi-yearly phone call given more out of duty, I suspected, than any sort of family feeling. Not that I disliked her; there was a certain presence about Allegra that had always struck me. I just didn't know her. She had been my mother's friend, and I knew nothing about her background, her history, her habits, her likes, her loves. I knew even less about Seal Island, where she lived. Which was why it seemed odd that I, a city girl, was now headed there for a visit of unspecified length, to tie up Allegra's affairs and determine what to do with the house and business that had been deeded to me at her death.

But where else was I to go? I had no job, no apartment, and the safe, walled place I had built for myself had proved to be founded on sand. So why not Seal Island? What more could it take from me than New York already had? At times, it seemed that my life was a series of losses tempered by brief, intermittent periods of constancy. But a false constancy—one that was snatched away from me the moment I began to feel comfortable with it.

Only. . . . That sounded melodramatic and self-pitying, and who was I to complain? I still had my life. Allegra Gordon, at forty-five, had been deprived of hers in an instant.

Part of me still felt numb at the thought. Not that I was a stranger to violent death; my parents had taught me that lesson well, one snowy night in December. But, as with all broken resolutions, Allegra was one of those people I had always wished I knew better, had always planned to acquaint myself with. Tomorrow, next week, when this next crisis was over, when there was time. . . . Only there was never time, and now it was too late.

I still wasn't clear how on she had died—something quick and unexpected like a stroke or an embolism, I assumed. The lawyer who had called me had seemed oddly reluctant to discuss it, but by the catch in his voice as he imparted the news, I imagined her passing must have been harder for him, who had known her, than for me, who had not. Yet, she had left me her house, her business, and all that she had acquired in life. To a girl she had met but twice. To a girl who accepted her phone calls happily enough but never quite managed to make one of her own in return.

I stared out the plane window, feeling a sluggish guilt unfurl as I rested my cheek against the cold plastic and watched the scenery of New England stream by below me. Maine. It conjured up images of blueberries, bears and boats, and beloved children's books. Of sea and fog and gulls and, presumably, seals. Perhaps I had heard so much about it as a child that it had taken on almost mystical proportions for me—a place where magic could exist, or dreams could come true. Or perhaps I had just heard one too many people extol its virtues. Regardless, I had always longed to go, someday. But now someday was here, and I was on my way with no more than a few remembered phrases and routes highlighted on a hastily purchased map to guide me.

What, by all that was precious, was I *doing*?

Panic seized me, sudden as my guilt, and I clutched at my armrests, trying to distract myself with the fields and forests scrolling away below me. I hated change. The last time it had almost destroyed me; how would I weather it again? What was that popular phrase, "that which doesn't kill you can only make you stronger?" Only, I wasn't quite sure I believed it. I don't think I became stronger, just harder. More brittle. Most days I muddled along cheerfully enough, but on others I felt as if a breath of wind might crack me.

I had spent eight years shoring up walls around my world, so that the wind might not penetrate, and now look at me. I was twenty-eight years old and just "downsized," as the popular term would have it. Six years of company loyalty—or, more accurately, mindless and generic office drudgery—and now I was unemployed with three months of severance between myself and the future. And homeless to boot. The lease on the ridiculous box I called an apartment had expired, and a recent bout of "renovations" had skyrocketed the rent beyond my means. So it was either hunt for a new job and a new apartment at the height of the summer crunch, or . . . retreat to Maine for a few months. Rest, re-energize, and regroup away from the crushing heat, humidity and stench of a true New York summer, then return in September renewed.

Clearly, I had chosen the latter course.

A coward's act? Perhaps. Then again, maybe it was just what I needed. As the roar of the plane's engines rumbled dully in my ears, I forced myself to evaluate what had become of my life. Or rather, my existence, because gradually— and without my even realizing it—my life had taken on a dull sheen of bare necessity. I had worked six years at a job I didn't care about, and its greatest advantage was that it required no particular talents or ambitions. Anyone could have done it; for me, it was simply biding time. I had scraped together a few friends, but none terribly close—or perhaps none that I let get terribly close. No boyfriends, no lovers— short term or otherwise. No one I really cared about. I lived alone in a box, and my main passions had become cooking and reading. The former half out of necessity, because I was too poor to eat out a lot, and half because it added a surface color to my life and gave me an excuse to invite my acquaintances around for meals. Because then, packed around my cramped table in my even more cramped apartment, while wine and laughter and conversation flowed, I felt a part of something—but a something that departed as naturally as the guests out the door, that cleaned up as tidily as a sink full of dishes.

The reading seemed self-evident.

I clutched the Thomas Moreland paperback on my lap. In times of stress, I retreated to old favorites, and there was something about Moreland's books that had always appealed. They were top-notch legal thrillers, of course—and as such a good distraction—but there was also something in them that went beyond that: a way of portraying characters that seemed intensely honest—and intensely real. Flawed people, struggling to do good. Struggling to uphold their convictions, sometimes against impossible odds. I had sometimes thought that if only I could act that way, then everything would be all right. The spell would be broken, the sleeping princess would come out of her shell, and I would lose my dull fear of the world and its consequences.

On my more cynical days, I even wondered if I *had* convictions, any more. There were days when not hiding seemed such a monumental task that I couldn't conceive of anyone ever managing it—the books' author included. Because, really, what did anyone know about him? He was as much a mystery to the world as my life was at times to me. No bio beyond the minimal: "Thomas Moreland served as a Boston A.D.A. before turning to writing full-time;" no author photo. So maybe he, too, was hiding—which could be another way to explain the connection I had always felt to his work.

I let a small laugh trickle through my lips and turned my attention back to the scenery below me. The further north we flew, the less it seemed that summer—let along spring— had penetrated the land. There were still large patches of bare, muddy ground, and where I could see the ocean it looked cold and grim. Yet, instead of depressing me, this gave me new heart. Maybe this was exactly what I needed. Maybe, like the coming summer, Maine could wake something in me that would enable me to return to the city with a new energy, a new outlook. And maybe all it took to wake the princess was simply a decent vacation.

I smiled to myself. Besides, the lawyer who had called me—Harry Cameron—had sounded quite attractive on the phone the few times we had spoken. There was a comforting

resonance to his voice, tinged ever so faintly with what I had
to assume was a New England accent. And as he had gotten
over the shock of Allegra's death, a natural sense of humor
had begun to assert itself that often had me smiling into my
end of the phone. Not that it would be easy, I reminded myself, coming into a small community and claiming the life
and possessions of a woman who had only been dead a
month; I had no doubt there would be repercussions I was
not even aware of now. But if Harry Cameron's demeanor
were any indication, there might still be more of a welcome
for me on Seal Island than in impersonal, suspicious New
York.

Even the weather seemed to support this, for the plane
eventually touched down into one of the most welcoming
days I had seen in a long time. It was sunny and in the six-
ties, crisp and cool in the shade, warmer in the sun. The air
held a sharp, ineffable freshness and I inhaled wonderingly,
amazed how I had existed all these years breathing the
choked haze of the city. Everything felt fresh here. Even the
potential complications of picking up my leased car did not
occur. The clerks were both friendly and courteous, and keys
in hand, I loaded my two suitcases and one carry-on into the
trunk, laid the map out beside me, and took the wheel, grateful I had not let the drivers' license I had gained in college
expire.

THE DRIVE TO SEAL Island was a long one, and could
have been tedious had I not been gripped by a continued excitement. But that delightful feeling of newness had not yet
faded, so I rolled the windows down and tuned the radio to
something joyous, aware beneath the music of the rumble of
the engine, the hiss of wheels on asphalt, the rush of wind
through the open windows. When it got cold, I turned up the

heat, unwilling to lose the freshness of the Maine air. And wondered why I hadn't done this years ago.

As it was, I smelled the ocean before I saw it. But soon it was before me, steel blue and frosted with white-caps in the breeze. At first it was revealed only in pockets, peeping shyly through dips in the hills and gaps in the pines. And later, in glittering stretches, revealing islands slabbed with granite ledges and capped with bristling pines. Sails dotted the water, the boats scudding before the wind. Picture-book perfect, but too much so to be real?

For once, I refused to let my suspicions spoil the moment.

Unerring signs directed me toward Seal Island, amidst markers for such places as Blue Hill, Sedgewick and Brooklin—the latter delighting my New York soul. I was deep in the heart of the country now, and the houses scattered along the side of the road were an odd mixture of tumble-down and gracious. They ranged from gleaming, whitewashed residences to little more than tarpaper shacks, their yards spanning a spectrum from manicured lawns and gardens to piles of rusted-out cars and appliances. Moreover, there seemed to be no rhyme nor reason to their placement—the posh shoulder to shoulder with the impoverished—and this delighted me as well. There was something so egalitarian about it.

I was aware from the signs that I was getting close to my destination, but even I was amazed at the suddenness with which my leased Honda seemed to be swept bodily around a curve and onto the Seal Island causeway. The scent of the ocean increased threefold, the salt stinging my nostrils, and the air grew perceptibly colder. Seal Island, as Harry Cameron had informed me, was a true island, but set close enough to the mainland that it didn't need a bridge to connect it, just this winding stretch of roadway across Jericho Bay. It must have been high tide, for the waves lapped aggressively against the large rocks bordering the causeway, as if given reason they would wash against my tires, driving me back. I imagined the water as a guardian spirit, carefully considering each visitor, choosing to grant or deny them access on the whims of its perception.

Fortunately, I must have passed the test, for four sweeping arcs of causeway later I was on Seal Island.

The houses were more unassuming, here—some clapboard, some shingle: the latter weathered to a ghostly silver-grey, the former painted white and red and pink and green. And once, even, an improbable purple. In the yards were lawn ornaments and more rusted cars; lobster traps and buoys. Quaint signs proclaimed bed-and-breakfasts, announced craftsmen and artisans. One, Cassel's Woodcrafts, made me laugh, for it advertised itself as a maker of signs, of all things, yet its own sign showed a distinct lack of planning, the letters dribbling off into a crooked heap at the end. Private drives yawned off the main road at intervals, presumably leading to the grander, sea-side dwellings such as I had passed on the mainland.

Then the road curved again and regained the coast, and I could see the smaller islands dotting the bay, giving shape to the view. Larger houses ghosted from clearings by the water: some traditional like the whitewashed Victorians, some more modern, often shingled and more than half glass. Save for a few exceptions—and those strewn with boulders as if from a giant's hand—the beaches seemed to consist of slablike ledges of pink-and-grey granite. One island, not far off the coast and consisting of no more than barren rock, was scattered with black blots, curved up at both ends like a series of miniature anvils.

The road turned inland again, the houses growing denser, then swept back out into a half-moon cove, around which clustered the town and the public docks. Boats bobbed at anchor—twenty or thirty, as near as I could tell—ranging from tiny motorboats to luxury sailboats, with a handful of what could only be working fishing boats thrown in. There seemed a bustle of activity around the longest of the docks; less so on the streets. A scattering of summer folk—the merest tickle before the seasonal flood, I would later discover—browsed the shops, dressed in outfits from J. Crew, Eddie Bauer, and L.L. Bean.

I had dressed carefully for the occasion—neither too formal nor too fancy, not wanting to either underdress or overwhelm—but now my jeans, boots and green V-necked sweater seemed hopelessly understated.

I pulled my car into parking space, rolled up the windows and locked it out of sheer force of habit, then shrugged into a brown leather jacket as I examined the main street. It stretched about two city blocks, anchored at one end by a brown and green post office, and at the other end by what looked to be an upscale restaurant and inn, backed by a garden that swept down to the water. There were tourist shops and galleries, a hardware store and a supermarket. And, to my delight, a smallish library. About three more streets angled off from the main road, seeming to contain further shops and galleries.

At a glance, none of the establishments seemed to boast a lawyer or house what might pass in these parts as a law office. So I headed for the library, as much to survey their collection as to ask for directions. But on second glance, taking in the darkened windows, I realized it must be closed. I stood uncertainly on the sidewalk for a moment, brushing back hair which the wind seemed determined to disorder, then chose a shop at random.

It was a tourist shop, but tasteful. It was called simply The Gull, and had a welcoming exterior with flower-boxes beneath the windows—though the blooms had been blown somewhat ragged by the breeze. As I opened the door, the wind chimes mounted above it tinkled merrily. Inside was an eclectic collection of cards, books and local crafts, mingled with the inevitable T-shirts and postcards. And, of course, stuffed seals.

Had I been the type to credit premonitions, I might have felt a frisson of inevitability. But as it was, I simply felt at home. Behind the counter, a woman—the shop owner, presumably—was engaged in a sale. She looked about thirty-five, slightly plump, with erratically curled reddish-blond hair and a sparkle in her hazel eyes. Her customer—as pampered and sour-faced as I have ever seen—could not seem to make up her mind between a blue T-shirt and a green sweatshirt, both with "Seal Island" imprinted on them. Judging from her comments, she seemed to dislike both equally.

The shopkeeper spared me a fraction of a glance—enough to assure her I was not a similarly high-maintenance prospect—then went back to her sale. Not wanting to interfere (and wishing her the best of luck with it), I drifted toward the back of the shop, delighted to discover a rack of paperbacks. Someone, it seemed, liked Thomas Moreland as much as I did. I skimmed though the titles, vaguely aware of the two women's voices behind me as they concluded their sale, the tinkle of chimes as the elder of the two departed, leaving me the sole customer.

Nonetheless, I still found myself startled when a soft voice from behind me said, "I'm sorry about that. Is there anything I can help you with?"

I jumped and whirled, restoring the book I was examining to its rack, feeling vaguely guilty about handling merchandise I had no intention of buying. But if my reaction was a bit extreme, I was not in the least prepared for the shopkeeper's.

She literally tottered two steps backwards, her face draining so severely of color that it revealed a scattering of freckles across her nose and cheeks like rocks uncovered at low tide. One hand was clutched to her chest as if to hold her heart within it by sheer force of will.

"Allegra?" she breathed.

2

HER WORDS CAUGHT ME completely by surprise.

"Excuse me?" I stammered, and the woman took a deep breath, pushing back her hair. The color flooded violently back into her cheeks, obscuring the freckles.

"It's nothing," she said, waving a hand. "Foolishness. You just caught me off guard is all." She fashioned a smile, then recognition flared in her eyes. "Of course; you must be Cecilia Hargrave. I knew you were coming, but I just didn't expect you to walk in so . . . well, unannounced!"

I blinked. "I'm sorry? I just got into town and was looking for Harry Cameron's office, and when I couldn't find it I just . . ."

". . . walked into the first place you found to ask directions?" The woman completed my sentence in chagrin. "Oh, dear. I really have made a muddle of things, haven't I?"

"I . . ."

"So you really don't know?"

Despite my best intentions, my voice became a little sharper. "Know what?"

She took another deep breath; it seemed to anchor her. "I'm sorry. I've gone about this all wrong. You *are* Cecilia Hargrave, aren't you?"

"Cecil," I said. "But yes."

She stuck out a hand, and I shook it automatically. "I'm Abby Cantwell," she said almost sheepishly, peering at me as if expecting recognition to dawn.

An instant later, it did. I knew that name from Harry Cameron's briefings. Abby Cantwell had been Allegra's assistant and second-in-command. She had even offered to buy Allegra's business if I was interested in selling—though Harry Cameron had seemed less than certain about that prospect. I felt another sluggish stirring of guilt. Here I was, come to tie up Allegra's affairs, and it had never occurred to me to determine exactly what the nature of her business was.

From what I recalled of Allegra, this was the last thing I would have expected. Yet, in another way, it made perfect sense. I looked around the shop with new eyes. It had Allegra's sense of style written all over it. But why she had chosen to deed it to me instead of to Abby, who had managed it with her for all those years, remained a mystery.

"Abby," I managed, since my new . . . employee, I suppose, was staring at me expectantly. "Good Lord. Well, it's . . . nice to meet you."

She smiled, revealing a faint trace of dimples. "And you," she said, adding more seriously, "I'm sorry for your loss."

I sighed. "I expect I should be sorrier for yours. I . . . didn't really know Allegra that well; she was more my mother's friend than mine. I don't know why she . . ."

I hesitated, not wanting to get into the ramifications of that quite yet, but Abby was already plowing ahead "I suppose Harry already told you about my offer to buy the shop?

I know you've only just got here, but . . ." Then she caught sight of my face and amended, "I'm sorry; you're right. There'll be plenty of time to talk about that later. Everyone always says I don't know when to take a hint . . ." She grinned at me then, a genuine expression that made her dimples dent in earnest. "Why don't we start this all over again? Hi, I'm Abby Cantwell."

"Cecil Hargrave," I said, echoing her smile, and this time our handshake was warmer. "And, Abby, I'm sorry, but I honestly don't know what I am going to do yet. Allegra just died; I just lost my job and my apartment. I probably will sell you the business and move back to New York in September, but I can't decide that right now. I just . . . Well, I need a little time to figure it all out."

"No, I'm sorry; I shouldn't have even brought it up. Believe me, there's time. Time is something we have in spades on Seal Island. And, frankly, the longer I have to save my money, the better. Businesses—even small ones—don't come cheaply. And there's my daughter to think of. Jessie; she's twelve. Besides, you seem a reasonable sort; I'm sure we'll get along just fine."

I had a feeling she was right. For all her scatter-brained exterior, there was a solid core of honesty to Abby Cantwell that I liked.

"Look," she added, "why don't we do this in the proper order? Go see Harry Cameron first; he's around the corner and three doors down on your left. Then come back and see me whenever, and we'll have a proper chat. And no pressure, I promise."

"Fair enough," I said, then, "Thank you. I'd like that."

"My pleasure." She smiled again and turned back to her post.

I walked to the door of the shop, then paused with my hand on the knob. "Abby," I said.

She looked up. "What?"

"That woman with the sour face. Did she end up buying the blue T-shirt or the green sweatshirt?"

Abby grinned. "Thanks to a little persuasion, both." And when I gaped at her, she laughed and added, "Whatever else has been said about me—and plenty has been—I do know how to do my job!"

SETTING OFF THE CHIMES in my wake, I left the shop. The wind tugged idly at my hair, blowing it into my eyes, my mouth. I pushed it back and rounded the corner, following Abby's directions.

CAMERON AND ROWE, the sign said, small but unmistakable. I swallowed another surge of panic and pushed open the door.

Somewhere in his mid-sixties, overweight and balding—with a wedding band planted firmly on his finger—Harry Cameron stood up from behind his desk to greet me.

I almost laughed. So much for expectations. Not to mention fairly emblematic of my life to date.

I was flustered, however, to see him, like Abby, go subtly pale at my appearance. Admittedly, Allegra and I may have shared a basic coloring. In fact, my mother had always used to joke about the fluke of the genetic draw that popped me out of her womb looking more like Allegra than like her. "It's a good thing your maternity is faultless," she'd say. "Otherwise, your dad might get suspicious." But I'd always thought the resemblance was far more superficial, limited to our shared dark blond hair and greenish-gold eyes. My memories of Allegra were of a profoundly beautiful woman with an impressive degree of poise. I, myself, had none of her flair, and knew it only too well. So why was everyone acting as if I were Allegra incarnate?

I would have to ask Abby, later.

To Harry Cameron's credit, it didn't take him long to pull himself together. "Cecil Hargrave, I presume?" he said, his voice as rich and resonant as I remembered. But, coming out of that body, it suddenly seemed less fraught, less flirtatious. Though it didn't change my impression that he was a nice man. He smiled and waved me to a seat. "Welcome to Seal Island."

"Thank you," I said, settling in across from him. "It's good to be here." I meant it. There was something about my brief view of the place that appealed to me—and not just because it was so different from the city. "Ironically, I went into The Gull to ask directions; I hadn't realized it was Allegra's shop."

"Yours, now," he said. "And she's done"—he winced—"she *did* some wonderful stuff with the place over the years. It's quite popular with the summer folk."

"I can see why. It's lovely. And Abby seems a darling."

"Yes," he said, though his voice seemed fractionally cooler. "Abby has run the place well enough since Allegra's . . . passing. But just remember that you don't have to make your mind up right away about The Gull. There are those of us who don't believe Abby Cantwell is quite sober enough to handle such a responsibility by herself."

A reference to her character, I wondered, or something more serious? I kept silent.

"It might even be best," Harry continued, "if you were to run the place with her for a while—that is, if you are planning to stay for the summer—to see what it is you are giving up before you do."

There was an unspoken question in his voice, and I didn't see the harm in answering it. "As I told Abby already, I'm not certain what my decision will be—about any of this. But

I will be staying at least through September, so I will have time to decide."

"Good." A definite expression of relief crossed his face, and he abruptly became more businesslike, handing me two bank statements. "Allegra's accounts; checking and savings." He frowned slightly. "Not very much, I'm afraid, which is odd, since The Gull can turn a tidy profit at the height of summer. When I checked into it, the bank manager said Allegra had been regularly withdrawing large sums of money out of her savings account throughout the late summer and early fall, claiming she was planning to invest them with a friend, but none of us have been able to find the records of those investments. But then, perhaps you'll find something in the house we overlooked. In any case, I'll see about getting the remaining balance transferred to your accounts. You'll want to open something local, I assume?"

"Most likely."

"Well, tomorrow will suffice for that. In the meantime . . . You've seen The Gull, you know her assets—at least, those we've been able to discover—so all that remains is the house."

"Yes, the house. Is it in town, or . . ." I doubted it would be one of the grand mansions by the ledges, but I had, I realized, been expecting a water view. The very name—Seal Island—conjured images. And until I had actually seen the island and the cluster of houses around the town, it hadn't occurred to me that the place might be inland.

"Not in town, no," Harry was saying. "It's about two miles out, on the Drewes Point Road. Would you like to go there now, or explore the town a bit more first?"

While the town did have a certain appeal, I had never owned a house before and found myself eager to see it, hoping I liked the proportions, the furniture. The setting. For even if it was only until September, it would be a welcome novelty to have a place I could completely call my own. So, "The house, please," I said. "If you don't mind."

"Not at all." He levered himself up from behind his desk, and as he moved around it, I noticed that he walked with a pronounced limp. I tried not to stare, uncertain if it was congenital or a recent injury, but he noticed my covert attention and smiled.

"Walking cast," he said ruefully, exhibiting it. He reached for a cane I hadn't noticed in one corner. "I'm afraid it plays havoc with my driving, which is why I was unable to offer to pick you up at the airport. And why I'll have to ask if you don't mind driving us to the house as well. I'll direct you, of course, and my wife will pick me up when we're through."

"It's no trouble at all," I assured him. "I'm parked a fair bit down the street, though. Will you be okay with the walk or shall I bring the car around?"

"No, no, my doctor said that walking is good for me; gets the circulation moving. So as long as you don't mind a slowish pace . . ."

"Not at all."

"Thank you," he said, patting my hand. "You're a sweet girl. I think you'll be a welcome addition to our little community—even if it is only for a summer."

From anyone else, such words would have sounded condescending, but from Harry Cameron—with his guileless, round face and spaniel-brown eyes—they merely seemed sincere. I wondered if he was as genuine as he appeared, or if that was all part of his lawyer's façade, playing the innocent to put people off their guards.

Then, as he locked the office door behind us and began his halting progress along the street, I chided myself for my suspicions. We were far from the city now, and things worked differently in small towns. Lawyers did not have to be sharks, and young heiresses did not have to look every gift horse in the mouth.

However, as we wended our slow way to my car, I did become aware of the attention we were drawing. Now that I was in Harry's presence and identified—no longer the anonymous tourist—every eye seemed to track me, aided by our snail's pace: curious, assessing. Allegra Gordon's not-quite-niece, coming to claim her inheritance. I wondered how many of them were judging me, and how many were finding me lacking.

Too young; too callow.

Maybe this town wasn't quite as accepting as I had assumed. The back of my neck was red and hot by the time we reached my car.

As I unlocked the door—there was no way not to make it a production—I blushed again at the lack of trust a locked door implied. But Harry must have noticed my distress, for he just smiled and said, "Don't mind the eyes. Everyone is curious, that's all. Allegra was an important part of this community." *You have big shoes to fill*, was my unspoken assumption, but all he added was, "She'll be missed."

I just nodded and opened the door for him. As he maneuvered himself in, hampered by the awkward cast, I went around to the driver's side and unlocked it. When we were both seated and underway, he turned to me and said, "And don't worry about people's opinions; you'd be wisest to continue locking your doors. This may seem like a small island, and safe, but we have our share of problems. And I don't mean to alarm you, but there have been rumors of some rather shady characters hanging about recently, and a few houses have been broken into. You'd be wise to keep everything locked as tightly as possible. Especially the house."

"Very well. But is it . . ."

"Dangerous? No." For the first time, his heartiness

sounded forced, but before I could elaborate he said, "Now, make a right out of the village and just keep going. I'll tell you where to turn."

Since I didn't feel comfortable pursuing the issue, I complied, continuing out a road that once again grew more wooded and isolated the farther we got from town. The houses out this way, while not exactly more affluent, at least seemed a little less run down. I was even happier when we turned right up a smaller, pine-lined road and I began to catch occasional glimpses of water through the trunks.

The road swooped closer to the shore, and a succession of clearings opened up, separated by stretches of pine, revealing green lawns sloping down to the same slabbed-granite ledges I had noticed earlier. The houses were widely separated, and further hidden from each other's view by the swooping curves of the road as it navigated the winding shoreline.

We passed one house painted a bilious, virulent blue. I was desperately afraid this was going to be my legacy—and my luck—but we continued on, passing a few more houses and another long stretch of woodland instead, before Harry said, "Turn here. And there. What do you think?"

I drew in a breath. A short hop of gravel road led through a clearing and down to grey-shingled house. It wasn't large and was built very simply in the New England style, but I loved it instantly. There were three gabled windows under the eaves, the wood trim painted white against the silvery cedar. Two large windows and one small one graced each side of the door, and what looked to be a sunroom was attached to one side, while a screened porch lay to the other. On the far side of the screened porch was a garden, once laid out with care but now gone rather badly to seed. Beyond the garden was a small greenhouse. And beyond that, far off to my right, was a dense stretch of woodlands.

There were more woods to the left, with a freestanding

garage tucked discretely beneath the branches. And—glory of glories—stretched out before me, the water, sparkling brightly in the sun. The beach was ledged and curved away to both sides, for the house lay on a smallish point. There were a few distant islands scattered in the bay, and—nearer to hand—a smattering of barely-exposed rocks, one of which bore at its top an oddly bulbous, anvil-shaped form much like the ones I had seen scattered across that rocky island, earlier.

"What *is* that?" I exclaimed, pointing.

Harry laughed. "Haven't you ever seen a seal before?" And when I stared at him, he added, "Where do you think our island gets its name? The harbor seals will often haul out on those rocks when they are exposed by the tide. It must be a good omen, welcoming you to the island. How do you like the house?"

"I . . . love it," I said, sounding oddly tentative—not from any lack of enthusiasm, but more because I was struggling to believe my good fortune.

Harry fished a set of keys from his pocket and handed them to me with a smile. "Then why don't you open it up and have a look around?"

I bumped the car to a stop near the side of the house where the road petered out and was out of it almost as fast as I could scramble, with Harry following more slowly behind. At the commotion, the seal slid from the rock and disappeared beneath the waves, but I paid it scant attention. I was so eager that I fumbled the keys on the first try, dropping them clanking to the stoop.

As I scooped them up, I froze, convinced that I had seen a flash of movement out of the corner of my eye: a shadowy figure disappearing into the trees behind the greenhouse. I glanced over at Harry to see if he had noticed, but he had pulled a cell phone out of his pocket and was dialing, unaware. I looked back at the woods, but now could see nothing: no hint of a figure, no motion among the densely packed trunks.

Most likely it had been my imagination, whetted by talk of unsavory lurkers. I retrieved the keys and examined the locks, both of which seemed uncharacteristically new and shiny. Recently replaced, perhaps? Harry or an associate had obligingly labeled the keys for me, so I inserted the proper one into the lock more cautiously, then pushed the door open.

The air inside the house was hot and somewhat stale, but even so I felt at home. The front vestibule was shaped like an upside down T, one side leading off into what looked to be the kitchen through a door at the base of the stairs. The other, longer hall to my right passed a row of windows before opening into the sunroom. Ahead of me, through a wide archway, was the living room, with three sets of French doors at its far end leading onto a wide deck.

I passed though the arch, intent on that deck, and was delighted to observe in passing that the living room contained not one fireplace but two, mirrored to either side. What a joy on winter nights, I thought, temporarily forgetting that I was leaving in September. But it seemed an unusual design—and now that I noticed it, something else struck me as unusual about this room as well. But such concerns quickly vanished as I reached the far wall, for then I was undoing the latches of the leftmost French door, pushing wide the panes and emerging onto the broad expanse of deck.

It was newer than the house, the wood still faintly golden rather than weathered into ghostly paleness. It should have looked odd, and yet it didn't. I leaned against the railing at the far end, letting the wind whip my hair, and listened to the whispered kiss of the waves against the ledges. The seal that had left the rocks bobbed up again, closer to shore, and I saw its head more clearly now. It seemed to be looking straight at me. Its long muzzle drooped mournfully into wide, W-shaped nostrils; its whiskers added the appearance of a walrus mustache. Whether through age or just particular coloration, the otherwise dark head seemed grizzled around the ears and whiskers, giving it a venerable look. It stared at me for several long seconds until I began to wonder uncomfortably if I should somehow hail it, then turned away, presenting me with an elongate profile, the nose curved and almost equine. I could now see that its coat was dark with white flecks, which perhaps explained the look of age and wisdom. Then it submerged again and was gone.

I became aware of footsteps off to my right. Remembering that half-seen glimpse of the figure in the woods, I was startled but it was only Harry Cameron coming around the side of the house, casted leg thumping awkwardly. He grabbed the railing of the side stairs and, grunting slightly with effort, pulled himself onto the deck.

"Lovely spot, isn't it?" he said, crossing to where I was standing. And when I voiced my agreement, he added, "This land has been in Allegra's family for generations, and she spent every summer up here as a child before settling in permanently. So I'm glad it doesn't have to pass out of family hands just yet."

"As am I," I said, envisioning the long, lazy summer ahead, getting acquainted with the house and the view. After another moment of silence, I added, "I saw the seal again. He came up closer to the shore, almost as if he were studying me."

My companion chuckled. "I'm sure you'll be seeing a lot of that in the months to come. Seals are naturally curious creatures, always willing to investigate a new sight or a new face. They also tend to return rather frequently to their favorite haul-outs. After a while, Allegra came to recognize individuals. She had even named a few, though I'll be damned if I can remember what she called them. Except, of course, for Ragnarok. A great woman for seals, our Allegra. She used to say they were her greatest passion."

I shivered slightly, remembering that dour, elongated face bobbing atop the waves, the steady regard of those obsidian eyes. I don't know why it struck me as sinister. Maybe because I had always thought of seals as playful creatures. But then again, maybe this particular seal *had* been far beyond its carefree youth. Certainly, there had been something about it that seemed almost ageless. Or timeless. And not just because of its markings.

"Cecil? Are you all right?" Harry asked, as my silence stretched out.

I blinked, then smiled. "I'm fine. I'm just . . . getting a little cold." The wind was stiff, and fierce. "Shall we go in?"

Harry hesitated, as if loath to intrude on my first moments in my new house. I was about to insist when I heard a crunch of tires on gravel, and moved curiously to the side rail of the deck. A battered, pea-green station wagon was rolling into the drive behind my car. "Ah, there's Martha, now," Harry said—though I could see no more of his wife than a curly grey head behind the steering wheel. "I'll introduce you later; for now I'll leave you to poke around on your own. Should you need anything, I left my number—and yours, by the way—on the fridge. I've kept the phone bills, the electric bills, and the heating bills paid and current, so you shouldn't have any problem with that. We haven't gone through any of Allegra's things, yet; we figured that was best left to you." His face closed off again, briefly. "But any clothes and such that you don't want can be donated. Just let me know, and I'll arrange it. The local market has a decent selection

should you want to cook in. Of the local restaurants, I'd recommend the Clam Digger. Or the Myrtle Inn if you want
something more upscale. Unless you'd care to join Martha
and me? I believe she has a roast . . ."

I felt suddenly overwhelmed. "Thanks, but I think I would
rather get settled in first. Another time?"

He smiled, seeming not the least put out by my refusal. "I
figured as much, but I wanted to extend the offer nonetheless.
How about next Friday?" It was Thursday, now. "We'll make
a small party of it, have some of the neighbors around."

"That sounds lovely," I said. "And thank you. For your
hospitality. For everything."

"It is," he said, "my pleasure. And please do call me if
there is anything you need. But, remember . . . Keep the
doors and windows locked when you are not around. Do you
promise?"

His tone was oddly intense, and I nodded. But I couldn't
help wondering—with another shiver—if there wasn't far
more to those simple words than he was admitting.

3

As Harry's car pulled away and silence descended
again over the clearing, I thrust his words from my mind and
turned my face from the water, studying the back side of my
house. It was as pleasantly symmetrical as the front, although more contoured. The roof, more steeply pitched on
this side, gave the impression of a one-story dwelling, and
the rooms to either side of the central living room sported
deep bay windows. The living room itself mirrored that
shape, its outermost corners sloped in at angles. Which
likely accounted for that nagging feeling of oddness I had
noticed upon entering.

Leaving the French doors open to circulate some air
though the house, I began to explore the rooms in more detail, starting with the bedroom which was behind the nearer
of the two bay windows. It was a light, airy room, with two
windows besides the bay, and a deep window seat cut into
the latter. The bed was big and crafted of wrought iron, with

steely roses and vines emerging from upright, white-painted bars. It looked to have been freshly made up, with pale green sheets and a green-and-white sprigged quilt. Small nightstands stood to either side, each bearing a shaded lamp. There was an antique trunk at its foot, and a braided rug before what had to be—joy of joys!—the back side of one of the living room fireplaces. There was also a comfortable armchair tucked into the corner between the mantel and the window seat.

Opposite the bay window was a dresser on the far wall, and a small table by the door. The former had a mirror above it, and another shaded lamp on its top; the latter held a cut-glass vase atop a crocheted doily. Between were two doors—one which led into a spacious bathroom complete with a claw-footed tub and shower and a wide console sink, and the other which opened into a walk-in closet. There was another dresser in the back of this, and two rods of hanging clothes on either side.

I had a momentary qualm at violating a dead woman's possessions, but then fascination took over and I spent the better part of an hour picking through outfits, both disturbed and elated that they seemed to be precisely my size. And my childhood impressions of Allegra were amply borne out by her closets. Indeed, it seemed that she both had exquisite taste and the ability to indulge it. I had never owned anything half this nice. Worse, it was exactly the sort of stuff I would have bought had I the money to spare and the confidence to carry it off.

I didn't know if I'd have the guts to wear a dead woman's clothes, but I found myself longing to do so. In fact, the more I examined my inheritance, the more an uncomfortable feeling began to grow in me that Allegra had somehow reached into my mind from beyond the grave and fashioned the perfect life for me to step into.

ıt was an impression that only grew as I abandoned the closets with a slight shiver and began to explore the rest of the house. The room next to the bedroom was a small, internal laundry room. The two narrow windows on either side of the front door were stained glass, and cast rainbow patterns across the polished wood floor. Down a side hallway, which held only another braided rug and a wooden bench of the sort you would see in old-fashioned waiting-rooms, was the sunroom. Bare hooks and chains for hanging pots and empty wrought-iron stands indicated that the place had once been alive with greenery. But whatever plants had been present were now gone—save for the lone rubber tree, wilting sadly in one corner.

I stabbed a finger into the soil. Dry as a bone.

Across from the sunroom was a kitchen of the type I had always dreamed of possessing: open and spacious, with plenty of light, miles of counter space, oak cabinets galore, and a refrigerator you could lose an army in. There was even an island with bar lights above it, and a hanging pot rack. The sink basin was deep and wide and stainless steel, as was the stove-top. Gas burners, I noted with relief; not electric. The pots were substandard, but that could be fixed. There was even a dishwasher.

I had a sudden urge to cook dinner, though I doubted there were any supplies in the house. Instead, I filled a nearby saucepan and retreated to water the rubber tree. The water pooled on the surface of the arid dirt, then slowly began to penetrate. From here, I supposed, it was simply a matter of crossing my fingers and praying. I returned the pot to the kitchen, emptied it, and continued my explorations.

Beyond the kitchen, mirroring the sunroom, was a screened dining porch. The dining room itself, separated from the kitchen by only a low counter, had a fireplace and a chandelier of brass and fluted glass. A small, four-person table was tucked halfway into the niche formed by the bay window. Two larger, drop-leafed console tables, which I assumed could be joined into a whole for more formal dining, were pushed against the walls.

My ambition escalated. I no longer wished to cook dinner; it was a dinner party I was after. Maybe in payback for the party Harry would throw me. I envisioned the long table set with linen, china and silver. There would be candles, and the chandelier would glow softly. And maybe there would be a local man: tall, dark and handsome . . .

Disgusted—these days, I wouldn't know what to do with someone tall, dark and handsome, even if I *could* find him— I shook off the vision and continued my explorations.

Upstairs, above the kitchen, was a slant-roofed guest bedroom with a large closet, one dormer window, and another window tucked flush against the side of the house. It was more spottily furnished than the rooms downstairs, with a double brass bed that had clearly seen better days and a bookshelf filled with dog-eared paperbacks. Across the landing was a second bedroom, this one with two single beds, another closet, and the other two dormer windows. It was shaped—by necessity, I supposed—into an oddly squat T that gave it two cozy nooks that had been turned into reading corners. More bookshelves lined the walls, filled with yet more paperbacks. When I had more time, I was eager to browse the titles, to see what Allegra had left me, but for now I continued to roam.

The upstairs landing curved around the staircase, then bent again. At the far end lay a bathroom, the virtual twin to mine downstairs, its window likewise overlooking the woods and the garage. The only other door led into the attic: a long, wide, badly cluttered space with windows to either side, in terrupted only by the twin thrust of the chimneys. Sorting through this mess—draped with dust and cobwebs—was not a task I looked forward to. I hastily retreated, leaving a track of footprints behind me in the dust.

That left only the living room to examine—or perhaps re-examine. I descended the stairs, still sneezing.

I hadn't been aware of how much time had passed during my explorations, but the air had grown noticeably cooler, the shadows lengthening across the lawn. I pulled the French doors shut and latched them, then turned my attention to the central room with its lovely twin fireplaces. But the more I looked, the more it struck me that something was wrong with this chamber—and not just because of its unusual shape. In fact, that almost worked, the two angled walls bearing book-shelves filled with well-preserved hardcovers rather than the dog-eared paperbacks I had discovered upstairs.

I couldn't resist a quick peek, wondering how Allegra had afforded so many expensive titles, then quickly realized that most must have come cheap from library sales. Some still bore acetone covers, their spines marked with Dewey designations. But there were a few newly purchased ones, including a complete set of Thomas Morelands. I smiled. Yet another example of Allegra's exceptional taste.

I turned my attention back to the living room, still wondering what it was about it that disturbed me.

For one thing, there was no TV; that would have to be remedied—though I did find a small stereo and CD player tucked discretely in a cabinet, the speakers mounted neatly on the bookshelves. But . . . The largest problem was the focus of the room. With the two fireplaces, neither side could dominate. Yet the furniture was all huddled off to the left-hand side of the room, circled about a large Oriental rug in deep reds and golds, leaving the other fireplace bizarrely exposed. That was the problem I had sensed—and frankly it surprised me. In all other rooms, Allegra's tastes had so closely mirrored my own that it was almost as if she had designed my ideal dwelling without either of us realizing it. Consequently, why she had gone so stunningly wrong here remained a mystery.

I backed up against the French doors, and squatted down on my heels to survey the space. Perhaps if I centered the rug, angled the two couches off to either side, and cornered the armchairs . . . Yes, that would work. I stood and resolutely seized one of the couches, dragging it into position. It was harder than I anticipated, the frame both heavy and cumbersome. But I persisted, and eventually got it properly placed. Then I did the same with its twin. Lastly, I dragged the rug to the center of the room, then stood back and surveyed my work, wiping my sweaty forehead with the edge of one sleeve.

The placement indeed was better. Almost harmonious but for . . .

Damn it! A large, dirty-brown stain marred the floorboards, previously hidden by the awkward conjunction of sofas and rug. No wonder the living room had been arranged as it had. There was something so distasteful about that mark. If only there was some way to hide it while keeping the furniture as it was . . .

My stomach rumbled audibly, distracting me from my musings. I glanced down at my watch, amazed to see that it was close to seven. I would run into town, buy some food, cook dinner, and deal with my living room later. I scooped up my jacket from where I had left it slung over the foot of the bed and shrugged into it. I patted the pocket, locating both house and car keys, then left the house, locking the door behind me as instructed—though not without one last glance back at that distressing stain.

As the key turned in the lock, I suddenly remembered the

half-glimpsed figure from earlier and, on a whim, walked over to the garden. The plots looked generous, and I had always wanted to try my hand at gardening, but it wasn't that sort of surveillance I was after. More than anything, I wanted to reassure myself that there was no sign of trespass, that it really had just been an illusion.

I circled the greenhouse and stopped dead in my tracks. For there, in the soft dirt by the far corner, was the unmistakable print of a man's work boot.

4

BY THE TIME I reached town, I had managed to convince myself that I was overreacting, that a footprint could mean anything. It could have been a gardener's print. An electrician's. The gas man's. The locksmith's. Some other workman reluctant to go inside and so surreptitiously relieving himself around the back of the greenhouse instead. After all, that made more sense than the alternative, which was that someone was watching the house. Watching me. And what did Allegra Gordon or I have that anyone could possibly want?

Still, I felt almost obscenely glad to see a familiar face when I pulled my car up before the market, belatedly realizing that I had forgotten to remove my suitcases from the trunk. I was just berating myself for the oversight when I saw Abby emerge from The Gull with a set of keys in her hand, flicking out the lights behind her.

I hailed her and she turned, smiling as she saw me. Locking the door behind her, she crossed over to where I was standing.

"Cecil," she exclaimed. "What brings you back to town?"

"Food," I admitted. "I figured I'd pick up a few things at the market, cook a quick dinner . . ."

She shook her head mischievously, her reddish curls dancing. "Not on your first night you shouldn't. Besides, we already got off on the wrong foot and I feel the need to make it up to you. So if it's not too forward of me . . ." She hesitated minutely, then laughed. "Damned if I know the etiquette of these things. But Jessie is off at a friend's tonight, so I'm on my own. And I was going to stop by the house and ask you anyway, so as long as you promise not to construe it as a bribe or a bid for the store . . . How about if I buy you dinner? That is, if you'd like the company."

I glanced around the town, now all but deserted as it shut down for the evening. Most of the stores save the grocery were closed, and only a few cars peppered the streets. It was the true twilight hour, the sky dark and heavy, the light purply-thick and almost palpable. All that remained of the sun was a salmon streak across the horizon, out beyond the now-silent docks and the boats that bobbed at anchor. The tide had retreated, leaving an unsullied stretch of flats that stank of mud and seaweed, salt and fish.

Not, I thought—recalling the footprint in the mud by my greenhouse—a time to be alone.

"That sounds wonderful," I said. "Only . . ."

I surveyed the town again. In one direction, welcoming lights proclaimed the Myrtle Inn open for business; the few cars still in town were clustered in its lot. Glancing in the other direction, toward the post-office and market, I was just in time to see the lights in the latter wink off decisively. I paused for a moment in shock—it was barely evening, after all—then smiled. I was no longer in New York. And fate, it seemed, had decided.

"Would it be considered employee harassment if I took you instead? You can tell me all about the business. After all, I don't even know what I pay you! And I'd really like to make it my treat."

"Well, who am I to say no?" Abby declared cheerfully, pocketing her keys. "After all, you *are* the boss. Where were you thinking of going?"

At a glance, there seemed little choice, but I said, "Harry recommended the Myrtle Inn. Is it any good?"

"One of the best. A bit pricey, though. Are you certain?"

"Absolutely," I said, expecting no more than a provincial inn furnished cozily in castoffs, serving a hearty fare from meatloaf to macaroni at one third of New York's prices.

Granted, the Myrtle Inn was imposing enough from the outside. It was a three-story wood colonial, painted a stately reddish-brown. Its windows were lace-curtained, spilling out warm yellow light against the gathering darkness. The front hall had parquet floors and white-painted walls, but instead of the expected cast-offs, it was furnished with antiques both beautifully restored and lovingly maintained. To one side was a gracious sitting room, a fire burning cheerfully in the grate, and to the other was a breakfast room. Beyond that—occupying a long, low addition built onto the side of the house—was the dining room, its walls painted a darker, richer red than the inn's exterior. The light was low, and candles winked from the tables, creating an atmosphere both cozy and romantic.

So much for my city prejudices. I drew a breath and Abby grinned.

"Not quite the backwaters, it is?" she remarked. "But are you sure this is all right? The Clam Digger is plenty good, and much cheaper . . ."

In truth, I was beginning to feel a bit intimidated by the surroundings. It wasn't the cost I was worried about—I came from New York, after all, where even the hot dogs were overpriced—but I was still wearing jeans and a sweater, and both, I realized, were streaked with dust from my brief foray into Allegra's attic. I was on the verge of at least begging time for a change of clothes when fate once again intervened, this time in the form of an elegant woman emerging from behind the dark wood bar as we paused uncertainly on the threshold of the dining room.

"Abby," she exclaimed. "What a surprise! What brings you here on a Thursday night?"

"My first dinner with my new boss," Abby answered promptly as the woman approached us. "She offered, and who am I to say no?"

The woman surveyed me speculatively. She had dark hair, stylishly bobbed to just above her shoulders, and dark blue eyes. She was slim and well-kept—somewhere in her mid-forties, I imagined—and was dressed impeccably in a black sweater belted over a long, straight maroon skirt. She was taller than I to begin with, and her smart black heels elevated her still further. Even to my untrained eyes, her wardrobe looked expensive.

"So you must be . . ."

"Cecil Hargrave," Abby interjected. "And Cecil, this is Joanna Mills. She and her husband Tom own and run the Myrtle Inn."

"A pleasure," I said, extending a hand. "This is a lovely place you've got."

"Thank you," she said, taking my hand in a firm, cool grasp. "We like it. And just wait until you try the food." She smiled, the expression not quite touching her eyes, which remained distant and appraising. "We lured Jean-Pierre away from Le Coq Basque in New York City. Which I understand is where you hail from as well?"

If she had planned to intimidate me, she had done so. Thoroughly. "Yes, I do—though not from such remotely exalted circles, I'm afraid. Lowly office workers of my stature do not get much chance to dine at Le Coq Basque."

She smiled again, and this time a hint of warmth touched her expression. "Well, we're not quite so snobbish here—though some of the summer folk do like to pretend. Tom and I are just lucky that Jean-Pierre fell in love with the area and decided to relocate. Although it seems almost too common an occurrence these days. How long are you planning to stay?"

The sooner gone, the better, her tone implied.

I winced, on the verge of explaining my plans—or lack thereof—again when Abby intervened. "Joanna!" she exclaimed. "At least get Cecil a drink before we start grilling her about the future."

The smile Joanna turned her way seemed genuine. "Very well. If you will follow me?" She led us to a table near a window and another crackling fireplace, twin to the one in the parlor. I sat, feeling uncomfortably the outsider. Abby took her place across from me, plucking a fluted cloth napkin from her water glass. She unfolded it across her lap, then planted her elbows firmly on the tablecloth, staring suggestively at Joanna.

"What?" the woman demanded. Then, "Oh, very well," as Abby grinned. She turned to me. "What can I get you to drink?"

"I suppose a bottle of wine for the table—if that's all right with you?" I said, looking hesitantly at Abby.

"Perfect."

"Red or white?" Joanna asked.

I glanced again at Abby, who promptly declared, "Red. If that's all right by you?"

I indicated my agreement.

"I'll see what I can dig up," Joanna said. "On the house, of course."

"No, you mustn't . . ."

For the first time, Joanna's composure softened into actual friendliness. "Oh, yes, I'm afraid I must, or Abby will never let me hear the end of it. I'll be right back with your menus."

Abby grinned at me as Joanna disappeared, and said, "Don't let the gruff demeanor fool you. Joanna's a cream puff—and one of my best friends on the island. She just gets a little over-protective of me at times. Worried, I think, that my new boss is going to turn me out of doors."

"I would never . . ." I began, horrified, but she waved me off.

"I know. I have a good instinct for people. Well, except for Brian the Bastard, my ex-husband. But men don't count. Joanna will soften up once she gets to know you. Isn't that right, Jo?"

"Isn't what right?" Joanna said, returning with our menus. "I'll be back in a minute with the wine."

I opened the leather folder and surveyed the contents: gourmet French fare, each item sounding more appetizing than the last. And at prices equivalent to a moderate New York restaurant.

I looked up to find Abby peering at me anxiously over the top of her menu. "Are you *sure* this is all right?" she asked again. "Joanna runs a lovely establishment. But, as I said before, it isn't exactly cheap . . ."

"No, it's fine," I assured her. "Cheaper than I'm used to, honestly."

She smiled, and gradually I began to feel more at home. I forgot about my substandard clothing as the red-walled room worked its comforting magic. There were brass and glass chandeliers like in Allegra's dining room—idly, I wondered who had gotten the idea from whom—and dark wood tables covered by white cloths. The chairs—reproductions, I imagined—were simple yet elegant with their dark-red cushions and fluted backs. The tableware was refined, and the whole atmosphere was one of peaceful tranquility.

I had to give Joanna credit. Classical music was playing in the background, and the few diners present filled the space below the music with quiet conversation. The fire crackled in the grate, bouncing shadows around the room that were echoed by the candlelight, until the very walls seemed to dance and shimmer.

"Are you from around here?" I asked Abby, grabbing for a neutral topic.

"No, I was one of the transplants: one of the summer folk who came up and fell in love. Unfortunately, one of the two things I fell in love with left me—or, more properly, I left him. But the place remains."

"You seem to have a real feel for the island." I could hear it in her voice, which had softened to the tones of a lover.

She smiled. "How could you not? In fact, I'll bet it won't be long before you get the bug yourself. No one can be up here more than a month without contracting it."

Like a disease? I thought, but didn't say it. Somehow I doubted I'd succumb. The place had a certain charm, but I was a city girl, born and bred; I had never imagined living anywhere else.

"So, how long have you been here?" I asked instead.

She calculated for a moment, studying the tablecloth intently, then looked up with twinkling eyes. "Good heavens, fourteen years! Can it really have been so long? I don't feel remotely old enough."

"You don't look remotely old enough," I told her, and she grinned.

"I'm thirty-four, and some days I feel every year of it. And you? Or is that a rude question?"

"Twenty-eight. And I usually feel about half that. Can I ask you another question?"

"That depends," she said promptly, and I smiled.

"Do I really look that much like Allegra? You and Harry both reacted as if I were Allegra incarnate today, and then seeing the house . . . I'm beginning to wonder if I have an identity of my own any longer."

She looked at me oddly for a moment, her face strangely tight, then relaxed into a smile. "There is a basic resemblance, yes, but not so severe as I seemed to imply this afternoon. You just startled me. I was always so used to seeing Allegra there at the back, sorting through the books, and when you turned around in that green sweater with your dark blond hair . . . Green was always Allegra's favorite color, and so few people have that shade of hair—that pure, unbottled gold—that for a minute . . ." She smiled faintly and shrugged. "I guess I'm just not used to having her gone."

"Mmm," I said, and then, "What was she like? I mean, really?"

Abby's face went still and quiet, and she looked down at the tablecloth again. Was that a gleam of tears in her eyes, hastily blinked away?

"She was lovely," she said at last. "Generous, warm, funny—a truly wonderful person. I used to wonder why she never married. She said it was by choice, but sometimes she just seemed so lonely . . . Still, she had a stubborn streak and was fiercely independent, so I suppose it wasn't easy giving up a lifetime's worth of habits. Not that she would have ever felt sorry for herself. Allegra was never one for self-indulgence; very much a pull-yourself-up-by-your-bootstraps type. I mean, just look at the hell she gave me after my divorce! No lying about moping for me." Abby grinned faintly.

I wasn't quite sure what to say to that. I had never been very comfortable with that level of personal talk—on the theory that what goes around often comes around—so I stayed silent. And in the sudden lull, Joanna arrived with a bottle of wine and an extra glass, the latter of which she set down on the table. She uncorked the bottle with aplomb, then decanted a small measure into the extra glass, sampling it.

"Lovely," she declared, and poured out two glasses. "Let it breathe for a bit, and enjoy it. It's the vintage I've been telling you about, Abby."

Ignoring instructions, Abby took a sip, then raised an appreciative eyebrow. "Lovely, indeed! I forgive you of all sins, Joanna." And she made a crossing motion in the air.

Our hostess laughed and departed.

"Take a taste," Abby urged. "Joanna's been saving this wine for years. And she must have decided she liked you if she uncorked this particular vintage!"

I took a sip as instructed. It was rich and mellow, and so deep in color it was almost black. "Amazing!"

Abby grinned. "Isn't it just?"

Briefly, I recalled Harry's comment about Abby's sobriety, but if she was a secret drinker, she was hiding it well. She seemed content to merely sip her wine, flashing an occasional appreciative smile. And it wasn't the sort of question one asked—especially not of a new employee. Instead, I asked, "Have you worked for Allegra long?"

"For about eleven years, ever since I left my husband. Mostly part-time at first, but less so in recent years." Her face darkened slightly. "By the end of last summer, I was pretty much running the place by myself."

"Why? Harry didn't say anything about Allegra being ill . . ." *Just about you being giddy*, I thought. *Or a drunk.*

Abby frowned. "Not ill—at least, so she claimed. Just . . . distant, I suppose. Actually, it was a little odd. Like I said, Allegra was never one to wallow in might-have-beens, but she changed over the winter. Became all secretive, or something. It's hard to really describe it, but we were all worried about her. We kept asking her what was up, but she wouldn't say. And that was, for her, unusual. Oh, she could be intensely private—not like me, who will reveal every bit of my life in excruciating detail should anyone show the slightest bit of interest, so be warned! But . . . when she was happy or proud of something, or wanted to share . . . You always knew. I mean, even though I knew he wasn't, I always felt that Ragnarok was as much mine as hers; we all did. She was like that. But this . . . This was different."

"Different how?" I demanded. Had Allegra committed suicide? Was that the reason people seemed to be skittering away from discussing her death? Was such a thing still a stigma in a small community like this?

But Abby set my mind partially at ease when she added, earnestly scrunching up her nose, "I don't know. Just . . . different. Initially, there was kind of an electric excitement to her, as if she had just met a guy or fallen in love or had the world's biggest secret that she couldn't tell a soul. I used to tease her about it—though I never got a damned thing from her."

"Really? When was this?"

"Last fall."

Right after she had begun pulling large chunks of money out of her accounts, I thought. Abby was right; something had clearly been up. But what?

"Then, as winter approached," Abby continued, "well, it's not like we all don't go into a bit of hibernation during the

winter; it's just too damned cold to be bothered with social-
izing. But Allegra pulled away completely. She said she
wasn't ill—and the autopsy confirmed it—but she looked
dreadful towards the end, all gaunt and hollow-eyed. It was
kind of like . . ." She paused, looking embarrassed, then
laughed faintly. "This is going to sound so ridiculous, I can
hardly bear to say it! And you're probably going to think that
I'm insane. But . . . it was almost as if all the light just went
out of her eyes. As if someone had sucked away her soul."

"And then she died," I added, almost in a whisper.

Abby's gaze sharpened. "I'm still not convinced it was
completely causal," she said bitterly. "Though sometimes I
wonder. There was certainly *something* going on. But to give
her credit, she didn't truly abandon me until after the height
of the summer madness; we usually have the shop closed in
the winter."

"No tourists?"

"Precisely." She took another sip of her wine, paused,
then said, with the same, strange intensity, "What did you
mean earlier, about the house?"

"Oh, that. I don't know. It sounds silly now to say it, but it
was so lovely, so perfect—so exactly suited to my tastes—
that part of me was convinced I had somehow furnished it
for myself without my knowledge. That part of me *was* Allegra." I attempted to lighten my words with a laugh, but it
came out sounding strained and forced. "Now you must
think *I'm* the one who's insane!"

"Not really. Allegra always had that effect on people,
made them feel warm, welcomed. I think it's part of why
The Gull did so well. I was just worried, because . . . Well,
I'm glad it wasn't a shock, anyway. I mean, not in the usual
sense. Tom must have cleaned it up pretty well, afterward.
Who knew he had it in him, to be a housekeeper?"

If she was talking about Joanna's husband, I didn't see why she should be so surprised. He ran a lovely inn—unless it was Joanna herself who did all the work.

"But enough about such grim topics," she added. "Tell me, how are you liking Seal Island so far?"

"It's beautiful. Though I must admit I was glad for the company tonight—not only for the conversation, which is lovely, but also because I was a bit shaken up when I ran into you this evening."

"Shaken up? Why?" she demanded, looking almost disproportionately concerned.

I swirled the wine in my glass, then took a sip. "Well, it sounds silly now, but I thought I saw someone lurking around the house earlier, when Harry and I first arrived. And then, on my way over here, I found a footprint by the greenhouse."

"Oh." She seemed caught between reassurance and concern. "It's probably nothing; just Harry's fears infecting you. He's been jumpy ever since Allegra's death." She smiled ruefully. "Did he tell you how he broke his ankle?"

"No."

"He was checking the house a few days after she . . . died, testing the new locks or something." So, I *had* been right; I wondered why he had seen fit to replace them. "Anyway, he thought he saw someone lurking around outside, panicked, and tripped over a root trying to get to his car. He was very embarrassed about it afterwards."

"Well, maybe that explains why he seemed so reluctant to come in."

Abby's face crunched in sympathy. "Oh, that," she said. "Look, Cecil, don't take it personally. Harry has always been a bit in love with Allegra. Rumor has it that he once asked her to marry him. When she refused, he moved to Boston and met Martha. But I don't think he's ever completely gotten over her, and her loss has hit him hard. So don't blame him for not wanting to go into the room . . . well, where it all happened."

"What do you mean, where it all happened? Where what happened?"

Abby looked stunned. "You mean you didn't know? I assumed all along that Harry had told you."

"Told me what?"

She hesitated, then said bluntly, "Allegra didn't die of natural causes, Cecil. She was murdered."

5

"Murdered?" I squeaked, drawing the attention of several other diners. I flushed, and lowered my voice. "Murdered?"

"Yes, I'm sorry; I thought you knew. It was . . . Well, no one knows exactly what happened, except that it was probably some isolated incident. At least, that's what the police are saying. It was Tom who found her, and he said the house was a total wreck, like a hurricane had gone through it."

Or like someone was searching for something, I thought with a shiver, remembering that odd flicker of movement from the woods.

"Or partially wrecked, anyway," Abby revised. "Tom thinks he might have scared the guy away in the act, because nothing valuable was missing. Nothing that he could find, anyway."

Except for how many thousands of dollars, drawn in chunks out of her savings and still unaccounted for. And whatever mysterious ailment had been troubling her over the winter, the secret that Abby had never been able to worm out of her . . .

"Anyway," she added hastily, seeing my expression, "I wouldn't worry. The police caught a guy trying to break into a house in Brooklin two weeks ago and they have him in custody now. He claims that he never went anywhere near Seal Island, but they don't believe him. The trial is coming up, and whether or not they can get him for the murder, he is going away for at least a year for the breaking and entering. And there have been no further attempts on the house since, so I'm certain they've got the guy."

She may have been right, but abruptly, I was grateful for those shiny new locks, and for Harry's foresight in changing them. Suddenly, my New York caution didn't seem so absurd. I was locking my doors at every opportunity, and to hell with what the neighbors thought.

"No wonder Harry was so insistent about the locks," I said, my voice still unpleasantly shaky. "That's advice I'm definitely heeding."

Abby nodded. "Never a bad idea. And while you never like to think of your home as unsafe, it seems that even our small island isn't free from the world's problems. Nonetheless, everyone says it *was* an isolated incident, so you shouldn't let it affect you. Or let it affect your feelings about the house, because it is a lovely one."

"What's a lovely one?" asked a new voice, almost suggestively.

I glanced up. A man stood by the table, peering down at us speculatively. He was fairly young—not much older than Abby, I imagined—and good looking in a clean-cut, boy-next-door sort of way. He was blond, with blue-grey eyes and an unassuming smile. Though perhaps taller and leaner than average, he had fine, even features and an air of casual confidence. Almost unbidden, the phrase popped into my mind: no distinguishing marks or features. But nonetheless, the not-so-remarkable pieces combined into a very attractive whole.

I found myself smiling at him and he returned the expression—his attention, for that instant, focused on me alone. It was both gratifying and disturbing; I wasn't used to being the subject of such scrutiny. I flushed, and—seeing that—his smile widened. Not maliciously, laughing at my weakness. But delightedly, as if the two of us shared some grand conspiracy.

"Let me guess," he said—his voice, now that I focused on it, a pleasant tenor. "You must be Cecilia Hargrave."

"Cecil," I corrected. "But . . . Yes."

"Excellent. May I join you for a minute?" Without waiting for a reply, he swiped a chair from a neighboring table and pulled it up, taking a seat. But this time, instead of looking at me, he turned his attention to Abby. "I stopped by the store, but by the time I got there you'd already gone, so I left you a message at home. However, it seems that house you were interested in won't be available, after all."

"Damn," she said, sounding genuinely disappointed. She turned to me. "The house I'm renting was just sold, and no one knows if the new owners will want a tenant or not. So I'm looking for a new place. But it's not easy, finding something year-round that is large enough for both Jessie and me, yet still affordable. And I don't want a buy a house, in case . . ."

"I decide to sell you the shop," I finished, and she shot me a watery smile.

"Exactly. Well, thanks for checking, Richard. And if you see anything else . . ."

"You'll be the first person to know, I promise," he said. He turned back to me, adding, "So, how was your flight from New York?"

"Fine," I answered, wondering if everyone on the island knew more about my business than I did.

"Looking for a scoop, Richard?" Abby teased, and he laughed, the expression lighting his face. "Cecil, this is Richard Feinman, the editor of our local paper. Which he likes to pretend is closer to the *New York Times* than the weekly shopping supplement, but we humor his delusions. And Richard, this—as you have deduced—is Cecil Hargrave."

"Pleased to meet you formally," he said, extending a hand. It was a nice hand, I noticed, sensitive and well-sculpted.

"Likewise," I replied, keeping my voice deliberately light.

"So what brings you to the Myrtle Inn?" Abby asked, leaning back in her chair to regard him. For myself, I was trying very hard not to regard him—though, despite my resolve, my eyes kept straying back.

He shrugged. "It was a long day at the office, so I thought I'd stop by Joanna's for a drink and a little company before I went home." He reached out and appropriated Abby's wine glass with the ease of long familiarity, taking a sip then arching his eyebrows in surprise. "But it must be quite an evening if Joanna is pulling out all the stops like this!"

She snatched the glass back, her brow furrowed with pretend fury. "Don't jump to conclusions; Joanna just likes me better than she likes you. Besides, you didn't have a bad day at work. You just wanted to see if Cecil had arrived, yet. Admit it."

"Well, it wasn't my *sole* motive," he temporized. "But still . . . Guilty as charged." He turned to me with a grin. "Curiosity is one of my worst faults, I'm afraid. Put it down to the foiled reporter in me. However, I don't regret succumbing to the impulse."

I wasn't sure what to say to that, but fortunately I didn't get the chance.

"And no doubt you're already composing the headline,"

Abby declared. "Something along the lines of: 'City Girl Gets Island Windfall.' "

"Actually, I was thinking more of: 'Attractive New Yorker Inherits Gordon Estate,' which sounds decidedly more friendly, not to mention professional. And also may explain why I edit the paper and not you."

Despite their bickering, I could tell they were not truly at odds. Rather, there was an affectionate undercurrent beneath the words, and I wondered briefly if they were involved. Therefore, I was not quite sure how to respond when he said, "I hope you'll let me buy you a drink someday. When you're settled."

"As long as it's only a drink," Abby inserted. "She doesn't know anything about Allegra's death."

"Heaven forfend!" Richard replied, sounding honestly offended. "I'm not a total shark, Abby. I do have a few decent bones in my body."

She laughed, then conceded, "Well, maybe one or two . . ." And leered at him cheerfully.

Emboldened by the by-play, I said, "I'd love a drink. And thank you, Richard." His gaze once more focused on me, and this time I managed not to blush. "And I understand that you have to do your job. If I did know anything about Allegra's death, I'd tell you. But I don't. I didn't even know she was . . ."

But the awful word wouldn't come. My face must have clenched, for he laid a hand on mine and squeezed my fingers lightly. "I'm sorry. I didn't mean to upset you, and I'm glad you understand. Not everyone would be quite so sympathetic." This with a pointed look at Abby, who stuck out her tongue in return. "And I know I'll be seeing you around soon, so why don't we set it up then? If that suits."

It suits, I wanted to say, but only nodded.

"Then," he added, "contrary to popular opinion, I did indeed come in to get a drink, and I see Joanna with one now, waiting for me at the bar. So if you ladies will excuse me, I'll let you get back to your business."

He stood and, with one last smile in my direction, restored his chair to its former position and retreated.

There was a moment of silence, then Abby grinned and said, "I think he likes you."

"I very much doubt that. And besides, aren't the two of you . . ." I waved my hands vaguely for emphasis, unable to come up with the polite euphemism.

"Richard and I? Heavens, no! Not," she added hastily, "that there's anything wrong with him. Richard is a total darling, very cute—and utterly single, to the despair of several aspiring wives-to-be. You should go for it, if you are interested; you could do a lot worse than Richard Feinman. It's just that he's too . . . I don't know. Too *Richard* for me, I suppose. I mean, not that he didn't pursue me for a while, but I tend to go for another type entirely—much to my detriment. I might have been better off if I had stuck with the Richards of this world."

"Why? What type do you go for?"

She laughed ruefully. "Tall, dark, brooding and antisocial, I suspect. And you?"

I don't know if it was the wine or the superb food that Joanna eventually brought us (although admittedly the raspberry vinaigrette could have used a bit more raspberry and a bit less vinaigrette) or the fact that I caught Richard shooting me the occasional glance from across the room before he departed (a knowledge that both terrified and delighted me), but somehow I found myself filled with a new resolve. Maybe now that I was in a new place—even if just for a summer—I could let down my metaphorical hair for a bit and release the tight strictures that told me not to trust, not to let anyone in, for fear of being hurt and abandoned again.

Besides, if everything did go belly-up, as it always seemed to, I could just run away from my shame in September and never return. How much easier could that be? So I found myself confessing to Abby, "I think I've always tended to go for the ones that are completely inaccessible. It's just seemed easier that way. No chance of it ever working out, if you know what I mean."

She grinned. "Do I ever! Believe me, I am a card-carrying member of the Commitment Avoidance club! Allegra used to have a theory that like wounds attracted, but I've always thought it was a bit more perverse than that. It's like cats, you know? How they always seem to bug the people who are most allergic? Well, for me, it's like the minute I sense a man is unavailable, I'm all over him. Whereas someone like Richard is . . ." She shivered slightly. "You know; too *there*."

The relief I felt at hearing her say this was nothing short of profound. So, I wasn't terminally screwed-up. Or if I was, I certainly wasn't alone. Still . . . "It might be nice to try something different," I hazarded. "For the past year, I've been wondering if it isn't about time to come out of the shell."

In truth, I'd been wondering a bit more than that—and most of it concerned with perversity. How was it possible to both want something so badly and be so scared of it at the same time? The conflicting impulses pulled at me endlessly—and worse so in the past year. But, so far, terror always won.

"Well, as I said before, you could do a lot worse than Richard," Abby said cheerfully. "So, I give you my blessing— not that you need it! Me, I'm not remotely ready yet." And—

apparently as I had evinced some interest in her life—she told me all about Brian the Bastard, who lied and cheated and screwed his way through the first years of their marriage, in the promised excruciating detail. Not that I hadn't been warned. In truth, I was fascinated by her honestly. It must have been so liberating, just to let it all hang out like that! The inaccessible man thing was enough of an admission to last me a year.

Still, I could see why she now possessed—as the media loves to put it—"trust issues." It was a pretty harrowing tale. And the day she left Brian the Bastard—with barely a penny to her name—Allegra had taken her in, engendering a loyalty that lasted for the next eleven years.

"I don't know what I'm going to do this summer," she confessed as I was working my way through a stellar crème brulée that even I could find no fault with. "The height of the season is always a madhouse, and I've never had to run the place by myself before. I suppose I'll have to look into hiring some help . . ."

She hadn't been fishing; I knew that. But Harry's words echoed through my head. I didn't know why he doubted her, but a little caution never hurt anyone. Besides, my severance wouldn't last forever, and I couldn't spend the whole summer reading my way through Allegra's library.

"I'll help," I offered.

She stared at me.

"I know I don't know much, but I'm a quick study—and how better to acquaint myself with the business and determine what's best for it? Just let me know when you want me to start."

She surveyed me speculatively, then laughed. "Despite the fact that you're still technically my boss . . . I'll give you a week to settle in. Well, a little more than a week. How does next Monday sound? It usually doesn't get crazy until after the Fourth, so that'll give you time to get adjusted before the summer folk pour in."

"It sounds perfect," I said. And strangely enough, it did.

She peered mournfully at the table. "But, we don't have any wine left to toast with. So I suppose this will have to do." Ever resourceful, she raised her coffee cup instead. "To us, and a successful summer."

"To us," I echoed, clinking cups.

We lingered late over our coffee, talking—and I had all but forgotten her unpleasant revelations about Allegra until I pulled my leased car into my newly-acquired driveway far later than I had intended. I shut off the headlights and killed the engine, and for a moment just sat there in the clearing. A faint moonlight frosted the trees and streaked the water, and when I got out of the car, shut the door and tipped back my head, I saw a glory of galaxy undimmed by the city lights— the likes of which I had never seen. I stood there for a moment in the sharp, chill evening with my back against the warm, ticking car, huddled in my too-thin jacket with my breath forming wintery ghosts before my face, and suddenly understood why that river of stars had been called 'the Milky Way.'

I understood, as well, the impulse that had led so many people to leave their lives for this small island. Even now, it worked its magic, enfolding me with sounds more peaceful than silence: the buzzing chorus of tree frogs, the lapping murmur of the waves against the rocks. And somewhere, faintly, the mournful sound of an imagined bagpipe.

This time, there were no phantom figures behind the greenhouse, and the solitude was comforting rather than menacing. Then I yawned, loudly, and abandoned my musings for more practical concerns. I would crawl into that wide brass-and-iron bed, open the windows to the surf, and bury down under the covers, letting the waves and thoughts of tall blond editors lull me into sleep.

I opened the car trunk and withdrew my bags. There was enough light from the moon to fit the key into the front door lock. I pushed open the door and switched on the lights in the entry, instantly transmuting the moon-washed night into impenetrable blackness beyond the windows. Locking the door behind me, I left my two suitcases in the hall and proceeded towards the bedroom with my small overnight bag slung over my shoulder. I had intended to go straight to the bedroom, but something drew me into the living room instead.

When I switched on the light, I saw it—the spattered stain across the floorboards that my previous rearrangements had revealed: rusty-brown and soaked into the porous wood. The sort of stain that no amount of scrubbing could erase.

A shiver traced up my spine as I regarded it, compelled to read in its patterns the truth behind Allegra's final moments.

Not a pretty death, it seemed, or an easy one.

And I hadn't even realized until this moment what it signified.

6

I PASSED AN UNEASY night, haunted by visions of that stain and the many, gruesome methods of its creation, burning the lamps late into the night and drifting into more solid slumber only when dawn brightened the sky and a cheerful chorus of birds made mockery of my fears. Then I slept deep and dreamlessly, waking only when the sun pouring through the tightly locked windows began baking the air into a heavy, unbreathable mix. Yet still I lay there, heat-logged and drowsing, until a series of angry, honking barks propelled me from my bed.

They echoed across the water, raucous and strident, and easily the oddest noises I had ever heard: rather like that of a dog crossed with an angry goose. I darted to the window, banging my shin painfully against the window seat. I let out a yelp that almost rivaled that of my intruders and peered out through the glass, visions of I don't know what flooding my mind. It took me a moment to locate the commotion, for at a glance all seemed peaceful. Then I saw it and abruptly felt foolish.

The tide was partway out, and on one of the rocks that humped from the water, two seals were fighting for possession, honking angrily as each tried to gain ascendancy. Their coats were lighter than my visitor of the previous afternoon, their faces less drawn and lugubrious. In fact, it seemed the whole shape of the head was different: pert and almost spaniel-like. One was larger, but the smaller made up in feistiness what it lacked in mass. For a while, the contest looked even. Then weight prevailed and the larger one triumphed, driving the smaller back into the water. Almost smugly, it took up position, curving itself into the odd anvil shape I had noticed yesterday, head and tail elevated from the rock.

That cannot be comfortable, I thought, and laughed. Then went in search of my watch.

It was nearly 1 P.M.—high time to be up and about. Still, reluctant to face the living room, I busied myself in the bedroom for a while, unpacking the suitcases I had carried in late last night and taking a long, hot shower in the deep, claw-footed tub. Finally, dressed and ready, with my hair brushed if not fully dried, I could procrastinate no longer. I opened the bedroom door decisively and proceeded through—only to find myself flying to the floor amidst a deafening clatter of pots and pans.

Caught between curses and laugher, I sat up and rubbed my knees, regarding my tripwire ruefully. My fears of the previous night suddenly seemed ridiculous in the light of day. Especially since I had apparently managed to forget the elaborate tower of kitchenware I had constructed the night before—protection against who knew what lurkers. And which I would now have to put away, pot by pot.

Allegra's killer was in custody, according to Abby, and

the stain looked more pitiful than menacing in the light: a sad testament to a life departed. I would simply have to buy a larger carpet to cover that stretch of floorboards.

Then my stomach rumbled imperiously and I stood, wincing as my bruised knee flexed. I had missed breakfast, and there was still no food in the house. Disinclined to deal with the pots and pans for now, I located the house and car keys, tucked them firmly into my bag, shrugged into my jacket, and left the house.

The air was fractionally warmer than yesterday, though still with a fresh tang to it that made me realize I might have to purchase a heavier jacket, and a stiff breeze was blowing off the water. I smiled as it whipped my hair about, for it was impossible to feel scared or threatened on such a day. Especially not with memories of the scorching heat of a true New York summer to make me appreciate my good fortune.

I opened the car door, tucked myself behind the wheel, and started the engine. I was quickly becoming familiar with the drive into town, letting a kind of peace steal over me as the trees flashed past my windshield, their trunks casting a dappled pattern of sun and shade across the road. The bay was calmer today, though still as deeply blue, and I knew I had made the right decision to come to Maine. Abby was right; Allegra's death probably had been a fluke. A tragic fluke, admittedly—but a fluke nonetheless. And there was no reason to let that one fact color my existence.

I pulled my car up in front of the grocery, but as I got out, my stomach rumbled again and I remembered one of my cardinal rules: never shop on an empty stomach. Unable to decide what I wanted, I would end up buying everything in the store—only to have it all rot in the fridge later. And it wasn't like I was on any sort of deadline. The only thing I was supposed to do today was visit the bank with Harry to transfer Allegra's money to my own accounts, and perhaps learn more about these mysterious withdrawals. So I would find a restaurant, eat, visit Harry and do the banking, then shop.

I couldn't, at a glance, locate the Clam Digger, but I wasn't much inclined to search for it. Not when there was a tantalizing smell of frying seafood wafting up from the docks—which was probably what was inciting my stomach to riot. I traced the scent down to a small shack at the near end of the public docks. It was painted red and badly weather-beaten, and there were a handful of tables inside. Out back were three wooden picnic tables, liberally splattered with guano. Perched on a pylon near one of the tables, a large gull regarded me speculatively, weighing my merits as a provider of food.

"Not me," I told it, firmly. "I'm hungry."

It turned its head away, feigning disinterest.

Grinning, I approached the take-out window, discovering a scarred and laminated menu held in place by a large rock. Torn between the lobster roll and the fried clams, I took forever to choose—and even longer to catch the attention of the lone attendant. Who, faced with a marked lack of customers, seemed content to continue the situation indefinitely.

She wasn't doing anything in particular that I could see; her movements about the kitchen were aimless. And I wasn't keen on playing the strident New Yorker, but I was hungry. After several tentative "Excuse me"s, I finally contrived to drop the rock that had been weighing down the menu.

That got her attention.

"May I have the lobster roll, a small order of the fried clams, and a lemonade?" I said, solving my dilemma in the simplest way possible.

"Ten minutes," she said, in a heavier, thicker version of the accent I had noticed in Harry's speech.

I nodded, wishing I had thought to bring a book, and settled down at the table closest to the gull. Not because I particularly relished the attention, but simply because that was the table nearest to the water. At this hour, the docks were active, filled with fishermen coming back from their morning runs or perhaps refueling for their next outings. The gas pumps were down at the far end of the dock, and several boats were tied up awaiting service. The murmur of voices and the buzz of outboard engines echoed across the water, punctuated at intervals by the piercing cries of gulls as they swooped above the chaos.

I watched—at first idly and then with more interest—as the fishermen joked amongst themselves, their voices both rough and lilting. Most wore thigh-high rubber waders, and shirts stained and redolent of fish. They were old and young, grizzled and clean-shaven, but each seemed to share some indefinable quality. Perhaps it was an ease or comfort on the water, or perhaps it was something more—a passion for the ocean that lit them up from within.

Salt in the veins, I thought. They were probably all as poor as dirt, struggling to make ends meet with long hours and longer weeks. Yet there was something about them—about their rough humor and unselfconscious bearing—that just seemed so . . . free.

Obscurely, I found myself envying them as they swung effortlessly from dock to boat, calling out cheerful taunts to rivals—jealous of the fact that they had found their niche while I was still struggling to discover mine. And resolutely ignoring the cynical voice inside me that insisted it was less a matter of passion than sheer necessity; there were likely few other jobs on this small an island. Still, I forgot the time and my hunger as I watched them, graceful in the ungainly waders, fueling boats and off-loading crates that scraped and scrabbled and occasionally clacked in a manner disturbingly reminiscent of damp insect carcasses rubbing together.

My laconic waitress threw open the take-out window and leaned out, grinning. "What ha'you brought me today, then, Ned?"

"Same as I bring you everyday," one of the fishermen responded, his sun-baked face crinkling up in a grin. His skin was prematurely aged with sun and salt, his sandy hair shot with grey, but his eyes were as blue as two slivers of sky as he hefted a box onto his shoulder. "Not that you're ever grateful."

She laughed.

"You got the boxes for the Myrtle, Tom?" he added.

The one named Tom nodded, said something inaudible to the other men that had them roaring, then followed Ned up the docks. He was younger than his companion—in his late thirties, I imagined, or maybe early forties—with softly-curling hair so dark a brown that it was almost black. But not blue-black; the sun teased out hints of auburn fire hidden deep within the strands. His features were rough and weathered, but there was nonetheless a precision to them, a strength, that not even the two-day's stubble of beard on his cheeks could hide. His eyes were what his hair was not: a true blue-black, and compelling, the pupil almost indistinguishable from the iris. He was wearing faded jeans under the thigh-high waders, and an Aran sweater that had clearly seen better days. It had gone grey with age and dirt—but somehow that only added to the image.

He wasn't precisely good-looking; he was a little too rough-cut for that. The word 'life-scarred' sprang to mind. But there was something mesmerizing about him nonetheless, and I was embarrassed to find myself staring.

"What was that, Mr. Fancy-Pants?" the one named Ned called back, obviously in response to the unheard comment.

"A girl in every port," Tom responded. "Eh, Ned?" His voice, unlike the others', was a deep, rich baritone, and bore no trace of an accent.

"And a port in every girl," Ned responded cheerfully, leering exaggeratedly at my chef-cum-waitress.

"Scoundrel," she responded, lobbing a hot dog bun at his head.

The seagull shrieked with glee, practically clipping my head with surprisingly vast wings as it dove after the treat, stabbing greedily at it with its long, yellow beak.

"Your order's ready," the girl added, almost as an afterthought, seeming to notice me for the first time.

Both of the lobstermen turned to regard me, and I went bright red as I moved to collect my fried gluttony. Ned smiled in a friendly way, but the one named Tom simply nodded absently in my direction and moved on. Just as well. The last thing I needed was to develop an inappropriate crush on a lobsterman, as compelling as he was. Nor could I see myself spending the summer discussing shellfish.

I lost myself in seafood and tried not to stare as Tom returned from his trip to the Myrtle, the box now empty in his hands, nodding again briefly at me as he passed. And, I had to admit, the seafood was not a bad distraction. I hadn't been expecting much from the shack, but the clams were piping hot and full-bellied, and the lobster as fresh and tender as if it had just come off a boat. Which, given what I had just witnessed, it no doubt had—perhaps that very morning.

I finished every scrap, despite the hovering gull's attentions.

Tom's boat, the *Sea Hag III*, was just pulling away from the dock as I finished. I could see his dark head at the wheel, while Ned stood on the back deck stowing empty boxes, shifting still-full ones, and coiling up the lines. The hum of the outboard motor sang them out of sight around the headland.

I should, I knew, head for Harry's office so we could take care of our business before the bank closed for the weekend, but I found myself oddly reluctant to move. Maybe it was the warm sun beating down on the leather of my jacket, off-setting the cool breeze off the water, or maybe it was the tang of salt on the wind. Or maybe a combination of the two, coupled with the heavy lassitude of a full belly, that made me sit there far longer than I had intended, my elbows propped on the dropping streaked table, my chin resting on interlaced fingers, gazing out over the water and the scattering of islands against the horizon.

But eventually, realizing that my lobsterman was unlikely to come back and that I was wasting a perfectly good afternoon, I gathered up the detritus of my lunch, threw it in the bin by the take-out window, then leaned briefly into the shack.

"Thank you," I called to the girl. "That was delicious."

She actually came to the window this time, looking almost friendly. "I'm glad you enjoyed it. Staying here long?" Her slow, laconic Maine drawl seemed to give each word three extra syllables.

"For a while," I answered. "The summer, anyway."

"You're the Gordon woman's niece, no?"

It was close enough. "Yes," I agreed. "That's me."

"Nice lady, your aunt. Liked her seafood, too. You have a good summer, hear? And come on back."

"That I will. I suspect you'll be seeing a lot of me this summer." And as there seemed nothing left to say, we exchanged courteous farewells and I went off in search of Harry.

I FOUND HIM IN his office, sitting at his desk with his casted leg thrust out before him. He straightened when he saw me and smiled in obvious delight. "Cecil!" he exclaimed. "I was just about to call you. You look lovely this afternoon. How are you settling in?"

Somewhat self-consciously, I fingered my wind-tossed hair, my wind-burned cheeks, and laughed. "Rather well, I think. I've just been down on the docks sampling your fried seafood."

Harry grinned. "Ah, yes. A particular vice of mine—though don't tell Martha!" He patted his ample stomach. "But back to the original topic, I have to admit I was a bit nervous leaving you out there on your own last night after, well . . ."

He colored vividly and I had to take pity on him. But nonetheless I couldn't help adding bluntly, "Yes, Abby told me what had happened. She also assured me that the police have caught the guy who did it, and are not letting him out of custody at any point soon, so I should be perfectly safe."

"She's right, you know—and that's exactly what Martha was telling me last night when I was all set to have her drive back over and rescue you. And I should have told you. I'm sorry. I just couldn't think how . . ."

He looked so distressed that I impulsively leaned over and patted his arm. "It's okay. I know now—and, trust me, I am not leaving because of it. Now, shall we head to the bank and see what we can do about these accounts?"

Harry looked almost disproportionately relieved as he pushed himself erect and reached for his cane. "Let us, indeed. Are you all right to drive again?"

The bank—a branch of Bar Harbor Trust—was a short way outside of town, at the crest of a hill. And if I had any doubts as to Harry's competence as a lawyer, they were quickly put to rest as he guided me expertly through the transfers and helped me to establish my own local accounts—for which, the bank manager assured me, I should have a working ATM card within days. Admittedly, I felt a little staggered when I looked at the balance of my new accounts. Including my recent severance—and discounting the still-missing money—it was more than I had ever possessed. And abruptly—remembering the pots and pans and rugs I wanted to replace or supplement—I felt a shopping expedition coming on.

Nonetheless, when the last of the paperwork was wrapped up and we were on the verge of concluding our business, I couldn't help asking, "About the money that Allegra had been withdrawing from her accounts . . . How much *did* she take out, in total?"

Both Harry and the bank manager looked chagrined. In the month since Allegra's death, had neither of them bothered to calculate this? Instantly and contritely efficient, the manager departed to check his records, and came back a few minutes later with a stunned look on his face. "I honestly hadn't realized how all the little pieces would add up. I'm afraid to say she pulled out close to eighty thousand over the course of ten months."

It was my turn to look a little stunned.

"We'll get to the bottom of this," Harry assured me, as I drove him back to town. Then, almost to himself, he added, "What could Allegra have been thinking?"

I found myself wondering if Abby knew about the missing money, if Harry had noticed Allegra's mood-swings. Was there more going on here than everybody seemed to assume?

I couldn't help a faint shiver at the thought.

7

WHEN WE ARRIVED BACK at the office, Harry informed me that he and Martha were still planning on holding a dinner in my honor a week from tonight. I thanked him and assured him I would be there, and asked where I might purchase supplies that the local shops might not have. Then I drove to the market, parked, and proceeded to stock my kitchen. It was a small store and the selection was not vast, but still I was pleasantly surprised to find a number of gourmet items I would have not expected at in a town this size. I filled a small cart and presented my credit card at the register, feeling oddly extravagant. Then I loaded my purchases into my car and started the engine.

The gas gauge, I noticed, as I drove out of town, was hovering somewhat lower than I normally liked. And while I could probably make it a few more days, I had noticed a tiny gas station between my house and the town. A few more minutes wouldn't hurt my groceries, so I impulsively swung my car in beside the lone set of pumps. A bell rang inside the small garage as my tires bumped over the rubber signal hose, but otherwise there was no sign of life. Still, the garage door was open, so I snugged optimistically up to the pump, rolled down my window and switched off the engine. And waited.

Nothing, save the occasional car whizzing past me on the main road.

Objectively, I knew that the pace of life in small towns was different, but still . . . Perhaps this was not a full service station? Usually such stations were, but there was an exception to every rule. And the last thing I wanted was to look like some spoiled tourist unable to pump her own gas. Granted, I hadn't pumped my own gas in more years than I cared to mention, but how hard could it be? I shoved my door open decisively—and nearly kneecapped the attendant, who had appeared, as if by magic, at my window.

It took me several seconds of babbled apologies before I actually looked at him, and when I did my voice stopped dead in my throat.

What *was* it about this island? If I had thought the lobsterman was gorgeous, then the gas station attendant was simply stunning. Literally.

Okay, I have to admit he was not classically good looking—at least not in the magazine-model sort of way. (Neither had Tom been, for that matter. I tended to distrust men who looked too polished and smooth. Well, okay, I tended to distrust men in general, but there you had it.) Still I had also never been rendered completely speechless by a guy before. And the weirdest part of it was, I couldn't even figure out why.

This man wasn't as tall as Tom, though his build was both leaner and sleeker. His hair, unlike Tom's curlier thatch, was thick and shiny and unrelentingly straight—albeit badly in need of a trim—and was as unrelentingly blue-black as his eyes. His features, though finer than Tom's, were charmingly incongruous, dominated by a nose that was long and aggressively roman, which lent his face an oddly equine cast. He was dressed in jeans and a blue-and-green plaid flannel shirt, both liberally streaked with oil.

Why this should be appealing, I don't know, but it was.

Worse, his eyes were fastened intently on me, as if drinking in every detail of my appearance. Or my humiliation.

A painful wave of color hit my cheeks. "Sorry again about the door thing," I said. "I wasn't sure if . . ."

He regarded me for a moment, his head cocked to the side like a bird's. Then slowly, his lips curved upwards in a smile. It was a devastating expression, only augmented by the liquid blackness of his eyes. In the light of that smile, the proud nose faded back and his face flared into handsomeness. And I felt as if a wave of complete acceptance had washed over me.

My blush retreated as I studied him.

Like I said, he was not traditionally good-looking—the nose ensured that. But if Tom were compelling, then this guy exuded raw, animal magnetism. His face was longer, his features thinner save for the nose—which, upon closer scrutiny, simply added character to his face. His skin, too, was darker—with an almost Mediterranean tint—and against it his teeth, small and precise, flashed blindingly white.

Admittedly, there was something odd about him—a sense of foreignness or maybe even feyness, if he was not quite all there. And that impression only increased when he spoke.

"Not a problem," he said, "How can I help you?" His voice was deep and somewhat rough—oddly reminiscent of the barking I had heard that morning—and yet with an undeniable music beneath it, like waves over rocks. I had grown so subtlely used to hearing the Maine accent over the past few hours that his speech also caught me completely by surprise. It had a lilt to it, almost a brogue—but it was like no brogue I had ever heard. Like a combination between Scottish, Irish, and something else I had never encountered before.

I found myself smiling up at him, and in response that mesmerizing grin increased in wattage. "Fill it up," I commanded recklessly.

I felt almost a physical sense of loss as he circled around the back of my car to comply. But even before I could start berating myself for my ridiculous attitude, he had inserted the nozzle into the gas tank and was back, leaning casually against the hood of my car and peering in the window at me with his startlingly liquid eyes.

"Fancy you turning up here," he said. "I was wondering when we were going to meet."

I came down to earth with a bump. "Excuse me?" I said, coldly. "Do I know you?"

He seemed unphased by my rudeness. "Not yet, but you will. I'm your neighbor."

"You are?" I said, somewhat stupidly.

He nodded, not seeming to mind my inanities. He held out a hand and I took it. It was hard with callus and streaked with dirt, yet surprisingly gentle for all that.

"Ronan Grey," he said, with a fluid trill on his Rs. "I live right up the road."

"Oh, that's nice. I mean . . . Cecil Hargrave," I replied.

One black brow winged upwards in surprise. "Cecil? What kind of name is that for a girl?"

I flushed again, but more faintly. "Actually, it's short for Cecilia."

His eyes widened then deepened, as if something in my given name delighted him. "Ah, now that's more like it.

Cecilia." His mouth drew out my name, and for a second I couldn't help feeling that there was something I was missing. Then the feeling was gone as he added, "I hope I didn't startle you yesterday. Since I live nearby, I've been keeping an unofficial eye on the place since Allegra died. I was there yesterday afternoon when you arrived, but I didn't think you were up to meeting the neighbors yet, so I nipped away through the woods."

A surge of relief flowed through me so strongly that I almost went limp in its wake; I hadn't realized until now how much that unexplained sighting had bothered me. "That was *you*?"

"Indeed it was. And I had a feeling you had seen me as I left. So when you pulled in here as if fate had sent you, I know it was time to come clean. After all, I didn't want you to think you were being stalked or anything."

"Heaven forfend," I said. "But thank you."

Behind us, the pump clicked off, but Ronan continued to linger.

"Thanks for keeping an eye on the place," I added. "And for introducing yourself. It's good to meet you."

"And you." His smile was fainter, but no less devastating. "I'm sure we'll be seeing more of each other in the future."

I couldn't think of anything nicer, I thought—and then found to my horror that I had actually said it.

But Ronan just twitched me half a smile and said, "In that, we are in agreed."

I don't know how long he might have lingered, chatting, if a battered pickup hadn't pulled in behind me, breaking the idyll. With a sudden efficiency, Ronan circled around to the back of my car, topped off my tank, and screwed on the gas cap. Then frowned in concentration as he made change from my twenty.

"See you around?" I ventured, as I started the engine back up.

"Oh, I think you most certainly will," he said with another devastating smile, and I drove away feeling absurdly cheerful.

MY DRIVEWAY FELT INFINITELY safer now that I had identified the boot print by the greenhouse, and a warm glow suffused me at the thought of Ronan looking after me. I laughed again at my foolishness, unloaded the groceries, then—still out of force of habit—locked both car and house behind me. But this time, I did throw open all three sets of French doors to the deck, letting the cool breeze blow though my house as I gathered up the scattered pots and pans, and found homes for all my new groceries.

It was growing later, the sun slanting low though the windows, when the strident ringing of the phone startled me.

"Oh, thank God you are there," Abby's voice said, when I answered. "I've been trying to call all afternoon and there's been no answer. I thought that maybe, with how suddenly I told you about Allegra, you'd just up and left." Or something more sinister, her tone implied.

"I'm fine," I assured her, not bothering to mention my night terrors. "I was just out running errands and shopping. Oh, and I discovered the owner of the boot print by my greenhouse: Ronan Grey."

I could almost hear Abby frowning down the phone lines. "Rowan who?"

"Ronan. Ronan Grey. Totally gorgeous? Works at the gas station just outside of town?"

"You mean the one with the nose?" Abby said, then laughed. "Well, to each his own—though I suppose he does have a certain rough charm. He only started working there this spring. Louis, who owns the place, says he looks to become a natural mechanic, but is still a bit unsocialized. Apparently, he comes from an island even more remote than Seal Island, if you can believe that. He's still in training with Louis, really. But if that's what floats your boat . . ." I had a sudden sharp image of Tom the lobsterman, and flushed. "Well, more power to you," she added. "Is it: Alas, Poor Richard, then?"

"Abby!" I exclaimed. "Of course not. He was just . . . nice. Said he was a neighbor, has been looking after the place a bit since Allegra died."

"Really? Funny that Allegra never said anything. But then, she wasn't exactly herself this spring, and he only arrived on the island a little before she died, so I suppose she wouldn't have. Still, nice for you."

"Don't be silly. And I'm probably leaving in September anyway, so it's all academic."

"I don't think Richard's offer of a drink was entirely academic," she teased. "But seriously, Cecil, I'd be a bit careful of the locals if I were you. Not that this guy's exactly local, but still . . . Relations between the transplants and the natives aren't exactly what one would call friendly. They see us as invading their island, taking away their land, and driving up their property values. And I can't exactly say I blame them. I tend to feel the same way about the summer folk; all of us transplants do. So, much as I hate to burst your bubble, don't pin your hopes on some native Mainer. I've been here for fourteen years, and they still consider me 'from away.'"

"Point taken. And as I said, I'm not pinning my hopes on anyone."

I could hear the grin in Abby's voice. "So Richard still has a chance? Oops, here comes a customer. Talk to you later?"

"Absolutely," I said as she hung up, then turned back to my silent kitchen, feeling a sudden, self-pitying moment of loneliness. I had considered inviting her around to dinner, but no doubt she had obligations to her daughter. I sighed, then distracted myself by sorting though the pots and pans I had employed in my failed booby-trap, separating out those I deemed worthy of salvage and bagging up the rest for disposal.

Admittedly, I felt a little guilty for so recklessly disposing of these parts of Allegra's life. Who was I to determine what should stay and what should go? Except that she had left me the house, and everything in it. And quite specifically, too. Harry had given me a copy of the will today. At first, I assumed I had inherited by default, as the only living relative, but no. My name had been there in solid black and white, incontrovertible. This place was meant for *me*. So despite a residual discomfort, I continued on, sorting through the kitchen drawer by drawer, making lists of all the things I would need.

For all Allegra's virtues, she obviously was not a particular cook—which in some ways was a relief, for I was beginning to feel we had entirely too much in common. Yet, once again, I found myself also saddened, wondering about this woman whose life I had taken over and yet knew so little about. What had she done each night when the sun began to sink over the water, when the shadows of the trees stretched long across the lawn? Had she, like I, used the rather battered corkscrew to open a bottle of the local blueberry wine I had discovered at the market? Had she poured some of the rich, dark liquid into one of the fine set of matched goblets I had discovered—along with the good dishes—in one of the kitchen cupboards? Had she carried that glass, as I did, though the living room—now burnished in rich golds by the late afternoon sun—and through the central set of French doors onto the deck beyond?

There must, at one point, have been deck furniture, but I hadn't spotted it in my quick scan of the attic, nor had I located the basement—if in fact there was one. But I didn't feel like indulging in any more explorations just now. So instead I sat on top of the central set of steps that led down to the lawn, sipping wine as I gazed across the grass to the rock ledges and the water beyond.

The wine was divine, both dry and fruity with a rich tang of oak, and the sinking sun turned the whole world to bronze. There was something both timeless and ancient about the quality of that light, as if I was part of a scene that had been enacted over and over throughout the years until I, too, had become a part of its existence. Perhaps, years from now, when other generations and other owners sat these steps in this antique light, they would sense my spirit in the same way that I now sensed the long line of all those that had come before me.

It was, I realized with a shock, the first time in years that I felt I truly belonged, that I was a part of something larger than myself. I had been anchorless for too long—admittedly, mostly at my own instigation—but now I had found a sense of community. And while it was only a community of ghosts, it was still a start. And I owed it all to a woman I had met but a twice, and who was now just another ghost in the long line of ghosts.

But instead of saddening me, this thought left me feeling oddly peaceful. If I, too, could pass this same legacy down at my death, then maybe it would all not have been in vain.

I raised my glass in silent toast to Allegra and took another sip of my wine. As I did, I became aware of a sleek, dark head breaking the surface of the water about six feet off the rocks. Snub-nosed and inquisitive, it bobbed at the surface of the water for a minute, regarding me out of large, dark eyes that reminded me strangely of Ronan's. Then it flipped onto its side in a liquid twist of movement and swam three times in a circle, regarding me steadily all the while.

When it halted again, its head once more bobbing on the

surface of the waves, it was about a foot closer to shore. It seemed to be waiting for something.

"Hello?" I said tentatively, my voice sounding unnaturally loud in the hush.

Startled, the seal flinched visibly and submerged. I felt an unaccountable pang of loss. Then it bobbed back to the surface again, its gaze warier but still curious. I remembered Harry talking about Allegra's bond with the seals and wondered if this had been one of the ones she had known. Now that I noticed it, there was a distinctive pattern on its head, almost like a lightning bolt of white against the dark coat. Had she given it a name? And if so, what had it been?

The seal bobbed fractionally closer.

"I wish I knew your name," I told it, more softly this time, trying to blend my voice in with the wind and waves.

It cocked its head at me this time instead of fleeing. Encouraged, I continued.

"You knew Allegra, didn't you? I'm Cecil. Cecilia, actually. It's nice to meet you."

A part of me realized how foolish this might have seemed, sitting here on Allegra's back steps talking to a seal, but somehow it didn't feel foolish at all. It felt as natural as breathing, as if this moment existed for no other reason.

The seal gave a tentative half bark and rolled onto its back, still regarding me out of large, liquid eyes. Then its mouth stretched wider as if it were grinning, and it went into a series of tumbled rolls expressly designed to impress. Half a dozen times it wheeled, then popped back up expectantly.

Obligingly, I clapped my hands and cheered, and its grin widened smugly: the well-trained human responding on cue. It seemed about to perform again when suddenly it froze— this time, I was sure, through no action of my own. It rotated its head slightly to the back, and I followed its gaze.

There, in the distance, silhouetted against the sinking sun, bobbed a lugubrious dark head, long-nosed and dour. I felt a shiver run through me that may or may not have had anything to do with a sudden spike of cold wind that arrowed off the water. Somehow, I felt he was watching us—judging us—me and the seal, both.

Then the seal closest to me barked again, reclaiming my attention, and when I glanced back at the horizon again, the second seal was gone, almost as if I had imagined it. But later, after my playful companion had departed and the mosquitoes had driven me inside, and as I stood in Allegra's kitchen cooking dinner—losing myself in the familiar tasks of chopping vegetables and garlic—I couldn't help recalling that dark, dour profile.

I had a feeling I hadn't seen the last of that particular creature.

I SLEPT WELL THAT night—and on the next few nights after that—exhausted from three delightful days of shopping. After relegating the unwanted pots and pans to a heap at the local dump, I drove to Ellsworth on Harry's instructions. Between Rooster Brothers, The Grasshopper Shop, and the series of strip malls along Coastal Route 1, I purchased most of what I needed—and ran up quite a substantial charge on my credit card. But I had never felt more alive.

I bought pots and pans and assorted kitchenware, rugs and candleholders and potted plants for the sunroom. And a warmer coat for the cool June nights—all the time ignoring the fact that I would be leaving in September. I told myself over and over that it was an investment, that a well-stocked house would be easier to sell in the long run. I likewise ignored the knowledge that the shopping was just plain good fun. I eventually did have to put a rein on myself when I started obsessing over the purely frivolous, like prints and decorative coasters. Though I still couldn't resist purchasing a hand-made pottery vase glazed with bold, abstract patterns in blacks and reds that I knew would look terrific on one of the living room mantels. And a scarlet dress, more vivid than any other piece of clothing I had ever owned but which somehow matched my mood, that I would wear to Harry's dinner on Friday night.

I drove home happily each day with my car laden, and spent the early parts of my evenings unloading all my purchases, maneuvering bags and boxes and rolls of rugs into the foyer. I was too busy to be lonely, and was delighted with how perfectly all my purchases worked.

My first task, of course, was to cover the stain in the living room. I hadn't been able to find another carpet as fine as the red Oriental, but I had found two small, matching area rugs in complimentary colors, and if I just shifted the couches back a bit and placed one of the small rugs before each, the stain vanished beneath the left hand rug like magic without affecting the balance of the room. In fact, it looked perfect—and perfectly intended. The room was whole once again.

Or almost, I realized, as I looked around. I hadn't been aware of it on any conscious level, but the mantels were off-balance. The left-hand mantel bore a decorative lacquer urn, almost oriental in style, enameled in reds and blacks. I hadn't really noticed it before, but I must have been aware of it on some level, for how else to explain the new vase that rested in a roll of bubble-wrap in one of my bags? I smiled, and gave my subconscious a mental pat for being on the ball even when I wasn't.

I unwrapped my new purchase and centered it on the right-hand mantel, smiling to myself as the balance of the room shifted into harmony. Then, curious about Allegra's urn, I crossed the room and picked it up.

It was heavier than it looked, with a hinged top and red

dragons chasing each other across a black background. It was a lovely piece, but as I turned it, something shifted within. I paused, turning it back upright and flipping up the lid, then shivered, for it was filled with ash. Hastily I placed it back. Someone's remains, I supposed. But whose? A loved one? A parent? Who close to Allegra had died? Perhaps I would ask Harry.

Then something else distracted me and I forgot all about it.

Other parts of my new house were also coming into order. The rubber plant had, improbably, survived. A few trips to a local nursery had provided it with company, so that the sunroom was now restored to its former glory.

Still, my favorite place to pass my time was on the back deck. I had made a tradition of having a glass of wine and some appetizers out there every night that it was fair—and so far I had been lucky in the weather. For while I had experienced a few grey days, it had yet to rain. And best yet was the company. For no sooner had I unloaded my purchases from my first day out and settled down on the back steps for some wine than the small seal with the lightning-bolt pattern on his head appeared. Over the days, I noticed that he grew bolder each time he performed. Though I had an increasing feeling he was disappointed in me, as if there was something I was supposed to be providing beyond applause and attention.

My other visitor soon became just as regular—and just as welcome. He, too, appeared after my first day out, materializing around the point of the shore with an almost uncanny timing, just after my seal had grown bored with me and departed. So that before I could feel bereft by the seal's absence, there was Ronan, a mischievous grin curving his lips as his sleek, dark head come into view.

He raised a hand, then hesitated fractionally on the verge of my lawn, as if uncertain whether to advance or not. I remembered Abby's words about the frictions between the natives and the transplants and gestured him forward eagerly. He advanced across the grass with a catlike grace.

"Good evening, Cecilia," he said, in his deep, rolling brogue. He seemed to take the same pleasure as before in drawing out my given name, the sounds like taffy in his mouth.

"Have a seat," I said, indicating the step beside me. "I'm sorry; I still haven't found the deck furniture yet. I assume it is somewhere, but . . ." I shrugged.

He smiled. "Try the garage." And, then, as I made to rise, he laid a light hand on my arm that seemed to raise the hairs like electricity to his touch and added with a laugh, "Later."

I almost flinched at the power of that all-too-casual touch and resumed my seat, trying not to feel bereft as his hand fell away. What was it about this man? No one had affected me like this in years. Well, ever, really.

I resumed breathing with a conscious effort, and forced a smile. "Well, if I can't offer you proper furniture, can I at least get you some wine and some salmon dip?"

His eyes lit visibly. "Salmon?" he said.

"Quite." My smile was more genuine this time. "Back in a minute."

I hastily gathered supplies, almost afraid to find him gone when I returned, but he had drawn his knees up to his chest and sat hugging them, gazing almost longingly out over the water. There was something oddly closed about his expression, and for an instant I hesitated to disturb him. Then I cleared my throat and he turned around, his smile so light and natural that I must have imagined his previous expression.

For lack of anything else to say, I extended a glass of my new favorite blueberry wine.

"Thank you," he said, reaching for the glass. His fingers, I noticed, were long and lean, his nails trimmed short and

square. Artistic hands. I wondered how they would feel
on . . .

Hastily, I shook myself out of my trance and released the
glass to him with a smile. I took my seat in turn, laying the
plate of salmon dip and crackers safely between us. He
raised his glass for a sip, then made a sound somewhere between a sneeze and a bark.

"What is it?" I asked.

He grinned, a purely mischievous expression. "Damned
mosquitoes," he replied, slapping at his arm.

And indeed, I had quickly discovered that the minutes before dusk brought out the mosquitoes, that I had a limited
window of daylight in which to enjoy the back deck before
being eaten alive. But I hadn't really noticed any this early
before. Still, some people were targets more than others.
Poor Ronan. I wondered if I should invite him in . . .

Then he took another more cautious sip of his wine, put
down his glass, and reached for a cracker and some of the
salmon dip I had made last night. He raised an eyebrow.
"Very good," he said, around a mouthful.

"Thank you." Searching for a topic, I added, "So, rumor
has it you haven't been on the island that long yourself. Is
that true?"

He looked almost disproportionately startled at my words,
sitting up hastily—but perhaps that was only the mosquitoes
again, for he slapped at his arm again and answered naturally
enough. "Says who?"

"A friend who was talking to your boss."

"Ah." His dark eyes danced. "He does consider me a bit of
a . . . what is the word?"

"Protégé?" I suggested.

He grinned. "Yeah, that. But it is quite true. I come from an
island so small it doesn't even have a name. But my family

has been there for . . . Well, as long as the sea's had tongue."
His lilting voice took on the cadence of a good Irish storyteller, all charm and blarney. Except that it was undoubtedly
true. No wonder he had looked oddly out of place in the gas
station—and why I had kept comparing him to Tom. Seeing
him now, with the water at his feet, seemed a far more natural thing, as if he, too, were born to the sea. Which I suppose
he had been.

"So why Seal Island?" I asked. "And why the gas station?"

"A change of pace?" He looked suddenly wistful. "I always wanted different things than my family, wanted a different life. I doubt you would call this the big city, but for me
it is. And I've always been fascinated by how things work.
All . . . I mean, everyone's always teased me about how I
love to take things apart." His eyes twinkled abruptly, all
mischief again. "I can't always get them back together quite
right, but . . . I'm learning."

"Good for you!" I said. "It's good to try new things."

"And is that why you are here?" he asked me. "To try new
things?"

I felt suddenly self-conscious under his liquid gaze. "Perhaps. I don't know. So how do you like Seal Island?"

His face went serious again. "It's not always been everything I imagined. But now . . ." Mercurial creature that he
was, his eyes again fastened on me and he smiled. "I think
things are starting to look up again."

"Stop," I said, blushing. I had never been comfortable
with overt flattery, as evidenced by the nervous pounding of
my heart in my chest. I sought to turn the conversation
again. "That accent . . . That's not from around here. Where
is your family from, originally?"

He grinned and drank more wine; he seemed as enamored
of it as I was. He loaded up another cracker with salmon dip,
ate it, then replied. "Ireland and Scotland, mostly—though

there are smaller branches of the family from Scandinavia and Iceland. But own my particular family comes from a very tiny island off the Outer Hebrides, in Scotland."

A remote sect; that might explain the brogue. "And when did your family come to America?"

"Oh, many years back. But we still stick rather closely to the old ways and don't tend to intermingle greatly. Or, at least, *they* don't." He paused. "As I've said, I've always been considered a bit of a rebel."

He was almost done with his wine, and I was about to offer him more when suddenly he stiffened, looking out over the water. I followed his gaze. The horse-headed seal had reappeared, and was now closer into the shore than I had ever seen him, his dark gaze somehow menacing. Dusk was falling, bringing with it the whining vanguard of the mosquito invasion. I felt one bite my neck, and jumped and swatted.

"I should go," Ronan said. "You need to get inside, and I just wanted to stop by to see how you were settling in."

"Well, thank you. Would you . . . would you like to come in? I have extra food."

He looked torn, his dark gaze flicking from me to the water. The seal had bobbed in closer, and I had an odd feeling he was protecting my shore—though I couldn't quite determine from what or why. But I wished he would go away.

"No, I must go," Ronan said at last, reluctantly. "Perhaps tomorrow, though, if the offer still stands?"

"It does."

"Tomorrow, then." He held out his hand and I took it, the hard, lean fingers closing over mine in a gesture that was almost a caress. Then, like a courtly knight of old, he leaned over, brushing his lips against the back of my hand.

The shock that went through me was disproportionate to the intensity of the kiss, and for an instant I was frozen to the spot. With a last glance out over the water, he left my deck, raising a hand to me as he vanished around the curve of the shoreline.

I don't know how long I stood staring after his vanished figure. But eventually I realized that I still stood motionless on the deck, a ready target for the thronging mosquitoes. I had almost unconsciously clutched the hand he had saluted to my breast, my other hand cradling its back as if I could hold in the kiss.

The skin still throbbed. The seal was gone.

Disgusted, I dropped the pose, grabbed the remainder of my wine, crackers, and dip, and headed inside, away from the insect hordes.

9

THANKS TO RONAN'S ADVICE, I finally located what passed for the basement next to the garage: an attached shed filled with some rather weathered deck furniture, a large sub-zero freezer, and an upright fridge smelling rather strongly of fish. On my second day back from shopping, I scrubbed out the latter and dragged the former out onto the lawn, cleaning it up as well before assorting it on the deck. There was a table with a green marble top, which I despaired of getting up the back steps by myself; six green metal chairs with mesh seats and two long matching green loungers which I carried up without problem; and four smaller, likewise marble-topped, tables which I also managed to wrestle up solo.

The table alone defeated me. But I needn't have worried. That evening, as soon as my seal had departed again, there was Ronan, advancing across the grass. He paused to peer at the large, marble-topped table that was still stranded on my lawn like a beached rowboat.

"You found it, I see," he said, his dark eyes—even from this distance—registering amusement.

"Hello, Ronan. Yes, thanks. But I can't budge it by myself. If I bribe you with another glass of wine, will you help me?"

"With pleasure," he said.

I descended onto the lawn to meet him. The last two times we had met, I had been sitting. Now I realized that, for all his lean grace, he was taller than he appeared. I was five foot seven; he must have been close to six feet. He grinned down at me, his eyes even more mesmerizing from up close, and said, "Well?"

He smelled, I noticed, of fresh air and salt, with a faint undercurrent of machine oil. It was not an unpleasant scent. I led him to the table and he placed his hands beneath one side while I took up position on the other.

"Right; on three," he said, then executed the count. Obligingly, I heaved on cue, but it was instantly clear that he was also far stronger than he looked and was taking the lion's share of the weight. Together, we wrestled the ungainly table up onto the deck. When we had placed it down with a certain degree of ceremony, I said, "Thank you. I could never have managed that on my own."

"Well, what else are neighbors for?" he said. "And if I ever want to," his eyes twinkled, "borrow a cup of sugar, I know where to come."

I laughed—as much at the idea of him borrowing sugar as anything—and said, "Right; I owe you. Pull up a lounger and I'll get you your promised reward."

We talked some more that evening, and on the evening after—I forget exactly about what—while he made headway though my wine and appetizers, and I soon realized I was coming to find his presence as much a part of my evening routine as visits from my seal. He ate everything I fed him, though seemed fonder of anything containing fish, and while there remained something mesmerizing about his presence, I soon began to discover there were large gaps in his knowledge of the world and popular culture that I could only put down to his being raised on a tiny island, but which sometimes made conversation more difficult without a common base of experience to draw on. I would mention something that, to me, seemed perfectly obvious, and he would stare at me blankly.

Another thing that seemed odd was that, occasionally, our conversation would derail under the strong sense of someone watching. Or perhaps I should say some*thing*, because when these distractions came and Ronan went stiff and silent, I would often look up to see a lugubrious, dark sealhead bobbing on or vanishing beneath the waves, and an unaccountable chill would shake me.

But, apart from this, I welcomed his presence—though I often found myself wondering why he left the sea and the fisherman's life. Because when he talked about his past and the ocean, his voice throbbed with an audible passion and nostalgia, his descriptions of the wind and waves almost rising to a rough poetry. But when I gathered up my courage enough to ask him, all he said was, sadly: "It's just not a life that works well anymore in this modern world."

And while Seal Island hardly seemed to be the modern world to a city girl like me, I supposed I could see his point. I had driven around the island and its surrounds a fair amount in the past few days, and even I was not oblivious to the signs of extreme poverty that cropped up at intervals. I didn't suppose it was easy making a living from the sea.

It made me feel a bit guilty about my recent orgy of spending, and perhaps this is why, the day after this conversation, I found myself feeling oddly at a loss. I had been in Maine for almost a week, although it felt like longer. I had shopped my fill, and I had no social engagements until Harry's party on Friday. Save for Ronan, I had barely seen another soul in days, and I suddenly felt a longing for town—not to mention the shack's lobster rolls and fried clams. I had spent the morning reading on the back deck and had somehow managed to miss lunch in the process. So now I gathered up purse and jacket, got into my car, and drove back to the nameless shack on the pier. And, if my fairly active subconscious had brought me there at approximately the same time as before, when the lobster boats came in, then what of it? The main lure, I told myself, was the food. And the fact that I could visit Abby after.

The waitress-cum-chef was friendlier today, perhaps recognizing the advantages of encouraging repeat business. She even smiled at me as she took my order. "Same thing as last time," she said. "Must be good, eh?"

I smiled my assent. "You don't get seafood this fresh in New York."

"Don't imagine you do," she said, dismissing my city with contempt; I suppose New York would be the ultimate in 'from away' to a Mainer. Then she grinned. "Have a seat. I'll give you a holler when your order's ready."

I complied, claiming my usual table by the water. The gull—obviously more of a regular than I—was still there, and clearly still awaiting people to feed it. But perhaps because I had rebuffed him before, he was more aggressive today, making brief, flying forays at my table as if to let me know what I was in for when my food arrived.

I sighed.

"You're not planning to feed him, are you?" a voice said, in a faintly disapproving baritone.

"God, no!" And I turned to find Tom the lobsterman behind me, a crate balanced on one of his broad shoulders. His eyes were cool and speculative, with a hint of darkness within, and I managed a tentative smile. "Quite the opposite in fact. I didn't feed him the last time, and now he's determined to bully me. I'm trying to figure out how to make him stop."

Tom shifted the crate on his shoulders. "Glad to hear it. They're flying vermin. I always tell Cheryl not to feed them; it just encourages them. We'll see how happy she is when that bold fellow finally attacks a tourist for table scraps."

I laughed. "Judging by his behavior, it might be me."

"Nonsense; you're not a tourist. But still . . ." He deposited the crate on a corner of my table and scooped up a handful of pebbles from the ground.

"What are you . . ." I began. But before I could complete my thought, he gave a loud shout and flung the pebbles at the gull. I heard the small thumps of impact, and the bird gave a screech. For an instant, it looked like it might attack him. But when he stepped forward, one gloved fist raised threateningly, it squawked again and took off, flapping low over the water.

Wise bird. There was a hard expression on Tom's face that made me understand why the gull might not want to tangle with him. But the girl in the shack—Cheryl, apparently—flung open the take-out window and shouted, "You stop that, Tom Moneghan, you great bully!"

He just raised an eyebrow, then turned back to me. "That should guarantee you a peaceful meal." And, with a surprisingly courtly bow for so rough a man, he scooped up his crate again, delivered it to the shack, and departed before I could say a word.

"Food's ready," Cheryl added.

I ate my meal in a bemused silence, wondering why all the Maine men seemed to be raised in the high medieval tradition. Then I retreated to The Gull.

Abby was a refreshing breath of clean, sane air. "Cecil!"

she exclaimed as I walked through the door to the tinkle of chimes. "What brings you here?"

"Nothing more substantial than boredom. Are you busy?"

"As you see." She gestured around the shop. There was not a customer to be seen.

"You must be bored, too."

"Heavens, no! Relishing it. Tourist season starts in less than a month, and then I shall get no rest until after Labor Day." She cocked her head, regarding me with half a smile. "Nor will you, for that matter, if you are still intent on helping me out."

"Still trying to scare me off?" I said. "So, any tips before I start on Monday?"

"Yes; relax. It's only retail, not rocket science. I'm sure you'll pick it up fast enough. Besides," she rested her elbows on the counter, "you still have two weeks before the rush starts."

I smiled and wandered over to the display of stuffed seals. I idly straightened them, stroking their furry heads. One was quite adorable, and sinfully soft; I couldn't quite resist picking it up and cuddling it.

Her elbows still propped against the counter, Abby looked over and me and grinned. "Cute, isn't it? I'm always tempted to buy that one myself, but somehow I manage to resist. Ultimately, it's not quite the real thing."

Still petting the seal, I wandered over to the counter, remembering my visitor of several nights back.

"Really?" I asked. "Are the seals around here particularly friendly?"

"Particularly?" She smiled. "Perhaps not anything out of the ordinary—unless you are someone special, of course." Reaching up to a shelf over the counter, she pulled down a framed photograph and handed it to me.

In it, a slim blond woman clad in jeans and a black sweater, her face half obscured by her hair, stood before a watery background, bent over something in her arms that looked up at her with wide, dark eyes. It was a seal pup, its coat still snowy. I felt a momentary twinge of envy for her closeness to the creature, then did an abrupt double take, focusing on her face. "My God, is that Allegra?"

Abby laughed. "And Ragnarok. You mean you didn't know?"

I laid the stuffed animal down on the counter, my attention focused on the picture now. "Once again, it seems not. Please, tell me."

Abby sat down on the stool behind the counter and crossed her arms, obviously settling in for a tale. "Well, it was a rather recent occurrence, as things on this island go. But about two years ago, in early June—in the wake of a rather bad storm—Allegra found this little guy washed up on the rocks in front of her house, abandoned, hurt, and crying piteously. She took him to a vet, had him fixed up, and nursed him back to health by hand. When his parents didn't arrive to claim him before the seals all migrated in the fall, she kept him. She named him Ragnarok and took him in, adopting him until the seals came back in the spring. I have never seen a woman so devoted to a seal, nor a seal to a woman. Allegra absolutely believed in the philosophy that if you love something, you set it free. When Ragnarok outgrew the bathtub and his kin came back, she let him join them. It nearly broke her heart when he went south with them this past fall. I almost wonder if that wasn't part of what contributed to her isolation last winter. No one knew if he was going to come back this year or not."

"And did he?" I asked. "Come back?"

Her face grew pensive. "I don't know. Allegra was killed

just before the seals returned in early May. There are days I wonder if Ragnarok isn't still out looking for her, wondering where she disappeared to." She took the photo from me, peering at it for a long moment, then set it back on the shelf. "Still," she added, "having known Ragnarok, if only briefly. . . . Stuffed seals don't quite cut it. He was a capital fellow, endlessly smart and charming. I hope he does come back."

"As do I." I set the stuffed seal back on the shelf, suddenly feeling inadequate.

Fortunately, we were distracted by the chiming of the shop bells as a handful of tourists appeared. While Abby was busy showing off bags and T-shirts, I found myself cornered by a middle-aged woman, anxious for something to read. Almost without thinking about it, I led her to the book corner and started talking up the benefits of the various Morelands—although she seemed to be leaning to the more insipid of the romances. But eventually I prevailed, and ushered her proudly to the counter, three Morelands in hand. "Honestly," I said, as Abby rang her up. "If you don't love them, come back and I'll give you one of the others you were looking at for free."

"There, you see, you're a natural," Abby said, as our customers departed. "Definitely supporting the local economy. But just remember, you can't give away all our stock!"

I flushed. "Sorry; I forgot where I was for a moment."

"No sweat," Abby said cheerfully. "After all, you're the boss. Officially, you're the one still buying the stock. So your money, your guarantees."

I stood stunned. I had forgotten for a moment that this was my place.

"Still," Abby added, speculatively, "that's not a bad idea. That woman looked like she'd actually enjoy the books, and that sort of salesmanship makes for a nice personal touch. She'll be back. How many of those books *can* you recommend?"

I grimaced. "Embarrassingly, a fair amount. Among my other faults, I read too much. One of the sidelines of having no life."

"And since when has reading too much been a fault?" Abby countered stoutly. "I only wish I had time myself. Selling the Morelands is a no-brainer, but I don't have the time to read all the other books. Maybe I should just put you in charge of that end of the business."

"I'd be delighted."

"But not until Monday. You have four days of vacation left; don't waste it in here. Go out; have fun."

I KILLED TWO MORE hours wandering through the town, acquainting myself with the other merchants and their wares. Unsurprisingly, most of them seemed to recognize me and introduced themselves as I appeared. But though I lost track of the names and faces, I did begin to get a sense of the community that held this island together—at least among the transplants. For there were very few of these merchants, I suspected, who had actually been born here.

My wandering eventually took me past the library, which was open—fortunately, as it happened, given the sign posted outside which announced the sadly limited hours of operation. I poked around happily. For such a small building, it had a satisfyingly complete collection, including all of my old favorites. I ended up applying for a card and checking out an armload—not to mention acquiring a lunch date with the librarian, a charming woman in her seventies named Mabel. She was a former schoolteacher who made some comment about young people and reading, smiled when I said I loved Thomas Moreland, said she knew Allegra, and invited me to the Clam Digger for lunch a week from Saturday.

I accepted with alacrity and left clutching my pile of books.

When I got home again, the tide was high, lapping up against the margins of the rocks. It was still too early for wine, so I poured myself a glass of lemonade and settled down on the back deck with one of my new books. A while later, absorbed in the story, I nonetheless became aware of something watching me.

My seal was back again, not five feet from shore, the lightning-bolt pattern clear on his head. The pert, spaniel-like face bobbed at the surface of the waves, the mouth stretched up in what could only seem like a hopeful grin. The dark eyes were fixed on me intently.

"Hello, again," I said.

After six days, the creature was no longer startling at the sound of my voice. Instead, it almost seemed to laugh. It executed a backward flip, bobbing back up two feet closer to shore.

Those liquid black eyes regarded me, almost as if they were prompting me.

And then, like a blinding flash, the revelation came.

"Ragnarok?" I asked.

The seal's mouth stretched wider and he barked, then spun three flips in rapid succession.

Slowly, I rose from my chair and crept down to the margin of the water to avoid startling him, but he only watched me until I had reached my desired spot: a bare two feet from his dog-like head. Then he barked again and rolled over on his back, regarding me speculatively across the expanse of his belly.

I smiled, filled with a sudden warmth. "Welcome home."

10

Friday dawned grey and chilly—still not raining, but hardly the ideal weather for Harry's party. It was too cold and gloomy to spend time outside, so I passed a peaceful day indoors, reading. Around noon I drove to town to run a few errands and cast an idle glance at the docks as I passed, but it was too early for any of the lobster boats to be in. So I returned home, fixed lunch, and read some more.

At four, I put down my book, then showered and changed for Harry's party. It was still too chilly to wear the red dress alone, so I compromised by adding a black cardigan and then examined myself critically in the mirror. Even I had to admit it was an effective outfit. I was not used to such bold colors, but they suited me. The scarlet of the dress swirled like flame about my ankles, and my hair shone a deep, brilliant gold against the sweater. Even my objectionable dishwater eyes seemed wider and greener than I had ever seen them. All it needed was the drama of a gold chain around my neck and a pair of decent earrings to complete the image.

I knew there would be something to suit among Allegra's jewelry boxes, which I had discovered a few days earlier in the top drawer of one of her dressers. Surely she wouldn't begrudge me the use of few pieces? But still I hesitated for a minute before pulling out the boxes and sorting through them.

The pieces were, in general, bold, dramatic creations I would never have dared to wear a month ago, yet had always secretly yearned to. I fastened a heavy-linked gold chain around my neck, inserted a pair of coiled button earrings into my ears, and marveled at how right they looked. I silently thanked Allegra again for her taste—and her bounty—and wondered if that attractive editor, Richard Feinman, might be at the party.

I had, I admitted to myself, almost forgotten his presence on the island, overshadowed as he was by the twin dark auras of Ronan Grey and Tom Moneghan. But for all that his nightly presence had become almost a fixture on my back deck, Ronan had made no move save for that first night's courtly hand-kiss to suggest that he saw me as anything more than a friend. And a large part of me was glad for that. My physical reaction to Ronan was too strong, too intense. A concerted assault at that wattage on my habitual walls stood a good chance of sending them tumbling to the ground, and that was the last thing I wanted.

No, far safer to remain as we were.

As for Tom Moneghan, who was he to me but an ambiguous figure glimpsed twice on a dock? That was the realm of dreams more than reality.

Whereas Richard was . . . real. Richard was interested. And if that wasn't its own kind of terror, I didn't know what was. But still, in my usual contradictory way, it was a good terror, one which left me oddly elated as well as scared. How long had it been it since there was anything resembling a real prospect in my life? Far too long. Maybe . . .

I dismissed the thought with a mental snort. Whatever was awaiting me on this island was not romance. And I was only too aware that part of my waffling over the jewelry—and men—was to help distract me from the fact that I was never at my best in social situations.

But the whole debate had made me recall that I had neglected to tell Ronan of my absence this evening. How would I alert him? I didn't know where he lived save 'nearby,' and I had no phone number. When I tried the local directory assistance, they had no listing whatsoever for a Ronan Grey. So for lack of anything better to do, I scrawled him an apologetic note and left it tacked down to my back deck with a large rock. It fluttered a bit in the stiff breeze off the water, but hopefully would stay put. Then I turned my attention back to the coming party.

WHEN I ARRIVED AT Harry's door at five past five, Richard was indeed there. I caught a glimpse of his sandy head on the back deck, talking to a tall, elegant women I thought might be Joanna. The Camerons' house was on the far side of the island from Allegra's, and was one of the large, modern creations that seemed to dominate the area. It wasn't the most impressive of the houses I had seen on my drive over, but it was still imposing. The front door opened into a single, vast room that seemed to serve as living room, dining room, and kitchen all at once, with one wall of solid glass looking out over the bay. The remaining walls—painted white and rising to a cathedral ceiling—were covered with large, bold canvases, their subjects abstract and seemingly by the same hand. Beyond, on the deck, several guests milled—Richard among them.

"Cecil!" Harry said, as he ushered me in and took my coat. He seemed as delighted to see me as before. "Come in. You look lovely!"

"Thank you. You have a gorgeous place here."

"Thanks. We like it."

"How long have you been here? I mean, didn't you say you've only been back on the island for two years?"

Harry laughed. "And she pays attention, too. Yes, we did just move back, but we've been summering up here for years; we built the house about fifteen years ago. The kids love it, and I just couldn't give the island up completely even when I wasn't living here permanently."

"You were born here, you said?"

"Yes. Martha's from Boston; we met down there in college, and stayed for twenty-odd years while raising the boys. After they left home, we decided to move back here full time."

"And your children?"

"The eldest, Bill, is married; he just moved to North Carolina with his wife. And Dan, the youngest, is still in Boston. Still single, too. He comes up here occasionally in the summer." And Harry's eyes twinkled expectantly.

I almost laughed. So that explained his somewhat paternalistic interest in me. I wondered what Dan Cameron was like.

"Can I get you a drink?" Harry added.

"Yes, please. A glass of wine would be wonderful."

"Red or white?"

"Red, please."

"Let me get it while I introduce my wife." He was, I noticed, still walking with cast and cane. But he gestured cheerfully across the room, summoning a short, plump woman with curling grey hair. From a distance, she looked the quintessential motherly type—until she got closer and I saw the tough, no-nonsense expression in her eyes, softened by a visibly apparent sense of humor. "Martha, this is our guest of honor tonight, Cecil Hargrave. And Cecil, this is my wife, Martha Cameron."

"Lovely to meet you," I said, extending a hand.

"Likewise," she said, gripping it firmly. "I'm supposed to entertain you while Harry hobbles his way to the bar. It might take a while, though, so why don't I start by asking how you like Seal Island?"

I laughed, liking her instantly. "I love it. Everyone's been so helpful and friendly. And your husband's been wonderful. I can't thank you enough."

"Well, much as I'd like to claim credit, I'm afraid that's Harry's doing, not mine. But I am glad that you could make it tonight." She peered at me, seeming to notice my necklace for the first time. "That's one of Allegra's, isn't it?" I flushed, but she forestalled my stammered apology. "Nonsense; I'm glad to see someone enjoying it. Ah, here comes Harry. And, damn it, there go the beans!"

Indeed, I could smell a sudden charring coming from the kitchen. She dashed off with a rueful twinkle as Harry arrived at my side, bearing a glass of red wine.

I accepted it with thanks and took a sip; it was divine.

"Come meet the others," he said, steering me across the room.

There was a door in one corner that led out onto the deck. Harry held it open for me, and I passed through. Richard looked up at my approach and smiled, abandoning his previous companion.

"Cecil," he said, extending a hand, then surprised me by leaning over to kiss me lightly on the cheek.

"Oh. You've met?" Harry sounded startled.

"Indeed. Abby introduced us about a week ago at the Myrtle Inn. It's lovely to see you again, Cecil. You look beautiful."

His blue eyes were fastened intently on me, and I felt a flush of happiness—and panic. He was wearing a tailored navy suit with a blue shirt and a blue-and-black tie that brought out the color of his eyes.

"Thank you. So do you." Then I flushed again and stammered, "That is . . . I mean . . ."

He smiled reassuringly and squeezed my hand—which I realized he still retained. "Never mind. I understand the intent, and I'm grateful for it." Then he released me, adding, "I figured I'd give you a few days to adjust to island life before I called you about that drink you promised me. Are you sufficiently adjusted?"

"I think so."

"Good, then."

Abruptly feeling awkward, I looked about the deck. "Where's Abby?"

I was hoping to see another familiar face, but Richard looked abruptly uncomfortable. "I very much doubt she's coming."

I glanced over at Harry, who was industriously studying the horizon, then back at Richard, but he just shook his head and mouthed: *I'll explain later.* And before I could comment further, Joanna came over, saying, "Good evening, Cecil. It's good to see you again."

"And you, too." She looked every inch as elegant as I remembered, and I suddenly felt eclipsed in my old black cardigan and borrowed jewelry—despite the new dress.

"I'm glad to see you are putting some of Allegra's things to use," she added. "It would be a crime to leave them moldering in a drawer. Harry, maybe you can settle a bet. Rumor has it that you've invited Tom."

I stared at her, baffled as to why she would be surprised at her own husband's presence; Abby hadn't said anything about a divorce or a rift. But Harry just laughed and said, "Rumor has it correct. I did invite him—though heaven only knows if he'll show."

Joanna laughed. "Well, if he does, it'll be the social coup of the season! I can't recall the last time he attended one of our parties."

Just then, a tall man more informally dressed than the others wandered over. He had brown hair and glasses, and a beard liberally streaked with grey. In his dark pants and flannel shirt he looked like a cross between a college professor and a lumberjack. But the elegant Joanna smiled fondly at him and put a hand on his arm. "You were right," she told him. "Tom is on the guest list."

He laughed. "I told you." He extended his hand. "You must be Cecil. I'm Tom Mills, Joanna's husband."

I muttered something polite, feeling more confused than ever.

Martha joined us with a grin, and a large gin and tonic in her hands. "Disaster averted," she declared. "Hell, Joanna, I don't know how you do it. It's all I can manage not to burn dinner every night. I feel almost guilty for making you eat my food after sampling yours."

"Jean-Pierre's, actually," Joanna returned. "Heaven protect you if you ever have to sample *my* cooking! Besides, you have other talents."

"Those are Martha's paintings on the walls," Richard informed me.

"Really?" I said, wishing I had had more of a chance to examine them. I tried peering back through the glass, but the sun was striking it at an angle, obscuring the room beyond.

"If you're interested," Martha said, "I'll give you a tour of my studio later."

"I'd like that."

"So, how are you liking Seal Island so far, Cecil?" Tom asked.

I suppressed a grin, wondering how many times I would have to answer that particular question tonight. "I love it. Everyone's been wonderfully welcoming. Especially . . ." And then I remembered that I did indeed have significant news, and smiled.

"What?" Richard prompted.

"Let me guess," said a deep and vaguely familiar voice from behind me. "Ragnarok's back."

I jumped and whirled. Casually elegant in dark trousers and a black cashmere sweater, Tom Moneghan the lobsterman smiled enigmatically back at me.

"Tom!" Joanna exclaimed. "Now here's a surprise! We never thought you'd show. What brings you here?"

He raised an eyebrow. "A desire not to be too predictable in my unsociability. Thanks for the invite Harry, Martha. I can't stay for dinner; I have a previous engagement, I'm afraid. But I did want to stop by and say 'hello.' "

"And scare the crap out Cecil while you are at it," Martha said acidly. But there was an undeniable hint of affection in her voice—though she did seem to be the only one in the group who felt it, for an odd tension had sprung up at Tom's arrival. Harry was acting deferential while Joanna was scowling at him suspiciously, as if trying to fathom his true motives. Richard was bristling visibly, while Tom—the other Tom; this must get confusing—was smiling in overt amusement. "By the way, you have met Cecil, haven't you?" Martha added.

He turned to me, his dark eyes speculative. "After a fashion," he said, extending a hand. "But to make it official . . . I'm Tom Moneghan."

"Cecil Hargrave," I responded almost automatically, shaking the proffered hand. As expected, his palm was hard and callused with wind, salt and lines.

"And I'm glad I arrived in time for such significant news," he added. "Tell me about Ragnarok."

"Yes," Joanna chimed in. "Are you certain he's back?"

"I think so." But with everyone's attention focused on me, I suddenly felt less certain of my conclusions. "I've . . . well, I've noticed two seals watching me ever since I arrived. One seems very reserved—almost morose if the truth be known—but the other is quite friendly. Comes right up to the shore as if he was expecting something. At first, I didn't think anything more about it. But then, after Abby showed me a picture of Allegra with Ragnarok, I put it together. And when I called him by name yesterday, he almost seemed to recognize it."

"No doubt he did," Tom Moneghan said. "Seals are quite intelligent. And Ragnarok was always a prince of the breed."

"Except I think I'm disappointing him," I confessed. "He keeps looking at me like he expects something more from me than just company and an audience."

A faint smile sketched itself across Tom Moneghan's lips. "I think I can help with that one. In addition to being highly intelligent, seals are also greedy bastards. I think he wants you to feed him—on the principle that it's easier than catching it himself."

Richard laughed, but I just felt a sudden surge of panic.

"But I have no idea what to feed a seal." I could sense my voice rising, and broke off in annoyance. I turned to Tom. "Any recommendations?"

He raised an eyebrow. "Mackerel is always a favorite."

"And where am I supposed to get mackerel?"

His dark eyes suddenly filled with such an exquisite mischief that I caught my breath, realizing I'd been set up. "Easily enough remedied," he said. "Who do you think used to keep Allegra supplied? I'll bring you a load tomorrow. I assume the refrigerator in the shed is still working?"

Remembering the fishy smelling fridge off the garage, I said, "If unplugging it and scrubbing it down didn't hurt. I'll plug it back in in the morning and check. And thanks."

He nodded, but there was a hooded reserve back in his eyes. In fact, in the few times I had met him, I had yet to see him really smile. Suddenly he struck me as a man with walls that could rival even mine. I peered at him curiously, as if to unlock his secrets, but his expression remained impenetrable.

"So," Joanna broke in, "if one of your two seals is Ragnarok, then who is the other? Allegra never mentioned anything about a second pet."

I just shrugged, and all eyes turned again to Tom.

Martha scowled at him. "Don't you dare!"

He raised an eyebrow. "Why not? It might be true."

"What might be true?" Joanna demanded.

"That Cecil may have gained herself the attention of a selkie," he said.

Joanna groaned loudly. "Good Lord, Tom, not those old stories again! There's no such thing as a selkie."

"According to you. The fishermen have another story entirely. And if you were out on the water as much as they were, you might change your opinion. Odd things can happen in the fog and the mist . . ."

His voice had taken on the unmistakable tones of a veteran storyteller, and—despite their skepticism—the group was hanging on his words in rapt silence, as if he were uttering prophecy. True, there was something mesmerizing in his dark gaze as his voice dropped in register, but still I couldn't help feeling like this was growing into a grand joke at my expense. So, breaking the spell a bit, I demanded, "And what exactly *is* a 'selkie?'"

His head turned and his eyes fixed on mine, and for a moment I had the sense that we were the only people on the deck, in this world. "The seal people," he responded. "The stories originated mostly from Scotland and Ireland. My family is of Scottish descent . . ."

Like Ronan, I thought absently; maybe that was the similarity I had sensed between them.

". . . and we are said to have the blood of the seals in our veins. The selkies are a race of seals who can become human at will, mostly co-existing with the fisherman who work their native waters. And those who are kind to them while they are in their seal form get nothing but rewards, while those who are cruel meet their eternal vengeance."

"Vengeance?" I asked, alarmed.

He smiled slightly. "You see, occasionally when a lonely fisherman is kind to the seals, a beautiful selkie woman will come from the sea to be his bride, forsaking her seal skin for that of a human. And so the selkie blood is mingled with the human, in their children. But it is hard to keep a seal from the water forever, and the selkie brides eventually long to return to their first and only home. But they cannot change back into their native form without their sealskins, which they shed when they became human. Many stories tell of the fisherman unwise enough to destroy the skin so his bride can no longer return to the sea. And when she dies of grief and yearning for her true home, her family comes from the sea for revenge."

"Revenge?" I demanded, as caught up now in the story as anyone. He did have a natural storyteller's gift, the cadence of his language low and even.

"The fisherman dies. A life for a life, you see. And if there are children, they take those too and return them to the sea. Maybe those half-seal children can reach into the depths of their seal blood and somehow transform to join their mother's family, or maybe they cannot and simply drown. But no one knows for certain, for they never return."

Despite myself, I suppressed a shiver. But Joanna just said, "So apart from the fact that there are no such things as shape-shifting seals, are you really trying to tell us that Cecil is in immanent danger of being carted off to the water on some dark and stormy night?"

"Of course not," he replied. "Allegra was nothing but kind to the seals, and Cecil is not her child. She is probably just being observed, to see how she treats Ragnarok." But even as he said this, he turned slightly to me, dropping me a surreptitious wink I was certain none of the others saw.

Comprehension dawned. This wasn't a gigantic joke at my expense; it was a gigantic joke at the expense of the others. Maybe designed to puncture their complacency, maybe for some other reason entirely. There were undercurrents here I couldn't begin to understand, not to mention a history I was clearly not privy to. But I couldn't help wondering why a crowd I suddenly realized was intensely socially conscious had invited a lobsterman to their party, and why that lobsterman had accepted. Was it only to scare me with his tales of shape-shifting seals? He had clearly known who I was; I recalled his words back at the docks: *You're not a tourist.* And he had known I would be here, at this party thrown in my honor. So why include me in his conspiracy? Was he trying to make me choose sides? And between what? What was happening on Seal Island?

Moreover, why did everyone seem to think that having this man at their party was such a social coup? Was it some sort of exercise in reverse-snobbism, since he was the only one that cleaned up nicely? *Look how magnanimous we are, inviting the locals to our party. At least, the ones that won't embarrass us.*

I felt vaguely disgusted.

In the past few days I had, I realized, fashioned a rosy utopia around Seal Island, imagining its denizens as one big, happy family. Now, my naïveté embarrassed me. In every group, there are tensions and petty rivalries. How could I have imagined it would be otherwise here? Just because people had been nice to me didn't mean they were kind to the world.

I would just have to start evaluating my surroundings more carefully. And try not to make assumptions.

But there was one thing I had to admit: Tom Moneghan did clean up nicely. Though even sartorially dressed, he still wasn't what you would call classically handsome. There was a roughness to him, a sense of lingering darkness, that wasn't aided by the combination of dark clothes and darker hair. No wonder his ancestors had claimed seal blood. His eyes were almost the same liquid black as Ragnarok's. And Ronan's.

Still, people were so foolish. Any hint of difference, and they built legends: tales designed to isolate, to exclude. And I, for one, was determined not to play that game. I was not going to judge Tom Moneghan simply for some accident of his birth. So I met those dark eyes boldly and managed a smile, just to let him know I was in on the joke.

He actually smiled back, the expression taking years off his face. And Martha, her face the picture of innocence, grinned.

"Tom Moneghan," she declared, "the day you stop telling stories is the day you die!"

He turned a rather rueful smile to her. "That may be truer than you know," he said, and suddenly everyone laughed, the tension all dispelled.

"Well, if only I was half so successful with my pictures as you are with your words," she added, and chuckled. "But, speaking of which, I promised Cecil a studio tour, and you might as well see my progress on those two pictures you commissioned. Anyone else interested?"

Joanna and Tom Mills elected to stay with Harry, but Richard seemed disinclined to leave me alone with the other Tom, so the three of us trailed across the lawn with Martha in the lead.

The studio, glass-walled and skylighted, was located in a separate building off to the far side of the main house, commanding the same water views. And whatever Martha might have said about her work, she did indeed have talent. Her canvases were both bold and brash, yet oddly indeterminate, their meanings sharpening almost to the point of comprehension before fading back to obscurity. Yet they conveyed a decided mood. And, more impressively, sometimes more than one, as if any picture, viewed from another angle, could morph into something entirely different.

In fact, I found myself almost mesmerized by a pair of large, matched canvases. While clearly unfinished, both still had that same ambiguous quality that seemed to characterize Martha's work. Both conveyed a sense of shoreline—sky and rocks and water and trees—the palette primarily one of smoky blues, greens, and greys. But while one was light and tranquil, like a perfect summer's day, the other was deeper, darker, more troubled: a winter's storm. And yet . . . If one looked closer, the sunny day seemed on the verge of storm, and the stormy on the edge of fair.

Even half-finished, they were breathtaking.

Gradually I became aware of Tom Moneghan at my side, one arm crossed at his waist, the other propping up his chin, regarding the two pieces with an intensity that was almost frightening. I snuck a sideways glance at him, and was amazed to see the sudden, proud grin that lit his features.

Then he shook his head, but I could still see the trace of awe in his eyes as he said, "Martha, you have utterly outdone yourself," and swept her up in a sudden, quick embrace, startling a squawk from her. Abruptly serious, he added, "How perfectly you understand."

Then I knew. His pieces, commissioned. And what exactly she understood I couldn't say, but somehow I knew he was right. Whatever the essential core of Tom Moneghan was, it was captured in those two, mirrored images.

I looked away from them, abruptly uncomfortable, as if I had caught a glimpse of something it wasn't my right to see.

"They're magnificent, Martha," Richard said, breaking the mood. "In fact, I'm almost jealous. If you were going to paint me, how would you do it?"

She smiled and cocked her head, regarding him. Then, rummaging through a rack of canvases, she said, "Well, it's not exactly perfect, but . . ." and pulled out a painting.

It was all in shades of sands and browns, with hints of blue, and again I sensed she was right. It wasn't perfect, but there was something of Richard in there. At least Richard as I knew him, which admittedly wasn't well. But there was the same sense of solidity and strength, coupled with the polished gentility that had first attracted me.

He seemed pleased as well, grinning at her. "Now do Cecil," he said.

I froze, startled like a deer in the headlights as her eyes fastened on me. That keen, grey gaze was suddenly unnerving, seeming to pick me into my component pieces. And she wasn't the only one staring. Richard was regarding me with a warm intensity, and Tom's gaze was dark and cool, once again unreadable. My fingers plucked nervously at the hem of my sweater, and I had the feeling my face was the same shade as my dress.

"I don't have anything to match, yet," she finally decided, and I let myself draw a breath. It was a diplomatic way for Martha to back out of analyzing someone she barely knew, even if a part of me did think she saw entirely too much in too short a time. "But I will, soon," she declared. "Just as soon as I finish yours, Tom. Meanwhile," and she smiled at me, "what do you think of this one?"

She drew out another canvas, this one in shades of rich yellows, velvet greens, smoky blues, and seal browns. There was something extraordinarily elegant and lovely about it, and yet at the same time profoundly lonely. Was that a tree reaching tall for the sun or the lone remains of a once-proud forest? And, though I didn't know how, I knew there was a seal in there somewhere. But whether the pert-nosed, playful seal or the lugubrious one, I couldn't say. Or maybe it was a bit of both at once.

Almost without my conscious volition, my hand reached toward the canvas.

I drew back hastily as Tom sucked in a sharp breath. Richard was smiling softly, sadly; he reached for my hand and squeezed. Then I understood.

Allegra.

I felt a prickle of tears in my eyes and reflexively clutched Richard's hand tighter. His grip was warm and firm, reassuring. On my other side, Tom seemed cool as a statue, and about a million miles away.

But even as I looked at the painting, I felt another prickle—this time completely different—run up my spine. Once again, I couldn't help feeling that Martha had tapped into something deeper than she intended. What was it with my almost-aunt and the seals? Not Tom's ridiculous selkie stories, clearly, but . . . something. Something that struck me as amazingly profound—if only I could tease it out of the blots and swirls of paint.

"Martha?" Harry said, sticking his head in through the studio door and shattering the mood. "Can you help me? Gilbert's arrived, and I have no idea where you've hidden the brandy."

And whatever the feeling was, it disappeared like a wisp of fog in the sun.

11

GILBERT ROWE, HARRY'S BUSINESS partner, fit my stereotype of a lawyer much more than Harry himself did, and I was suddenly glad it was Harry and not Gilbert who was handling Allegra's affairs. Gilbert was about sixty, grey-haired and handsome in a completely conventional way, and seemed aware that he was good-looking but not that he was conventional. Worse, his manner was just a shade too hearty, and began to grate on me badly as the evening wore on.

His wife, Linda, closer to my age than his, likewise seemed obsessed with appearances—and with as little comprehension about what she was seeing. She wrinkled her nose visibly at Tom Moneghan as if she could still smell the fish on him rather than the woodsy, outdoors scent he had carried into the studio.

The lobsterman greeted them coolly, then vanished off to whatever other appointment awaited him just after the Rowes arrived, bidding me a similarly cool farewell that contained no hint of our previous conspiracy. And I found myself on the back deck, a fresh glass of wine in hand, chatting with Tom Mills, who it turned out had also grown up in New York City. We compared neighborhoods and other such trivia for a bit, then Tom drifted off and I found myself alone with Richard.

I was leaning against the deck railing, looking out over the water with my glass of wine beside me. Richard came to stand next to me, too close for purely casual contact, his hand brushing against mine. He was silent for a long moment, then said, in a voice as soft as the waves, "A penny for them?"

I forced a laugh. "Hasn't inflation had an effect, yet? Or is it only me that's so cheap?"

"Far from it," he said, his voice almost a caress. I turned slightly, startled to see his head so close to my own. "I'm sorry about that business earlier, with Tom," he added. "I hope it didn't upset you."

I wasn't sure if he was referring to Tom's stories of the seal people or his compatriots' treatment of the lobsterman. But I suspected it might be the former and so mustered the polite lie. "No, not at all. Martha's quite the artist, isn't she?"

"That she is. She was building a very solid career in Boston before coming here. She still exhibits in some of the Boston galleries and also in Portland, though she hasn't yet broken into New York. There are some who say it was a mistake for her to relocate to Maine because it is so isolated, but I disagree. This place seems to feed her art in a way that no place else ever could. I think that coming here was the best thing she could have done."

"It seems so," I responded, thinking: *gallery exhibitions?* I had figured she was strictly amateur since Tom Moneghan could afford a commission. The quality of her work should have told me otherwise, but still . . . How *was* Tom Moneghan affording two such glorious pieces?

". . . that drink?" Richard was saying.

"Huh?" I dragged my attention back to the matter at hand.

Richard was looking at me quizzically, one eyebrow slightly arched. "I was asking if you were still interested in that drink I had mentioned."

My heart pounded, but I managed too reply with reasonable aplomb. "Yes, that sounds lovely, Richard. Thanks. When?"

His eyes warmed again, and I managed not to flush. "I was thinking tomorrow night. Are you free? We could even combine it with dinner, if you'd like."

"That sounds . . . Yes. I mean . . . yes. Yes," I said more firmly. "I'd like that."

"Even if it took you a while to reach that decision?"

There was no hiding the blush this time. "Yes. I mean . . . no. That is . . ." I sighed. "I'm sorry, I'm just a little out of practice at all this."

"At all what?"

"Getting asked out." Despite my presence at this party of adults, I suddenly felt about fifteen years old. "I mean, that is what this is, isn't it?" I added, then suddenly wondered what I would do if he said no.

But all he said was, softly, "Yes, it most definitely is. And pardon me if I find that hard to believe. A woman as lovely as you should get asked out all the time. But if not, then all the better for me; far less competition. So, shall I pick you up at seven?"

"That sounds lovely." Really, this was getting easier by the minute, augmented by the warmth in his eyes and the broad solidity of his shoulders. This was a man you could depend on: a true New England rock, solid as the slabbed ledges before us, now darkening in the dying light. "The Myrtle?" I added.

He laughed. "Hell, no! Much as I love Joanna, she is too damn nosy by half. And besides"—he dropped his voice again—"I want you to myself, tomorrow."

Well, maybe not as easy as I had thought. My heart was pounding unnaturally fast again, making it hard to think, let alone talk.

But again he seemed to sense my limits, backing off like the gentleman he was.

"Actually, I was thinking about Jonathan's in Blue Hill," he said. "That is, if you don't mind a bit of a drive?"

"Not at all. But that reminds me; I've been meaning to ask. Why is it called Blue Hill?" I had driven through the town on my way to Ellsworth earlier in the week, and it hadn't seemed particularly hilly to me. Or blue.

He smiled. "Some people say it's called Blue Hill because of the blueberries. But I think it's really because of how it looks when you see it from the water. Or from Mount Desert Island."

He pronounced it like "dessert," and I frowned, images of heaping ice cream sundaes and mountains of profiteroles springing to mind. He just chuckled, and added, "From the French, meaning "descrted." This whole area was first settled by the French. Unlike today, they apparently found very few people around. But you can tell why they loved it. Look, that's Mount Desert Island, there." And he gestured out across the water. There were more islands scattered off the Cameron's part of the shore than off Allegra's—although Allegra's had the sunsets. Here, the sinking sun was almost at our backs, casting long shadows across the lawn. And the islands, instead of being vividly backlit, were slowly fading into twilight. But still I discerned the large landmass he was indicating, rising high into view.

"Cadillac Mountain," he said, "the highest point on the

Eastern seaboard. A lot of Mount Desert Island is taken up by Acadia National Park; I'll take you there some time. No one should experience the Down East without a taste of popovers and tea at the Jordan Pond House."

I turned back to him, letting a teasing note slip into my voice. "Indeed?"

But before he could respond, Martha's voice echoed across the deck. "Stop monopolizing our guest of honor, Richard, and bring her in here. Dinner is served. Such as it is," she added with a laugh.

Richard smiled and extended an arm.

"Shall we?" he said.

DINNER WAS VERY PLEASANT—and though Martha was no Jean-Pierre when it came to food, the atmosphere was impeccable. The lights were kept low and the candles lit, and as the sun disappeared behind the trees, the huge room took on the feel of a cave, the cathedral ceiling vanishing into darkness. The plate glass windows, with the night behind them, reflected back the interior light, glowing a soft, dusky bronze. And the two large canvases hung one atop the other on the protruding sweep of chimney—holding, I suspected, much of Harry in them—were similarly bronze-toned. But not in any metallic way. Rather, the soft, matte colors seemed to glow from within, in much the same way that the window seemed to trap and hold the light, adding to the room's luminosity.

At the table, the same bronze tones were picked up by the dishes, which looked to be handcrafted, with a vague, metallic sheen to the glaze. When I asked, Martha told me that they were indeed made by a local potter, and promised to take me by the studio. The combination of the painting and the pottery stirred something nebulous inside me, some ill-defined longing I couldn't put a name to.

Then Richard distracted me, pouring me wine, and I forgot the sensation.

The company was quite pleasant—apart from Gilbert and Linda, whom I just couldn't warm up to—but it was also surreal as well. Few of my acquaintances had ever been married, and fewer still were older. I had rarely been to "adult" dinner parties. And the few times I had, I was invariably the charity case. Poor Cecil, who had no one left in the world. I was always the third wheel. Or the fifth. Or some odd number, anyway. And if, by chance, a date had been invited for me, he was usually the same as me: another lame charity case.

Except this time.

I had expected to feel the odd one out again, to have little to say. But with a handsome man beside me and a host of kind people determined to make me feel at home—coupled, I have to admit, with a few I could feel superior to—I felt, if not completely at home, then at least welcomed. And very much a part of the evening's festivities.

We chatted about New York, and about my job; about my plans for the future. About movies and books. When they asked me about my favorite writer, I immediately responded "Thomas Moreland," to which Joanna laughed and countered, "You would say that!"

Richard pouted, then brightened as I said liked classical music and vowed to take me to some place called Kneisel Hall when it opened for the season.

Rural Maine, it seemed, was not a cultural wasteland.

When I—rather naively, I suppose—made a comment to that effect, they all laughed and told me: "Summer folk." I received quite an education on the economics of Maine that evening. I hadn't realized quite how dependent the state was on its tourist trade. Or how busy small islands like this would become once the flocks arrived. Wealthy families from Boston and New York and often points further south migrated north, escaping the summer heat but determined not to abandon their creature comforts or designated lifestyle. It was such people who kept Joanna and her ilk in business. And, I supposed, myself, now that I was the temporary owner of The Gull.

The year-rounds, such as this crowd, were essentially the support staff for the summer folk. They were the people who ran the businesses, and kept the wheels of tourism running smoothly. Most of them had strayed up here for a summer, fallen in love, and remained. Or their parents had. Or their parents' parents. Like Harry: a third-generation islander whom the natives still considered "from away."

In contrast to that were the locals—the true Maine natives. People such as Ronan Grey and Tom Moneghan, though both lacked somewhat of the local accent. And the latter, I suspected, somewhat of the local poverty. The natives were primarily fishermen, tradesmen, skilled or unskilled laborers, whose families had been Mainers for generations untold. The money was tight, and the resentments between the locals and the transplants high. Which made me wonder more than ever about tonight's inclusion of Tom Moneghan, but I didn't have the nerve to ask. Oddly, these people seemed to consider me one of them rather than one of the dreaded summer folk, and I didn't want to alienate them. Still, I found a certain narrowness to their thinking that bothered me. A tendency to lump people into groups, regardless of personality or merit.

Truly, I thought, Ronan's comment about the fisherman's life made more sense than ever.

Nonetheless, the evening passed fast, and when Joanna

and Tom rose to leave, I was surprised to discover that it was almost one. I helped Martha clear the table, but couldn't quite stop an involuntary yawn from slipping out as I worked. Once my body knew the time, it seemed to be conspiring against me, sending me off to bed with or without my permission.

Two more yawns later, there was no hiding it. Richard offered to walk me to my car and we said our good-byes, leaving Gilbert and Linda sharing a last cognac with the Camerons.

After the cozy warmth of the house, the night was black as pitch, with a damp, biting chill and the scent of cold salt permeating the air. The moon—if there had been one—was long since set. I shivered slightly in my jacket, and didn't object as Richard put an arm around my shoulders. He was warm and solid, a comforting presence in the chilly dark. And after the city, I had forgotten how black a country night could be.

I leaned into him slightly and he tightened his arm, then paused beside my car, turning me to face him.

My heart started pounding again and I stiffened, part of me not sure if I wanted this and another part of me wanting it desperately. And yet another part, despite all evidence to the contrary, not believing that this could happen—regardless of my desires.

Cecil Hargrave wasn't the one who got the guys. That just wasn't the way the world worked. Except, perhaps, this time it was.

"Tomorrow?" Richard said, softly.

I managed to nod. "Yes. At seven, right?"

He moved slightly closer, one hand brushing a wayward strand of hair from my face, as if awaiting permission to kiss me. I couldn't move and he didn't push me—even though a part of me wished he would, for I knew there was no way I could make that first move on my own. But in the end, he

simply feathered a light kiss on my cheek and dropped his
hand to mine, squeezing it lightly. "See you at seven, then.
Will you be okay to drive, or do you want me to follow you
home?"

I shook my head and attempted to steady my voice.
"Thanks, but I'll be fine."

"Tomorrow, then," he said. "Good night, Cecil. I'm glad
you came to Seal Island." And with another light kiss he was
gone, crunching across the gravel to his car.

I smiled slightly to myself in the darkness, thinking: *So
am I.* This sort of sophisticated interaction suddenly seemed
a far cry from my casual evenings of appetizers and wine
with Ronan on the back deck, and I found myself yearning
to be a part of it in a way I never had before. Maybe Seal Island was having an effect, or maybe just age and time and
distance, but again I found myself thinking that it might not
be a bad thing if my walls fell just a bit. Then, with a snort of
laughter at my foolishness, I fumbled for the car keys in my
purse.

Richard's engine growled to life, the headlights stabbing
through the darkness, before I had my keys in my hand. He
pulled his car—a dark-colored SUV—to a halt beside mine,
but I just smiled and waved him on.

He drove away, his car rumbling off down the road,
bathing the drive in the dim red glow of the taillights. Then,
as blackness once again descended over the clearing, I unlocked my car door and slid in behind the wheel.

It was cold as an icebox inside, and mist had condensed
on all the windows. The road ahead of me was swallowed in
darkness. I turned on the headlights, the heat and the de-
froster; I ran the wipers until a patch of windshield had
cleared. Then, still shivering, I pulled out of the drive in the
opposite direction from Richard.

Fortunately, I didn't have far to go, for the road was

stygian—and far more torturous than I had remembered. Only the unbroken yellow line, shining like a beacon under my high beams, kept me from vcering off into the trees as the road dipped and curved.

There were no street lights; no other cars, either. As I drove, I had the impression of shadowy figures emerging out of the woods to menace me. Once I startled a deer, foraging at the margin of the road. It bounded off into the trees, its white tail erect. And I almost ran over a rabbit, which hopped madly out in front of my car.

In the hollows, a thin fog was gathering over the asphalt.

But then there was my drive and my house, and I turned off gratefully, my tires crunching down the gravel drive. And is my headlights swept across the lawn, I saw it. Another shadowy figure—this one erect—caught in stark black by the bright glare of my headlights. It stood, framed against the house, a vertical slash of darkness against the silvery shingles. And then, in a swirl of motion, it was gone, darting beyond the narrow circle of illumination.

"Ronan?" I whispered, but even if he could have heard me, there was no answer, no lean, handsome face materializing out of the darkness. Besides, at this hour, even the most vigilant of neighbors should be asleep.

Unsure of what I should do or even if I had really seen it, I sat there frozen. What if the lurker was still out there, just beyond my circle of vision? If I turned off the engine, could I hear it breathing? Despite the heat cranking out of the vents, I felt like I was encased in ice. Even my fingers were numb; I couldn't turn the key.

Besides, I didn't want to hear it breathing. I didn't want to hear anything. What I really wanted to do was to turn this car around and drive back to the Camerons'. Or New York. I was haunted by sudden visions of that stain in my living room, of Allegra lying violently dead. Of Tom's selkie tales, and creatures only half-human lingering in the moist blackness. I wished I were the type of person to leap out of the car, beard the shadows, order this creature to get the hell out of my yard and the hell out of my life.

Only I wasn't. So for five interminable minutes I did nothing but sit and listen to the whir of the heater, trying to convince myself I had only imagined it. That it had only been an odd concatenation of circumstances, the shadow of a fleeting animal, cast large across the house. A tree, caught in the sweep of my headlight beams.

So why did I still have the feeling I was being watched? That someone—or something—was lurking just beyond the borders of my vision, evaluating me as I sat paralyzed in my car?

Damn Tom and his stories. I could almost see the amphibious shape of that half-seal creature lurking out there among the trees. But I was not Allegra's child, and I had never been cruel to Ragnarok. So what had I done to attract its attention?

Then, berating myself for being fifty different kinds of fool, I slowly fished in my purse for the house keys, then threw open the car door and ran for the front steps—leaving the engine on and the headlights blazing. I fumbled my keys into the front door lock, almost expecting to see my car driven off by that shadowy menace. But the car rumbled on, unmolested, as the door swung open and I hit the switch wildly for the porch lights.

A wide circle of yellow illumination bathed the lawn. But if there had ever been anything there, it was gone. All that was left was a muddy footprint at the center of my top stair, and a snaking path through the wet grass—punctuated by a hollow where something might have stood and waited.

12

I SLEPT FITFULLY AGAIN that night, my dreams haunted by shadowy figures and violence, and awoke with the sun. I rose and dressed, wishing I had a way to talk to Ronan. I wanted to know what he knew about my mysterious visitor—if indeed there had been a visitor. Had he gotten my note or not? Had he simply been checking to make sure I had got home safely? But if so, why hadn't he identified himself?

The rock remained planted on my back porch, but the note was gone. Taken or blown away? When I checked outside my door, the dew was uniformly heavy on the grass. If there had ever been a path, the night wind had ruffled it back into place. Only the footprint remained, but that could have been left at any time.

Besides, there were no shadowy figures on my lawn now, not even a lugubrious seal head bobbing on the waves between the blowing layers of fog. And Ronan would be by again this evening or the next, as he always was. So I tried to lose myself in a book and my preparations for lunch, but I was still jumpy enough that I had to muffle a shriek when a battered blue pickup came bouncing down my drive a little past two. I had been having coffee on the back deck, already feeling the effects of my near-sleepless night and marveling at the clear, cloudless sky that had been revealed when the last of the mist had burned away. But as my visitor arrived, I hastily put down the cup before I spilled it, then peered around the side of my house as the truck came to an inelegant halt.

From its condition, I almost expected Ronan to step out from behind the wheel, but instead Tom Moneghan unfolded himself from the driver's side, the sun sparking reddish lights off his dark curls, and I was abruptly aware of my appearance. I was wearing faded jeans and a sweatshirt, my hair bound up in a ponytail, my feet bare and not a trace of makeup on my face. It had somehow seemed appropriate for facing Ronan, but Tom Moneghan was another thing entirely—even though he had clearly just come off the boat. His rubber waders were gone, but his jeans were streaked with engine grease, and the Aran sweater was still as grey with age and toil.

"All hail the house," he called. "I brought bounty, as promised." Then he caught sight of me peering around the side of the deck, and his face abruptly altered. "Cecil. What's the matter?" he said, without even the preliminaries of a "Hello" or "How are you?" to follow his greeting.

I laughed ruefully and padded barefoot down the steps and across the grass. "Is it that obvious?"

He cocked his head, his expression more approachable than I had yet seen it. "I have the oddest feeling that if I so much as look at you wrong, you will run screaming. Is there anything I can do to help?"

"I very much doubt it, but thanks for offering. I just didn't sleep very well last night."

"Why not?"

"Nothing really; just foolishness. I thought I saw someone lurking around the house last night when I got home, but it was late and I was tired, and probably imagining things." I didn't say anything about the footprint, or about Ronan. That was between us—for now.

Again, Tom's gaze seemed to pull inwards. "I'm sorry. I hope it wasn't my fault for filling your head with all those silly stories at the party. I wasn't exactly on my best behavior, but then there's something about that crowd that always brings out the worst in me. I do enjoy challenging their expectations, because I never jump quite as they want me to."

"So why did you come, then?"

"Because I wanted to meet you. I was . . . good friends with Allegra. And because what I said to Joanna was true: I don't like to be too predictable in my unsociability. But I didn't scare you, did I?"

He suddenly looked so earnest standing there in his fisher garb that I didn't have the heart to lie. "Well, maybe a bit, but nothing that isn't more than half my own fault. Everyone's always told me I have far too much imagination, and I am constantly blowing things up way out of proportion."

"Nonsense. There's no such thing as too much imagination," Tom said stoutly. "But I do know what you mean, being guilty of the same thing myself, and I do apologize again for providing the fodder, however inadvertently. If I promise to act in a civilized manner in future, can we start this all again?"

I stared at him for a moment. His lips were actually curving in a smile, and I found myself smiling back. "There is nothing to apologize for. But tell me . . . You don't really believe in all that salkie stuff, do you?" I meant to sound skeptical, but to my annoyance a hint of wonder crept into my voice, as if he could still prove to me that magic existed.

Tom just laughed. "Selkies," he corrected. "And hell, no! I'll admit the water does strange things to your mind, sometimes. I have seen . . . Well, I can't always explain it, and I do think there are more things in heaven and earth, Horatio. But . . ." He grinned, and my heart turned over. "No, I don't believe that the selkies are one of them. Though I wasn't lying when I said that some of the fishermen do, nor that there is rumored to be selkie blood in my family tree. But I come from a long line of fishermen, and fishermen are notoriously superstitious. And notorious tale-tellers. All men seem to be who give their lives to the sea."

"Including you?"

He forced a smile. "Oh, especially me," he said, far too lightly, and brushed a hand through his hair. "I've got it worse than most, for all that my life is given but imperfectly to the sea." Before I could ask what he meant, he turned to the bed of his truck and drew out two buckets and a cheap picnic cooler so decisively that I knew the subject was closed. The buckets stank strongly of fish, and were filled almost to overflowing with silvery bodies.

"I figured you probably hadn't had time to buy one of these," he added, handing me the plastic cooler as he swung down the two buckets of fish, "so I thought I would supply the lack."

I gaped at him stupidly. In all the upset of last night, I had forgotten that he had come to bring me fish for Ragnarok; I hadn't even had a chance to plug in the spare refrigerator again.

He looked embarrassed. "I'm sorry. I should have confirmed last night, but I'm afraid I ran out rather abruptly when Gilbert and Linda arrived. I really cannot abide those two, though I am perfectly fond of Harry and adore Martha. But this is for . . ."

"Ragnarok; I remember. And thank you. I haven't had a chance to check that fridge yet, let alone . . ."

"Well, then, there's something I can help with. Lead on."

Feeling somewhat bemused, I led him to the utility shed tacked onto the garage, and opened the door. It was well-shaded under the trees, and little light penetrated the room's shadowy interior. But Tom must indeed have known Allegra well, because he moved unerringly for the back corner, plugging in the refrigerator and fiddling with the controls as the motor hummed into life.

"All in working order," he said. "Wait here; let me get the cooler."

He left the dim chamber and returned a short while later, bearing the cooler, which he wrestled into the bottom of the empty fridge. "There," he said, and opened the lid, showing me a heap of fish. "Enough for four days, at least. I'll bring you more as needed."

"Thanks again," I said. "I owe you."

The shed was too dark for me to properly decipher his expression, but I thought I saw a smile light his eyes. "Don't worry," he said, "I'll hold you to that."

Something about the dank, close darkness of the shed made me suddenly blurt out: "Do you really believe in the break-in story? About Allegra, I mean?"

I still couldn't see his face, but I felt his whole body go still, torn between the desire for truth and a comforting lie. "I honestly don't know," he said at last, slowly. "They do say that the vast majority of murders are caused by someone the victim knows, but . . ." A chill blew though me at his tone. "This is a small community. I know pretty much everyone that Allegra did, and I can't imagine any of them capable of an act like that. So I guess I have to believe the break-in story."

His voice was grim; I couldn't blame him. Faces floated though my mind: Abby, Richard, Joanna, Harry . . .

He took a step towards me in the gloom and I flinched involuntarily, but he simply said, "You're shivering," and escorted me out of the shed with one hand to my elbow. Which was just as well; the cold flagstoned floor was starting to hurt my feet.

As we emerged into the startling blaze of sunlight, my fears suddenly seemed foolish. Of course he was right; it had to be a break-in, a random act of violence. The alternative was unspeakable.

"So, shall we see if we can't persuade the little guy to come in?" he added. He walked over to the side of the house and grabbed one of the buckets, still half-full of fish, from where it rested by one of the deck supports and continued down towards the water.

I followed. The tide was retreating, leaving a slick of seaweed across the lower reaches of the rock ledges. I made my way tentatively across in my bare feet, trying to avoid barnacles and sharp bits of hidden shell, but Tom just strode confidently through it, the air bladders popping rhythmically under his heels. When he stopped, the water was kissing the rubber toes of his battered hiking boots.

Having already felt its frigid embrace, I stayed farther back. "What now?" I said. "Call him and he comes?"

"Essentially," he answered, and began emitting a series of liquid noises not unlike the sound of the water lapping on the rocks. "What they really like," he added in the intervals, "is music. I'll show you someday. Meanwhile . . . Ah, look. We have an audience."

And, indeed, a head had popped up just off shore. Ragnarok—if it was indeed he—surveyed me for a moment, then turned his fickle attention to the man with the bucket.

Tom laughed. "Hey, buddy," he said, in a softer tone than I would have imagined coming from a man of his demeanor. Nor was it a condescending croon, like the meaningless baby noises some people feel compelled to utter around small children and fuzzy animals. Rather, it had a depth of respect and welcome to it that surprised me. "Look what Cecil and I have brought to welcome you home." Reaching into the bucket, Tom drew out a single, gleaming mackerel, holding it aloft by the tail.

Ragnarok seemed very aware of what Tom had brought him and flipped his way closer to shore. About two feet from the margin of the ledge he stopped and bobbed back to the surface, watching us. Waiting.

"That's called 'bottling,'" Tom explained. "When they float with their heads up like that. Look at him, the devil. He's waiting for us to make the first move."

It seemed he was, the dark eyes flicking between the fish and Tom. Tom wiggled the fish, testing him. Ragnarok barked once, loudly—imperiously—that odd honking that still, to my ears, sounded midway between a goose and a dog.

I glanced over at Tom, startled to see the darkness back in his gaze. "Not quite Hoover, my lad," he said softly. "But you'll do." Then, shaking off the mood, he lifted his arm and flung the fish wide. Its silver scales winked and glittered as it tumbled end over end in the sun.

Ragnarok, his mouth widening in a grin, flipped backward, rolled one hundred and eighty degrees, and streaked off after the prize. Then, surging from the depths, he caught it in mid-air, and I found myself whooping and cheering like some demented tourist at Sea World.

Tom looked over at me and smiled. "You try," he said, and handed me a fish.

I took it gingerly, holding it by the tail between my thumb and forefinger. Ragnarok had bottled back to the surface and was watching me expectantly.

"Here goes nothing," I told him, and lobbed the fish at him underhanded. It transcribed a low, wobbling arc, then plopped into the water two feet from shore.

Ragnarok stared at me reproachfully. Clearly, it wasn't even worth his effort to go after it.

I flushed.

Tom just laughed and took my hand, wrapping it around the tail of another mackerel. "Don't worry," he said, "it's not going to hurt you, and the smell washes off. Eventually."

I smiled nervously, all too aware of the warm pressure of his fingers around mine. His hands were hard and strong. *Competent*, I thought. *Human*.

"Now, grab it like this," he continued, "pull your arm back like this . . . no, like this"—he made an adjustment—"and then . . . there! You have it."

Indeed, this time the fish soared a respectable distance, and Ragnarok uttered a happy yip before giving chase.

He caught it effortlessly and grinned up at me.

"Right. Now me." Tom feinted right then threw left. Ragnarok leapt, snapped, and swallowed.

For a short while we alternated fish, laughing as Ragnarok leaped and dove and cavorted, exhibiting his skills. Then Tom said, "Let's see if we can bring him in to shore."

Instead of throwing his next fish, he continued to hold it, wiggling it slightly to get the seal's attention. "Come on, Ragnarok," he said. "Say hello."

Ragnarok, clearly piqued at being deprived of his game, rolled onto his side and regarded the fisherman dubiously.

"You know me," Tom added. "I helped bottle-feed you when you were a pup, or have you forgotten already, you ungrateful wretch?"

Ragnarok inched closer, eyeing me.

"And you know you're dying to meet Cecil. Come along, then." Oblivious to the water that soaked his jeans, Tom knelt on the seaweed and extended his arm out long over the waves, the shiny mackerel still in his hand.

Ragnarok swam in a circle that left him one foot closer to shore.

"Still not ready to commit, yet?" Tom said, and leaned even farther out over the water. He wriggled the mackerel enticingly.

Ragnarok drew nearer.

With one foot braced in a crevice between the ledges, Tom leaned out so far I thought he would overbalance, and I readied to grab him should the need arise.

Which it almost did. Ragnarok darted in so quickly he left foam in his wake, snatching the fish from Tom's fingers. My companion started to slip and I grabbed him by the belt at the same moment he steadied himself, then let go hastily as my fingers brushed the bare skin of his back.

"Thanks," he said unnecessarily, clambering back to more solid ground. "Do you want to have a go?"

I eyed the slippery seaweed dubiously. I was still in bare feet, but Ragnarok was watching me, closer than he'd been before, so I took the fish and knelt in the weed, reaching out as far as my arm would extend.

He was bolder this time, taking the fish delicately from between my fingers.

I was entranced by his nearness, by the brush of his whiskers against my skin. "More?" I said eagerly.

Tom shook his head regretfully. "Nope, he's had his share. You are never supposed to feed wild seals too much. It spoils their appetite and they forget how to fend for themselves. So promise me you won't overdo it."

"I promise," I said, obviously feeling the same regret as

Ragnarok when he realized that playtime was over. I had never seen a seal sulk before, but that was clearly what Ragnarok was doing. Though . . . Some residual mischief in his eyes told me he was also milking the pity factor for everything it was worth.

"Oh, no you don't," Tom said with a chuckle, taking the empty pail and moving it firmly up onto the lawn. "Cecil will feed you tomorrow, if she's around. And in the meantime . . ." He lowered himself onto the rock, stretching out across the sunbaked ledges with his hands crossed behind his head, staring up at the now flawless arch of the summer sky. "Have a seat, Cecil, and let's see what happens."

I was suddenly nervous. "What do you mean?"

"We're about to try some psychological warfare. So lie down; enjoy the day." He was still staring up at the sky, so I stretched out tentatively beside him—not too close and not too far away, still not sure what he had in mind. Or how I would react were it something to do with me.

But he made no move toward me, just stared up at the sky and said casually, "So, how was the rest of your evening apart from seeing shadowy figures in the woods?" His casual tone instantly put me at ease and made my nighttime fears seem silly. "Did Martha make too much of a mess of the food?"

This seemed innocuous enough and I began to relax, admiring the impeccable blueness of the sky. As I reached up to cross my hands behind my head, our arms briefly touched. I tried not to jump. "It was lovely. And no."

He laughed. "Don't lie; you're no good at it. Martha is a wonderful artist, but somewhat of a disaster as a chef. But at least you are still alive to tell the tale."

Tom Moneghan was full of surprises. This was neither the coolly taciturn fisherman of the docks, nor the enigmatic cipher of the night before. This man was chatty and almost friendly, the darkness buried so deep I could almost not discern it in his eyes when I glanced his way.

I decided to test my limits by asking, "And your evening? How was that other engagement you had?"

He actually laughed. "If by that you mean a solitary dinner over a book, marvelous." When I stared over at him, he added, "There was no other engagement, just a polite, social lie to get me out of having to sit across from Gilbert and Linda. Though perhaps if they had been indisposed, I might have been persuaded to stay." He peered over at me and arched an eyebrow. "Are you shocked?"

I was a bit—but more at his candor than the revelation itself. "On that subject, I tend to agree with you," I admitted.

"Ah, a woman of taste and discernment. I suspected as much; otherwise, Ragnarok would not be making overtures. And speaking of which . . . Don't move and keep talking. But I think we've got him."

I hadn't been aware that our conversation had an ulterior motive—though I suppose I should have expected it. But as I let my attention drift off Tom, I realized that Ragnarok, far from disappearing, was lurking closer to shore than ever. And with the attention off him, he was free to indulge his curiosity. Either that, or he was piqued at being ignored. But whichever the case, he had one flipper on shore. I tried to watch him without being obvious, but apparently I failed miserably because Tom said, "No, just keep talking and ignore him. He'll only come up if he thinks he's not being observed."

"Oh." I felt suddenly awkward. "What do you want me to say?"

"Whatever you want," he responded, with a faint chuckle.

"Very well, then," I cast my mind back to a previous remark. "Who is Hoover?"

He seemed startled. "What?"

"Hoover," I said. "When Ragnarok barked at you, and you said he wasn't Hoover but he'd do . . ."

I could sense the darkness was back in his gaze again, but all he said was, "There was a seal down at the New England Aquarium in Boston named Hoover who used to mimic human speech. He had a small repertoire of phrases like 'Hello there,' and 'Get out of here' that he would bark at visitors."

"Is Hoover still alive?" I asked, wondering if that was what accounted for the sudden bleakness in his gaze.

But Tom just smiled somewhat sadly and said, "I don't know." His face closed further as he added, "I haven't been to Boston in a long time, and to the aquarium in even longer. Though I suppose you could always call and ask . . ."

Such was Tom's power of distraction that I had managed to forget about Ragnarok again. So I shrieked and jerked involuntarily when something cold and wet brushed the bare sole of my foot.

The seal slid hastily back into the water, and Tom sighed. "Well, we've lost him for the day," he said, sitting up briskly. Further startled by his sharp motion, Ragnarok vanished. "But if you lie out like this every day being still and nonthreatening, he may decide you have seal blood in you yet and come up to join you."

I suddenly wondered how much of Tom's affability had been for me and how much had simply been an excuse to reconnect with the seal, but I quickly quashed the feeling. I had no right to feel disappointed. Besides, I had a date with a very eligible man tonight.

I climbed to my feet and Tom followed suit. "I should wash my hands," I said. "Can I get you coffee or anything?"

"No thanks. I should go." The coolness was back in his tone. So it *had* been Ragnarok that was the lure.

"Well, thanks again for the fish. How long do I have to let them warm up out of the fridge before I feed him tomorrow?"

"Thank you for reminding me. And good thinking. You see, you're a natural." And this time his smile seemed for me alone. "About an hour should do it—less in the sun. Coldish is okay—the ocean is cold—but fridge temperature is not."

"Right. Thanks again."

"Think nothing of it," he said carelessly, and got back into his truck. Then he waved briefly and drove away, leaving me feeling oddly bereft.

13

BY THE TIME RICHARD arrived at seven, I was feeling better. I had taken a nap, had a proper shower, and had washed the last of the fish from my hands. It didn't even bother me when I opened the door to see Richard standing half on, half off the muddy footprint on my front steps, smearing its lines. How bad could a place that had a seal like Ragnarok be? And even if Tom had been using me to get at the creature, I was incredibly grateful for the experience. Still euphoric at feeling the brush of a damp seal nose against my foot.

"You look elated," Richard said, as I bounded out of the house, locked the front door behind me, and climbed into his SUV almost without invitation. In the light of the sinking sun, it was revealed to be a dark, forest green with deep leather seats. He looked somewhat nonplussed as he got in beside me and asked, "What's up?"

"Ragnarok," I replied happily, then realized belatedly that

he might have been hoping the cause was him. "Tom came by today," I explained, "and brought me mackerel, as promised. We fed Ragnarok and almost got him up on shore."

"That's wonderful," Richard replied, and if his smile lacked something in wattage, I suppose that could be understood. He started the car, backing out of the drive, and I pulled my attention off the seal and gave him a more committed look.

He was dressed more casually tonight, in slacks and a navy sweater that brought out the blue in his eyes. I couldn't imagine Richard kneeling in seaweed, teasing a seal with fish, but I was happy to see him nonetheless. I didn't think there was a dark bone in the man's body—unlike certain fishermen who seemed prone to unexpected fits of moodiness.

Then I started slightly as I realized I had forgotten to leave a second note for Ronan.

"What is it?" Richard asked.

"Nothing," I replied, feeling suddenly resentful that I should have to justify myself to a man I'd barely met and merely shared cocktails with for four nights. That wasn't any sort of a life commitment; I owed him nothing. I was free to do what I wanted.

Free . . .

I looked out the car window for a moment, watching the way the light slanted low and golden through the trees, casting palpable rays across the road, and realized that I was, indeed, feeling a palpable rush of lightness fill me as the road unscrolled beneath the SUV's tires.

I turned to Richard and smiled. "It's good to see you. And good to be getting off the island for a bit. I had a bit of a scare when I got home last night, so thank you for this." A scare that had, apparently, still left me jumpy, for as I cast my mind back to my behavior on Richard's arrival, I suddenly realized how quickly I had seized the opportunity to get free of my house and the island. He had probably expected to be invited in for a civilized drink, but instead was faced with a date who had practically bowled him over on her way to the car. I laughed. "I'm sorry. You must think me a complete nut. First I get all reticent on you last night, and now this. I'm surprised you even let me in your car."

He grinned, the expression lending a boyishness to his face. "You actually didn't give me much of a choice. But let's leave last night out of it for a moment. Do you want to tell me what's troubling you now?"

The causeway was spiraling past beneath our wheels, leading us off Seal Island, and I felt my spirits rise another notch. "I'd like nothing better."

So, on the drive to Blue Hill, I told him everything. The midnight visitor, the sense of eyes watching, the footprint on the step, the path in the grass. It was a long drive and I spared him nothing. I even mentioned the figure I thought I saw that very first day, with Harry, and how it had turned out to be Ronan.

He kept his eyes on the road as he drove—which relieved me; I don't think I could have spilled all the details with those brilliant blue eyes fixed so intently on me—but I could see his face grow longer and more concerned as I continued. And that, too, was a relief. In the daylight—on the mainland—the whole thing seemed more ridiculous than ever, the product of an overwrought imagination. That he took me seriously . . . Well, suddenly I felt a whole lot less foolish. And, perhaps, a whole lot more scared.

"Maybe you should get a dog," he suggested, when I had finished.

I shook my head. "I'm going back to New York in September, and it's cruel to keep a dog in the city—especially considering the size of the average apartment."

"Then an alarm system?"

I shook my head again. That seemed even more foolish, to install more stringent security measures on a tiny island than I would in the big, bad city. I didn't want to turn into a paranoiac. "Really, I'll be fine. I'm just not used to the country, that's all. I probably imagined the whole thing."

He raised an eyebrow. "The figure?"

"An animal. A shadow from the headlights."

"And the footprint?"

"I probably left it myself, on my mad rush to the front door." Never mind that my best pair of heels were more versatile than I had envisioned if they were able to mimic the print of a man's work boot.

"And what of the path?" Richard persisted.

"A sort of anti-wish-fulfillment. What I expected to see."

"You have an answer for everything, don't you?"

"Yes. Besides, everyone has always said I have too much imagination for my own good."

Unlike Tom, he didn't try to defend me. All he said was, "Ever thought of writing?" And when I looked at him askance, he added, "Sorry, it's the editor in me coming out. But I'm glad you told me. Are you feeling better about it now?"

"Yes, I am. And I'm glad I told you, too."

"Good. Then shall we start this over?" He glanced at me out of the corner of his eye. "Hello, Cecil. Have I told you that you look lovely tonight?"

I felt myself flush, suddenly glad that I had made an effort with my outfit. I had discovered a black dress of Allegra's that I simply had to try. And, once tried, I couldn't give it up—despite the residual oddness I felt from wearing my dead aunt's garments. It was far worse than wearing her jewelry.

However, I assured myself again, she had wanted me to have the house; I didn't see that she would begrudge me a few dresses. Especially not this one. It was a black wool jersey but soft as cashmere, with long sleeves and a V-neck into which I had set one of her more dramatic torques—heavy gold with a darkly brilliant cabochon garnet. The top of the dress clung sleekly; the bottom flowed in a sensual swirl to mid-calf. And against it my hair shone more brightly than the gold of the necklace. Matching earrings and my own nicest set of black heels completed the outfit.

"That's one of Allegra's, isn't it?" Richard added. Then he blushed and stammered, "That is . . . I didn't mean . . ." He seemed to recover himself and grinned. "Let's just say that you do things to it that Allegra hadn't been able to do for years—much as I adored her."

"Thank you," I said. Then, "You were friends with Allegra?"

"Most people on this island were. She was very personable—even if she did have a few odd quirks. But then, which of us don't?"

I wanted to ask him more about Allegra, but instead—unwilling to admit the depths of my ignorance—said, "And what would yours be?"

"My quirks, you mean?" He laughed. "How about my attempts to delude myself that the paper I edit actually accounts for something simply because I fell in love with Seal Island and can't imagine living anywhere else? Let's face it; my life's work is not exactly setting the world on fire."

"And whose is?" I said. "Certainly not mine."

He grinned. "That might be debatable. But what about you? What are your quirks?"

I shrugged, suddenly uncomfortable. I had not realized that this line of questioning had the potential to turn and bite me. Did he want the whole list, or just the annotated version? I laughed nervously.

"But of course," he added, "you are likely perfect and have no quirks."

I laughed again, this time in genuine amusement, and managed to say, "Oh, trust me, I have plenty. I will just leave it to you to discover them." And amazed myself that I actually managed to make it sound flirtatious rather than just the panicked escape it was.

To my relief, we shifted off to more neutral topics for the remainder of the drive, and I was feeling considerably more relaxed by the time we finally reached the outskirts of Blue Hill. Richard was a charming companion, and it was hard to feel out of sorts in such a beautiful setting. The sun had been sinking as we drove, filtering more and more golden though the trees. As we swooped down the hill into the town, the light cast long shadows across the road, and the white clapboard church that guarded the town's fringes shone with the patina of antique bronze.

The stores were shutting down, the houses and restaurants beginning to glow against the encroaching dusk, as Richard pulled into the lot a few doors down from Jonathan's and handed me out before I could so much as open my door. Unlike me, he left his car unlocked. Then we strolled up the street to the restaurant, passing a bookstore along the way. I cast a curious glance at the window, but there were no Morelands. So, it must be a Seal Island phenomenon only.

Dinner was lovely, the first true date I had had in longer than I cared to remember. The room was high and airy, beamed with pale pine and featuring local art on the walls—I thought I saw one of Martha's pieces towards the back—and candles and flowers glowed on the widely-spaced tables. Richard was an exemplary companion, charming and erudite. We chatted about our lives and about our pasts—though I deftly, and with the ease of long practice, glossed past that dreadful December night which had deprived me of both parents and support net. Instead, we kept to innocuous topics, and Richard made me feel both relaxed and admired—not an easy combination. We even discovered we had attended the same college and vainly played the name-game for a few moments. Vainly, because he had graduated ten years ahead of me, and the chances of us knowing anyone in common was remote.

Still, it made me feel a connection with him, and by the end of the evening I felt positively chummy, laughing as naturally over trivialities as I ever had in my life. And if, on occasion, a warmer glance from those blue eyes made me blush, I was actually coming to enjoy it. There was something heady about feeling admired.

Maybe this dating thing wasn't so traumatic, after all.

I indulged myself with a warm salad of smoked mussels, local chevre, and seasonal greens with a sherry vinaigrette, and cedar-planked Atlantic salmon so fresh it might have been plucked from the sea mere minutes before. And I don't know how much Richard paid for the wine, but it was a fine Pinot Grigio, smooth as sin going down. We lingered over coffee and dessert—for me, a wonderful crème brulée—until gradually the restaurant emptied around us and it became obvious we were the only ones keeping it open. When one of the waiters pointedly started inverting chairs atop a nearby table, I said, "I suppose we had better go."

Richard smiled and stood. "Not quite New York hours, is it?"

I looked down at my watch. It was nearly ten. "Not by half." I was, I suspected, somewhat drunk. Richard—perhaps in the interests of driving—had emptied more than half of the bottle into my glass. Which, perhaps, accounted for some of my mellow mood. But not so much that I forgot we had seen neither hide nor hair of the check. "Don't we need to pay first, though?" I asked, wondering how I would broach the awkward etiquette of the bill.

I needn't have worried. "It's already taken care of," Richard responded cheerfully. Suave bastard that he was, he must have paid while I was in the rest room, over an hour ago. If I hadn't been impressed by Richard before, I was now. And not because he had paid the bill, but because he had managed it so unobtrusively.

Still, as we drove home on roads that seemed as dark and narrow as tunnels, illuminated only by the sweep of the headlights, blindingly white against the black macadam and the blacker sky, I couldn't help feeling a creeping sense of oppression. Each mile brought us closer to Seal Island. And while I desperately didn't want to be afraid, a part of me still was. For no matter how much I told myself that what I had seen was only a figment of my imagination, I knew it for a lie. There had been something on my lawn last night, be it man or beast. And the footprint on my step, though perhaps made by someone in a frantic haste, had been printed by a solid sole. And I had been wearing heels.

As the distance shrank, I felt a chill creep over me that not even the sweep of night sky, brilliantly freckled with stars, could dispel.

Richard drove in silence—perhaps sensing my need for reflection, or perhaps because we had run out of neutral topics. But still, it wasn't an uncomfortable silence; I felt no need to fill it with chatter as I was so often impelled to. And maybe my fear was a good thing, for it managed to distract me from the lesser matter of end-of-date etiquette that normally would have had me in a panic. But, as it was, the issue of whether or not I would let Richard kiss me seemed unimportant when compared to the knowledge that I might well be facing another unwanted visitor on my lawn. Or, worse yet, as I was sleeping.

Maybe I should get a dog. Or an alarm system. Or just go back to New York before the summer was up.

Yet I think what surprised me most, the closer we got to Seal Island, was how my resolve mounted. I had, in my short life, been forced to face a lot. And I had coped with the situations that fate threw at me—barely. But I had never considered myself a strong person or seen myself as any particular sort of survivor. In fact, I had spent most of my life—at least, the parts I had any control over—trying to avoid all possible conflicts. As far as I was concerned, the less I was tested, the better, because I had no faith that I would stand up to another assault. Yet now, instead of feeling myself collapse, I felt an odd stiffening of my mental sinews, and a growing determination not to be intimidated out of the one vacation I had managed to snatch in years.

It surprised me—endlessly. But it also felt astoundingly good. And so by the time the causeway unwound before us, I was almost ready to face my house. Although not even my newfound determination could quite stop a shiver.

Seeing it, Richard reached over and turned up the heat a notch. I only wish it could have been that simple.

He piloted the car expertly into my drive, and all was still and silent in the sweep of the headlights. No menacing figures, no attenuated shadows. No rustles from the woods. Just my house, silver and silent in the starlight. And when Richard killed the engine, there was no more sound around us than the waves over the rocks and the occasional electric screech of a cicada.

He was more slow to move this time, so I opened the car door for myself and climbed out. And shivered again as a cold wind blew through me. But no supernatural wind this time; just the chill of a Maine evening, still unexpected after the steamy heat of the city.

The headlights bathed the house. I stared at it, and it

seemed to stare back, the darkened windows reflecting the car lights in silvery glints.

I was barely aware that Richard had joined me beside the car until his hand, startlingly warm in the cool air, brushed back my hair, trailed lightly along my cheek.

I stiffened slightly, a whole new panic seizing me.

"Are you sure you'll be all right here alone?" he said, misinterpreting. "I could stay if you want . . ."

I managed a laugh—somewhat strangled, but still genuine for all that. "Richard, if I didn't know better, I'd think you were trying to take advantage."

He looked almost embarrassed. "I meant in the spare room."

"I know you did. And thanks for the offer. I do appreciate it, but I'll be fine. Really, I will. Look." I gestured around the clearing. "No ghosts; no bogeymen. Nothing whatsoever to hurt me."

He cocked his head. "Are you sure?"

"Quite sure. But thank you so much for a lovely evening." And, greatly daring, I laid a hand on his arm. "It was precisely what I needed."

"You weren't the only one," he responded. And reached for me.

It was surprisingly easy, after all. His arms closed around me and his lips touched mine, warm and tentative, giving me ample room to pull away. But I didn't.

It was sweet and tremulous and assured all at once—rather like Richard himself. All my life, I had dreamed of kisses that would sweep me away like a strong wind, carrying me out of the conscious part of my mind. This wasn't it, and I was beginning to doubt that such a thing existed. But still, it was lovely in its way, as warm and comforting as a familiar blanket.

I let my lips part beneath his, deepening the kiss.

"Are you sure you don't want me to stay?" he asked again, somewhat breathlessly, as he released me. "There are benefits to being taken advantage of . . ."

I smiled. "No doubt. But you wouldn't do it."

He sounded almost offended. "What makes you so certain?"

"You're too much of a gentleman. And don't try to make me think that you aren't."

"Well, damn me for being so transparent," he said with a somewhat stiffled laugh. "You're right, of course. Though I like to think I'm a capable of a little misbehavior every now and then. Another time?"

"I'd like that."

"Well, then. Let me at least walk you to your door, see you safe inside."

He did, and kissed me again in the open doorway.

I flipped on my porch lights and watched him walk back to the car, climb in behind the wheel. I waved to him, waited until he reversed the car and began to drive away, then shut and locked the door behind me with a smile on my face.

It wasn't grand passion, but I could get used to it.

Feeling almost euphoric, I killed the porch lights and walked through to the living room. I had intended to go straight through to the bedroom, but instead something drew me out onto the back deck—perhaps that same sense of determination I had felt in the car. I unlatched the central set of French doors and threw them open, walking out to lean against the far rail. Behind me, yellow light bled across the planks, casting a warm circle of protection around me, blotting out the stars.

I leaned my elbows against the railing, feeling the weight of Allegra's cabochon in the hollow of my throat, the stir of her dress around my calves. I wondered how often Allegra had stood here like this, at one with the night, surveying her domain. I felt oddly close to her in that instant, as if there were two of us standing on that deck, sharing the one body.

Family, I thought. *This is what family means, that sense of continuity from one generation to the next.*

"Listen to me," I said into the night. And had the odd sense that someone was. "I'm here, and I'm not going away, so you'd better damn well get used to it!"

A childish impulse. So why did I have the sudden impression that something was approving of my words, lauding my courage, even as it still weighed my ultimate worth? And as my eyes adjusted to the darkness in front of me, I thought I saw twin glints of light on the waves, as if two eyes looked back at me.

On some strange inclination I couldn't fathom, I bowed to the water. There was a liquid splash, like water curling around a rock, then the eyes were gone—if indeed they had ever been there.

And as I stood there in the night, the sound of bagpipes whispered in my ears.

14

I PASSED A LAZY Sunday reading and tidying and trying to entice a reluctant Ragnarok up onto the shore. But the seal, while perfectly happy to devour his treats, seemed disinclined to venture too close to the ledges without Tom's familiar presence, and I wasn't about to betray his trust by forcing the issue. Though still I couldn't help feeling a little hurt; I had hoped I rated better than that.

But perhaps there was another reason. Because, with two mackerel left to go, Ragnarok abruptly stiffened, his eyes taking on a wary cast. I looked up and down the shore, but saw nothing strange. So I cast another fish, which plopped into the water bare inches from his nose.

He made no move to go after it.

"What's the matter with you?" I demanded.

"Perhaps he's just not hungry," a liquid voice said from behind me, Rs rolling like surf over the rocks.

I looked up, startled. I hadn't heard anyone approach yet

there was Ronan, closer to me than Ragnarok, his dark eyes
hooded yet somehow strangely expectant. I had a sudden, insane urge to throw my last fish to him, just to see how he'd
react.

Ragnarok, perhaps sensing my urge, moved fractionally
closer, sparing me a brief, reproachful glance. But mostly
his eyes were fixed on Ronan. He seemed both fascinated
and apprehensive, and there was none of the playful friendliness he had shown towards Tom in his demeanor. Suddenly
I felt a little better. Ragnarok was clearly a seal slow to trust.
He was patently not going anywhere near Ronan for all he
kept staring at him; every taut, bristling line bore that out.
But the fact that he had chosen to let me in this close . . . It
was downright flattering.

I found myself basking in the warmth of my seal's loyalty
and reached for the last fish in the bucket Tom had left me. I
waved it in Ragnarok's direction and his gaze finally left Ronan, returning to me and the treat I proffered. Fickle, yes,
and like all creatures governed by his stomach, but still his
body uncoiled, regaining some of its former fluidity. I tossed
him the fish, and while he made none of his usual, flashy
moves as he retrieved it, he did gulp it down and gape a scaly
grin at me. Then he streaked away towards the horizon, his
sleek, dark body submerging about forty feet from shore.

I stared out over the waves for a moment, half expecting
to see the other seal lurking lugubriously against the back-
drop of the islands, but for once there was no elongate profile bobbing on the waves.

I turned back to Ronan. He was wearing fading jeans and
a plaid flannel shirt in blues and greens that complemented
his dark coloring. I didn't think he'd been around an engine
all day.

"Where have you been?" he asked me, not quite accusing.
"I came by the past two days and you weren't here."

I had expected to feel a renewal of the resentment I had experienced when I was out with Richard. But faced with Ronan's slightly hurt dark eyes, my anger evaporated like mist in the sun.

"Didn't you get my note?" I asked.

He stared at me blankly; it must have blown away, then.

"I left you a note the first night," I explained, "tacked down to the deck with a rock, in case you came by, telling you that I'd be out." No sense in mentioning that, distracted by Richard and Ragnarok, I hadn't left him a note the second night. If he hadn't gotten the first one, I could take the moral high ground and pretend it had been inclusive. "It probably blew away. But I didn't know how else to get in touch with you. *Do* you have a phone?"

Another blank look, and then his eyes cleared and he shook his head.

"Well, then," I said. "I can't always be around, Ronan; I do sometimes have other obligations." Then, realizing that this sounded unaccountably condescending to someone who probably just missed one of his few friends on the island, I added, "You know you are always welcome when I am here, but if I have no easy way of contacting you when I'm going to be out . . ." I shrugged. "But I was meaning to ask: Did you come looking for me fairly late on Friday night?"

He looked puzzled. "Why? Was I supposed to have?"

"No. It's just . . ." Suddenly, it all seemed so silly. I gazed back out over the water, sparkling in the afternoon sunshine, and masked a flush. "I got home late from Harry's party that night and thought I saw someone lurking in the shadows." Ridiculous, really. I turned back to him. "It wasn't . . . I mean . . ."

"Me?" he said, and laughed somewhat tightly. "What would I be doing around here this late?"

I had probably hurt him with my accusations, but if it had

not been Ronan, then who was it? Allegra's killer, back for me? And why? Besides, Abby claimed they already had the guy in custody.

I shook myself out of the spiral of my thoughts with disgust. "I'm sorry," I told Ronan. "You must think me a complete nut! I survived twenty-eight years of New York City without a problem, and now the peaceful countryside turns me into a raving paranoic! But never mind. I'm being a terrible hostess. Can I get you a cup of coffee? A drink? Some salmon dip?"

He seemed to debate for a minute, looking out over the waves, then turned back to me and grinned. A lock of straight dark hair blew boyishly across his brow and made my fingers itch to brush it back. "Might you happen to have any of that raspberry tea Allegra liked so well?"

"I don't know, but I can check. Umm . . . do you happen to know where she kept it?"

There was something odd about seeing Ronan in my house. Under the artificial lights of my kitchen he seemed somehow smaller and paler, out of his element.

"Where *do* you live?" I asked him as I boiled water and he pointed out the tea. I suddenly couldn't imagine him living in a house at all; could not so much as picture where it might be and what it might look like.

"Five doors down the road," he said. "The ugly one, painted blue." And in response to my look: "I rent. I'd invite you around, but your house is nicer."

"Yes, I like it," I said, and served the tea. And we were friends again.

ON MONDAY MORNING, THE alarm went off at far too early, rousing me from a peaceful slumber It was time for my first day of work—which prompted another anxiety all together. Was I cut out for this, or would I make a complete fool of myself? What was I even supposed to wear?

I settled for black dress slacks and a pea-green cashmere sweater, debated the whole concept of jewelry, then abandoned it as a lost cause. I had nothing nice enough for the sweater, and Allegra had nothing casual enough. Then I drove into town with my stomach all in a flutter.

But the day went far better than expected. Abby was a godsend, and explained everything to me with an admirable clarity that made even the most complex tasks seem simple. Again I wondered at her exclusion from Harry's party, and wished I had remembered to ask Richard for that explanation he had promised me. As she coped cheerfully with my first-day fidgets and a series of fractious customers, I marveled at how anyone could possibly take issue with her. Her boundless energy seemed to bring a smile to even the sourest of faces.

In fact, I felt vaguely inadequate next to her, but I acquitted myself well enough. And after a time, I began to have fun. Oddly enough, I discovered that years in an office, dealing with office politics, had given me a fair sense of people. And I likewise uncovered a stubborn core to myself that held no truck with waffling shoppers. I simply turned on the charm and quietly bullied them into what I wanted, all the while convincing them that it was their idea to begin with.

After I had persuaded the third indecisive customer into a purchase and the store had emptied again, Abby turned to me with an amazed look and said, "Well, that's another thing you've inherited. You've certainly got Allegra's gift of gab."

"She was good at this, then?"

"The best." Abby grinned and pushed back her reddish curls. "Who do you think taught me?"

"Tell me about her. I mean, I keep feeling that I'd like to know her better, even if it is a bit after the fact."

Abby sighed, leaning one hip against the counter and surveying the packed shelves. "I've already told you that I thought Allegra was wonderful, but then I have a bias. She took me in when everyone else was against me, condemning me for leaving that cheating bastard simply because . . . It was not what wives were supposed to do, I guess. But the best thing about Allegra was that she didn't give a flip about public opinion. She liked herself and she liked her life, and she expected others to like her right back—but on her own terms, not theirs. I respected her for that. She was intensely practical and yet still capable of great passions." Abby grinned. "Mostly centered around Ragnarok, I'll admit. She engaged in some fearsome battles for that seal."

I glanced up again at the photo, still in its place of honor on the shelf. "Why? Surely there wasn't controversy over Ragnarok."

My companion chuckled. "On the contrary, there was tons of it. Some people felt that raising Ragnarok by herself was irresponsible, that he should be sent to an aquarium, brought up among his own kind. Because otherwise he would never be able to return to the wild if he developed too many human habits, or grew too dependent on human care.

"Still, in a way, no one knew seals better than Allegra. She had lived with them for years, watching them off these shores as she grew up. She sometimes said that Ragnarok was her gift for a lifetime of devotion to the creatures, and the only child she was ever likely to have." Abby looked pensive for a moment. "Which is a pity, because Allegra would have made a fantastic mother. Jessie adored her, and she had a real knack for kids."

"Yes, I remember that," I said softly.

"And troublesome customers." Abby laughed. "Of which we have another one now, so look sharp!"

But after that one had been dispatched, she added, "In any case, that's why I'm so delighted to hear that he returned.

Not only because he is a love, but also because it gives her detractors something to chew on. And I hope it chokes them!"

I, too, was glad that Allegra had been vindicated—and that Ragnarok had returned. But still, "Do you think it was just depression over his absence that was affecting her so badly this past winter?" I asked.

Annoyingly, the bell jingled again and we were forced to drop the topic. About half an hour passed before we could resume the conversation, and then it was over cans of Coke that Abby had grabbed from the market across the street.

"What were we talking about?" Abby said. "Oh, Allegra. I told you already how she changed over the winter, became so reclusive. She would beg off work more often than not— she who had always been so conscientious. About three years ago, she came in to work with a full-blown flu and it was all I could do to get her to go home. Then suddenly a headache was felling her. Or dreams. She told me once that she had actually been becoming a seal in her dreams, or something; she certainly looked like she was getting no sleep whatsoever. But when I questioned her about it later, she denied the whole thing."

"What did you think?"

"That she probably *was* suffering from some sort of depression. I think Ragnarok's absence that first winter made her realize how lonely she truly was. Winter is never an easy time up here: too cold, too dark, too grim. I think it would have been all too easy to sink into despair on those long, dark nights. Especially when the store closed for the season and she had no more excuses to come to town.

"I was worried about her; we all were. But when I asked her, she kept saying that she was fine, that she was happy, and she almost had me convinced. Except that she just withdrew more and more. I went over on a few occasions. Sometimes she wouldn't let me in, even though I knew she was home. When she did let me in, she looked horrible, like I said—all dull and hollow-eyed—although again she claimed she had never been happier.

"Finally, one night when I no longer knew what to do, Tom called." Abby was silent for a long moment. "He found her, you know. Dead. My first thought, when Tom told me, was that it had been suicide. But Tom said no. There was no way those marks could have been . . ." she swallowed audibly, ". . . self-inflicted."

She seemed to come to her senses then, shaking herself visibly. "But enough of grim topics. It's a lovely day; too pretty to be morbid. So, on a more cheerful topic . . . How was your date with Richard on Saturday?"

I gaped at her.

She just grinned. "Small island. So, how was it?"

I tried not to blush. "Very nice," I said, as casually as I could manage.

"Oh, come now, you're going to have to do better than that! Richard's been unattainable for years. Well, okay, so he was after me for a while. Which was kind of flattering. But not," she added hastily, "that I was interested. I mean, he's a great guy, but . . . Well, we've been through that." She laughed, I thought nervously. "Truth to tell, I'm just as happy to have you here, to take the pressure off me. It was beginning to get a bit embarrassing. For him, I mean. I'm glad he's found someone else."

"I think I am, too. But . . . Are you sure you're okay with this?"

"Absolutely," she said, emphatically. "More power to you. And him. I have it from a very reliable source that he didn't leave you alone for a minute at Harry's party."

"Let me guess," I said, dryly—avoiding, for the moment, the reason why she hadn't been at Harry's herself. "Joanna."

"One and the same. So. Was he an absolute gentleman, or did he misbehave?"

"A gentleman."

She sighed deeply and shook her head. "That Richard. When will he ever learn? So, are you seeing him again?"

"Abby!"

"Sorry," she said again, completely unrepentant. "I have to get my adventures vicariously these days. You can tell me to go to hell if you really want to, but I'd far prefer it if you tell me all the gory details." She waggled her eyebrows at me suggestively. "Did he at least kiss you?"

My flaming cheeks must have given her the answer, but suddenly I found myself not quite so averse to talking. It was kind of nice to have an appreciative audience. We ended up giggling like two teenagers until the shop bells chimed again and a handful of tourists clamored in.

AND SO WENT MY first week at work. I gossiped with Abby, sold some souvenirs, vastly depleted our stock of Morelands, and went home every night to Ragnarok and Ronan. The seal still wouldn't come up onto the rocks, but had made somewhat of a tradition of lurking about the shore after he had been fed, watching me as I sat on the back deck with some appetizers and a glass of wine—at least until Ronan appeared.

On Wednesday, just as I was beginning to run low on fish, Tom came rumbling up in his rusty pickup in the late afternon with a fresh load and dangled one for Ragnarok, who came swimming up ecstatically to meet him.

I was rather pleased to see Tom myself and persuaded him to join me for a glass of wine on the deck. I had just prepared some homemade crab dip, and he absently devoured half the bowl and almost a full package of crackers as he prompted me to relate stories of my first few days of work. I had half-expected Ronan to join us, but if he had come by looking for me, Tom's presence must have scared him away.

Richard called me again on Thursday to ask me out for Saturday. I accepted with alacrity, wondering if I had finally managed to find myself a life. The frantic pace of New York had enabled me to hide out far too easily, but the quiet, gentle pace of the island seemed to be luring me inexorably out, like a hermit crab from its shell. And while I still wasn't sure what I felt about the presence of three men in my formerly sterile existence—although admittedly only one seemed interested— it did add a certain excitement to things.

Still, there was a pleasure even in eating my solo dinners, looking out through the dining room windows as the sun sank nightly behind the islands; sometimes placidly, the sky showing no more than a pale line of salmon on the horizon, and other times in great washes of fire that left me gasping.

On Saturday, I had a lovely lunch with Mabel, the librarian, at the Clam Digger, which turned out to be a slightly shopworn diner a little outside of town. We ate bowls of piping hot clam chowder and discussed our favorite novels, and each went home with a list of titles we urged the other to try.

The only odd part of the meal was when she asked me if I knew how far Allegra had gotten on her book.

"Her book?" I echoed. It was getting embarrassing, how little I seemed to know about the woman who had deeded me her life. "What book?"

Mabel herself looked briefly confused. "Perhaps I was mistaken," she said, "but over the winter she was taking out a lot of children's books from the library. I assumed she was trying to write one herself about Ragnarok, using them as a model. A pity, too. I suspect it would have been a wonderful story. She was a talented woman, Allegra."

When I got home, I phoned Abby to ask her about the book, but a blank silence just hissed down the phone lines. "I haven't a clue," she said eventually. "If Allegra was working on such a thing, she never said a word to me."

I put it down to yet another mystery of Allegra's final months—of which there seemed to be many. Still, I realized, as I hung up the phone, I had completely forgotten to be scared of my home. I had seen no more of Tom's shadows; nothing had happened to upset my new-found equilibrium. In fact, though I had only been on Seal Island for a little over two weeks, I already felt as if I had been here my whole life. Allegra's house felt like home, and I had more friends here than I had ever had in New York. And then there was my date with Richard.

He had called me Friday night to confirm, and to throw out suggestions for what we might do. He named a few restaurants that sounded upscale, but I was just as happy to keep it low key—and, besides, I was feeling movie deprived. So I persuaded him that we should drive to Ellsworth early enough to get tickets for an evening show. He arranged to pick me up at four.

Because it was just dinner and a movie, I hadn't bothered to change out of the jeans and sweater I had worn to meet Mabel. I was out on the ledges feeding Ragnarok when Richard arrived. It was another of those blissfully perfect days that I had come to associate with Maine—still chilly, but with the sun lancing through a cloudless sky, the water almost navy and capped with lacy crests of foam, the islands sparkling like jewels against the horizon. I had left my hair unbound, and it was whipping around my face as I tossed fish to Ragnarok, who was in a particularly playful mood. He wheeled and dived, and was in the middle of a rather spectacular leap when Richard's SUV crunched into my driveway. I heard the sound of his motor turn off, the car door open then close again.

"Cecil?" he called.

"Back here," I responded, hoping my voice would carry over the wind.

Ragnarok started a bit at the sound of my voice and eyed me disapprovingly.

I could hear Richard's footsteps crunching through the gravel, but Ragnarok seemed oblivious. So when Richard abruptly appeared from around the side of the house, his blond hair tousled by the wind—wearing chino pants, a sweater and a windbreaker—the seal spooked badly and vanished. He popped up several seconds later, much farther from the shore, torn between the desire to flee and the lure of the fish still in my bucket.

"So this is Ragnarok, I take it?" Richard asked.

"Indeed it is. Come on, Ragnarok, be a good boy and say 'hello,'" I cajoled, but the seal, as usual, had his own ideas on the matter. He swam in a foot closer, then refused to budge another inch despite the fish I tossed deliberately short. But he was not so far away that I couldn't see the reproach in his eyes for wasting perfectly good fish on a dirty trick when he had clearly made up his mind. So I quickly abandoned that tactic like the well-trained human I was and tossed long instead. And, in return, he even condescended to do a trick or two—though he made it clear they were for me alone. For when Richard clapped and cheered, the seal shot him a series of contemptuous glances that seemed to say: *and just what does this have to do with you?*

"I'm sorry," I said to Richard when my bucket was empty, feeling slightly embarrassed by my seal's behavior. "It's nothing personal. He's just a little shy and doesn't tend to like strangers. He won't even come near Ronan."

Richard frowned faintly. "Who's Ronan?"

"My neighbor—and I assume a friend of Allegra's. He lives a few houses along; often comes by for drinks in the evening."

Richard looked suddenly jealous, and I cursed myself for mentioning Ronan at all. Male posturing was the last thing I needed to deal with. Fortunately, we would not be interrupted by Ronan himself at this unfortunate moment; he already knew I'd be out for the evening.

"So why haven't I met this Ronan?" Richard said.

I sighed faintly. "You probably have. He works at Louis' gas station. But he's fairly new to the island." In response to Richard's continued gaze, I added, "We're just friends, honestly."

"Good," he said, decisively.

I sighed again and looked around. Ragnarok was long gone, and it seemed pointless to linger on the rocks any longer.

"Let me just go wash my hands," I said, "then we can leave."

15

ON THE WAY TO Ellsworth, I told Richard more stories of Ragnarok. Eventually he said, "Would you mind if I did a local interest story on you and your seal?"

I was slightly taken aback. "Why? I mean, who would care?"

"Well, you've certainly piqued my interest," he said, cheerfully.

I wasn't sure what to say to this, so—as usual in such situations—I said nothing.

"I know," he continued, sounding almost embarrassed. "It's an awfully work-oriented request for a date, but apart from my personal interest in the matter, I really do think it would make a great story. Everyone here knows about Ragnarok—well, knew about him, because of Allegra—and I know they'd be interested to hear he's back. Besides, everyone loves seals; it could get you wider coverage. Maybe even as far south as Boston."

"With your by-line?" I said, meaning to tease him, but he flushed, concentrating studiously on driving.

"Well, I admit," he said, his eyes fixed resolutely to the road, "I do know my audience, and I've made a comfortable life as a small-town editor. But even the most mundane of us do have our ambitions. I know I couldn't make it in a big city—I just don't have the talent for that, much as I like to delude myself—but it would be nice to get the occasional recognition. So." He turned and grinned at me. "Mind if I ride you and Ragnarok to glory?"

I laughed. "Well, I don't know if it will be precisely glory, but . . . Feel free. Give me a week or so to get Ragnarok more comfortable around me—despite appearances, he's still debating my merits—and then we'll see if we can't get you a good photo op. He does love performing. But . . ." I paused. "How would you feel about an agenda?"

He glanced at me briefly before negotiating a turn. "What agenda?"

There was something profoundly refreshing about stating your opinions, I found. "Abby told me that Allegra had taken a lot of flack for raising Ragnarok by herself, that people didn't believe he could survive in the wild after that. If I agree to cooperate with you, you'll have to make it clear that she was right and they were wrong."

He raised eyebrow. "That might catch you a lot of flak, as well. Are you sure you want to do it that way?"

"Absolutely," I said. It would be a vindication of Allegra. And, after all she had done for me, it was the least I could do in return.

WHEN WE GOT TO Ellsworth, we joined one of the oddest conglomeration of movie goers I had ever seen, ranging from local families and their kids to blushing teenagers out on date-night to a handful of obviously affluent summer folks. Richard and I cheerfully dickered over movie choices. He wanted something more highbrow and serious; I was in the mood for frivolous. I practiced the salesmanship I had been learning with Abby at the store, and he finally laughed and capitulated, purchasing the tickets I had wanted.

We had about an hour before the show, so we grabbed a hasty dinner at The Mex, and I made a conscious effort to open up to him, holding hands as we stood in the movie line, letting him put his arm around me as we sat in the dim theater waiting for the feature to begin. In front of us were two teenagers, clearly on their first or second date. I found myself watching them, wincing empathetically at the tremulous awkwardness between them. Each clearly wanted to make a move; each was just as clearly terrified of doing so. Afraid of opening themselves up to rejection, perhaps, or of revealing their vulnerability.

Nervous giggles abounded.

I felt for them, but I also—obscurely—envied them. Despite their tension, they both wanted the same thing. Whereas I didn't know what I wanted. Hadn't for years.

"Any time I feel any regret about getting older," Richard whispered, his breath warm against my ear, "I just try to remember what it was actually like being young. I wouldn't go back for all the world. Not knowing what you wanted, not knowing what lay ahead . . ." He shuddered in mock horror.

I just muttered something non-committal, because he was very wrong. They knew exactly what they wanted because wants were simpler then, with fewer perceived consequences and complexities. As for knowing what lay ahead . . . No one ever knew that, no matter how old they got. The only difference was, the young hadn't learned to fear the unknown.

"Would you go back?" Richard added. "If you could?"

I tried to tell myself it was the brush of his lips against my

ear that made me shiver. "No," I said, but not for the reason
he intended. The two kids in front of us looked about seven-
teen: a year younger than I had been when the anvil had
dropped on my life.

Like Richard, I would not go back for all the world. I
never wanted to live through that sort of pain again.

Richard seemed on the verge of saying something more,
but then the movie started and we were distracted.

It was precisely the type of thing I had needed: foolish
and mindless, and utterly charming. For all his objections,
Richard laughed himself silly. And I felt my spirits rise, all
my sober reflections forgotten.

Midway through the film, I suddenly became aware of our
teenage neighbors. Inhibitions forgotten, they were locked
together. I hadn't seen who had made the first move, but
Richard smiled beside me, his eyes meeting mine. They
seemed to twinkle in the darkness of the theater; *not a bad
idea*, they seemed to say. And before I even knew what was
happening, Richard's lips claimed mine. Soft and gentle at
first, then more assured.

I couldn't say it was a lightning bolt and the world disappearing. But it was infinitely sweet, and the movie did vanish
for a while. Then a disgusted noise sounded behind us and
we broke apart, Richard's chuckle ghosting across my
mouth.

He tightened his arm around me and, after a moment, I
rested my head against his shoulder, thinking: *I could get
used to this. I really could.*

When the movie ended and the couple before us disentan-
gled and departed, Richard chuckled again, extending a
hand to help me to my feet. "Again," he said softly, "nice to
be an adult."

He retained my hand out into the lobby. But there, in the

lights and the crowds, I felt suddenly self-conscious and
stiffened a bit. Being Richard, he let me reclaim my hand.
We walked to the car in a silence that was not exactly uncomfortable, but certainly fraught. He waited until we had
negotiated the traffic through the strip of Route 1 and turned
onto Route 15 before saying, "Shall we talk about it? Or just
repeat the experience again as soon as possible?"

I squeaked out a laugh that was not all that different from
the teenagers in its awkwardness.

"Is that a 'yes?' " he persisted.

"It's a . . . I . . ."

We swept down past Rooster Brothers, and up the hill that
led out of town. As the streetlights vanished and darkness
swallowed the interior of the car, I felt bold enough to say,
"I'm sorry, Richard. This is all . . . a little new to me."

In the reflected glow of the headlights off the macadam, I
saw him turn briefly to me. "As I said before," he replied, "I
find that hard to believe."

"And as I answered before, it's very true."

"But surely you've had boyfriends before."

"Of course," I said defensively. No point in admitting just
how long ago those few boyfriends had been. Or how young
I had been, at the time. "It's just . . ." I laughed nervously.
I'm sorry. You'll have to be a bit patient with me."

"I can do that," he said, but something in his voice
sounded unconvinced.

Unable to help myself, I laughed—genuinely, this time—
and placed a hand on his knee, squeezing it in wordless
thanks for at least contemplating the task. He jumped slightly.
And then, in the bright slice of headlights from an approaching car, I saw his answering smile, wide and exuberant.

He reached down and twined his fingers in mine, lifting
my hand briefly to his lips. He kissed it lightly, his tongue

brushing against my knuckles, then released it, and I spent the rest of the drive home in a state of high nervousness I couldn't quite understand.

Richard, on the other hand, was in high spirits. And words, at least, were not awkward between us. His cheerfulness was infectious.

Still, as we swept across the causeway, the water beyond the rocks as dark as an abyss, my anxiety, which had begun to fade to a dull throb, suddenly spiked. What would happen now? He would want to kiss me again. And—this much I had to admit—I was not precisely adverse to the idea. But should I invite him in? Was I even ready for that? I had made a lot of progress that night—at least, within myself—but I still had a long way to go.

But as usual with life, the fears you anticipate are never the ones that catch you out. I had been so preoccupied with the matter of Richard that I almost didn't notice the unmistakable silhouette of a human figure darting through the sweep of Richard's headlights as we turned into my drive.

"What the hell?" Richard exclaimed, stomping on the brakes so hard that I had to brace a hand against the dashboard to avoid being flung through the windshield.

Just like last Friday, only this time I had a witness—proving it had not been just my imagination.

My heart set up a frantic tattoo as Richard flung off his seatbelt, whipped open the door, and leapt from the car. I made a futile grab, as if to say *don't leave me*, but it was too late. Richard had vanished, and so had the intruder. A chill wind blew through the open car door, and I shivered. Then a dark figure loomed in the driver's side door, and a small, involuntary shriek escaped my lips.

"Damn it; nothing!" Richard exclaimed. Then, "I'm sorry. Did I scare you?"

I muttered something incoherent even to myself, and he suddenly seemed aware of my condition. He became briskly practical. "Come on. Inside with you," he said, and there was something comforting in having all decisions temporarily pre-empted.

He bundled me into the house, half-carrying me up the steps and wresting the keys from my frigid fingers. Then, unlocking the door, he flipped on the lights, casting a comforting glow over the lawn. Electricity: by its very nature so antithetical to the things that lurked in the darkness. What had our ancestors done without it?

Dimly, a part of me wondered why I was reacting so strangely. Or was I? Perhaps I was just cold. The air seemed more frigid than usual tonight.

Richard shut the door decisively behind us and locked it with a gratifying click. And, as simply as that, he was in.

A vaguely hysterical giggle escaped me.

"Cecil?" he said. "Cecil!"

"What?"

"What's so funny?"

"I don't know."

"Then why won't you stop laughing?"

The next thing I knew, a glass was thrust into my hand. I took a deep gulp . . . then almost choked as the liquor seared my throat. I sniffed, and took a sip. And then another.

I smiled. Trust Richard to revive me with an expensive Laphroaig.

I took another sip, reflecting that they could have called it Scotch courage as easily as Dutch. The smooth, smoky liquid seemed to stroke every muscle into submission.

Richard had taken advantage of my condition to pour himself a glass as well. When I started to laugh, he peered at me nervously for a moment. Then, seeing my expression, he relaxed. "What?"

"I hadn't intended to ask you in," I told him. "Is this your idea of taking it slowly?"

He chuckled ruefully and peered down into his glass, swirling the liquor reflectively. "Not precisely." He looked up. "I didn't imagine that, did I?"

I shook my head. "Not unless I did as well."

He exhaled gustily and took another drink. Then he smiled. "Good scotch."

"Allegra had taste."

"That she did. But I'm beginning to question her sense— especially when it came to leaving this place to you. Maybe you should find another house."

"Or go back to New York?"

"That wouldn't be one of my first choices, but . . . You might be safer." He grimaced. "What was I thinking, chasing after that thing in the dark? I could have gotten myself killed!"

He was right. Though he was tall and solidly built, he didn't have the innate scrappiness to take down a mysterious prowler. Granted I had seen little more of my intruder than I had the night before, but my few fleeting glimpses had hinted at a wiry strength and a sleek economy of motion. More a match for Tom, perhaps. Or Ronan, who for all his lean grace had a core of steel to him. But Richard?

His ego was looking wounded, so I said, "My hero."

He chuckled in a deprecating sort of way. "Fine hero. I rush out boldly, then get the shakes and have to be coddled back into shape."

He must have been feeling better, for he looked at me hopefully. I laughed.

"Fat chance, hero. Especially if this is your idea of taking it slowly."

He sighed, then grinned. "Well, it was worth a shot." He drained his glass and set it down on the table by the door, and I suddenly realized I had never made it out of the front hall. "Are you sure you don't want me to stay? In the spare room,

I meant," he added hastily. "It might make you feel more comfortable to at least know someone else was around."

I shook my head. Oddly enough, I didn't feel scared any more; just angry at the phantom intruder who kept invading my privacy. If I ever caught him, I would . . .

I would what? If Richard couldn't take him, what made me think I could?

Besides, the choice between having Richard in the house or the stranger outside was a simple one. My intruder hadn't yet managed to penetrate my locks, and my feelings about Richard were more complicated. I both wanted to fling myself into his arms and burn out the last of my fear and anger in pure physical sensation, and to close the door firmly behind him and retreat into my customary solitude.

Knowing that my impulse to the former was teetering on a knife-edge of indecision, I chose the latter course. No sense needlessly confusing the issue—for anything that transpired tonight would be less about us and more about me.

"I'll be fine," I assured him. "Really. No one's managed to break into the house yet."

"There's always a first time," he said darkly, then flushed. "I'm sorry. I . . ."

"Forget it. I'll call the police in the morning, I promise, and report this. And put a motion sensor on my porch lights. But in the meantime, we probably scared him as much as he scared us; I doubt he'll be back tonight."

"And tomorrow? And the next night?"

"We'll take that as it comes, Richard. We'll take of it all as it comes."

He seemed to take my meaning and smiled slightly. "Fair enough, Cecil." He stepped closer and ran a finger lightly around the edge of my jaw, then tipped my face to his.

I guess I was feeling needier than I had expected, for I

clutched at him. And fueled by our shared emotions, this kiss was more intense. His lips seized mine almost greedily, perhaps grasping for the same illusory comfort I was after. My mouth fell open under his assault, returning need for need until my breath came hard and fast.

Then, seeming to recollect himself, he pulled back, gentling the kiss for a moment before releasing me.

We stared at each other for a moment in renewed awkwardness. Then I opened the door wordlessly.

"Thank you for the movie, Richard," I finally managed.

He laughed faintly. "My pleasure. Good-night, Cecil."

"Good-night."

I shut the door slowly behind him.

"I won't leave until I hear the lock turn," he said though the panels.

Obligingly, I shot the bolt home, listening to his footsteps retreating down the steps. I heard him close the car door and key the engine to life.

The car crunched off and I sank to the floor in the hallway, my back against the door, staring through my living room to the dark night beyond the three French doors. I wrapped my arms around my legs, rested my chin on my knees, and wondered what I was going to do next.

16

I DID CALL THE police, as promised, on Sunday morning, but as I had suspected, there was little they could do beyond showing up, drinking lots of my coffee, and filing an incident report. There were not even any footprints for them to examine, only Richard's and my testimony. They gave me some of the same variation on the shadows theme—although I suspected it was more because they thought me a hysterical city girl rather than because, like Tom, they too had seen things they could not explain.

On Monday, since business was still slow enough, Abby dispatched me to the local hardware store to have a motion detector installed on the porch lights—after she had quizzed me thoroughly and obsessively about Richard. And something about her questions made me begin to wonder if perhaps she wasn't regretting her decision to reject him, just a bit, now that he had shifted camps, but it wasn't anything I could say to her. So instead I escaped work with an almost palpable sense of relief, and headed off for Eaton's. I negotiated the price and had the workmen out at my place within the hour. By five, I had lights that would come on the minute I pulled into the driveway and, more important, would be triggered by midnight visitors, hopefully scaring them off. Or at least revealing their identity.

When that was finished, I drove back to town to pick up groceries, and by the time I got home, I found a second mackerel-filled cooler resting atop my front steps.

I think you can probably leave the shed door unlocked without incident, the note, stuck half in and half out of it, read. *Or else give me a key. I'll be by tomorrow for the cooler. Just leave it outside the front door tonight.*

It was signed, simply, *T*.

I grimaced in regret and wrestled it across the lawn to the utility shed. Then I filled the cooler already in the refrigerator, rinsed the second cooler in the sea, and fed my seal.

Ragnarok seemed a little out of sorts that evening, upset at being forced to wait a full hour more for his feeding, and it took me some time to coax him back into a good humor. But eventually—after some very silly capering on my part that left me very glad none of my neighbors could see—he conceded to leap and wheel for me. And by the end of our session, I realized that the little wretch had managed to guilt me into giving him an extra portion of fish and was looking quite smugly pleased with his ploy.

"You are incorrigible!" I accused, and he barked at me happily.

Ronan and I shared a drink, and then I had a peaceful dinner—which was not interrupted by a single flicker of my porch lights—and was back at work on Tuesday morning without incident. Or so I assumed.

"It's the Fourth of July a week from today," Abby informed me gleefully as I walked in the door of the shop.

I looked at her, baffled, as I stowed my jacket beneath the counter. "Meaning our work load is about to increase?"

"Among other things. But first is the day itself."

"Why? What happens around here on the Fourth of July?"

Abby's eyebrows soared. "You mean no one has told you?" And when I shook my head, she laughed and hopped down from her stool. "It's quite a big to-do. Parades and an islandwide cookout, and some of the most pitiful fireworks you have ever seen. It's endlessly fun! You have to come, of course. Jessie and I will be depending on you."

I very much doubted if her daughter cared whether I was there or not. Jessie was finishing off her school term, so I hadn't even met her yet. But Abby was looking at me anxiously, so I laughed and said, "How could I miss it?"

"Then what sort of costume are you wearing?"

"Costume?" I exclaimed.

Abby chuckled. "All the local merchants get dressed up. This year's theme, predictably, is life on the island, coupled with a dash of island history. I'm going as a rather dreadful-looking Penobscot Indian. Jessie's school is going as seafood. And if you think making an Indian costume is bad, try sewing a clam suit! Allegra always came up with the greatest costumes. But then I suppose, being new, no one will expect you to participate this year."

"Well, thank heavens for that!" I declared.

"But you must come witness the festivities, costume or no. The whole town will be there, and, like I said, there's quite a stupendous lobster cookout."

"Really?" My interest peaked at that. I had long heard tales of the Maine lobsters, but had yet to experience one. None of the local supermarkets seemed to sell them, and I didn't know the secret places to purchase them. And while I suppose I could have asked someone like Tom Moneghan, I think I was rather intimidated by the idea of buying some overgrown bug and popping it in a pot without even the faintest clue what I was doing. The cookbooks I had read had always made it sound enormously complicated. But perhaps there was some local trick I was missing that I could learn next Tuesday.

The week passed both fast and slowly in anticipation. It started raining Tuesday night, and the water leaked steadily from a leaden sky for the next three days. Business slowed to a crawl, and I found myself hoping this would let up before the Fourth. But from the look of the unrelenting sky, the rain might have continued indefinitely.

Richard called several times and asked me out again for Saturday, but I had already promised Abby a girl's night in. Jessie was staying at a friend's that night, so Abby was free. I explained this to Richard as I regretfully declined. But, not to be discouraged, he invited me instead to join him for at least part of the Fourth, which I did accept. And the same with the Thursday night dinner at the Myrtle, which we passed in pleasant conversation while the rain pattered soothingly on the roof. Though—poor Richard—I had still not resolved my conflict about him. I was attracted to him, but something was holding me back, preventing me from making any kind of full commitment. He was very good about it, though I did sense a part of him was growing impatient with me.

I felt for the guy; I really did. I wouldn't have wanted to be dating me right then for the world. But I was also not about to let a certain fellow-feeling guilt me into making a leap that, for me, was equivalent to hurling myself blind and headlong into an abyss.

Consequences cluttered up my head. How well I knew that caring only led to heartbreak! No, the wall I had built around myself was not that easily breached—but to give Richard credit, he was melting it by slow degrees.

The rain also drove Ronan and me inside for our drinks—

though oddly this didn't deter him. There was, in fact, something refreshing about seeing him rounding the curve of my shore dressed in rain gear but with the hook of the slicker flung back and the rain pouring down his cheeks and hair. He seemed to take a genuine pleasure in the damp, and once I caught an almost ecstatic smile on his face as he paused on my lawn and turned his face up to the weeping sky, the rain running like quicksilver over his skin.

Of course, the first night, he managed to scare us both nearly senseless when he set off the exterior lights in the rainy gloom. I had been laying out my appetizers, and had jumped and almost dropped the dish when my alert lights had flickered on without warning. A small, involuntary squeak escaped my lips, followed immediately by a louder, tenor yip from the back porch. It sounded oddly like the noise Ragnarok had made a few days back when a mackerel from one of my slightly over-energetic tosses had clipped his nose: sheer, animalistic surprise. I set the dish down and peered out through French doors. And was relieved to see Ronan stranded on my back deck like a shipwreck survivor, streaming with water, a baffled expression on his face.

I padded to the nearest door and pushed it open. "Good evening, Ronan."

He was still staring at the light as if it might bite him. "How did you . . ."

I grinned. "Sorry if it startled you. I put in a motion detector yesterday. The lights now go on the moment someone wanders past."

"Oh." He uttered it on one, long-drawn breath, then focused his attention more firmly on me. He peered at my face for a moment as if assessing, then said, "Another incident?"

I smiled ruefully. "With witnesses, no less, so I know it's not my imagination. Please, come in." And I opened the door wider and stood aside.

Still, he hesitated for a moment. "Only the lights?" he said. "No . . ." He waved his hands vaguely.

"Alarm?" I said. "No. And no booby traps, either." And when he stared at me blankly, I added, "Honestly, just the lights. Please." I gestured him inside a second time. "I made salmon dip."

That seemed to decide him. In he came—then paused, sneezed, and shook his head like a dog, spraying water everywhere.

There was, I had to admit, something refreshing about the almost childlike enthusiasm with which he sometimes embraced the world. So much was still new to him that at times he made me feel old and cynical. I handed him a towel, and he rubbed it vigorously over his head until his hair stood up in damp spikes about his head.

It was odd having Ronan inside, though. I noticed he always entered the house somewhat warily, like a cat. Each time I shut the door behind him, I felt it was almost as much to keep him in than to keep others out. And for all his fluid grace outdoors, he still seemed oddly uncomfortable inside, his eyes flicking about my domain as if searching for the traps I had assured him weren't there. Nor would he go near the left-hand sofa, as if instinctually aware of the violence that had taken place close by.

But gradually he seemed to relax—or I ceased to notice his behavior.

By Friday, the rain finally ceased, but the sky remained heavy and oppressive. Tom stopped by that evening with more fish. I had hoped to catch him on Tuesday when he returned for his cooler, but by the time I awoke on Tuesday morning, it was already gone from my stoop. Now, we fed Ragnarok together, and the seal acted like Tom's absence had been the height of betrayal. Tom had to work even harder than I had on Monday night to win him back, and as I looked over at Tom's tall form, silhouetted against the steely sky, his fingers wrapped purposefully around a silvery mackerel, I found myself saying, "I think you'll just have to help feed him more often."

He turned slightly to regard me. There was an almost surprised expression in his eyes. "I would love to," he said. "But . . . I didn't want to intrude."

"You wouldn't be," I assured him, and somehow managed to refrain from adding: *Ever*.

I convinced him to stay for dinner that night, and I forget what we talked about as the sky faded from violet to black. I think mostly books. He was remarkably well-read for a lobsterman; but then I supposed there was little else to do during the long, dark winter than to curl up with a novel or three. And he praised me lavishly for the food—though in truth it was just something I had thrown together at the last minute from whatever I had in the fridge, since I had not been expecting company.

"At least I'll bring the wine, next time," he said to me at one point in the evening—I think after we had emptied the bottle—and I felt a flush of pleasure that he so simply assumed there would be other times. And it was true, my house did feel oddly vacant after he had departed.

I had never realized how many empty corners existed for the echoes to pile up in. And that night, for the first time, I began to regret that I never had managed to purchase a TV, to fill up the house with the sounds of artificial company.

Then there was my night with Abby, which was also much more pleasant than I had anticipated—especially since I discovered at the last moment that she had also invited Joanna. But that night, I began to see the real person beneath Joanna's cool façade, and I began to understand the affection Abby had for her. I wouldn't say we became close, but sitting around Abby's kitchen table that night, watching Joanna grow slowly and somewhat rambunctiously drunk, was not an experience I would have missed. And it was hard to feel intimidated by a woman relating some of the more embarrassing incidents from her first year of running the Myrtle with a self-deprecating smile on her face.

And the following Tuesday at noon, I showed up at the town center—dressed casually as both Richard and Abby had recommended—and watched the Fourth of July festivities begin. It was, as Abby had promised, a true spectacle, reeking of provinciality. For one thing, it took almost half an hour to start, as aimless groups of costumed people clotted up the road just outside the town while someone with a bullhorn barked out indecipherable commands. A few were mounted on horses, which fretted and stamped in the growing heat. And just as everything seemed about ready to go, one of the antique cars that always seemed a requisite part of such parades drove up, its horn wheezing, and the horses spooked and scattered.

But finally the parade commenced: a ragged line spurred on by what could only be a high school marching band. There were about three antique cars, their horns echoing like dyspeptic cows, and the volunteer fire department on their truck. The school kids wore homemade costumes, and all looked impossibly angelic. While the local merchants in equally homemade guises appeared patently ridiculous. The lines stuttered and staggered, and the nervous horses dropped piles of manure in the middle of the street.

And I found myself whooping and hollering along with the rest of the viewing public, losing myself in a spectacle which would have earned nothing but my scorn in New York.

I couldn't tell which of the handful of ingenious clams was Abby's daughter, but Abby herself looked more like a brunette Raggedy Ann in her brown yarn braids and freckles than any sort of Native American I had ever seen. She smiled and waved at the crowd, strands of her reddish blond hair springing from beneath her wig. I could tell from her eyes that she knew just what an incongruous sight she created. And that she cared not a whit.

I redoubled my cries, clapping and cheering, and she shot me a jaunty wink.

"Quite a far cry from New York City, isn't it?" said a voice from behind me, and I whirled. Tom Moneghan was gazing down at me, the indecipherable expression back in his gaze. Today he was wearing a pristinely white short sleeved T-shirt that only seemed to emphasize the athletic fitness of his arms and chest, and a pair of worn, faded—and remarkably clean—jeans that made his legs look impossibly long and lean. And though his words could have been construed as cynical, his mouth slowly curved into a teasing smile that took away their sting.

"Exactly," I said, with a smile of my own. "And thank God for it! I heard on the news that it was supposed to go above a hundred degrees in New York today." Here on Seal Island it was all of seventy, finally warm enough for shorts, sandals, and a sleeveless top, but not too hot to be oppressive. "But what is it about such events?" I added. "Back in New York, I would have been sneering at such a parade. So why am I enjoying it so much today?"

He raised an eyebrow, and the sudden flare of his smile transformed his face. "Perhaps because everyone else is enjoying themselves as much?" he said, and he was right. Despite the ridiculous costumes and the relative paucity of paraders, a festive air reigned.

It was just a matter of perspective, I realized. All in your perception. And thought it was a pity that Ronan was missing this. I had invited him to join us, but he had just smiled faintly and told me that someone had to work. "Besides," he added, "I'm not very good with crowds."

"Look, there's Joanna," Tom now added, leaning over my shoulder to point.

I sputtered with laughter. Joanna and her husband were dressed as salad fixings—he as a tomato and she as celery—being herded by a white-hatted chef who could only be Jean-Pierre, bearing a pair of oversized tongs.

And there was Richard, garbed as Shakespeare, leading the crew of the local paper, all likewise clad in various literary outfits. Except for one who didn't seem to fit the theme. He was dressed in a worn Aran sweater and rubber waders rather like those Tom wore on his lobster boat. But then, perhaps he hadn't had time to change.

Behind me, Tom snorted, a mixture of disgust and amusement—at Richard's pretension, I assumed. It did seem a bit much for the editor of the local paper to disguise himself as one of the greatest bards of all time. But then who was I to judge him? Especially since he seemed to be enjoying the role so greatly.

Before long, the parade trailed off, its participants gathering into a milling knot at the opposite end of town, rather equivalent to the configuration they had started in a mere fifteen minutes before.

Tom cocked an eyebrow. "All will be chaos for a while. So what do say to some refreshments while we wait for Abby to uncostume? The tables should be set up by now."

I hadn't been aware that Tom Moneghan was part of our party, or that he knew Abby so well, but who was I to complain? This was the Tom Moneghan I was coming to know from our seal-feeding adventures: a decided improvement over the rather surly lobsterman that seemed his more public persona. And I couldn't think of a better companion for a holiday afternoon.

He offered me his arm as the crowds of observers began to disperse, and I looped my elbow through his, trying to ignore the vague tingle that went through me as flesh met flesh—not as startling as those from some of Ronan's rare touches, but somehow more potent for all that. Deftly, he guided me though the crowd—for which his height had to have been an advantage—delivering us without incident to a set of tables on the far end of town, clustered in the Myrtle Inn's parking lot. They were spread with cookies and donuts, sandwiches and chips.

"What can I get you?" he said.

Our arms unlinked as we surveyed the tables.

"I don't see prices . . ." I began.

"For a good reason: there are none. Whatever else you might say about Seal Island, it knows how to put on the Fourth. Lunch has been on the Myrtle Inn for years, and we fishermen supply the lobsters for the cookout. Island government, such as it is, supplies the rest. Plate?" he added, handing me one.

I took what appeared to be a ham and cheese sandwich, some chips and two cookies. Tom had piled his plate with two sandwiches, a minor mountain of chips, and four cookies. "Growing boy," he said with a grin as he noticed my reaction. "Though in which direction, these days, I really couldn't say. Drink?"

He had almost effortlessly guided me to another table, this one with a selection of sodas and juice and bottles of water in bins of ice. I was reaching for a lemonade when Tom arced an eyebrow at me.

"Are you sure?" he asked, reaching for a brimming plastic cup of beer that a man had passed across the counter to him, dispensed from a keg I had only just noticed. "Thanks, John," he added.

"Sure thing. And for the lady?"

"The same," I said, throwing caution to the wind. After all, it was the Fourth. And what was an American holiday without beer?

Tom Moneghan passed me the cup he had just accepted and received another in return. Then, juggling our booty, we retreated to a shady hillock by the side of the Myrtle where a crowd was already gathering.

"Damn," he said, "I forgot the blanket in the truck. Here, this looks like a prime spot. Guard it for us." And laying his plate and cup on the ground, he dashed off, like an oversized boy.

I smiled and took a sip of my beer, surveying the crowd around me. Some were clearly summer folk, though perhaps of long-standing, and others were just as obviously locals. And despite the air of festivity, there was nonetheless a tension between the two, a visible drawing of boundaries fostered by resentment on one side and prejudice on the other. And I began to understand what Ronan had meant about crowds.

I flushed slightly as Tom returned, wondering if I would be seen to be conspiring with the enemy, but he seemed not to notice, shaking out the blanket and laying it across the grass, settling down with his plate and cup. He patted the space beside him, adding, "Don't worry; Abby will find us."

I took a seat, settling the plate onto my lap with the beer beside me. "I didn't realize you and Abby were such friends."

He smiled ruefully, and took a large bite of his sandwich. "Nor," he said, eventually, "did you expect a lobsterman to appear at one of Harry's parties, no matter how well he cleans up."

Somewhat embarrassed, I wondered if he had successfully read my face that day, but when I glanced over at him, his gaze had turned inward, contemplative.

"In truth," he added, "I don't know quite where I belong in this community, and neither does anyone else. I was born here, and my father was a lobsterman. But unlike most of my childhood friends, I was determined to escape. So I went to college. Worse, I went away to college. And I stayed away for a good number of years." The gloom was increasing in his expression and I didn't know what to say to him. But before I could utter any embarrassingly trite pleasantries, he continued, "The locals feel betrayed because I went away, proved myself other than they were. And because I showed no signs of coming back until recently, and very unexpectedly. I've been back for eight years, but they trust my reasons for returning no more than they trusted my reasons for going away. So they still regard me with suspicion, whether it be from jealousy or narrow-mindedness. They're a clannish lot, the locals, and I betrayed them.

"As for the transplants, or the children of transplants . . . Well, I suppose I'm their charity case, the local boy made good. Which endears me even less to my childhood companions. But I have the taint of the sea on me, and I chose to go back to lobstering when I clearly didn't have to. Which makes the transplants suspicious in turn. Why would a man choose to dirty his hands that way? Except that I genuinely love it, and couldn't imagine doing anything else when my world crashed in on me. Sometimes I wonder if it isn't cowardly, retreating to what I knew best rather than trying something new. But it is in my blood, and I did miss it, all those years away. There's nothing like the sunrise over the water, the feeling of freedom that comes from being in a boat with nothing but ocean around you."

He was going far beyond my depths, and I didn't know what to say. This was far from my casual companion of the seal-feeding afternoons; even at dinner he hadn't opened up so greatly. I wanted to ask him what he meant by his world crashing, but then he laughed, his expression lightening again. "I think I only showed up at Harry's party to see how they'd all react. I would find it endlessly amusing if it weren't all so patently ridiculous."

A million questions were running through my head. *What were you doing all those years you were away? And what, precisely, crashed? And how many scars has it left?* But those questions were impossible. I couldn't possibly broach a subject so clearly off-limits.

The most pressing question plaguing me, however, was: *Why me? Why are you telling me all this?*

I think he realized that, too, adding, "I don't even know why I'm spilling my guts this way, except that"—and here his expression sharpened, his gaze fixing on me—"I have the sense that you know something about all this; that there's something in your life that you are hiding as well. Or hiding from. Am I right?"

I opened my mouth but no words came out. I literally couldn't think of a thing to say.

It was almost with a sense of divine deliverance that I heard Abby's voice exclaim above us, "Cecil, there you are. And Tom! What in blazes are you doing here?"

Her face registered open amazement, and my companion smiled somewhat sheepishly. I realized that he never had been part of the party, as I had assumed from his behavior. "Horning in on the festivities," he admitted. "I hope you don't mind. I do offer blankets and food in recompense." And he held up his half-empty plate like an offering.

I hadn't realized how much he had eaten in the interim. I had barely touched my food, rapt by his words, but he had managed to decimate most of his. The plate he now offered contained only half a sandwich—very obviously bitten into—a few crumbs of chips, and two cookies.

Abby had divested herself of the Indian outfit and the dreadful yarn wig. She was dressed comfortably in shorts, sandals, and a Seal Island T-shirt, her hair curling in an unrestrained bush about her face. She snagged one of the remaining cookies, her face lighting in a grin.

"I'm delighted, of course," she said, "but you're going to have to do better than this if you truly want to win me over. A proper sandwich will suffice. And a beer. That damn wig was hot!"

Tom jumped to his feet, saluting her in teasing mockery. "Yes, ma'am. Your wish is my command."

Abby flung herself down to the blanket at my side, heaving a sigh, and we both watched him as he departed, his impressively tall, jeans-clad figure weaving through the crowd, nodding affably at people as he passed.

I wondered again at his words. It seemed to me that he straddled both worlds rather than fitting into neither, and I wondered what it was in his make-up that made him perceive it so differently.

Then I was distracted again by Abby rolling over and heaving another sigh. "Damn," she laughed, wrinkling her freckled nose. "Remember what I said about those dark, brooding, inaccessible—and ultimately unattainable—types? Not that I mind Tom's company, but did he even give you a choice?"

I shook my head ruefully, and she laughed again.

"I thought not. Well, it will be an interesting Fourth, anyway. And there is far worse company to have than Tom Moneghan."

As my eyes again sought out his tall, dark form in the crowd, I couldn't help but agree.

17

"So," Abby said, sitting up after a moment and regarding me with a grin. "Was I patently awful? Don't worry; you can tell the truth."

"You were wonderful," I began, then smiled as she regarded me dubiously. "Right," I added. "So you looked more like Raggedy Ann than a self-respecting Native American, but . . ."

"I was afraid of that." She laughed. "Oh, well; live and learn. But thank God, here comes Tom with my food!"

He was indeed approaching, more heavily laden than I had expected. He grinned at Abby as he put down the plates and sat.

"Honestly, Thomas. Do you think I'm that much of a pig?" she demanded, staring at the assortment of at least half a dozen sandwiches, the plateful of chips, and about a dozen cookies he had brought.

"And what makes you think it's all for you?" he retorted

in a similar tone, snagging another of the sandwiches for himself.

"Oh I might have known," she declared. "First you invite yourself along, and then you eat all our food."

"Which I procured," he reminded her.

There seemed such an easy banter between them that I found myself wondering if he might be as interested in her as she clearly was in him, and was startled by the sudden kick of jealousy that went through me at the thought. That was the last thing I had any right to, as far as Tom was concerned.

"Uninvited guests must endeavor to please all the party," he added, "and I thought Cecil might want another. And besides, there's always . . ."

"Tom!" shrieked a delighted voice and a young girl dove at him, almost toppling him from his seated position. I had a brief impression of dark hair in pigtails and a length of gangly leg as she went by. "You found us!"

"That I did," he said, wrestling her cheerfully for a moment. Then he grinned at Abby over the child's head. "Not so uninvited after all, I think."

"Wouldn't you know," she said sourly, but she was smiling. "Sit up, Jess, and let Tom eat in peace."

The girl complied, gazing briefly at her mother before adding to Tom, "Are we still going out on the boat on Sunday?"

"I wouldn't miss it for the world," he answered.

She seemed satisfied with this answer, and turned her attention to me instead. We studied each other in silence for a moment. She was a boyish child who showed every sign of growing into a tearing beauty someday. She wore cut-off jeans and a T-shirt, and elbows and knees bore a liberal spattering of old scabs. Despite the pigtails, her hair was dark and curled at the ends, though it seemed less determinedly frizzy than Abby's. She had a narrow face with a firm, determined chin, a tip-tilted nose, and a liberal scattering of freckles. And disconcertingly frank hazel eyes, which seemed intent on seeing straight through me.

For an instant, she looked so strongly like Tom that I wondered . . .

I glanced over at him. He was stretched out lengthwise, propped up on one elbow, regarding us. There was a faint smile on his lips.

"Jess, this is my new boss, Cecil Hargrave," Abby said. "So . . ."

"Be nice to her, I know." The girl regarded me for another long moment, then stuck out her hand. "Nice to meet you," she said, in a startlingly business-like tone. "I've been wanting to talk to you."

"About what?" I asked, apprehensive as a wayward child suddenly summoned to the principal's office.

Abby smiled. "Cecil, this is my daughter, Jessie Rowe. Twelve going on fifty, if you hadn't guessed."

"Don't be ridiculous," Jessie said scornfully, confirming the impression.

Twelve year olds, I reflected, didn't have the right to be that self-assured. She already seemed more mature that I did at over twice her age . . .

And then it hit me. *Rowe?*

Abby must have seen my surprise, for she added, "Just so. Brian the Bastard is Gilbert Rowe's son, and Gilbert has never forgiven me for walking out on his precious boy."

"Mom!" Jessie exclaimed.

Abby just winked at me. "I'll bet you were wondering why I wasn't at Harry's welcome party. By association, Harry Cameron hasn't quite forgiven me either—not that he was here when any of it happened. Blissful island we live on, isn't it?"

I didn't know what to say to that, so I said nothing, and Jessie broke the silence, her eyes still fixed speculatively on me. I had the sudden sense that she was not one to give up when she had something specific in mind. "Mom says that Ragnarok is back."

"Indeed he is. Would you like to come see him?"

Apparently this was the right answer, for her face lit like a torch. "When?"

"Any time you like."

"Don't tell her that," Abby said. "She'll move in with you and never leave."

"Mom!"

"And I've gotten rather used to having her around," my partner added mischievously, reaching over to ruffle her daughter's bangs. "Though I know moms don't rate as high as seals."

Jessie made a face, then studied me again, idly picking at a scab. "Are you really going to be working with my mom?"

"I'm going to try. I can't say that I've had that much experience with retail, but I suppose one is never to old to learn."

"I like that attitude," said Tom, and I suddenly remembered his words of earlier. Did he really think of his return to fishing as that much of an escape? And what had he been doing before that required escaping? There was a complexity to this man that intrigued me, as if I were missing some piece of the puzzle that everyone else comprehended.

But I couldn't exactly ask, and any formless impulses I might have had in that direction were halted when he said, looking between me and Jessie, "I have an idea. Jess, what do you say we invite Cecil to go seal watching with us this Sunday?"

I felt a sudden surge of excitement at the idea, but waited for Jessie's decision. She glanced at Tom as if trying to fathom his motive, then surveyed me again with that curiously adult gaze.

I fidgeted slightly, trying not to drop my eyes, unused to being measured so many times in one conversation. Nonetheless, I had the sense that, once Jessie made up her mind, her loyalty was guaranteed. And I suddenly felt it would be a fine thing indeed to be in Jessie Rowe's camp.

Maybe she saw that in my eyes—or maybe she just remembered who had offered to let her visit Ragnarok—for she grinned and said, "Yes, let's. Cecil, do you want to come seal watching with us on Tom's boat? He knows all the best spots."

"I'd love to," I said, looking between her and Tom. "And thank you."

She nodded soberly and Tom laughed, tugging on one pigtail. "Lighten up, Jess." He turned to Abby. "You're welcome to come with us, you know."

She shuddered. "Not likely. I'll leave the boats to you three."

"Can we go to the mating grounds?" Jessie asked. "And see the pups?"

"I don't see why not," Tom answered. "As long as you are . . ."

"Quiet; I know," Jessie said. "The pups," she told me, "are adorable. Some of them are white as snow when they are born."

"Like the pictures," I said, thinking of the anti-fur campaign posters, featuring ice-white seal pups with wide, dark eyes. "But isn't that mostly for the artic seals?"

"Mostly, yes," Tom confirmed. "But about twenty-five percent of the harbor seals are born with similar coats. It's a long, white fur called 'lanugo,' from the Latin for downy. But don't expect to see any this time around. That fur is usually shed two weeks from birth and replaced with the adult coat. And our pups are far older than two weeks at this time of year."

"Pups," I said with a grin, thinking of Ragnarok's behavior, which did have a certain doglike enthusiasm to it. "Are all seals described in such canine terms?"

"Only the harbor seals," Jessie answered eagerly. "They are often described as having a very spaniel-like look. Short, upturned noses, concave profile, v-ed nose. I think they are one of the cutest seals, and I'm glad they are the ones we have up here."

"Really?" I asked. "Because my other visitor looked distinctly un-doglike."

Tom's face went still, and he turned to me with a sudden intentness in his dark eyes. "Is this the one I was teasing you about being a selkie?" When I nodded, he added, "I had assumed it was just another harbor seal. But . . . Describe it to me."

I shivered slightly, picturing that long, lugubrious face in my mind. "It was dark grey with white flecks on its coat, and its profile looked almost equine . . . What?" I demanded, suddenly aware of the frown that pinched between Tom's eyes.

"That's odd," Abby answered, half under her breath.

"What's odd?" I insisted, feeling a genuine frisson of fear this time. Had I been right all along? Was there really something to fear from that seal? Even Ragnarok had seemed to treat it with a certain respect . . .

"And you saw this one from your house?" Tom asked. "Right off the shore? Are you sure?"

"Quite," I said, almost testy in my nervousness. "Why? What's wrong?"

Tom shook his head in amazement. "Now *I'm* almost beginning to believe my own stories about the selkies," he said, then laughed. "It sounds like you've seen a grey seal. They are pretty rare in these parts—about four hundred to the estimated fourteen thousand harbor seals. They primarily haul out in remote areas where riptides and rough seas make it hard for fishermen like me to approach, so even we don't see them all that often. They almost never come in as close to shore as you've seen them."

"So should I feel honored, or . . . Why did you say that about the selkies?"

He gave a little half-smile. "Harbor seals are relatively small seals. The males average about five feet in length and the females about four foot eight. But the grey seals are man-sized. Males can get up to eight feet, and females up to seven. Over half the world's population of grey seals live off the British Isles, where the legends of the selkies originated. And perhaps because they are such secretive seals . . . Well, were I remotely superstitious, I'd say my previous words were confirmed."

"Still spinning tales, Moneghan?" Richard said in a disgusted voice from above me. He had changed out of his costume, and was wearing khakis and a polo shirt, still looking every inch the boy next door.

Tom glanced up, smiling sardonically. "Occupational hazard," he said. Then, dryly, "Tell John I liked his costume. Who put him up to it?"

Richard just grinned. "Amazingly enough, he came up with it all on his own. But I'll tell him you said so." He turned to me even as I was wondering who John was and why Tom should have commented on his costume. What had I missed? Again? "Care to take a walk, Cecil?" he added, holding out his hand. "The games are about to start."

"Games?" I said even as Jessie squealed and vaulted to her feet as if on springs.

"You'll see," he said. And, as I extended my hand, he pulled me to my feet.

* * *

"**What is the Fourth** of July without games?"
Richard said as we left the picnic spot under the trees, and
perhaps he was right. Though the cynical New Yorker in me
might have been as cutting about the games as the parade, I
found myself clamoring as avidly as anyone for a chance at
the ring-toss, horseshoes, and cup and ball.

Sometime during the course of our picnic, a series of
tables had been lined along the main street of the town, some
hawking games, and others manned by local craftsmen exhibiting their wares. The throng that meandered between
them was loud and festive, and it was impossible not to be
swayed. There were tables dispensing beverages and beer,
and some local radio station had set up a deejay at one end
of town and was spinning tunes.

Richard bought me game tickets, cheered on my freshman efforts, and didn't mind when I laughed at his. He was
the perfect gentleman, respecting my boundaries, and
didn't even try to touch me after that initial hands-up.
Though I did feel his eyes on me several times as I tried my
luck at the games, and he did manage to secure a date for
Saturday . . . but how could one be annoyed with an attentive
man—especially one so willing to indulge my whims? After
several turns at the cup and ball, which turned out to be surprisingly addictive, I managed to win a ridiculous, hand-
painted clam shell of which I was enormously proud.
Though I did notice Tom at an adjacent table, trailed by
Abby and her daughter, efficiently winning goldfish for
Jessie. She had at least three in the bag she clutched.

Training for surrogate fatherhood? I thought with another
flash of jealousy, then turned and smiled at Richard.

"I need a drink," I said.

We adjourned to the drinks table, and when I glanced

back, I noticed Abby staring after us, her expression unreadable. Beside her, Jessie was jumping up and down excitedly. It seemed Tom had won her yet another fish.

I smiled faintly at her, then turned back to Richard, who had just bought me a beer and himself an iced tea.

"Teetotalling?" I teased, and he grimaced.

"No, just a complete dislike of beer. Very unmanly of me, I know, but there you have it. I just can't abide the stuff. I brought a nice bottle of wine for later."

"Ah," I said, sipping my beer and obscurely pitying him. There was nothing quite like a cold beer on a hot day. Then, peering down at me, he saw my faintly supercilious expression, and we both burst out laughing. "Right," I added. "That's reverse snobbism for you. Where to next?"

"More game tickets?" he said. "I'm nearly out. Or do you need to morally support Abby some more?"

I glanced over at Abby, but her attention was back on Tom and her daughter, cheering him on in the ring-toss. I said, a little more sharply than I intended, "No, I think she's doing fine by herself." And when Richard peered at me speculatively, I flushed and added, "More tickets, please. Do you think they have support groups for cup and ball addicts?"

He grinned and led the way to the ticket counter, saying, "If I recall correctly, Allegra had a fair amount of glassware stashed away. Maybe you could set some of them up on the back deck and toss wads of tinfoil at them when you feel withdrawal setting in."

I pictured myself hurling bits of garbage into Allegra's prized crystal, watched by an audience of two curious seals, and laughed. "Maybe I'll just do that."

There was a different man behind the ticket counter this time. Unlike the last one, he looked vaguely familiar—though I wasn't sure from where.

"John." Richard greeted him with a grin. "Four dollars

more, please. Oh, and by the way, Tom said to tell you that he liked your costume."

I peered at him more closely, only now recognizing him as the one in the fisherman's clothing in the parade. So that had been a *costume*?

John chuckled, handing over the requisite tickets. "Yes, he told me as well. He seemed a little less than thrilled."

"Well, he's got to expect something like that after all this time. And if you ask me, I think he secretly loved it, but just didn't want to admit that."

"My thoughts exactly," John said as he waved us off. "Enjoy."

We played a few more rounds of cup and ball and ringtoss, garnering me a second shell, then wandered by the crafts tables.

There was one jewelry display that sucked me in, and I spent a good ten minutes admiring the intricate whorls of copper and silver set with semi-precious stones. There was one set in particular that drew me: a copper torque set with a graded triplet of unusual green and yellow stones that almost matched my eyes. The earrings, set with smaller stones, were matching double drops.

Richard waited patiently while I waffled, holding up the necklace and earrings, trying to determine the effect in the shard of mirror that graced the table. The ensemble looked ridiculous against my T-shirt and cost more than I had ever spent on a piece of jewelry before, but . . .

I was holding the pieces up for a third time when a voice behind me said, "Do it properly. Do you mind, Sarah?"

The woman behind the table shook her head, and Tom picked up the necklace, gesturing for me to lift my hair. I hesitated for a moment then complied, and he placed the necklace around my throat, his fingers brushing the back of my neck as he fastened it. I let my hair back down as he handed me the earrings. I stared at him for a moment; his eyes challenged me.

I grinned back and slipped them on.

"Turn around," he said. And when I did, feeling somewhat self-conscious, he said, "Oh, yes. Sarah, where's the larger mirror?"

The grey-haired artisan pulled a bigger hand-mirror out from under the counter and handed it to him. He passed it to me.

"Well?" he challenged.

I laughed. "Give the guy a commission. He's just made a sale."

Sarah smiled. "It could have been made for you," she said, and reached for a box. I was just about to pull out my money when a hand reached around me.

"Let me," Tom said, extending the requisite four twenties.

I gaped at him. "You can't possibly! I mean . . ." How did one politely say that, even as a newly employed shopkeeper, I probably earned more money than he did as a fisherman?

"Don't worry," he assured me, seeming to read my thoughts. "I can spare it."

"I . . ."

"Won't take no for an answer," he finished, his eyes once more enigmatic.

"Then thank you," I said. "Really."

"My pleasure," he answered. Then, more softly, he added, "Call it grateful payment for giving Ragnarok something to come home to. And now . . . The lobster cookout begins. If you will excuse me?"

And as silently as he had appeared, he vanished.

Feeling almost numb, I divested myself of the necklace and earrings, handing them to Sarah, who boxed them for me.

Richard was scowling after Tom's retreating back. And, across the crowd, I noticed Abby's gaze fixed on us. We walked over to meet her, and Jessie proudly displayed the five fish Tom had won for her.

"Don't get too attached, sweetie," Abby told her. "Fish like that usually die in under two days."

"Mom!" she protested.

I smiled. "She's right, you know—mostly. But sometimes extraordinary things can happen. Feed them regularly, don't overfeed them, change the water once a week making sure to add about a third of the old water back, give them some toys and some stimulation, talk to them occasionally, and they may surprise you. I once had a fish I won stay alive for five years."

"Really? What eventually killed him?"

"Age," I answered shortly. But the truth was that, after five years of doting care, I killed him in one awful week of neglect. I didn't think Jessie was ready to hear that, however, and I certainly wasn't ready to admit it. True, I had been barely capable of taking care of myself at the time, but seeing his small body floating, bloated and dull, at the top of the bowl had seemed the final straw.

Fortunately, Jessie seemed to know when to drop the subject, but Abby did say to me, as we walked off together, "Thank you. I tend to get too negative with Jess, probably because I don't want her as disappointed by her life as I was by large chunks of mine. But you were right; sometimes she needs to be reminded that things can work out for the best."

Not long after that, we ran into Joanna and her husband, who were walking along with Harry and Martha, and once again I wondered at the odd tensions that at times seemed to govern this island. Joanna and Company reclaimed Richard, who it seemed had been part of their original group, and Abby, Jessie, and I continued on alone. But not before Richard said, "Until Saturday, then, Cecil, if not before."

"Are you dating him?" Jessie asked bluntly, as soon as he was out of earshot.

"Jess!" Abby exclaimed, and this time the scandalized tone was hers. "That's none of your business."

"Where's Tom?" I asked, if only to get the attention off me for a moment.

"Off supervising the lobster cook," Abby answered. And now that I noticed it, the festival booths were shutting down for the evening and a tantalizing smell was starting to filter through the streets. My stomach rumbled appreciatively.

"You did bring food?" she added. "Shall we go get it?"

She had warned me earlier that people often augmented the lobster with their own contributions and I had come prepared, making my favorite potato salad and a tin of chocolate chip cookies for the occasion. With Jessie's help, we unloaded the coolers from our respective cars and progressed back to our picnic spot. Tom's blanket was no longer under the trees. Instead, he had moved it off to a more open location, overlooking the bay.

Of the man himself, there was no sign.

Abby laid out a second blanket and began unloading her contributions. She had brought a green salad and some rolls. I added my potato salad and the plate of cookies. Jessie's eyes lit at the sight, but Abby said, "Not until after dinner." Then winked at me and snuck one for herself when her daughter's back was turned. She rolled her eyes appreciatively and gave me a cheerful thumbs-up for my efforts.

She also had a large roll of paper towels, and a stack of three elongate oval plates. She handed me one of the latter, along with a nutcracker and a tiny, two-pronged fork, saying, "I didn't think you'd know to bring these, so I figured I would supply the lack. Tom will just have to fend for himself, the opportunistic bastard."

I peered down at the plate in dismay. "I can't say I've ever eaten lobster directly out of the shell, before."

"Not to worry," Abby said cheerfully. "If anyone can teach you properly, it's Tom."

And she was right. When he appeared about half an hour later, bearing four massive red crustaceans on a plate, drawing the straying Jessie back from her friends as inevitably as a flame draws a moth, he simply laughed as he was informed of my virgin state. "Don't worry," he said. "I'll take care of you."

So he did, after sending Jessie off for styrofoam cups of drawn butter. He showed me how to crack the shell and how to extract the meat from both claws and tail. Then, he demonstrated how to suck the bounty out of the little claws like straws, and how to extract every piece of meat possible out of the body.

When I exclaimed in disgust over the green stuff that leaked out when I tore off the tail, he grinned and said, "That's the liver, though in lobsters we call it the tomally. And everyone says you shouldn't eat it because that's where all the toxins from industrial pollution and such build up. But it's so wonderful," he added, sopping up the revolting stuff with one of Abby's rolls, "that I think the universe has to turn a blind eye every once in a while."

Tentatively, I sampled my own—and had to concur with his opinion. He even showed me how high to eat up into the head.

"Some people," he instructed, "say that there are poison glands in the head. That's a fallacy. What's really up there is the digestive system. First, the stomach. Then, higher up, the urinary glands, which empty out right at the base of the antennae, over the mouth."

I made a face, and he laughed. "Well, nature does the best it can with what it has, but if it has designed a perfect organism, I have yet to see it. I mean, look at us. Our bodies aren't even remotely designed to walk upright, and yet here were are. Lower back problems and all. Show her the stomach, Jess."

Obligingly, Jessie dissected the stomach out of her all-but-devoured lobster, and showed me the hard shell-like teeth inside that served to grin up the food. "Lobsters are scavengers," Tom said. "Sort of like the jackals of the sea bed. And whoever first fished one of these big, blue bugs off the sea floor, said 'let's try eating that,' and didn't die of shock when it turned bright red with cooking . . . Well, I owe him or her a huge debt of gratitude. Especially since I doubt I would have been so bold without a vast tradition behind me. There's nothing better than a well-cooked lobster."

I had to agree with him. I had never tasted anything so succulent and sweet, and amazed myself by eating every last bit—including the green stuff—until all that was left was a pile of shell. "Are all Maine lobsters this wonderful?"

"Yes, if they are done right. Unfortunately, most restaurants overcook them until they get a sort of dry, rubbery texture. Tragic, really. But even so, the demand for them is still high enough to keep people like me in a job for years to come."

Stuffed, we lounged about on the blankets for a while until we were ready to tackle the salads. And to my delight, my potato salad drew raves both from Abby and Tom, and later from Joanna and Richard, when they stopped by to say hello.

"I'll have you all over for dinner," I promised recklessly, starting to run through potential menus in my head.

Then there were my cookies—equally well praised—and an enormous bowl of freshly picked native strawberries supplied by Tom, which were as succulent and sweet as the lobsters had been.

Dusk had begun to fall as we finished our meal, the sun

sinking out over the harbor in all its persimmon glory. And
as the light faded, the chill that I had begun to associate so
uniquely with Maine crept into the air. I shivered, regretting
that I had not thought to bring a jacket.

Tom noticed, excusing himself for a moment. When he
returned, it was with an extra blanket that he handed to me,
and two bottles of champagne that even to my untrained
eyes looked expensive. When I raised an eyebrow at him, he
just grinned and added, "For the fireworks."

"We get fireworks, too?" I had never been so full and con-
tented in my life; I couldn't imagine the evening could hold
any more.

Abby just laughed. "Don't get your hopes up."

"Meaning?"

Tom smiled. "You'll see."

So I waited, wrapping the spare blanket around my shoulders and lapping it over my bare legs, noticing as I did so
how it smelled every so faintly of fish and pine, like Tom.
And when the last traces of light had leaked from the sky
and blackness reigned, the fireworks began.

Like the parade, it was one of the most pitiful displays I
had ever seen—cut-rate fireworks, about half of which didn't
even go off properly. But as Tom popped the champagne and
dispensed it—even Jessie got a small cup, though she just
wrinkled her nose at it in profound disgust—such a festive
air reigned that I found myself laughing myself almost sick
as the crowd 'oohed' and 'aahed' over the loud bangs and
white flashes of light that signaled misfired rockets.

It was about 1 A.M. before I got home—rumpled and still
wrapped in Tom's borrowed blanket. And as content as I had
ever been in my life. Somehow it seemed that, with the festivities, I had come through some sort of rite of passage that
had left me profoundly changed. Though exactly where the

change lay, I couldn't have said. Except that part of me instinctively understood I had been accepted, that I had become one of them.

I let myself into the house, almost tripping over the hall table en route to the bedroom; I could have sworn it had been in a different place when I had left. But perhaps I was just too tired to recall.

I smiled to myself as I showered, then climbed into bed, drifting into one of the most profound slumbers I had had since arriving on Seal Island.

18

UNFORTUNATELY, THE SHEER EUPHORIA of the night before was harder to recapture with the alarm shrilling in my ear on another grey morning, summoning me back to work. Abby grinned at me as I trailed in, bleary-eyed and ten minutes late.

"I take it you enjoyed the Fourth?" she said.

I smiled ruefully. "Probably too much. You?"

She nodded. "I'm glad Tom joined us. And that Jessie accepted you. Thank you for agreeing to let her visit Ragnarok. She's already been bugging me to bring her over."

"Anytime; I mean it," I said. "You're lucky; she's a great kid."

"That she is—amazingly enough. I don't know how she turned out so well when she's got two such flaky parents."

"Well, sometimes rebellion takes an odd path," I temporized.

Abby laughed. "I like that. And it's true; she couldn't be

more different from me. For which I remain eternally grateful. But I think Tom's influence has been good for her."

"Yes, Tom," I said, with a sudden sinking feeling. "Are you and he . . ."

"Involved?" she asked, with a rueful grimace. "Why?"

It was a damned good question. I didn't know why I had asked, or even what answer I wanted to hear. He was just a fisherman, for God's sake, but . . . My stomach clenched in anticipation.

"I don't know," I managed. "When I saw you two together last night, you and he just seemed so close. I guess I was just wondering if . . ."

She heaved a sigh. "Remember what I said about liking the inappropriate ones? It does seem to be my personal curse in life. In answer to your question . . ." My stomach fluttered again. "No, we are not involved. We were, once. But I knew it was never going to last because I never seemed quite . . . good enough for him, I suppose. Not that he ever implied that, but he's just so frighteningly intelligent, and multi-talented, and . . ." She grinned, and I suddenly found it a lot easier to breathe. "I'm over it now—mostly. Even though he'd make a phenomenal father for Jessie, I know it's not meant to be. And probably just as well. I think it'll take an extraordinary woman to get that one out of his shell."

I wanted to ask what she meant, but we were interrupted by the arrival of our first customer of the day. And at our next break, the opportunity had vanished as Abby asked: "And how did you enjoy the Fourth?"

"It was amazing!" I said with a grin. "You guys sure know how to party here on Seal Island. I only wish Ronan could have seen it."

"Ronan?" she said. "The gas station guy? Is he still around?"

I felt an odd moment of dislocation that she didn't know.

"Around?" I said. "He's over almost every night for drinks and appetizers."

She stared at me. "*Every* night?"

"Well, nearly. When I'm not otherwise engaged."

"And you're not dating?"

I shook my head, frowning faintly. "It's just . . . No. He's never . . . I mean, we're just friends." It had never struck me as odd until now, when I sat here with Abby's curious and slightly accusing gaze fixed on me, but now I wondered. I had never been the type of person to welcome someone in as nonchalantly as I seemed to have accepted Ronan into my life—in whatever capacity. But somehow having him in my house and my life seemed as natural and inevitable as breathing. Not like the conflicted confusion Richard engendered in me, or the deep attraction I felt for Tom. And why, after a slew of hints and half-remembered phrases—not to mention the undeniable attraction that occasionally sparked between us—had he never made a move? Was he even less socially apt than I was?

Remembering some of his behavior, I began to suspect that was indeed the case. But still . . . "I think he's just lonely," I concluded.

She looked like she didn't quite believe me. I didn't blame her. I didn't quite believe me, either.

"I'm not leading anyone on," I said defensively. "Really, I'm not."

"And what about you and Richard? Don't you have another date on Saturday?"

I still wasn't convinced that Abby was quite as sanguine about Richard as she pretended. "Abby, are you sure . . ."

"What?" she interrupted. "That I'm okay with you and Richard?" I'd never heard anyone snort with derision before, but that was unmistakably what she did. "I told you, I'm just trying to live vicariously. Hell, if this Ronan guy is not making the moves on you, maybe I'll have to date him myself! You'll have to introduce us."

"I can do that," I said. "In fact, was hoping to switch my date with Richard to Friday, instead. I was thinking about what I said to Joanna last night, about throwing a dinner party. I love to cook, and I'd love to have you all over to thank you for the hospitality you've shown me since my arrival. Would you be free Saturday night, or is that too short notice?"

She laughed. "With my bustling social life? Of course I am free—and would be delighted to come! That is, if Richard agrees."

"Yes, I suppose I should ask him."

Abby smiled and plucked the phone off the wall. "No time like the present," she said, handing me the earpiece.

I swallowed. "I don't . . . That is, I have his number written down at home, but . . ."

"He's at work, anyway. Here, let me. Aren't you lucky that I know the number?"

Richard was there and said yes—especially when I assured him that he was invited to the dinner party as well. I had been a little nervous, airing our private dealings so publicly, but Richard, as usual, made it easy.

"How could I object," he said, "when I get to see you twice in one weekend instead of once?"

I blushed hotly, still unused to being the object of anyone's affections, and when I hung up the phone after a bit more inconsequential chatter, Abby grinned and said, "What was that? Was he being unfailingly gallant, again?" And when I flushed anew, she added, "That boy needs a bit more of the rebel in his veins. But never mind. Are we on, then?"

"We are on," I confirmed, feeling a surge of excitement at the prospect. I would invite Joanna and Tom, Harry and Martha. Tom Moneghan, and Richard. Abby and myself. Ronan. Maybe I could get Harry and Abby to forget their differences; find Ronan some new friends. I had euphoric visions of creating peace among all the factions before I left in September.

Allegra's legacy.

The thought kept me bemused for the rest of the afternoon, and when I got home that evening, I continued my calls after I had fed Ragnarok, securing confirmations from Harry and Martha, Joanna and Tom. I was just hanging up with the latter when I heard a rumble in the distance and then the sound of tires crunching into my driveway. I padded onto the deck in time to see Tom Moneghan's truck bounce to a halt mere feet from the side stairs.

"More fish," Tom said, as he exited the vehicle.

"Indeed." I came down the stairs to meet him, absurdly aware of my bare feet, T-shirt, faded shorts, and ponytailed hair. I had changed into my most comfortable clothes when I got home, not expecting to see anyone, and now couldn't help wondering what sort of picture I must be creating, padding across the cool grass to meet him.

This was twice now he had surprised me.

"You look about thirteen," he said as I approached. Which, annoyingly, answered my question. "Fresh-scrubbed and carefree, with all your best years ahead of you."

I smiled, marveling at how he had managed to turn a potential insult into an almost-compliment. Reaching into the bed of the truck, he drew out two more buckets. He was back to fisherman's garb: filthy jeans, a stained sweatshirt, and knee-high rubber waders. So why did the look work on him whereas I only felt vaguely ridiculous?

"Jewelry, and bi-weekly deliveries of fish," I said, half-embarrassed, as I took one of the pails from him. "How am I ever going to repay you?"

He looked at me soberly for a moment. Then, just as my heart began to pound uncomfortably, he raised an eyebrow and answered, "Invite me to this dinner party that rumor has it you are throwing."

"Damn it! Can I even have an hour to myself without the entire island knowing my business? I was going to ask you, of course, but then the rumor mill took over . . ."

He smiled. "I think you're learning the disadvantages of small town life."

"Quite! So can you come, then? Saturday, seven o'clock?"

He bowed formally—or as formally as a man carrying a brimming bucket of fish can bow—and smiled. "I'd be honored."

"Good."

Only Ronan to go, and I would have a full house. Of course, nine was an uneven number, but I would just have to make do.

As we walked to the utility shed, Tom said, "So, how's work been treating you?"

Innocent query, or inquiry about Abby? I decided to test the waters, suddenly wanting confirmation from both sides as to the nature of their relationship.

"Fine," I said. "Abby's a mensch. I'm really having fun working with her."

"Yes, she does have her charms," Tom said, casually enough. "Even if she does tend to infect Jessie a little too much with her negative attitude. Kids have little enough time to believe in the fairness of the world before they learn the truth."

"Which is?"

He laughed shortly. "That life's a bitch and then you die."

I paused slightly in my march to the garage, half turning to regard him. But I could read nothing from his face, which was shuttered tightly.

"That sounds a bit clichéd," I ventured.

"But true."

I didn't know what to say to that, and when I said nothing, he continued.

"Much as I love Abby, she should learn to keep her problems away from Jessie. I mean, even on my worst days, I never . . ."

He paused for a long moment, pulling open the shed door, then went on, his voice unfathomable in the gloom. "Jessie's a great kid, but I think because she and Abby were on their own for so long, Abby's begun treating her more like a peer than a daughter, and I'm not convinced it's entirely healthy. For one thing, being her mom's support net has left that kid way too wise for her years. She has a way of seeing though you that is almost . . ."

He shrugged and I nodded, pulling open the fridge door. "I know exactly what you mean. I do like the girl, but that ability of hers is almost uncanny."

He paused in the process of unloading the fish into the cooler and turned to me, raising an eyebrow. "And why do I suspect you have as many secrets you want to hide as I do?"

Because like wounds attract? I thought, recalling the words Allegra had once said to Abby, aware again of that darkness in him that seemed to mirror something lurking deep inside myself. I don't think I could have spoken at that minute if my life depended on it, but not even I could have been unaware of the tension swelling between us. Thoughts of Abby fled, and I was acutely aware of how close he was to me and how far we both were from the rest of the world. I was dating Richard; Ronan was over practically every night. I had no right to be attracted to other men. Especially unsuitable ones.

Cold reality returned and I drew back slightly. Sensing my withdrawal, Tom finished dumping his bucket into the cooler and added, his voice rigidly neutral, "By the way, do you mind if I bring Jessie by tomorrow? I know she would love to see Ragnarok again."

I sighed slightly, both regretful and relieved that we were

back on familiar footing. "No, I don't mind at all. Please, bring her."

RONAN, WITH HIS USUAL uncanny timing, showed up again as soon as everyone disappeared, and as we lingered over wine and crab dip, I extended him an official invitation to my dinner party. Then I stared at him as he hesitated, again trying to make sense of the strangeness of this relationship. Or maybe its lack of strangeness, given the circumstances.

With his attention momentarily turned inward, pondering my offer, he was not that handsome, or even that magnetic. He just looked faintly worried, his brows pulling together over that prow of a nose. Then his gaze returned to me, his expression lightening, and that frisson was back between us again.

How could I not keep him around? He needed me.

"I've told you I'm not good with crowds . . ." he began.

"It's not crowds," I countered. "Just eight other people. My friends. People you should know. Especially if . . ."

"If what?"

I suddenly couldn't bear to make him face my likely departure in September. There was time enough for that, when he was a more integrated part of this community. So, "Nothing," I said. "Please say you'll come. It'd mean a lot to me."

"Well, in that case," he said, and I smiled.

My party was complete.

19

TOM DID INDEED SHOW up the next day with Jessie, who was rapturous with delight. And while her enthusiasm was infectious, it did seem to dominate the day. In contrast to the intensity that had briefly sparked between us in the shed, Tom had retreated to a studied coolness and barely spoke to me—barely looked at me, for that matter—and even Ragnarok seemed more reticent than usual. He refused to come up to the shoreline, and declined to take fish directly from our fingers. Maybe he was upset that new people kept getting added to his feeding routine, or maybe he was just being perverse. Jessie wanted him to come to shore so badly that there must have been a certain pleasure in playing coy.

In fact, after they had left, I said to him, "You're a wicked one, aren't you?"

He was still lurking about offshore as I said this and stretched his mouth in a grin. He swam in closer, as if anticipating his reward

Of course I gave it to him. Who was I to fault loyalty?

So, inevitably, I was back again to Richard. Whom I had to admit was unfailingly charming and gallant. And I did enjoy my time with him. There was an undeniable comfort between us as we drove again to Ellsworth, cinema-bound. I had promised to let him pick the movie this time, and while silence did reign between us for large chunks of the drive, it was far from awkward. On the contrary, I liked the fact that we did not need to fill the spaces with chatter. My mind was more than half on my dinner party anyway, and as the trees and houses flashed by, I stared idly out the window, mentally juggling menus and seating plans, trying to distract myself from a certain dread growing in my belly.

"A dollar for them?" Richard said at one point, after I heaved a rather heartfelt sigh. We were just dipping down the hill into the town of Surrey, and the late afternoon sun was striking golden lights off the small cluster of houses and stores.

I smiled because he had recalled my demand for inflation, then added, "I think I may have done something very foolish."

He cocked his head and regarded me soberly for a moment. Then, "How foolish?" he asked, returning his attention to the road.

"I invited both Abby and Harry tomorrow night without telling the other, hoping they might make peace. But now I'm wondering if I haven't made a very stupid mistake."

Richard looked thoughtful rather than reassuring, as I had hoped. "Well," he said eventually, "I wish you luck. It's a nice thought, though you are hardly the first to try it. Many others have failed in that particular act."

Something about the quality of his grimace made me ask, "You among them?"

"Me most definitely among them. I was the brash new arrival to the island, determined to unite the community through my words and deeds. I mean, I might not have been the editor of some big-city paper, but I was determined to be a man of the people—of all the people. Locals, transplants, and summer folk alike." He smiled ruefully again. "I suppose you could say I learned my lesson the hard way. There are some battles that are just not meant to be won—no matter how hard you may fight them. Abby and Harry are both inordinately stubborn people." But I had the feeling he had not been talking entirely about them. "Would you like me to arrive a little early tomorrow, to provide moral support and maybe a bit of an emotional buffer?"

He really is a very nice man, I thought. A rush of affection washed over me, and impulsively I reached out and squeezed his hand, which rested on the gearbox between us.

His face lit up and he squeezed back, his fingers strong and comforting. I felt a flush suffuse my cheeks. It was flattering to be wanted, and perhaps I *was* only avoiding Richard out of fear. I hadn't committed to anything in far too long, and while the part of me still terrified of becoming dependent gibbered somewhere inside, I was beginning to realize it might not be the best voice to listen to. My attraction to Tom was probably based on nothing more than the fact that he was unattainable. After all, hadn't Abby mentioned something about his fear of involvement? And for all his friendliness, both on the Fourth and with Ragnarok, I could still sense his walls.

No, liking Tom was safe; it would take a major cataclysm for him to let me close. And Ronan . . . Well, Ronan was Ronan. I couldn't even begin to explain that one.

But Richard was dangerous because, with him, I had only to reach out my hand—like now. Still, maybe it was time to start living again. And maybe, this time, fate would let me have a little happiness for a change.

When we got to the theaters, Richard chose a drama that was absorbing enough to keep my mind off my party, and I let him hold my hand throughout the film, thinking again how lucky I was to have found such a decent guy. Salt of the earth; that was Richard. Nor did he let me down the following day. In fact, he was so punctual I could have killed him—if I wasn't so grateful for his support.

I had spent the morning in the kitchen, burning off my energy in a frenzy of creative cooking. I had decided on a menu of Mediterranean chicken breasts with olives, capers and prunes, served with a saffron rice pilaf and a side of sautéed local zucchini. For starters, asparagus soup. A simple mesclun/tomato salad for after the meal, with the special citrus vinaigrette I had invented years ago and had been perfecting ever since. And for dessert, a strawberry and custard tart. The wine was Australian—Sauvignon Blanc for those who wanted white (the New Zealands were better, but if such were available, I hadn't yet located the store that sold them), and a Cabernet-Shiraz for the red-lovers. And I had also located a nice muscat to accompany dessert.

I think part of me hoped that the food would avert disaster.

So I chopped and stirred and baked and boiled all morning, breaking only once for a disheveled run to the local market for fresh bread, losing myself in the familiar routines. Cooking had always been my therapy, and part of me wondered if I shouldn't have tried harder to make it a career. But I was too old to start now, and moreover had no idea of how to begin. Although it would have been a fine life had circumstances been different.

By five-thirty my house was filled with delectable smells, the table was set with Allegra's best crystal and china, and I had completed all but the finishing touches. With the soup on a low simmer and the rest in covered bowls and pans and pots in the fridge or on the counter, I went out onto the back deck, picking up the bowl of mackerel I had left out to warm earlier.

Ragnarok was waiting for me, and by the expression on his face, had been for some time. Since yesterday, in fact; he informed me of my dereliction with wordless contempt.

I cajoled myself back into his good graces with capers and fish, and eventually he relented, leaping and diving after my throws. I tossed him his regular allotment, then glanced down at the four extra fish in the bottom of the bucket: my predetermined penance for yesterday's abandonment. Yet while the occasional treat couldn't hurt, I had decided that today there was to be a stipulation.

"If you want any more," I informed him firmly, "you're going to have to come up here and get it." And I held out a fish, extending my arm long over the water.

Ragnarok swam closer and regarded me, then made a leap and a snap, soaking me thoroughly.

"You devil!" I exclaimed as he gulped down the fish, his dark eyes smirking. It had been a very deliberate move, paying me back for imposing my conditions.

Still, a little water wasn't going to stop me. I held up the next fish. Then, before he could grab it, I deliberately backed up two paces.

Ragnorak surveyed me again, as if weighing my motives. I don't know how sincere I could have looked with my oldest T-shirt plastered to my body and my hair dripping down my back. But I must have convinced him, for he swam closer and took the treat more delicately.

Yet even as he did so, I felt a presence watching me. I glanced briefly across the water, numbly unsurprised to see the large grey seal regarding us. Was he hoping for some of the fish himself or did he have some other motives I couldn't begin to fathom?

Resolutely ignoring him, I turned my attention back to Ragnarok, dangling the next fish right over the margin of the water. The tide was high enough that the seaweed was underwater; only bare rock greeted him. Slowly, tentatively, he placed first one flipper on the rock and then the other, bracing himself for the grab.

I let him take it, then held up the last and final treat, backing away another two paces. This time, if he wanted the fish, he was going to have to come all the way onto the rock to get it.

Though Ragnarok didn't remove his two front flippers from the ledge, he seemed less certain about advancing. We regarded each other for a long, silent moment. Then, very slowly, very tentatively, he humped his body an inch closer, then another . . .

So intent was I on my silent battle of wills with Ragnarok, I never even heard the car approach. But at the slam of the door and a voice calling, loudly, "Cecil?" I jumped, startled. Ragnarok, nearly all the way onto shore, reversed course with alacrity, the fish forgotten.

"Damn it!" I exclaimed, stamping one foot impotently against the rock.

"Am I too early?" Richard asked in concern, coming around the side of the house. He was impeccably dressed in a sweater and dress trousers, his hair shining in the sun. He was carrying a bouquet of flowers and a bottle of wine.

I glared at him for a moment, soaked with seawater and stinking of fish. Then I laughed. "What do you think?"

He glanced down ruefully at the bottle of wine in his hand. "I think I should have brought you something stronger. Do you want me to go away and come back later?"

"No," I said. "No need." I went to brush back the dripping

tendril of hair from my face before I realized I still had a
fish in my hand. I grimaced, employing the crook of my elbow instead. "A fine mess I must look. But Ragnarok was
feeling playful today—and punishing me for yesterday's
inattention."

"Which I suppose is partly my fault." Richard smiled.
"But I think you look marvelous." His eyes wandered over
my T-shirt, which I hadn't realize was plastered to my chest
quite so revealingly. I blushed. "Is that him there?" Richard
added. "Do you suppose I should apologize?"

Though startled, Ragnarok had realized that there was
still another fish in the offing; he hadn't wandered far. At
least, not out of throwing range. He was bottled in the water,
regarding us. The grey seal had vanished.

"Yes," I said. "That's the wretch. Richard has apologized
for depriving you of my company last night," I called to
him. "Now, are you going to apologize for making me late
to my own party? I hadn't been intending to take another
shower . . ."

Ragnarok barked imperiously. Good enough. Laughing, I
tossed him the fish.

Aware that he was on display, he leapt high, executing a
half spin, and caught the fish on its downward arc.

"Show-off," I told him as Richard put down his gifts and
cheered.

He flipped his rear end at us and vanished.

Richard turned to me. "What can I do?"

I cocked my head at the flowers. "Put those in water," I
said. "Then open up the bar, put ice in the bucket, and fix me
a drink!"

He nodded and scooped up his gifts.

"Oh, and Richard?" I said, halting him halfway to the
deck. He turned back with a curious expression.

"Thanks," I said softly, and his smile returned.

"Your wish is my command," he replied, his eyes both warm and suggestive, and I flushed. "Have a good shower."

I fled for the bathroom, trying not to picture him two rooms over, fully dressed and no doubt imagining me naked. I took a shower that might have broken records for its speedy efficiency, all the while telling myself that time was my main concern. That it was rude to leave guests unattended, even if they had arrived unfashionably early. At my request.

I washed the saltwater off my body and the fish-stink off my hands. Then I brushed and hastily dried my hair, applied a light touch of makeup, and donned another of Allegra's outfits—this time a black pants-suit in a heavy silk, the jacket embroidered with abstract and vaguely oriental designs in gold and copper thread. Perhaps a little formal for the occasion, but when I had fastened the copper torque and earrings Tom had bought for me around my throat and in my ears, I no longer cared.

I looked fantastic.

When I emerged from my room, Richard did an abrupt double-take, leapt up from the left-hand sofa—vaguely, I wondered if he realized he was sitting directly over Allegra's bloodstain—and nearly spilled his drink.

"Cecil . . . You look fantastic!"

I tried not to look smug. "Thank you."

He stared at me for a moment more. Then, recovering himself, he said smoothly, "Here's your drink. There are your flowers. And where's my kiss?"

He had arranged the flowers into my new red and black vase. And, unlike most men, he had not stuck them in all higgeldy-piggeldy, but rather had arranged them with an expert hand. The drink he handed me was a tumbler of Laphroaig, neat.

I kissed him lightly. And then, caught up in the moment, more deeply. But when he groaned, pulling me more tightly against him, I recollected myself and placed a hand on his chest, pushing him gently away. "Not now," I said. "The guests are coming, and I'm still not fully set up." Then I looked around. He had opened the bar and put ice in the silver bucket. He had even remembered the tongs. "Everything looks marvelous. Thanks, Richard."

"Everything smells marvelous," he said, trailing me hopefully to the kitchen. "You've outdone yourself, Cecil."

I laughed. "Don't pass judgment until you've tried the food." I gave the soup a stir, and popped the covered chicken, rice and zucchini into a slow oven to heat. Then, just as he was trying—very unsuccessfully—to sneak up on me again, I swung open the refrigerator and handed him several blocks of cheese. I followed this with a cheese board.

"Unwrap those for me, would you?"

He rushed through the unwrapping as if it were a race. Meanwhile, I arranged some crackers and bread slices on a plate, decanted a container of fresh, mixed olives into a bowl, and emptied a bag of chili crackers into another bowl. Never one to go at things half-measures—and showing a surprisingly familiarity with Allegra's kitchen—Richard had added a knife and cheese-slicer to the board.

Sometimes I forgot that I had not inherited this house blindly, but that I had instead invaded a history I still knew frighteningly little about.

At least Richard had no more opportunities to corner me, for the doorbell rang just as I was laying out the last bowl. I went to open it.

It was Harry and Martha, bang on time. "Welcome . . ." I began, then halted. Martha was staring at me, and Harry's face had gone ashen. He was clutching his cane with white-knuckled hands.

I had forgotten until this minute that Harry disliked entering my house. As his injury attested.

"Are you all right?" I asked nervously, not liking the tint of his skin.

Martha recovered first, saying, "You'll have to pardon us, Cecil, but for a moment, standing there . . . You looked just like Allegra, back from the grave."

"That was one of her favorite outfits," Harry added softly.

I blushed a violent red. "I'm sorry. I shouldn't have worn this. I . . ."

"No, it's we who are sorry," Harry said, touching my arm. "Allegra would have wanted you to enjoy her things. You just gave us a bit of a start is all. Everything smells wonderful, my dear. Aren't you going to invite us in?"

I stepped aside hastily. "Of course. Come in, come in."

So that had explained Richard's reaction, I thought, looking back. Not awe at my appearance, but rather startlement at my resemblance to Allegra. A younger Allegra, I hoped.

"Hello, Richard," Martha called. "We saw your car in the drive. How long have you been here?"

"Since entirely too early," Richard responded, emerging from the living room to greet them. "Can I get you a drink?"

"Making yourself at home already?" Martha teased, and he colored. "A gin and tonic for me, if you can manage it."

"I think I can do that," Richard said, recovering his aplomb. "Harry?"

"If that's Allegra's famous Laphroaig, then a glass of the same for me." He still seemed nervous at being in the house, casting the furtive glances about him as if searching for signs of violence. But the liquor seemed to calm him, and by the time the doorbell went again, I was almost beginning to believe this would work.

It was Joanna and Tom this time, and Joanna's face reflected unexpected approval when she smelled the odors coming out of my kitchen. "I think we might survive this, after all," she joked. "Much as I love Martha, her cooking leaves much to be desired. And if everything tastes as good as it smells, Cecil, you might be giving Jean-Pierre a run for his money! You look wonderful, by the way. Allegra always said you couldn't go wrong in that outfit, and apparently she was right. Are the drinks through there?"

I nodded, regretting again my impulse to wear this particular garment. But I also couldn't help wondering if this couldn't be used as a litmus test for how well people knew Allegra. By that criterion, Joanna and Tom had been no more than casual acquaintances.

Richard was doing bartender duties admirably so I left him to it, ushering Joanna and Tom inside just as the doorbell sounded again.

I opened the door. Tom Moneghan looked me over—a long, slow scrutiny. There was a surprising depth of sadness in his eyes. I found myself flushing, awaiting his opinion.

"Allegra would be proud," he said at last, softly, and handed me a bottle of wine easily twice as expensive as what I was serving. "Hello, Cecil."

Like Richard, he also wore a sweater and dress slacks, but when he walked into the living room he instantly became its focus. Maybe it was just his height, more impressive when measured against such standards as chairs and doors. Or maybe it was the vague impression of wildness he carried— admittedly not as strong as Ronan's, but still as if he bore a part of the ocean within him.

"Tom!" Joanna exclaimed. "Well, blow me over. What does this make it, twice in one month?"

His eyes held a mocking humor, whether at her or at himself I couldn't tell. "I know. Amazing, isn't it? It fairly staggers me."

I couldn't help myself; I laughed. He dropped me a wink.

"What brings you?" Martha asked.

His eyes sparkled. "I wouldn't miss it for the world."

"Why?"

He answered obliquely. "We're still short at least one guest, aren't we, Cecil?"

I felt the same creeping sense of dread that had plagued me all day.

Harry looked sour. "Is Abby coming, then?"

"So she claimed, when I spoke to her this afternoon. Late as usual, of course, but . . . Definitely coming." Tom grinned at me.

Charming smile and hint of a dimple aside, I could cheerfully have slaughtered him. I scowled, but he just looked supremely innocent. "I'm going to get a drink. Can I get you a refill, Cecil?" He held out his hand for my glass.

Somehow I refrained from chucking it at him. "I'll go with you," I said tightly.

He seemed to sense my anger, saying quietly as he fiddled among the bottles, "I admire what you're trying to do, I really do. But the sooner it gets out in the open, the better." He smiled at me, reaching for the Laphroaig, refreshing my glass before pouring one for himself. "And if you survive this, I promise I will cook you a special dinner myself tomorrow, after our the seal watching trip."

I smiled sourly at him, taking a bracing gulp of my drink. "You're not exactly reassuring me, but you're on. I'm beginning to suspect I'll need some pampering when this is all over." Besides, I was dying to know more about him, to see how he lived. Maybe his house would give me some more clues about this enigma of a man who made his living netting crustaceans off the sea floor, yet who gifted me with expensive wines and jewelry as if were nothing.

Reflexively, I touched a hand to my necklace.

"Have I mentioned recently how much I like your jewelry?" he added.

"Not since Tuesday." Softening, I pitched my voice lower. "But thanks again, Tom. For everything."

"My pleasure," he said, his voice filled with the same low intimacy. "And if I didn't mention it before, you've done a great job restoring the place to its proper proportions." He tilted his head knowingly toward the left-hand sofa. "I did the best I could under the circumstances, but it certainly looks better this way. As Allegra had intended."

"Wait. *You* moved the furniture?"

"Guilty as charged. I . . ."

"How long does it take to fix a drink?" Richard said cheerfully, coming to join us.

"Oh, hello, Richard," Tom said carelessly.

"Tom," Richard said tightly, and I sensed an imminent bristling of male ego.

I groaned softly. Did *anyone* here like each other? I sighed, hoping Richard and Tom didn't kill each other beside my bar. This house had seen too much death already.

I felt a sudden presence at my back door, and looked up. Ronan, clad in his usual flannel shirt and jeans, was staring in at my impeccably-clad guests with an expression resembling panic on his face. Before I could so much as rise to detain him, he spun about abruptly and vanished down the shore.

I was about to go after him when the doorbell rang again.

I pulled open the door. "Hello, Abby," I said. "Save me. I think I've made a dreadful mistake."

20

AS EXPECTED, THE EVENING was a disaster, and I woke
at an ungodly hour the next morning to the dull throb of a
hangover and the unwelcome knowledge that I had to make
myself presentable before Tom Moneghan arrived. Though
in reality, the last thing I wanted was to be out on a boat—
seals or Tom notwithstanding. My world felt unsteady
enough as it was.

Both Abby and I had survived the evening thanks to liberal
infusions of alcohol. Which in retrospect may not have been
the wisest of ideas, but had certainly seemed so at the time. In
fact, I think we reached that decision simultaneously, from almost the moment she arrived at my front door, staring at me in
response to my opening words. Or my appearance. Or both.

"Don't," I had said, shutting the door behind us and tow-
ing her into a quiet corner. "I know I look like Allegra; I've
gotten that response from everyone else already. That's not
what's important. What's important is that I think I've just

served you up on the altar of good intentions, and I wanted
to apologize before all hell breaks loose."

She regarded me in silence for a moment, then grimaced.
"Don't tell me; Harry's here." She let a little sigh trickle from
her lips. "You're sweet, Cecil—and not the first one who has
tried. The difference, I'm afraid, is irreconcilable. Just point
me to the bar so I can fortify myself, and I'll try not to make
any obnoxious comments. At least, not unless provoked."

I smiled ruefully. "Don't worry. I'm afraid Tom's already
made that role his own."

"Joy." She heaved a martyred sigh. "Is the mysterious Ronan here, at least? I was going to say something to him the
other day at the garage, but he hasn't been working the
pumps for the past few days."

I grimaced. "He took one look at the company and vanished up the shore just moments before you arrived. And
now it is too late to go after him."

"Can you call him?"

"No phone," I said.

She cocked an eyebrow. "Probably just as well for him,
then; it may not be the most convivial evening. Well, there
will be plenty of time to meet him later. For now, let's go
face the music. And Cecil? Don't worry; I don't blame you
for any of what is about to happen."

Feeling glummer than ever, I trailed her to the bar.

"Hello, Jo; Tom," she said in passing. "Harry. Martha." She
nodded at them curtly. Then she peered at Richard and Tom
Moneghan, both of whom were still holding court at the bar—
and neither of whom seemed inclined to yield to the other.

Richard's motives I thought I understood; he was clearly
trying to establish his bonafides as my co-host. Tom's, as
usual, were harder to fathom.

"Well," Abby said, surveying each in turn "Which of you
is going to get me a drink?"

I was just as curious myself to see what would happen. But Tom, his lips curved in an enigmatic smile, made no move to help. He was, damn the man, just observing—and all too keenly. It was Richard, ever the gentleman, who wordlessly fixed Abby what looked to be a stiff gin and tonic.

Equally silent, she slipped him a grateful smile and took a sip. And then another.

"So, is this the lot of us?" Joanna asked, looking around.

I managed a smile. "Yes. Unfortunately Ronan couldn't make it."

"Ronan?" Joanna inquired, looking puzzled. She wasn't the only one.

"Ronan Grey. He's a neighbor. Apparently he was friends with Allegra, too."

"Funny," Tom Moneghan said. "She never mentioned him."

More silence. Abby took another sip of her drink, and for a brief moment a strained silence hung like a pall in the air. Then I managed to steer everyone to the olives, crackers, and cheese, and civilized conversation reigned. For a while. Until someone said something—I can't even remember what or who—and the sniping began.

Throughout the evening, the only thing everyone seemed to agree on was the food, making my nebulous fantasies of uniting a community with my cooking strangely accurate. Because in the brief moments after I introduced each new dish and everyone was busy complimenting me, a blissful accord settled over the table.

If only it could have lasted more than a few seconds at a time.

I had worked hard for this evening, wanting to pay everyone back for all the courtesy they had shown me. I had kept the lights in the dining room deliberately low, letting the candlelight take over as darkness fell. The silver, china, and crystal winked and twinkled in the dancing firelight, and it should have been both civilized and romantic.

And it was, in the brief intervals when I introduced the new courses. Then the sly comments would start again, sides would be taken, and tempers would flare. And I began to drink in earnest.

In fact, the only one who seemed to be truly enjoying himself was Tom Moneghan. He watched the proceedings with a cynical twinkle in his eyes, never actually taking sides but always seeming to insert the worst possible comments at the worst possible moments. I would have been furious if he had not been the one who also got me through the evening with my sanity relatively intact. I had a feeling my guests would have found something to argue about with or without his encouragement, and every time I was about to lose it, I would look over at Tom and see him glancing over at me with a wicked gleam in his eye that said, plainly as words: *Aren't people ridiculous?* And I would just have to laugh, my sense of perspective restored.

Though I had to admit that it had been a singularly ill-advised idea on my part to attempt such a thing, and I supposed I deserved this for my hubris—to think I could step in and solve a problem that a host of better people before me had tried and failed to find a solution to. By the time the night was over, I had the headache to end all headaches. Still, the most amazing part of the evening had been when Joanna had said, "So, how would you like to be a guest chef at the Myrtle some evening?"

I stared at her, stunned that I had not only been compared favorably to the inestimable Jean-Pierre but had also been dubbed a suitable replacement. I glanced over at Abby, but I think she had already realized that running a store was not my ultimate vocation. She nodded encouragingly.

"I would love it," I said, my voice annoyingly small and

tremulous. "But I know nothing about the dynamics of cooking—or even for a large crowd."

"Nor did I, when I first started out," Joanna informed me briskly. "But I talked to people who did, and I soon learned what I needed to—not that I do the cooking myself." She laughed. "But frankly, you are wasted in retail. What you need is a mentor, someone to teach you the ropes. Because you could be famous off that salad dressing alone!"

"And you're offering to be that mentor?"

"Why not? I know talent when I see it. And my years of experience have to count for something."

"Joanna . . . Thank you," I said, almost humbly.

"Hell," Abby said, into the silence. "Forget the occasional guest chef gigs, Cecil. What you should be doing is opening your own restaurant."

For once, no one disagreed with her. Richard was staring at me speculatively, and Tom was smiling quietly to himself.

"I . . . I couldn't," I stammered. "I mean, I can't compete with you, Joanna, not after you've so generously offered to help me . . ."

She just surveyed me, then smiled at Abby. "Actually, that's not a half-bad idea. I always have to turn people away during the height of the season, so there's room enough for both of us." She fixed me with a gimlet eye. "As long as you don't try to outdo me, that is. I still want the Myrtle to be the classiest restaurant in town. But if you are willing to run a more modest place—a little cheaper, a little more family-oriented—I believe an arrangement can be reached. And in that case, I would have no trouble recommending your place to my overflow patrons."

"Honestly, I don't think I'd have the guts to tread on your toes, Joanna!" I said, only half in jest. Yet, even as I considered it, the ideas were beginning to run away with me. "I don't think I could handle a large place; I'd prefer to keep it small and intimate. That way, I could still do most of the cooking myself, which is what I really love. And I could decorate it with artwork from local artists . . . Martha, would you exhibit with me?"

"I'd be honored," she said. "Although . . . I suppose I'd have to make you some smaller pieces instead of my usual monstrosities."

"And I could use local potters to craft the dishes. Martha, will you give me the name of that guy who did your stuff?"

"Absolutely," she said.

"There's that space on Bay Street," Richard suggested, "which has been empty since Irena's gallery closed. It might be just the right size, though it isn't on the main drag."

"Yeah, but it'll be cheaper than Main Street property," Abby interjected.

Harry frowned. "As your lawyer, Cecil, I have to inject a bit of practicality into the discussion. Starting a restaurant requires quite a bit of capital outlay. Can you handle that?"

"You tell me," I said, energized. "I have what Allegra left me, and I still have most of my severance package; that has to be useful for something."

"Besides," Abby added, "if I buy the store, that gives her even more capital to play with."

Harry scowled and seemed on the verge of a condescending remark—probably something to do with lack of responsibility and maturity which would lead to more disparaging comments about Abby's parenting skills, of which I had heard plenty tonight. And then she would respond with disparaging remarks about Harry's misguided loyalties, taste in friends, and taste in general . . . I couldn't handle that again, so I broke in, suddenly feeling genuinely overwhelmed.

"This is all a little much for me. Yes, the idea appeals more than anything I've heard in a long time. But I'm not sure I'm ready for this. Financially, emotionally . . ."

"Plus which," Tom said quietly, "you haven't even addressed the central issue, yet."

Everyone turned to stare at him, myself included.

"Which is?"

"Aren't you returning to New York in September? Because if you are going to open this restaurant, that pretty much means staying on Seal Island for good. Are you ready for that?"

No, I thought, almost instantly. *No, I'm not*. Tom was right; I had gotten so caught up in all the side issues, I had forgotten the central problem. I had been thinking in terms of a summer-only restaurant, but how practical was that? And I had never been one to make any decision lightly. Could I leave New York and settle permanently on a small Maine island, no matter how beautiful? Was I ready for that? Maybe opening a restaurant was too much responsibility.

My ambivalence must have shown in my lack of response, and a crashing silence stretched out. I was suddenly mortified, feeling that I had personally rejected each and every one of my new friends with my inability to commit to their world.

"I . . ." I began, but I couldn't think of any way to finish that sentence. So, for lack of anything better to do, I went to fetch the dessert.

But despite the sniping, the party had gone shockingly late, and when I finally retreated to bed after cleaning up the detritus, it was to a night troubled by uneasy dreams of failed prospects and restaurants going up in flames—both literally and figuratively. I had, somewhere in the depths of the night, admitted to the seduction of the idea; that was why I was so conflicted. Could I do it? Did I have it in me?

I had always expected that my first real commitment would be to a person, not a place. But Joanna had offered me a shot at a dream, and Seal Island *was* growing on me. In many ways, it frightened me how easily I could see myself living here, growing old here. But you couldn't make a life-long decision based on a month, could you? Was my very own restaurant enough of a lure to disrupt the comfortable routine I had established, the soporific security of the groove I had dug for myself? Was I ready to live out on the edge again, open to risks?

Fortunately, it was not a problem I had to face right away. It was Sunday, the banks were closed, and Harry was on his day off. Even if I had wanted to see the property Richard had spoken of, I was unable to. Besides, Tom had already arranged to pick me up at ten for our sealwatching trip.

Given my hangover, the thought of being on a boat hardly appealed. Worse, there was a wet, grey dampness to the sky that did not seem to make for ideal boating weather. But then, I would be spending the day with Tom—a thought that had begun to have an increasing appeal. And I couldn't quite suppress the small voice in the back of my head that wondered how a decision to remain on Seal Island would affect my future with him.

How much simpler life had been when the possibility of remaining hadn't been an issue. Having choices wasn't liberating; it just needlessly complicated things.

I gulped water and aspirins and forced myself into the shower. Then I dressed in my warmest, though grubbiest, clothes, packed a change of outfit as Tom had advised me, and rooted about for the waterproof windbreaker I had bought in case of emergency. Between the water and the rushing around, I was feeling almost human by the time Tom showed up, two large cups of coffee in hand.

"I figured you might need this," he said, holding one out.

I seized it eagerly—I had been running too slow and too late to make any of my own—and heaved a grateful sigh when the familiar buzz of caffeine showed signs of restoring my humanity.

"How did you know?" I said, when I had drunk enough to be coherent.

He just chuckled. "How do you think I felt this morning? And I didn't even have to clean up after the party. Though I did offer, remember . . ."

I remembered—barely. I had been too drunk at the time, and had too much of a headache, to tolerate any more company—no matter how useful it was inclined to be.

"It looks good in here," he added. "But since I'm sure you don't want to see another pot or pan for the next few days, and I always make good on a promise . . . Dinner is on me tonight."

I didn't remember this one quite as well, and another image sprang irrepressibly to mind. But I clamped down on my improper thoughts, searched my memory, and came up with the answer.

"I survived," I said, with a smile.

"You did," he agreed. "And you even acquitted yourself nobly, under very trying circumstances."

"Right," I said, staring at him. He was wearing his fisherman's clothes again: waterproof pants, boots, and that greying Aran. And for all he cleaned up nicely and behaved well at parties—when he wasn't quietly inciting my guests to riot—this still seemed to me the quintessential Tom, as if this were his real skin and everything else an illusion. But what fisherman used language like 'acquit yourself nobly' and 'trying circumstances?' And offered to help clean up after parties?

But perhaps I was just coming smack up against stereotypes again. Clearly, not all fishermen born were earthy and uneducated; for an instant, Ronan's lilting accent rolled through my mind. Though it was equally clear that this fisherman wanted to be moving along. So, clutching the coffee cup in one hand, I scooped up my jacket and sweater and gestured for him to proceed me out the door.

"I'm not trying to be condescending," he said, misinterpreting my tone as I shut the door behind us and stared up disconsolately at the sky. It was cold and not precisely raining, but a faint mist was beading across my coffee cup and skin. "Who do you think was one of the other people who attempted a reconciliation?"

I paused in my contemplation of the sky and peered over at him. "You?" I said, amazed. He didn't strike me as the altruistic type. Besides, he hadn't exactly been trying to foster any good relations last night.

"Well, for Jessie's sake, mainly," he admitted. "The kid has enough to deal with without all the family feuds. So I thought that maybe I could hammer out a compromise. After all, I used to do it on a daily basis in the Boston courts. And a law degree has to come in handy for something other than lawyering."

The comment was uttered so off-handedly that I almost missed it. I was on the verge of getting into the truck, trying to remember whether or not I had locked the door and wondering whether I should go back and check it, when I suddenly stopped dead. "Excuse me? What law degree?"

He smiled ruefully. "Well, you can't exactly be an A.D.A. without one." And when I stared at him blankly, he added, "Not only did I go away to school, I became a lawyer—the ultimate traitor to my background, I suppose. In my day, I put innumerable bad guys behind bars in the public name— and witnessed even more dirty dealings that kept them out. Not exactly the kind of job that gives you a lot of faith in humanity. So now do you see why I prefer the life of a simple fisherman?"

21

IF I HAD BEEN expecting any sort of revelation from Tom Moneghan this morning, this certainly wasn't it. But as I gaped at him somewhat stupidly, a few more pieces of the puzzle fell into place. Such as why he got invited to all the local parties. I supposed that a former lawyer would seem more acceptable to that crowd than a simple fisherman. At least he used to be one of them.

"Well," he added sharply, interrupting my thoughts, "are you getting in or not?"

Absently, I climbed into the cab, and he put the truck in gear with a clunk of antique transmission and rattled out of the driveway before I could utter another word—or go back to check whether or not I had locked the door.

The raindrops had started to fall more fatly, in counterpoint to the rhythmic slapping of the windshield wipers, as we pulled up before an undistinguished house at the outskirts of town. Tom idled the truck, then turned to me for a minute.

"I'm sorry I snapped at you. They're not really days I like to remember."

His eyes were dark with an unexpressed pain, and it was all I could do to say, "No, that's all right. I'm sorry, Tom. I honestly didn't . . ." *Know? Mean to pry?*

"No, really, the apology is mine. I'm a cranky old bear most of the time. It just goes to show how uneasy the sheen of civilization sits on this fisher-boy."

I was about to make some wordless sound of protest when I saw one side of his mouth quirk up in a small half-smile. An oddly fraught silence settled over the cab of the truck as that dark gaze caught and held mine.

Unable to handle anything more time-consuming this morning, I had bundled my hair into a simple ponytail. Now, a few strands had escaped it, and for an instant I thought he was going to reach over and brush them back, and my heart started to hammer uncontrollably. But instead, he turned off the engine and nodded his head at the windscreen. "Don't worry about the rain; it should clear up in an hour or two, and I have extra so'westers should you need one. Besides, seals don't mind the damp."

I bumped back to reality with a jolt and regarded him dubiously. I doubted his claims—not about the seals and the so'westers, but about the weather. The sky seemed unrelievedly grey, with nary a break between the low-hanging clouds. "I don't mind," I said, not entirely dishonestly. The rain seemed to suit my mood.

The other side of his mouth joined its fellow, quirking up into a full-fledged grin. Then he opened the car door, letting in a wash of damp air, and got out, his dark hair curling wetly in the rain.

I followed suit. Abby answered the door, wrapped in an old, terrycloth robe, looking hollow-eyed and bleary in the half light, her hair more of a wild bush than ever about her face.

"Jessie," she called, then added more softly, looking at me with an almost sheepish expression, "I'm sorry I was such an ass last night. I never have been able to take Harry's comments in good spirits. I was too young when I married Brian, and too meek. And maybe half of what Harry says about me is right, but I'm tired of not fighting back."

"Amen," I said, and reached out impulsively to hug her. She felt so small and vulnerable in that worn robe. "Abby, I can't play middleman in this game. I'm not choosing sides . . ."

"Nor would I expect you to," she said, horrified.

". . . but you know I'm with you, nonetheless."

She laughed, a light coming on behind her eyes. "Of course," she said. "But why you would want to . . ."

"Want to what?" Jessie said, thumping down the stairs behind her. Like Tom, she was dressed for the weather in waterproof pants and fisherman's boots, her face bright and eager beneath a floppy yellow rain hat that most girls her age would not have been caught dead wearing.

I felt distinctly out of place.

"Hello, Tom. Hey, Cecil. Bye, Mom," she called, breezing past us and out the door like a small, dark hurricane.

Abby laughed, another notch of weariness leaving her face. It couldn't be easy, raising a daughter like Jessie all by herself, and no doubt she valued her time alone. Not that I questioned her love for her daughter, but . . . Part of me could tell she was looking forward to this trip as much as Jessie was—although for entirely different reasons.

"Have a good time, guys," she said.

"And you," I responded, with a smile.

She grinned wickedly at us. "I intend to," she said, and shut the door.

Jessie was already in the truck's cab, awaiting us. Tom slid in to one side of her, and I got in to the other. I had expected we would drive the rest of the way into town, to the public docks, but instead Tom pulled a U-turn and bounced us back out the road in the direction we had come. We passed the turn—off to my road, and two more besides, then bumped down a small side road that led to a point on the far side of the island.

We passed a number of large and increasingly impressive houses, then a patch empty of habitation, then a larger and even more imposing dwelling—or so I assumed from the soaring rooftops; I could see little more of it from this vantage—isolated behind a screen of trees and a gated drive. Then more wooded wilderness until the road finally terminated in a large clearing with what looked to be open ocean in one direction and the islands of Acadia in the other. The clearing itself boasted a long, white house with multiple additions, somewhat in need of a fresh coat of paint, two outbuildings, and a vast docking complex with at least five boats in residence.

Two dogs ran out, barking, as Tom pulled into the central drive.

"Is this where you live?" I asked. It was not even remotely what I had expected.

Jessie snickered.

Tom just smiled and said, "Heaven forfend! That is entirely too much house for me to paint, as I keep telling Larry. No, this is Seal Island's main lobster pound. Larry buys up most of our catch and sells it in turn to many of the mainland restaurants. He's one of Boston's biggest suppliers. And because I sort of work for him and live nearby, he lets me dock my boat here—for a modest fee, of course. So be nice to

Larry. If you do choose to stay and open that restaurant, you will have to work though him for your lobsters."

"Oh," I said, and Jessie scowled. "I don't really know how to cook lobster correctly, though."

"I'll show you," Tom promised. "I . . ."

"Are we going, or not?" Jessie interrupted, jostling him.

"Right," he said, and shut off the engine, climbing out of the cab. The two dogs—a black lab and a golden retriever—bounded over to him, barking. Matt Rosen, one of my favorite Thomas Moreland heroes, had two dogs like this. The black lab had been named Dante, and the golden retriever . . .

"Down, Dante. Down, Beatrice," Tom said, trying to calm the eager canines.

I gaped.

Jessie hopped down after him, making a fuss over the dogs, and I followed more slowly, feeling uneasily out of place, again. Was Matt Rosen about to walk out of that peeling, white monstrosity?

Fortunately for my continued sanity, Larry was nothing like Matt Rosen. He had sandy hair, slightly frosted with grey, blue eyes, and a scruffy thatch of day-old stubble. I judged his age somewhere between fifty and fifty-five—though it was hard to make an accurate assessment, for his skin was lined and leathered through years of salt and sun. He had clearly been a fisherman in his younger days, and still had the hard, ropy strength I was coming to associate with a life on the water.

There was a puckish playfulness to him, combined with the obvious savvy of a hardheaded business man, that I liked instantly.

He was also—I was soon to learn—one of the most loquacious people I had ever met.

"Larry Hogarth, Cecil Hargrave. Cecil Hargrave, Larry Hogarth." Tom performed the introductions, and I felt a niggling familiarity at the name. Where had I heard it before? But before I could figure it out, my hand was seized in a firm, non-nonsense grip, and pumped soundly.

"Nice to meet you," Larry said. "Any friend of Tom's . . ." And he was off. He followed us down to the docks, talking incessantly. And, despite—or maybe because of—his heavy Maine accent, he had a natural storyteller's gift. He was, I suspected, the kind of man who could turn a trip to the store into a grand high adventure.

As Tom tended to his boat with Jessie's help—an activity I was aware of only in the periphery of my vision—Larry regaled me with tales of his life, and it had been one rich in experience. He had backpacked all over Europe in his early twenties before settling down to work his father's business. Which I learned when—allowed to get a word in edgewise— I asked about his dogs' names and was regaled with tales of Italy and his discovery of Dante's Divine Comedy, which he had apparently read in its entirety and greatly enjoyed.

I was feeling increasingly inadequate, my preconceptions about fishermen falling by the thousands. At most, I had assumed he had read the Thomas Morelands, but clearly he had read far more than that. And the dogs' names were no more than coincidence. He was heading off into the Faerie Queen when Tom interrupted, obviously amused by my discomfiture. "Ready, Cecil?"

I nodded. His boat, contrary to expectations, was not the *Sea Hag III*. This one was smaller: maybe fifteen feet at the outside (and probably closer to twelve), with a small, covered wheelhouse and a large, outboard motor. And I no longer wondered about his comments about the weather. Even if the rain didn't stop, we could ride perfectly dry under the shelter.

Or so I assumed.

The boat's name, painted jauntily on the transom, was *Revenant*.

"Have a nice trip," Larry said, not seeming the slightest bit put out at being halted midword. He handed me into the boat, then peered up at the sky. "Gonna clear up for you nicely this afternoon," he predicted, and cast off the towline. Then, with a cheerful wave, he retreated back up the dock.

Tom gunned the engine expertly, maneuvering the boat out of dock. The wind wasn't high—at least, not close to the shore—but the boat bounced aggressively over the waves, throwing rhythmic gouts of spray up over the sides. And despite the shelter of the open wheelhouse, I was soon thoroughly damp.

Nonetheless, it was exhilarating, and Tom's sure hand at the wheel gave me confidence. Bundled into one of Tom's spare so'wester jackets that was bright yellow and miles too large for me, I rode the deck at his side, laughing as an eager Jessie ran from bow to stern, alert for signs of the seals.

More than anywhere, Tom seemed in his element here: his hands strong on the wheel, his dark eyes fixed on the horizon, his damp hair ruffled in the wind. There was a light behind his eyes that I had never seen before, and I could understand how such a thing was an escape for him. I found the same was true for me, as well. Out on the water, the wind seemed to snatch up your worries, burying them beneath the rolling waves. Here, there were no thoughts of the future, or the past. There was only the wind and the bouncing boat, the salt spray of the sea.

"There," Tom said, pointing ahead, raising his voice over the roar of the engines. "While some of our local seals congregate off Seal Island, the highest conglomeration is usually off Mount Desert Island, in Jericho and Frenchman's Bay. We're heading into Jericho Bay now, and will probably circle around later into Frenchman's. That's Mount Desert Island, right ahead."

I peered though the windscreen, damp with spray and smeared by the windshield wipers. "How can you even see anything?" I demanded.

"Practice," he responded, and grinned. His expression was infinitely lighter than anything I had yet seen on his face. "Actually, much as I hate to admit it, any idiot could pilot a boat through these waters. The Down East region offers some of the best sailing in the world. Very deep waters; very few shoals. That's partly what brings so many people up here each summer. But if you want to have a proper look, lean out over the gunwales."

By that, I could only assume he meant the sides of the boat. So, unmindful of the rain, I thrust my head around the sides of the wheelhouse, peering through the spray.

There, in the distance, rising misty and indistinct from the grey water, was Mount Desert Island. From this distance, it looked like a fairy island, something not quite of this world. And huddled about its feet like subjects about a throne were a scattering of lesser isles, some of which would contain the seals we were seeking.

I smiled into the wind. The rain had lessened—and was that actually sun on the horizon, leaching through the thinning clouds in an electric streak? I pulled my head in, my face beaded with spray, and Tom laughed at me again, his dark eyes sparkling. And this time he did reach out to brush the dampness off my cheeks with fingers that were both cool and searingly hot all at once.

"You look like a seawife," he teased, his voice low and intimate, barely audible above the roar of the engine. There was a burr to his voice that I hadn't heard before. Our eyes met and locked. A wave of panic and euphoria tore through me, buffeting me like the waves that battered the boat.

"Cecil . . ." he began.

"I see one!" Jessie called, from the stern.

The spell, whatever it had been, was broken. Tom brought the boat to a halt, then shut off the engine. The silence was almost deafening. We bobbed on the waves, some miles out into the depths of the bay. I wondered if this was what Ragnarok felt, this random, rocking motion, as he bottled off my shore. It was oddly comforting.

"Where?" Tom asked.

Jessie pointed. Off to the left of the boat was a ridge of rocky island, jutting jaggedly out of the water. The waves crashed rhythmically against it, throwing up gouts of spray. Currents swirled at its base, forming miniature whirlpools.

We all stood at the side of the now silently-rocking boat, peering at the rocks. Clearly not wanting to risk his boat in the currents, Tom had stopped a good bit off the island. It had stopped raining, and was it my imagination or was the heavy sky lightening, the low clouds parting like a misty curtain? A stiff wind was whipping my hair about—or at least whatever part of it had escaped confinement. Still, I peered dubiously at the inhospitable stretch of rocks; it didn't seem very conducive to marine life to me. But Tom was grinning, his dark eyes sage.

"What do you know that I don't?" I demanded.

He laughed. "Very little, I suspect. Except, perhaps, when it comes to the sea. And this time I think . . . Ah," he said, on an outdrawn breath. "Horseheads. You were right, Jess. Good eye."

She smiled proudly, but I felt a shiver go through me. Did he mean the grey seals, like the one that watched me? I stared apprehensively at the rocks, trying to see what he did.

After a moment, he moved around to stand behind me, laying a hand on my shoulder; I could feel its warmth even through the hard rubber of the rain slicker. With his other hand, he pointed, his sweater sleeve just grazing my cheek. I suppressed the urge to lean into him and followed his pointing finger. And gasped.

What I had taken for streaks of gull guano against the grey rocks were really seals, their sleek bodies humped languidly against the wind. There were about a dozen of them, some darker than others. In fact, now that I looked more closely, some seemed to be dark with whiter spots, and some white with darker spots.

Tom moved away, standing at the rail between Jessie and me. "Grey seals are one of the few species in which you can tell male from female at a glance," Tom informed me. "The darker ones with light spots are the males, the lighter ones with dark spots the females."

Even as he spoke, one of the darker males slipped from the rocks and into the water, and I drew a quick breath, for it was both like and unlike my visitor. The same drooping, lugubrious face, the same convex, equine profile that gave them their common name. But not the same. Not remotely the same at all.

"There's a rare sight," said Tom. "As I said before, there are maybe four hundred horseheads off the coast of Maine. You'll often see one grey amongst a bunch of harbor seals, but to see a full colony . . . They mostly frequent places like this, where even the fisherman can't go. Though it may not look it, the currents off those rocks are fierce."

They looked plenty fierce to me, the water foaming and boiling angrily about the base of the island. The only one that didn't seem bothered by it was the seal. He bobbed in the current for a moment, then submerged.

Our boat drifted closer to the rocks, though still keeping clear of the currents.

The sky *was* lightening, streaked with paler greys and silvery blues in layered patterns that seemed to mirror the breaking waves.

One by one, the horseheads on the rocks appeared to notice our presence. Head after head raised in a wave, and the knot of sleek, dark bodies seemed to contract protectively around something at their center. For an instant, though a chink in the wall of flesh and flippers, I thought I caught a glimpse of something pink and squirming. Then a large bull towards the center of the rock swung his head around and met our eyes, and again I suppressed a shiver. It was still not my seal, but . . . There was something oddly familiar—and disturbing—about this one. Though perhaps it was only the preternatural intelligence that seemed to sparkle in those liquid black eyes.

Tom seemed to sense it, too, because I felt him stiffen beside me. The seal and he held glances, as if in challenge. I didn't know if I expected it to attack or flee, but it did neither. Instead—as if sensing the salt in Tom's veins, some kinship between them—it inclined its head regally, as if acknowledging a subject, and the tight knot of bodies on the rock began to relax.

And then, briefly, as if a curtain had parted, we saw it— white as new-fallen snow, its eyes wide pools of darkness in its face as it gazed back at us. Jessie gasped rapturously, and Tom's face held an almost reverent expression.

I just stared. My initial impression of its color had been off—no more than a trick of reflected light off the rocks. The pup could not have been more than a month old, its face not yet elongated into the lugubrious profile of its species.

"Late for lanugo," Tom muttered.

And then, as suddenly as the seals had parted to reveal their baby, they closed ranks again. The large bull reared up, as if warning us off, and Tom seemed to startle back to awareness. Our boat was drifting dangerously close to the rocks.

He leapt for the starter and the motor roared to life. With a terse efficiency of motion, he swung the boat hard to the right, away from the rocks. We caught the tail end of a wave, and bounced out of range as if shot from a catapult.

With Jessie quivering excitedly in the stern and Tom intent on the wheel, I think I was the only one to look back at the rocks. For an instant, I thought I saw a familiar head bobbing off the rocks, guarding the rookery. But I must have imagined that, too, for as a wave crashed over the rocks and retreated, there was nothing there but the empty sea. Even the knot of horseheads seemed to have vanished into the rocks, their camouflage intact.

"Rare, indeed," Tom said to me when I joined him at the wheel. "I know I told you that the greys pupped far earlier in the year than this, but I suppose there is always an exception. I'm glad you got to see that."

"It was beautiful, wasn't it?"

He looked oddly pensive. "That it was." Then he grinned. "And look there," he said. "What did I tell you?"

I followed his finger. Ahead the clouds had parted, a shaft of gold lancing through the silver, making the sea sparkle like a handful of cast diamonds.

I laughed aloud and threw off the yellow rubber jacket. I removed the elastic from my hair, intent on tidying my ponytail, then decided I liked the feeling of the wind whipping through my hair. It was wild and freeing.

I laughed again and tossed back the mane. Tom was smiling down at me.

"Want to drive?" he said.

"So I fall into the 'any idiot' category?" I said, recalling his words.

His look was strangely intense. "What do you think?"

My stomach did another flip-flop, but all I said was, "I don't care what you think as long as you let me drive!"

I had never spent much time on boats or on the water, growing up as I did in New York City. The last thing I had expected was to feel the madness of obsession creeping in under my skin. But madness it was. I no longer sympathized with Tom's love for the sea; I was beginning to share it. And

I could understand why he had run back to its familiar embrace when whatever had annihilated his life had hit.

He stepped aside and I wrapped my hands around the wheel. The thrumming of the engine vibrated through my arms, up through my feet, and I laughed. He showed me the throttle, the basics of the controls, then stepped back, arms folded across his chest as he leaned against the wall of the wheelhouse and watched me with a faint half-smile.

I let out the throttle and spun the boat through two test loops, whooping. Then, eyes to the horizon, I straightened my course and guided it into the sun.

22

WHEN WE ARRIVED BACK at Larry's dock at four in the afternoon, I was both sleepier and more elated than I had ever been in my life. The fresh sea air was exhilarating, and made me feel I had been gone for days rather than a mere six hours.

I couldn't decide if the high point of the day had been seeing the seals, or driving the boat. Both had been special in their way. I loved the feel of my hands on the wheel, the way the hull bounced over the waves, the slap of impact each time we hit a dip. Then, as we got closer in towards the islands, Tom took over the controls, gliding in expertly along the margins of the rockier beaches, and there we saw seals galore. Mostly the harbor seals, small and dappled like Ragnarok, their pert faces swinging curiously towards us as we approached. Some postured, protecting territory and infants. Some were indifferent. But most seemed intent on play, pouring off the rocks and bottling up alongside the boat like dogs begging for scraps.

And, as Tom had predicted, there were gray seals as well—though not, I sensed, like that colony out on the rock. These were scattered in ones and twos among the harbor seal colonies, and in contrast, seemed almost dull: oddly lethargic and ungraceful when compared to their more dog-like cousins.

We saw more pups, too—but again, it somehow didn't seem quite as special. Maybe I was becoming jaded, or maybe there was something about that snowy coat that altered everything. Tom was right; these pups were older. They had all lost their lanugo, if they had had any to begin with, and were growing into their adult colorings. But they were still playful and curious, and Jessie and I exclaimed over them delightedly. And when I mentioned something about not seeing much of this when I returned to New York in September, her face changed and she warmed to me significantly.

So perhaps it was Jessie more than Abby who was grooming Tom as a second father. At times, I did note a jealous possessiveness towards him which I tried my best not to come between. The kid obviously needed some sort of father figure, and if she had chosen Tom, then who was I—the interloper—to stand in her way?

As for Tom, he seemed to accept the role with a calm, unstudied assurance that made me wonder why he had never married nor had children of his own. He would, I suspected, have made a phenomenal father.

We spent several hours weaving in and out of the coves of the various small islands, and then—a special treat—docked the boat briefly at Bar Harbor. Jessie was lobbying for ice cream. By this point, Abby's daughter seemed to have accepted me as a companion-in-arms, so when Tom decided to stay with the boat, the two of us ventured into the streets, window-shopping and laughing at the tourists along Main Street, until we reached Jordan Pond's ice-cream store. We both ordered cones of homemade ice cream—hers chocolate and mine cinnamon—and when I handed over the money to the clerk, I felt a warm rush of maternal feeling, almost startling in its intensity. I had never given the idea of kids much thought before, but suddenly—with a warm, adolescent body jostling against mine, laughingly pointing out the sights—I felt a longing so strong it almost choked me. And I found myself envying Abby with all my heart.

I suppose I still must have looked a bit stunned when we arrived back at the boat, for Tom looked at me sharply and said, "Are you okay?"

I nodded, shaking off the spell, and he extended his hand, helping me back into the boat. Jessie scrambled nimbly in after me, and for an instant I entertained the fantasy that we were a family. Then Tom started the motor and the rumble of the engine drowned out all such foolish fancies.

He let Jessie take a turn at the wheel on the way back while I looked out over the water and wondered again at the lure of the ocean, why men had, for untold centuries, felt the need to be a part of this environment so fundamentally inimical to human life. But then, maybe that was the answer right there. The sea—impossible to tame, impossible to master—was the one place over which man still had no dominion. It was the last of the great unknowns and thus possessed of an awesome power. And not only for its ability to reach out and kill without warning. How could people live in cities, denied access to its lure?

How could I?

I shivered, then scanned the waves, searching for that familiar, convex profile, but this time there was nothing present but my own strange fancies.

When Tom finally pulled the boat up to Larry's dock, Abby was waiting with her car, and I saw a faintly relieved expression flit over his face. Evidently, we had been out longer than expected—or promised.

"There you are!" she exclaimed.

I glanced over at Tom as he vaulted over the sides of the boat and tied off the lines. "Sorry," he said, matter-of-factly. "There was some good viewing today." He didn't mention our sighting of the horsehead baby, for which I was glad. That suddenly struck me as a private moment, meant only for those of us privileged enough to witness it.

"It's just that I have to get up early tomorrow for the store," Abby said, hustling a protesting Jessie toward the car.

"I'll see you, then," I said, and Jessie shot me a betrayed glance as she was driven away—I suppose because I got to stay with Tom. Not that he seemed to be paying me any attention as he swiftly and efficiently, and with an admirable economy of motion, battened down the boat for the evening. However, when he looked up again, his attention was focused solely on me, and I felt another annoying flush beginning and resolutely pulled myself under control. But fortunately he seemed unaware of my lapse. What he did seem aware of, however, was our comparative isolation, or so I assumed from the oddly guarded look that came into his eyes. Then he seemed to shake himself, said, "Come on, Cecil," and held out a hand.

I hesitated for a minute, unsure of exactly where, or how far, I was expected to go, then placed my hand in his. His fingers, strong and callused, closed around mine, then he turned and led me decisively down the dock.

When we reached the sliding ramp that led from the lower dock to the upper, he released my hand and proceeded me up, then led me around a corner and down another ramp to an even larger dock, this one over deeper water and sprouting a tail of buoyed wooden boxes behind it. Hinging back a trap door toward the center of the dock, he grabbed what looked like a grappling hook and extracted a wooden crate, drawing it up out of the water and onto the dock.

The box, dripping water, clacked and rustled.

Untying the box's top hinge, Tom flipped back the lid to reveal a scrabbling mass of bluish crustaceans. I suppose I had forgotten, thanks to the popular media, what color lobsters really were when alive. But there was something subtly beautiful about their coloring, which shaded almost into green at the tips of their claws and the joints of their shells.

Reaching a hand in amongst them—their formidable claws had already been banded—Tom fished out two large specimens that flung their claws wide in protest as they were lifted into the air. They flapped their tails, and scrabbled frantically with their back legs. He handed them to me, one after the other, and I held them gingerly until they began to go quiescent.

I didn't know exactly how he planned to get them home. I had visions of myself, carrying them back on my lap like dogs. Then, after tying the box back up, sliding it back into the water, and shutting the trap door behind it, Tom reached into an upright box on the dock and pulled out a rather battered plastic bag. He held it open, indicating I should drop the lobsters inside.

"Dinner," he said, proudly. "As promised."

"Umm . . . don't they need to be in water?" I said.

Tom just laughed. "What you don't know about lobsters, lady . . . Now, pop 'em in, and I'll teach you the fine art of boiling a lobster."

I tried, but the minute I got the damnable creatures anywhere near the mouth of the bag, they flapped and flailed and flung their claws out wide, turning instantly into pound-and-a-quarter bundles of resistance. It was rather like trying to put a cat in a bath. Though I suppose, ultimately, their fate was far worse.

Just as I was starting to feel supremely guilty, Tom rescued me, taking the lobsters and indicating that I should hold open the bag instead. Then, expertly, he slotted them in one after another—tail-first, I noticed.

"So, there *is* a trick to it," I said, almost sourly.

Tom just laughed. "There's a trick to everything." Then with the bag swinging loosely in one hand, he led the way off the docks, ushering me into the cab of his truck. I was, I suddenly realized, feeling distinctly grimy—salt-crusted and sweaty. It was a good thing that Tom had advised me to bring a spare set of clothing, because I suddenly couldn't stomach the thought of spending the rest of the night in this ensemble. I wondered if he would let me grab a quick shower, either at my place or at his, and that led to further speculations of exactly what sort of house a man like Tom Moneghan would live in.

It would be something masculine, I decided, studying his profile covertly. Spare and functional, maybe a bit rugged. But modest, perhaps a bit run down. He had said he lived near Larry, but how close, really? Obviously not that gated mansion we had passed on the way in, but. . . .

"What?" he said, as if aware of my scrutiny, turning to shoot me a sidelong glance.

"I was . . . I was just wondering if I could trouble you for a shower. Do you think we could stop briefly at my place, first?" The thought of using his shower suddenly seemed far too intimate to be contemplated, let alone voiced.

"No need to detour," he said. "I have a guest bathroom at my place, and plenty of spare towels. Unless . . ." He hesitated. "Would you feel more comfortable stopping at your place?"

I managed to get the words out. "No, yours is fine." We were driving back out along the peninsula road, on the verge of passing the hidden mansion that had so intrigued me on the way out. This time, I would look at it more closely, see if I couldn't catch more of a glimpse than before. "Why?" I added. "How much closer is your place?"

There was an unmistakable twitch of humor at the corners of his mouth. "A lot," he said, obligingly slowing as we passed the screen of trees that masked the mansion. He reached up to punch a button on a small remote clipped to the driver's side sunshade and the gate retracted soundlessly.

"I told you Larry and I were neighbors," he added, clearly enjoying my confusion as the battered truck turned and bounced down the drive, the gates sliding soundlessly shut behind us.

I SUPPOSE I SHOULD have expected something based on the 'guest bathroom' remark but, even then, I would never have expected Tom Moneghan to live like this. Though I suppose I did get some bits of it right. Like "masculine." And "rugged."

Behind the screen of trees, the house rose in multi-tiered splendor, slabbed in the same hard, bold angles as the rock ledges that made up the beach. It was shingled the same silver-grey as Allegra's house, but there all similarity ended. For one thing, there were very few actual walls. Most of the house seemed composed of vast sheets of plate glass that reflected the sky and would probably make it a bitch to heat in winter. Nor did it have a regular symmetry, but seemed to sprout from the earth like a crystal, rising from one story in places to as high as three in others. It had, I suspected, been designed by either a genius or a madman—and only time would tell which.

I drew a deep, awed breath—purely involuntarily, I might add—as Tom said, "So? What do you think?"

"Who designed this?"

"One of the local architects." He shot me a sidelong glance. "With a little help from yours truly."

I had thought, for a moment, that I had actually had Tom Moneghan figured out, but each time he threw me for another loop.

"I had no idea lobstering made so much money," I blurted, then could have kicked myself for saying it.

He just laughed. "It doesn't," he replied.

Family money? I thought, which he all but confirmed seconds later, adding, "The land has been in my family for generations. I just decided to do something . . . a little different with it. And it's not as much of an energy drain as it looks. Thanks to all the glass, a good chunk of it runs off solar power; I'm trying to cause as little impact as possible with my obsession." He paused for a moment, then continued, almost as if begging for approval, "I'm actually quite proud of it."

"So you should be," I said. "It's astounding!"

He beamed. "Just wait until you see the inside."

I did, and instantly decided it was the kind of house that could quickly make you run out of adjectives. "Staggering" sprang to mind. As did "electrifying."

The central room had ceilings that rose almost two stories in height, with wide picture-windows looking out over the ocean, and a series of high, cut-out windows, like square portholes, on the upper walls. There were double fireplaces to either side, like at Allegra's, with an expanse of bare wall above that I knew would soon house Martha's paintings. And the wild storminess of her images perfectly reflected the bold dominance of the room.

A large, open kitchen to one side drew a curious glance, as did the stairs leading up to what I sensed was the master wing above—probably because of the presence of the low-slung deck off to the right side of the structure. To the left, rooms rose up in a series of graded steps.

"You'll probably want a shower, first," he said. "Then I'll give you the grand tour. Let me show you to the guest suite."

Guest suite it was, complete with bedroom, sitting room, dressing room, and a cavernous bath with a glass-bricked but otherwise open shower. Bed and bath both looked out onto the water.

"The towels are all clean," he said. "Feel free to take your time." And he disappeared through the door, still—I noticed idly—holding the bag of lobsters.

I laid down my own bag, containing my spare clothing, on the bed, and thanked all the gods at once for my foresight in bringing an outfit that wouldn't be completely overshadowed by the house. At first, I was worried it might have been too dressy. Now I was thinking that it just might pass. Barely.

I stripped off my salt-logged clothes, idly wondering if Tom weren't doing the same somewhere else in the depths of this cavernous house, and resolutely tried to ignore the warmth that went through me at the thought. I didn't know whether this was a date or not. Mostly, it was something so completely outside my realm of experience that I had nothing to compare it with. But I couldn't quite help wondering what would happen if it were.

Concentrate, Cecil, I chided, and went through to the bathroom, turning on the hot water.

I took a long, steamy, undisturbed shower. Then, as Tom had suggested, took my time dressing, suddenly reluctant to meet this person whom I realized I knew so little about. But eventually I gathered my courage, slipped on the jewelry he had bought me, and ventured out into the main part of the house.

I found him on the back deck, dressed in jeans and a white T-shirt, his hair still curling damply from the shower.

"Cecil," he said, as I approached. His gaze took in my outfit—black slacks and bronze-toned buttoned blouse— then fastened on my necklace. His eyes warmed perceptibly. "How about that tour?"

The house was not furnished cheaply, or shoddily. The kitchen, gleaming with restaurant-quality stainless steel appliances, was a chef's wet dream, and I stared enviously at the Viking stove. I had once priced one of those; the purchase would have put me back half a year's salary.

Who the hell *was* this man?

There were at least five bedrooms, and the master bedroom was easily the size of three of them put together, furnished with what looked to be oriental antiques—huge, solid pieces with clean-cut lines. The bed was king-sized and similarly grand, and I managed to control my blush, trying resolutely not to picture Tom among the sheets. It was a masculine room, yet not unwelcoming.

Still, I was rather glad when we continued on to safer quarters.

Toward the tail end of the tour, I finally said, "Well, this explains the gate. You must have a fortune in antiques, here. I suppose it would be a temptation to most thieves."

He looked somewhat startled. "Really? I suppose I seldom think about it. My great-grandfather—or was it great-great?—was a sea captain, so I guess you can say the sea really is in my family's blood. Anyway, he worked the spice route, and picked up most of this stuff dirt-cheap, from the source, as it were." He smiled. "No, the gate is mainly to discourage the occasional over-eager groupie who has managed to ferret out my whereabouts. Obviously, I like my privacy."

That struck me as an oddly egotistical statement from a man who had no ego I had been able to discern. It was almost as if he considered himself some sort of minor celebrity, which seemed highly uncharacteristic. But then, he had foiled my assumptions on several previous occasions, so maybe he was someone whose unpleasant qualities only came out gradually. Which might explain how such a good-looking man with such a glorious house was still rattling around in it alone.

I thought back to the occasional dark, brooding expression I had seen on his face, and congratulated myself—rather smugly—for discerning the trouble before I got too deeply involved.

"So," he said, oblivious to my musings, "now all that's left to see is my work room." So why did he sound strangely nervous? "I put it off to the side of the house to ensure privacy, back in the days when I was building this house for my wife and kids."

His expression closed off, and I felt an almost physical pain grip my stomach. *Wife? Kids?* "What . . . what happened?" I managed.

"Dead," he answered tightly.

I had been expecting 'divorced.' I stared at him in horrified silence for a moment, then fumbled, "I'm sorry. I . . ." But I didn't think he wanted to hear the whole sordid story of my parents, so I remained silent, and he forced his face into a lighter expression.

"It's years behind me, now," he said, and almost managed to sound as if he meant it. "Come along; I'll show you my study."

He led me through a breezeway and into a separate structure large enough to be a guest cottage in its own right. It, too, had large windows overlooking the water. And leather armchairs, and a heavy desk on which sat a top-of-the-line computer. There was a bathroom off to one side, and the walls were lined floor-to-ceiling in bookshelves, filled with a delightfully eclectic collection of titles.

It was like my own personal paradise: a self-contained library, far away from anything else. I recognized a number of the titles, including the inevitable Thomas Morelands. At least ten each of the inevitable Thomas Morelands, both in paperback and hardcover. And foreign language editions.

I stared at the few, exposed patches of wall, where framed Moreland covers stared back at me, then turned to gape at Tom, the inevitable pouring in like a wave, making me feel an utter idiot. How I hadn't managed to put it together before now, when I had had every one of the clues in front of me . . .

"*You're* Thomas Moreland?" I exclaimed.

To my amazement, Tom Moneghan turned a startling shade of crimson, muttered something that may have been, "Good Lord, I thought you knew," then recovered enough to sweep me a curt little bow.

"Guilty as charged," he said.

23

FOR THE SECOND NIGHT in a row, dinner was a disaster. There I sat, across the table from Tom the lobsterman, and just kept thinking: "Thomas Moreland." Down-to-earth Tom Moneghan, with whom I had spent one of the most delightful days of my life and now couldn't even talk to. Words just wouldn't go together, and when they did, the inevitable thoughts would crop up. *Thomas Moreland*. And *Thomas Moreland bought me jewelry*. And everything would derail.

At least this explained John's costume during the parade. *Good Lord.*

I did try to explain myself, to tell him how much I had always admired his novels, his characters. But all my attempts to sound logical and reasoned likewise derailed, and I ended up babbling like a star-struck teenager, which only made things so much worse.

Tom seemed as embarrassed as I was, and one by one all our attempts at conversation stumbled into the wall of my hero-worship and his sudden reticence. The only safe topic was lobster—and he did, as promised, teach me how to cook it properly. Though I had the feeling that, from that day forward, the words: "Bring a pot of seawater to a boil, put the lobsters in, remove them eight minutes after the second boil" would forever be associated with a searing humiliation.

Eventually, it did get a little better, if only because I had known the man across from me as Tom Moneghan longer than as Thomas Moreland. Besides, as he had assured me, that was his real identity. Thomas Moreland was smooth and suave and filthy rich—which both made me feel a little better and perversely more annoyed about the jewelry. I suppose Tom had been right when he said it was nothing; he must get twice that amount each day in royalties. Still, Thomas Moreland was the creation and Tom Moneghan the lobsterman's boy who had grown up on Seal Island with the ocean in his blood.

And while it didn't exactly seem incongruous to think of all my favorite creations coming from the mind of this man, it wasn't something I found I could wrap my head around on a moment-to-moment basis. Not when I had just seen Tom out on his boat, so clearly in his element. His head flung back in the salty spray, the wind in his face, his dark eyes alight, the sun picking out auburn glints in his soft, dark curls. No, that was something that belonged to Tom Moneghan alone; it was something that Thomas Moreland had never shared.

But if eventually my awe faded, it was replaced by a crippling shyness that would affect me at odd moments. So that, all in all, I think he was more than ready to get rid of me as our dinner drew to a close.

I climbed into the cab of his truck, feeling a creeping depression settling over me that not only could I not talk to a man I had always felt akin to since the moment I had read his first novel, but also that, by doing so, I had managed to destroy a relationship that had rapidly been growing more important to me. And whether it had just been friendship or something more, it was all academic now, and I mourned its loss.

I felt even more of an idiot when I realized, more than halfway home, that I had left my salt-encrusted clothing in his spare bedroom. Which he would no doubt assume was some fannish ploy to return when he so clearly wanted nothing more to do with me. How could I convince him that it had been no more than a stupid mistake, all thoughts of dirty laundry driven from my mind by the night's disturbing revelations? Maybe if I just wrote them off as lost and never went back.

We arrived at Allegra's house in silence and I climbed out of the truck. I almost expected him to turn around and drive off in a shower of gravel and screeching tires, but he was too much of a gentleman for that. Of course. David Maxwell always walked Patricia Neill home after their dinners, so why not his creator? Still, an uneasy restraint reigned between us so unlike the wordless companionship of this morning that I felt depressed all over again.

I reached into my pocket for my house keys, then realized, with a sinking feeling, that I had likewise left them back at his house, in the pocket of my dirty jeans.

I put my hand on the knob solely out of desperation. If I were even remotely lucky . . .

It turned easily under my hand, and I couldn't help the sudden chill that went through me. No big deal. I had simply forgotten to lock it that morning, as I suspected. This wasn't theft-plagued New York, and I should be grateful for my oversight. So why couldn't I shake the frigid feeling that continued to run through me?

Tom must have seen the look on my face, for he said, sounding more like himself than at any other point in the evening, "Cecil? What's the matter?"

All thoughts of Thomas Moreland were driven from my head, and I was absurdly grateful for his reassuring bulk behind me as I whispered, "I'm not sure," and pushed the door open. "I'm probably being silly, but . . ."

The sight that greeted me when I flipped on the light stopped me dead in my tracks.

The house looked like a tornado had gone through it. Furniture had been overturned, cushions slashed, drawers emptied, books tumbled haphazardly off the shelves. Someone had clearly been searching for something with brutal disregard for my possessions.

I gave an inarticulate squeak—all the protest I could manage—and heard Tom gasp behind me. I surveyed the carnage for another second, then turned to him, my face frozen into a mask. I must have been pale as a ghost; my eyes felt like wide, black pits in my face. My mouth moved soundlessly, but no words came out.

He looked down at me for a moment, and then I was in his arms, my head buried against his chest, his heart beating a strong, rhythmic cadence beneath my ear. *No wonder puppies like sleeping with clocks.* I thought irrelevantly, then began to shake.

"Cecil, shhh. It's all right," he murmured, along with a dozen other mindless platitudes which I only half heard. It wasn't that I feared my invader might still be present; I knew with an instinctual certainty that the house was now empty, maybe from the desolate quality of the silence that enveloped it. It roared at me, until I felt that I could almost hear the piles of Allegra's possessions settling in their unsteady new equilibrium.

I came back to myself with the sound of Tom cursing in

my ear, and managed to disentangle myself from his arms and stand erect—a feeble attempt to restore some sort of dignity to the situation.

"Right; come with me," he said, our awkwardness momentarily forgotten, and led me unerringly to the kitchen phone, where he calmly and efficiently phoned the police. "They'll be here shortly," he said, when he hung up. "Should we look around, see if anything is missing? But . . ."

"Don't touch. I know."

I felt wobbly as a new-born colt as I tottered about my house on legs that seemed barely cohesive, surveying the damage. Tom trailed behind me, silent and bristling at my back, like some oversized guard dog.

Just having him present made me feel calmer. But as for the rest . . . The more I looked, the more it felt like a personal attack. Especially since nothing of value had been taken. Allegra's jewelry was untouched, as was the small stash of twenties I had stowed in one of the bedroom dresser drawers. But the drawer itself lay upside-down on the floor, its contents strewn across the rug. Several of Allegra's dresses had been slashed, and the jagged, fraying edges were as disturbing to me as genuine wounds—probably because of the spiteful violence with which they had been inflicted.

My own clothing was largely untouched, save for being flung about and trampled by muddy feet.

I wondered what further damage had been done to the upstairs bedrooms, but all the jewels in India could not have induced me to climb up and check. And I wasn't going anywhere near the attic for at least a week!

The kitchen was another matter. I had expected to find it awash with shards of glass and broken pottery, and was disproportionately relieved to discover that was not the case. Whatever this person had been searching for, it was not here. Two of my new and bigger pots had been flung furiously to the floor, denting their edges and cracking a few of the kitchen tiles. But over all, the order was lovely—especially in contrast to the living room. There, books lay tumbled with broken spines; there was a stamp of muddy footprint across the crumpled pages of one of the Morelands. Seeing it, I wasn't sure if I wanted to rage or weep. Instead, I just stared down at the shattered fragments of the new red-and-black vase of which I had been so proud, now smashed into smithereens with the remains of Richard's flowers against the left-hand hearth.

Oddly, its companion piece on the opposite mantel was the only thing in the room left standing, almost like an eyesore of order in the midst of such chaos.

The cops and crime scene techs showed up not long later, tramping through the house and making even more of a mess of things with black dustings of fingerprint powder. The whine and burst of high-powered flash bulbs snapped at intervals. And throughout it all, I sat on the edge of one of the couches, staring at the one standing urn, numbly answering whatever questions I was asked. No, I didn't have any enemies. No, nothing was missing. No, I didn't have a clue what was going on.

"It's this damned house," I overheard one cop saying to another, at one point. "Nothing ever happens on this island except here!"

"Well, at least in the past few months," the other added.

A grunt of acknowledgement met that statement.

About two hours later, my house was "processed," and the hordes retreated, promising to call me if there was any information, and Tom and I were left alone again the house echoed around us. It was ridiculously late.

I crossed the room, superstitiously avoiding the stained floorboards that had once again been unveiled, and picked it the red-and-black urn, hinging back the lid. It was still full of the same grey, powdery ash. I tipped some into my hand, watched it trickle though my fingers.

"What the devil is that?" Tom demanded.

"Damned if I know," I answered. Startled back to reality, I sheepishly restored the rest of the handful to the urn. "Obviously not something important."

"Or something too important," he muttered, almost absently.

I stared at him and he smiled ruefully, plucking the object out of my fingers and putting it back on the mantel.

"I'm staying, of course," he said—and I couldn't help noticing that, unlike Richard, he didn't bother to offer. An offer I would have felt obliged to turn down, especially after the fiasco of our dinner. But he had neatly circumvented all my foolish posings of pride and independence. The truth was, I wouldn't have slept a wink without him in the house.

Though, how well I would sleep with him there likewise remained to be seen.

A little shiver went though me—part fear and part anticipation—and I moved away from him to hide it. Instead I knelt, picking up the muddy, broken-backed Moreland. "Your poor book," I mourned, closing it gently, my fingers lingering on the spine. Absurdly, I felt my eyes fill again with tears. Of all the things to get upset about.

"There's plenty more where that came from," he said with a wry chuckle, then knelt beside me. "Honey, stop that," he added, his hands closing over mine, halting me in my attempts to gather up all the broken, trampled books.

A slight, involuntary squawk trickled from my lips, which he misinterpreted as denial.

"There will be plenty of time to clean up later," he said, wresting the books from my hands—though I noticed he piled them neatly and carefully to one side. Then he stood and lifted me almost bodily to my feet. "You've had a nasty shock," he said, propelling me toward the bedroom with a hand to my back. "What you need now is a drink and some sleep."

Maybe he was right; I felt oddly numb.

Sweeping a path through the worst of the mess, he placed the cushion back on the window-seat—slashed side down— and placed me on top of it. "Stay there," he ordered.

I complied, sitting like a mannequin as I was placed: knees together, toes turned in, head drooping. I heard random cursing from the living room and the sounds of clutter being shifted, then he was back, pressing something into my hands.

"Here; drink up," he said.

I took a reflexive gulp, then choked and sputtered as the liquor seared its way down my throat. My eyes flew wide open, and I took another sip. And another.

He laughed. "Never underestimate the power of a really good Laphroaig. Feeling better?"

"A little."

"Keep drinking," he advised, and began to wrestle the mattresses back onto my bed. The sheets were hopeless, ripped and muddied. He balled them into a corner and looked at me inquiringly.

"Chest," I said, pointing.

It was lying on its side, the topmost layers spilled out and trampled, but he must have found what he was looking for several layers down. He made the bed with a practiced efficiency, then righted the bedside lamps. The bulb in one was smashed, but the other trailed a comforting glow across the fresh linens.

"There," he said. "Now . . ." He surveyed me. "Are you going to get into bed, or am I going to have to undress you?"

My head snapped up.

"Well, at least that woke you up." Was that relief or regret in his voice? I couldn't tell.

He cocked an eyebrow at me and I rose, shuffling along

his cleared path to the bathroom, wondering what would have happened had I been able to feign shock just a few moments longer . . .

"Cecil," he said.

"What?"

"You're drifting again. Go on; get ready for bed."

I blinked. ". . . You?"

His mouth quirked. "I'll be fine on the couch. Once I reassemble it."

"There are . . ."

"Spare bedrooms. I know. But having me half a house away does no good for the reassurance factor. Besides"—he laughed faintly—"I'm not sure I want to be up there alone myself. Now go."

I went, nudging aside overturned shampoo bottles and bars of soap. My toothbrush was upside-down in the waste bin, but I was too tired to care. I rinsed it haphazardly, and located my toothpaste behind the toilet tank. I brushed my teeth, washed my face with the nearest shard of soap, and looked about for something to double as a nightgown. An old T-shirt would have suited my mood. Perversely, what came to hand was my slinkiest bit of lingerie: a scrap of black lace and satin with the barest of spaghetti straps.

I donned it, then hovered uncertainly in the doorway. From the sound of it, Tom was cleaning my living room. I drifted toward him.

He glanced up as my shadow fell across him, then jumped abruptly to his feet, his eyes dark and unreadable. He muttered something I couldn't hear.

"What?" I asked.

He managed a smile. "I said: 'That's damned unfair.' "

"I know. You shouldn't be cleaning my living room. I . . ."

His mouth quirked. "That wasn't quite what I meant. Come along; I'll tuck you in."

I balked, planting my feet. "No, I . . ."

"Now," he said, and lifted me off my feet as if I weighed no more than a child, carrying me to the bed. He laid me down and tucked the covers around me. Then, rising, he shut off the overhead light, so that only the single lamp illuminated the bed. The shade was on crookedly, casting a slanting light across his features that made them impossible to read.

"Cecil," he said tightly, "if you had any idea how much of a trial you are to me . . ."

"I know," I babbled. "And I'm sorry. I've been such an ass tonight, and you've been wonderful, and . . ."

". . . you have no idea what you're saying," he said. Or, at least that's what I thought he said, but he was right. Apparently, my reaction to burglary was narcolepsy; I could barely keep my eyes open. But then again, it was close to three in the morning. I just wanted to sink into the pillows and be gone.

"It's all right," he said. "Sleep."

I think I tried to mumble some vague apology, but the words never even made it out. I felt his hand on my forehead, and then nothing more.

24

I AWOKE, WITH A start, to the utter absence of bleating alarms. *Monday*, my brain told me, but the sun was too high for a work morning. Unless I had overslept.

My eyes popped open and I raised myself half off my pillows, then sank back again as I took in the chaos that had become my room. Memory flooded back and, with it, the insidious smell of coffee, drifting in from the kitchen. Or perhaps from even closer.

More memories returned. Tom Moneghan. Who must have been listening right outside my door, because my involuntary squawk brought his voice through the portal.

"Ah, I thought this might wake you. And don't worry; I already called Abby. She knows everything."

Then, before I could answer, my door swung open and Tom entered, two mugs of coffee in his hands. I sat up and reached for one reflexively. His eyes widened and hot coffee slopped out of one of the mugs, spilling across his foot.

He yelped and I colored, abruptly conscious of my appearance. I must look a fright: my eyes bleary, my hair a tangled mess about my face. One of the straps of my gown was in the process of doing a slow slide off my shoulder.

I yanked it back, and by the time I reached for the coffee—successfully, this time—Tom had his face back under control.

I felt for the guy; I really did. Here I was, once again being a source of embarrassment, forcing him to attend to the wreck I'd become. Well, no more. Resolutely, I took a gulp of my coffee, put the mug down on the bedside table next to the sole remaining lamp, said: "Excuse me," with as much dignity as I could muster, and rose from the sheets like Athena emerging new born from Zeus' head.

I entered the bathroom, reached automatically behind the door for my robe, then cursed under my breath and spent the next few seconds pawing through the heap of towels and cosmetics on the floor. Was my life destined to become an endless comedy routine this morning?

By the time I emerged with both my robe and my dignity relatively intact, Tom had taken a seat on the end of my bed and was sipping his coffee with a speculative look on his face.

"I think," he said, as I settled cross-legged against the pillows and tucked the skirts of my robe demurely around my knees, "that we've managed to get off on somewhat the wrong foot, the two of us. What do you say we start this all over again fresh?"

I nodded and picked up my coffee, taking another gulp. "I think that's a very good idea."

"Well, then," he said. "Hello. I'm Tom Moneghan, who has sometimes been known to write books as Thomas Moreland, but who really bears no resemblance to that particular literary persona. That's the beauty of fiction; you get to make it all up." And he smiled faintly.

I smiled back, though I still wasn't buying that particular

argument. The more I was becoming accustomed to the idea that he was Thomas Moreland, the more I began to suspect that there was indeed a lot more of him than he acknowledged in his books. Maybe too much. For a man whose life was bounded by walls, a pseudonym was yet another barrier to hide behind. And to encounter someone who knew as much about his works, and in as much detail, as I did must have been intimidating.

So I didn't argue the point, but gave him the distance he required. "Cecil Hargrave," I replied instead. "Not-quite niece of Allegra Gordon, and nothing very particular beyond that."

His eyes went dark, and the look he shot me was oddly intense. "Don't sell yourself short. At the very least, how about soon to be founder of the second-best restaurant on all of Seal Island?"

I raised my eyebrows. "Second best?"

He laughed. "Well, I don't dare cross Joanna, either!"

I felt an answering grin tug at my lips. "I wouldn't go that far. I haven't even decided if I'm going to stay past September, let alone start up a local restaurant."

He just shrugged, as if he didn't believe a word of my protestations. And the damnable thing was that he was right. I was coming to believe them less and less myself.

But what he said was: "Well, for however long you choose to stay . . . Friends?" And he held out a hand.

I placed mine within it, expecting we would shake on the bargain, but instead his fingers closed warmly, almost caressingly over mine, and he just sat there in silence for a moment, holding my hand within his. My heart slammed painfully into my throat, and at that moment the last thing I wanted to hear from him were words of friendship. But it was a start—and a better start than we had possessed until now—so in a rather choked voice I repeated the word back to him, then rather blindly withdrew my hand for fear I might give something away that he was clearly unwilling to face.

Instead I reached for my coffee, now growing cool, and took another sip. And though I knew it was supposed to be a serious moment between us, in the continuing private farce that seemed to be my lot that morning, my mind couldn't help tossing up: *Thomas Moreland is in my bedroom.* And: *Damn, but he really makes good coffee! Is there anything the boy can't do?*

Not that I could discover, at any rate. Sometime during the night or early that morning, he had cleaned up my house, tidying away the worst of the chaos. When I finally rose and left the bedroom, lured by his promise of breakfast, I found my living room as immaculate as he could get it, given the circumstances. The cushions were all back on the couches, though some were clearly in need of repair; the rugs were straightened, once more concealing the stain; and the books had been returned to the shelves. The shards of the vase, the remains of Richard's flowers, and the ash I had spilled had all been swept away.

"Thank you," I said, feeling oddly unworthy. "This is . . ."

"The least I could do," my companion responded. "Besides, it's not a task I am precisely unfamiliar with. And this time was infinitely preferable to the time before."

For an instant, I was puzzled—and then I remembered Tom's words at my party, another piece of the puzzle falling into place. "You were the one," I said. "The one who found her."

He nodded curtly.

I felt a rush of shame. "I . . . I'm sorry, Tom. I . . . Well, clearly I've been less than great at putting things together, lately. Forgive me?"

His expression lightened fractionally. "Yes, well, enough of that." He took my arm, steering me into the kitchen. He sat me down at the table. "What do you say to a frittata?" When I stared at him, he added, "Don't look so impressed. Apart from lobster, it's one of the few things I'm actually able to cook. In fact, my wife used to say it was a good thing I was so talented as a lawyer, because I would have made a hopeless domestic."

The words, meant to be so casual, shattered between us like a breaking glass. An awkward silence descended. I was not yet ready to hear about his dead wife. And, judging by his expression, he was equally unready to discuss her. Then he muttered something under his breath that might have been: "Wrong time; wrong place," and distracted me by opening the cabinets and searching for my skillet.

I was more than happy to be diverted, and soon the smells of frying eggs and mushrooms sizzling in butter filled my kitchen. Despite his protestations to the contrary, what he eventually turned onto my plate was a fully professional frittata, as fine as any I had seen—or tasted—in any New York restaurant.

"Tom, this is amazing!" I said as I bit into it. It was both crisp and fluffy, stuffed with vegetables and expertly seasoned. *Can I keep you?* I wanted to add, but didn't.

He smiled ruefully, and took a seat across from me, thumping down his own plate. "Well, the few things I know how to do I apparently do rather well."

"As any number of best-seller lists will confirm," I said dryly, and he grinned.

"See how quickly the respect fades once you know my true identity? You would never have dared say that to Thomas Moreland, but poor old Tom Moneghan can be the butt of infinitely many jokes."

He was right, of course. I could never have been friends

with Thomas Moreland; he was too far beyond me. But Tom Moneghan . . . I began to think this might work, after all. Then suddenly I remembered Tom's other profession.

"What about the boat? Aren't I keeping you from work?"

"Oh." He looked almost embarrassed. "They can manage without me. As the demand for lobsters grows, the fishing license becomes increasingly rare. A son can inherit one from his father, but what of the second son? Or the third? For conservation reasons, so few new licenses are being granted that many families find themselves without a source of legal income. When I left the island, I deeded my family license to one of those third sons. Through obligation and friendship, he lets me come along with him—though lobstermen mostly work alone. Still, you never sneer at free labor. Nor will I take a dime of his profits. The books . . ." He flushed faintly. "Even in my wildest dreams, I'd never imagined they'd be so successful. I started writing as therapy, and then they became . . . Well, the dreadful truth is that I'm stinking rich, and haven't the faintest clue what to do with all the money, except for occasionally buying jewelry for beautiful women."

But before I could respond to that, the doorbell rang loudly, startling me.

"Who . . ." I began.

Tom smiled. "I suspect that would be your new alarm system. I called this morning about installation. Did I mention that part about being stinking rich?"

My heart sank. "But I can't . . ."

"Nonsense." He rose and padded toward the door, pausing with one hand on the kitchen doorjamb as he turned to look back at me. "Cecil, please. I'm not trying to turn you into a charity case, or flaunt my financial superiority. Part of me hates it, if the truth be known. But I'd feel better if you were protected, and alarm systems don't come cheap. Let me do this for you, as a gift to a friend. A friend I have come to value quite highly. Please?"

What could I say? I nodded numbly, torn between relief and annoyance. But I did find myself wishing, on a quite conscious level, that he wasn't emphasizing the word "friend" quite so much.

25

THE ALARM INSTALLATION TOOK about half the day, and Tom stuck around dutifully for the lot—in part, I suspect, because he didn't want me to see the bill. But the workman seemed competent, and I soon learned to stay out of their way as they wired doors and windows. Tom wouldn't even let me clean up the breakfast dishes, so feeling singularly useless, I trailed about the living room and bedroom, contemplating the damage and making lists of items I would need to replace.

Abby called a little before noon, sounding breathless and anxious. How I was, did I need anything, was there anything she could do? I assured her I was fine, on all counts, and hung up with a warm feeling inside, reflecting that it was nice to have friends.

But perhaps my protestations weren't convincing enough, for half an hour later the doorbell rang again, and there was Abby, her red-gold hair a halo about her head. She was grinning somewhat sheepishly, holding out two steaming boxes of pizza like an offering. When I stared at her, she said, "Kind of like coals to Newcastle, I know, but I figured the last thing you'd want to handle this afternoon was cooking, especially with so many people in your house."

She was, of course, absolutely correct. "Not to mention that I am temporarily banned from the kitchen." There were workmen swarming all over it. "But how did you know I had company?"

She laughed. "News travels. Besides, I heard them banging around when I called earlier. Now, where do I put these?"

"Abby, you're a godsend. How about the kitchen table?"

"All right," she said, "but make sure you get a few pieces first."

"Why?" I asked, as I helped her lay out the boxes and got out two plates. I handed her one, but she shook her head.

"I've already eaten, and besides, I have to get back to the store. I left one of those 'Back in ten minutes' signs on the door. A blatant lie, but no one will hang around waiting if you say half an hour. And in answer to your question . . . Boys," she called, raising her voice, "lunch is served!"

It was a good thing I had followed her advice, saving out two pieces on my plate, because within seconds the workmen descended and the boxes were stripped clean of pizza as if devoured by a swarm of hungry locusts. When Tom trailed in a few minutes later, looking hopeful, the look he cast at the empty boxes was so mournful that I offered him my second piece. Abby had already departed with a warm hug and a promise to stop by later, so we sat side by side on the stairs, out of the way of the workmen, and ate.

It was an oddly companionable meal. We were crammed on the narrow step, our thighs touching, while we both ate off my plate. And if my heart beat a little faster each time his arm brushed against mine, I did my best to ignore it.

There was still a reticence to him, but even that was beginning to fade. Not that he was any closer to telling me his life story, but his body was looser, some of the tension I had always sensed in him slackened.

He was probably inordinately relieved that I wasn't going to turn into some psycho fan girl, after all.

When we had finished, we sat there for a few moments longer, then he trailed off to supervise the workers. "Not that I have the slightest idea what they're doing," he admitted, "but I think they consider it my manly duty. So who am I to disappoint?"

Left once more at loose ends and somewhat reassured by the presence of so many people in my house, I decided to brave the upstairs at last.

The covers were off the beds here, too, and the mattresses tossed about. The books were tumbled off the shelves and more assorted knick-knacks were lying upside down or broken on the floor. I straightened up as best I could—finding a few treasures amongst the worn paperbacks, including a full set of Mary Stewarts and Barbara Michaelses—then decided to brave the attic. I padded across the hall and pushed open the door with a shiver of apprehension, but between the workmen and the police, whatever I had expected to see was lost under a chaos of dusty footprints and broken cobwebs.

Between the police and the alarm guys, if there had been a clear footprint, it had long since been obscured.

Still, I told myself firmly, what had I expected to do? Memorize the pattern of the treads then line up every man from one end of Seal Island to the other and demand to see their boots? Feeling abruptly foolish, I trundled down to the utility closet under the stairs, dragged out the vacuum, and got to work.

I wasn't up for sorting through the volumes of stuff in the attic, but at least I could eliminate the worst of the dust. I bundled up my hair and vacuumed away. Then, feeling inspired by the large patches of clean flooring, I went for rags and brooms and bottles of Windex, and tackled both the dusty windows and the rafters. I was so caught up in my task that I had almost forgotten what was going on in the house below until an alarm started blaring loudly, nearly scaring me from my skin.

I had been batting somewhat ineffectually at a mass of cobwebs in one of the most inaccessible corners with an upraised broom when the alarm went off, and I jumped and whirled. A shadowed figure was standing backlit against the now clean windows. With the sunlight streaming in from behind, I could see no more than a broad-shouldered silhouette, looming menacingly. It took a step forward.

The alarm was whooping mindlessly, and a jolt of pure terror ran through me. The workmen had gone and my intruder had come back. He had gotten in despite the alarm and now was coming for me, to demand whatever it was he was searching for . . . I screamed and started to swing the broom, but it caught on the rafter and I went down hard.

The alarm cut off abruptly.

Trying to suppress his laughter, Tom Moneghan leaned down and extended a hand, helping me to my feet.

"What are you doing up here?" I demanded irritably.

"Narrowly avoiding getting brained by brooms, it seems. And a good thing, too; that was winding up into one hell of a swing. Are you okay?"

I nodded and swiped an arm across my face. It came back streaked with sweat and dust. I grimaced.

"Actually," he added, "I came up to warn you they were going to test the alarm, but then got distracted by the sight of you fighting with that cobweb. Sorry. I hope I didn't scare you too badly."

"Not at all," I lied.

He reached out almost idly and plucked a tangle of cobweb from my hair.

Great. "Well, now that you're here, why not make yourself useful?" I scooped up the broom and thrust it toward him with a certain malice.

With Tom's greater reach, we had the rafters cleared in no time. And then with a clomp of boots on the stairs, the foreman came up and poked his head through the attic door. "All done," he said. "We just need the young lady to set the codes." And he cocked his head at me in bemusement, taking in my dusty, cobwebbed appearance.

Tom was grinning broadly. I shot him a freezing look, reflecting that my private farce had suddenly become a lot more public, then gathered up the shreds of my dignity and stepped around both him and the foreman, leading the way downstairs.

WHEN I HAD PERFORMED all of my alarm-related duties to the foreman's satisfaction, the team of workers departed, followed shortly thereafter by Tom, who indeed had managed to intercept the bill without my being aware of it. As he left, he said, "I'll call you. After you've showered." When I scowled at him, he reached out a finger and ran it along my cheek, then held it out for inspection.

It was black with dirt.

"Ah," I said. "Right."

He got into his truck and started up the engine. As he drove away, I remembered something. "You've still got my keys!" I yelled. "They're at your house." But he was already gone.

What the hell; I would figure it out later. I went back into the house and shut the door, then rather self-consciously activated the alarm. I made my way into the bathroom, which, along with my bedroom, Tom also seemed to have cleaned while I was upstairs. The bedroom floor was free of clutter, the furniture righted, the bulb replaced in the lamp. In the bathroom, my cosmetics were restored to almost their original positions. *Damn*, I thought again. *Why can't I have something like this?* Then I caught a glimpse of myself in the bathroom mirror and had to laugh. There was my answer right there.

My hair had gone prematurely white with cobwebs, and my cheeks were corpse-grey I couldn't remember what color my shirt had been originally, but it was now a similar hue. With a little sputter of laughter, I stripped off my filthy clothes and climbed into the shower, then lathered up until the water ran clear.

After my shower and feeling more confident, I decided that a soothing bask in the sun was just what I needed to finish unwinding. So I changed into my bathing suit, grabbed a towel, and threw open the French doors.

The alarm went off with a deafening whoop. Cursing, I dropped the towel and ran back across the room, punching my code into the keypad. The whooping stuttered, then blissfully went silent. Instead, the phone began to ring.

"No," I explained sheepishly to the alarm company. "I'm sorry. I was my fault. I set it off by mistake. No, really, I'm fine. Oh, right; sorry. Cecil Hargrave. Cecilia, I mean. Yes. My code word? Oh; selkie." I felt a bit foolish; it had been Tom's idea.

That settled, I retrieved my towel and took up position on the slabbed rocks along the shore. The tide was neither low nor high. It was still too early to feed Ragnarok (who would undoubtedly be annoyed at his abandonment yesterday, anyway), and Ronan wouldn't be back from work yet, so I laid out my towel and stretched out on my back on the warm rock, feeling rather like a seal myself in my functional brown one-piece. Maybe it was time to get a sexier suit, but the sun was warm and I felt too lazy to deal with it now. I closed my eyes instead and distracted myself with nebulous thoughts of Tom, which soon drifted into nebulous thoughts, and then into not much of anything at all.

How long I lay there I don't know, but I was brought back to reality by a wet nudging against my side. I was too tired to startle, and perhaps that was my salvation. I muttered something and struggled to open my eyes, wondering if it was Tom, back with my keys.

The nudging grew more insistent, and this time was accompanied by an imperious bark. A bark I knew only too well.

My eyes flew open and I raised my head. Ragnarok looked up from where he was butting his nose against my side and regarded me out of liquid black eyes.

For an instant I lay there, poised in indecision, wanting to touch him but not wanting to scare him. My heart was pounding. I couldn't bear for a return to my private farce; not here, not now. Ever so slowly I raised up on one elbow and watched the tension ripple through him.

"Sweetie," I said, trying to keep my voice low and even. "You came up!" But even I could hear the excitement in my voice.

The seal cocked his dappled grey head, the lightning bolt marking more prominent than ever between his eyes.

Again, with infinite caution, I stretched out my free hand. The moment froze, drew out; Ragnarok was strung as tight as a bow. Then he hunched his neck and butted his head into my palm.

Releasing the breath I hadn't realized I was holding, I ran my hand along his back. His fur was sleek and damp, his body hard with muscle. He wriggled slightly, then butted me again, apparently deciding it was safe to play. I ran my hands over his head, his sides, his flippers while he snuffled curiously at my neck, my belly, between my breasts.

"Ragnarok," I exclaimed. "Behave!"

He looked up, grinned, barked, and butted me in the chest.

"You want fish? Is that it?" I rose slowly, tentatively. "Don't go away, okay?"

He looked up at me quizzically.

"Don't go away," I ordered more firmly. "I'll be right back." And darted for the shed.

I needn't have worried. When it came to fish, Ragnarok was single-minded. Not only hadn't he moved when I returned with the bucket, he had humped up farther onto shore and had, in fact, appropriated my towel. He had a corner of it in his mouth and was chewing it idly.

"Ragnarok!" He looked up, the corner of the towel falling forgotten from his mouth; it slapped damply against the rock. "Wouldn't this be better?"

He humped further up my towel and barked again, his eyes alight. No longer shy, he seemed intent on diving nose-first into the bucket. On shore, he was larger than I had expected, almost five feet in length and probably upward of a hundred pounds of solid muscle. I had a feeling he might knock me flat in his enthusiasm. So instead I fished a mackerel out by its tail and held it out. He took it straight from my fingers without a qualm, his sharp teeth flashing. And then he barked for another.

He was far less graceful on land than in the water. His front flippers scrabbled for purchase on the rock, his back ones trailing uselessly behind. He humped his body along the ledge like an oversized slug. But he was lovely. His dappled fur shone silver-grey in the sun, and his pert, doglike face and dark liquid eyes lent him a charming piquancy.

I could see why Allegra had fallen head over ears in love.

I fed him more fish and petted him in between, getting him used to my touch, but I wasn't sure even that precaution was necessary. Ragnarok seemed eager for affection.

"Good lord! You actually got him out."

The voice startled us both; I hadn't been aware anyone was near. Yet there was Tom, freshly showered and dressed in new clothes, my bag of dirty ones slung over his shoulder. His hair was still damp, his dark eyes grinning, and I couldn't help feeling there was an odd kinship between him and the seal.

But maybe it was simply that they were both healthy male animals with lean, well-muscled bodies and the sea in their blood.

Ragnarok seemed equally flustered by his presence, but perhaps for different reasons. He stiffened and inched backwards, seeming torn between flight and fish.

"Oh, no, you devil," Tom said, in a low, sexy, liquid voice that almost took my knees out from under me. "You know me perfectly well, so no playing games. Your little act doesn't fool me for a moment."

Ragnarok stopped and cocked his head, considering.

"Besides, who do you think brings the fish?" Tom added. He reached down into my bucket and pulled one out. "Do you mind?"

I shook my head.

He waved the fish tantalizingly before the seal, then extended it. Ragnarok snatched it from his fingers, chewing contentedly.

Tom straightened and took the opportunity to say: "Sorry to barge in, but I figured you might be needing these." He fished my keys out of his pocket and dangled them before me, much as he had dangled the fish before Ragnarok, his dark eyes dancing.

So, he had heard me, after all. Because there was no other way he would have known that my keys were in the pocket of my jeans, which in turn were in the bag with all my other dirty clothes.

He wiggled the keys, and the sun flashed silver off the metal.

Ragnarok looked up, interested.

"No, not for you. For your mom," Tom told him, then smiled at me, tossing me the keys. I caught them with a jingle.

"I've set off the alarm by mistake once already," I admitted, slipping them under my bathing suit through one leg hole. Tom stared, seeming fascinated by the bump they made against my hip, then looked up and laughed.

"I expect you'll do that several more times before you're used to it," he said. "I certainly did. Just don't get frustrated and keep it off entirely. Promise?"

"I promise."

Ragnarok barked, humped his body back, then plowed into Tom's leg with more force than he had used for me.

"Someone's jealous," Tom said. He handed my bag of clothing back to me. I transferred the keys into it, then tossed the whole thing high up on the lawn. Tom, meanwhile, had gone down on one knee and was scrubbing both hands along Ragnarok's back as one would do to a large dog. The seal's mouth was stretched wide with delight, and he wriggled beneath Tom's touch.

Lucky bastard. I gave him another fish, which he gulped down eagerly.

We alternated fish, feeding Ragnarok until the mackerel were gone and the seal stretched out on my towel, replete.

Tom sat back on his heels and glanced over at me. "You've been supplanted," he said.

I smiled. "He does take advantage, doesn't he? A lawn chair will do me just as well. And fortunately, that wasn't one of my better towels." Because Ragnarok was chewing it again, his eyes half-lidded.

"Make yourself at home," I told him, half facetiously.

His eyes opened wide enough to peer at me lazily, then he shut them dismissively.

"Apparently it's basking time," Tom said.

"Right; then I'm getting a lounger. Can I get you one as well?"

Tom glanced between me and the seal for a moment, then said, "Sure, why not?" with the air of a man coming to a major decision. I wasn't sure if the seal or I had swung it, but I suspected it was the former.

We fetched two loungers from the back deck and stretched out, me in my bathing suit and Tom in his jeans and T-shirt. The sun was meltingly warm, and we sat in somnolent silence for a while, listening to the lap of the waves against the shore. Every so often, a gust of wind off the sea would blow over us: a cool, silken caress against my bare skin. Like Ragnarok, my eyes drifted shut.

I wasn't quite asleep or quite awake, hovering in that numinous realm between dream and thought. Once, I sensed a rustle of movement off to my side and turned to see if Tom had gone, but instead I discovered that he had simply stripped of his shirt and shoes and was lying full-length on the lounger, a smooth curve of chest rising out of one end of his jeans, his bare feet extending out the other. His eyes were closed, and his nose rose in smooth profile. His hair was mostly dried and looked so soft I wondered what if would feel like to touch.

A jolt of panic went through me as my mind again tossed up: *Thomas Moreland*. But the sweep of chest distracted me, bronzed the same deep shade as his arms. I could picture

him on the boat, shirtless, muscles shifting as he bent and
hauled out laden traps then tossed them in again, empty. His
skin stretched taut over a form as lean and powerful as Ragnarok's. There was no wasted flesh on the swell of pectorals,
the slightly concave belly that descended into his jeans.
There was dark hair on his forearms; little above. And on his
chest, only a dusting around each nipple, and a dark line that
descended into regions I didn't want to think too hard about.

Flushing, I turned away lest he catch me staring, and was
in time to see the tail end of a flipper sliding into the water as
Ragnarok vanished. Then the phone began ringing, slicing
through the silence with an almost surgical brutality.

I ran for it, my bare feet slapping against the boards of the
deck. It was Abby. "Right," she said, cheerfully. "The shop
is closed and I'm coming over for dinner. What supplies do
you want me to bring?"

26

BY THE TIME ABBY and I had figured out our menu, Tom was up and dressed. He had carried both loungers back onto the deck and had followed that with my bag, which was now resting against the side of the house, near the margin of the French doors.

"Thank you," he said, and surprised me by leaning over to drop a light kiss my cheek. "I needed that."

"You're welcome," I said.

I didn't know what to do from there. Fortunately, he took over. "So who was that on the phone?"

"Abby. She's coming for dinner."

"Good," he said. "And I expect she won't be your only call."

He was right. Immediately after he left, the phone rang again. It was Richard. "I heard there was a break-in," he said. "Are you all right?"

"Yes. Tom helped out." I gave him a brief précis of the

night's events. He seemed less than delighted to hear of Tom's involvement, but happy to hear that I had survived unscathed.

"Shall I do a story?" he said. "Try to flush the villain out of hiding?"

"I doubt that is necessary. But thank you. However," I could hear the excitement rising in my voice. "If you were serious about doing that story on Ragnarok . . ."

"Of course. Contrary to appearances, I am not using your seal to get at you. What happened?"

"He came up on shore! So if you want pictures for your story, I can probably guarantee you a good one."

"Really." There was a studied tone in his voice that told me he had his professional hat on. "Shall I come around with a photographer on Friday?"

"That sounds perfect."

"And then," his voice softened and he became Richard again, "I can take you out for dinner afterward, in celebration."

I hesitated only slightly. "That sounds great as well. Friday it is."

"And are you sure you'll be all right for tonight?" he added. "I mean, you don't want company or anything?"

I almost laughed. "No, I'll be fine. Abby's coming over."

"Oh." He sounded glum, and this time I did laugh.

"Thanks, though, Richard; I do appreciate the offer."

"Right," he said, and hung up shortly thereafter.

"So, HOW FAST DID Richard volunteer to come look after you?" Abby asked later that night as we sat at dinner, looking out over the lawn and the water though the curve of the bay window. Dusk was falling, sketching violet shadows between the blades of grass and the limbs of the trees; an electric streak of salmon on the horizon, out beyond the scattered islands, was all that remained of the sun. I was abruptly glad of her company, not realizing until this point how little I had wanted to sit around my house by myself, watching the corners fill up with darkness.

But her cheerful practicality seemed to banish all such fears, and I smiled in response to her words. "I don't think you are his most favorite person right now, if that's what you mean."

"Ah, well." She smiled faintly. And then her face went abruptly serious.

I paused with a forkful of food to my mouth, my experimental variant of crabcakes forgotten. "What is it, Abby?"

She sighed deeply and pushed the zucchini on her plate around a bit before replying. "This is probably not the best night to tell you," she said, "but I figured you'd hear it soon enough anyway, and it is probably better that it come from me."

"What?" I said again, genuinely worried now.

"That guy," she said slowly, "the one who was found breaking into a house over in Brooklin?"

"The one they thought was Allegra's killer?"

She nodded tersely.

"What about him?"

"The trial just ended today. He was acquitted of the murder."

"You mean there wasn't enough evidence?"

Abby shook her head, seeming uncertain how to continue. Then she took a deep breath and jumped in; her voice, I noticed, seemed terse and strained. "On the contrary, there was evidence aplenty. He was definitively proved to be breaking into another house that night, which gives him an airtight alibi for Allegra's. So there's no way he could have been anywhere near here."

In the somewhat tense silence that followed this announcement, the lights suddenly flooded across my lawn as the motion detectors tripped, washing across deck and grass in harsh and brilliant white, casting the trunks of the trees into stark negative. Abby actually shrieked, but I was cast into frozen silence, unable to move, unable to even utter a sound, as the dark shape creeping across my back lawn was revealed.

And then, as my brain caught up with reality, I went sodden with relief. A somewhat hysterical giggle trickled past my lips, and Abby cursed, because the deer looked even more startled than both of us, its neck a taut curve of suspended motion, eyes wide, one hoof still upraised. Then it fled for the far woods, tail raised behind it like a white flag of surrender, and in five bounds was gone.

"Damn it!" Abby exclaimed, torn between annoyance and laughter.

"Yeah, welcome to my personal farce," I told her. "Sorry about that. The lights should go out in a bit. So Allegra's case remains open?"

"Or officially cold. I'm sorry, Cecil."

I didn't answer. I had never bought the burglary theory, anyway. It seemed a little too pat, too convenient, for a woman whose life had contained so many mysteries. If nothing else, last night had convinced me that whatever Allegra had died for was far from over.

"Are you all right, Cecil?" Abby asked after a bit.

Surprisingly enough, I was. And maybe it was only the touch of a wet head against my side that afternoon that had done it, but I no longer wanted to flee to safe anonymity in New York. I wanted to stay here and make my stand against whatever powers wanted to drive me away. I wanted to open my restaurant. I wanted to maintain the friendships that had suddenly begun to be so vital to my existence. I wanted to be part of something again—and if that involved eventually uncovering the last mystery behind Allegra's death, so much the better.

Seeing my expression, Abby said, "Does this mean I should start interviewing for a replacement helper at the store?"

I peered over at her. "I'm not leaving, you know."

"I know." Her smile was wide and proud. "I just figured you might have other things on your mind than retail in the future. Am I right?"

"You might be. Would you mind?"

"Nothing would make me happier. Not because it means I get to buy you out, or anything," she added hastily, "but because . . . Oh, hell, Cecil, you've become a better friend than I expected. And you belong here; we both know that. Let's just let the future sort itself out as it will. I trust you to make the right decision—for both of us."

I felt my eyes prickle with tears, and impulsively I got up from the table and went around to hug her. She returned my embrace warmly, and I found myself wondering if this was what frostbite victims must feel, this achingly sweet pain of feeling returning as life and hope stole back.

"Abby, you are . . ." I fumbled impotently for words to express the sensations that flooded me. "Your friendship, your support . . . I am . . ." *Humbled. Honored. Awestruck.*

She punched me on one shoulder. "Stop it," she said, "or you'll make *me* cry." And, indeed, her eyes were somewhat suspiciously damp. "Now, sit down and let me eat, because someone needs to do justice to these crab cakes of yours. What did you put in them?"

The conversation flowed back into more mundane topics, but the resolution didn't evaporate. The following morning, Abby placed the Help Wanted ad in the local papers and I started calling realtors, checking out the available properties. Joanna, who had called slightly after Richard to check up on me, now offered her company. "After all," she said, when I phoned her Tuesday morning for pointers, "I've had some experience with this."

So for the next few evenings after work, Joanna and I went from storefront to house to storefront, searching. We debated the merits of in town versus out, space versus accessibility. But in the end, everyone seemed to be right. The place on Bay Street was the nicest, and the best suited to my purposes. It would be only a small restaurant—especially since I would need space for the kitchen at the back—but that felt right for a novice venture. I could probably only seat about forty people at a time, but since I was planning on doing most of the cooking myself, that would probably be the most I could handle. And, despite its small size, it was a cozy space. I could almost envision the placement of the tables, the intimate lighting, the soft colors on the walls, Martha's art. I would have to contact the potter about the dishes, and I wondered if there was a maker of local flatware.

I had also discovered, in the course of my conversations with realtors, that one of the gallery owners on Main Street was thinking of selling, and that the photo shop was thinking of taking over that space and expanding, leaving his space next to The Gull open. Ideas began to escalate—none of which I was quite ready to share with Abby, but still . . . She trusted me, and that made all the difference in the world.

I was more excited than I could have imagined.

I did, however, have one weird experience with one of the realtors. Cynically, I was getting used to the gasps and cries of "Allegra!" when people met me. But after I had disabused this particular realtor of her illusions, she added, "So, did your aunt ever find the house she was looking for?"

I must have been staring at her blankly, because Joanna said sharply, "What house?"

The realtor looked somewhat nonplussed as she answered.

"Allegra called me sometime in late November, asking if I had a property available on the island. When I asked if she was planning on selling her own house she said no; that she wanted to buy a place for her niece. Which, now that I think of it, must have meant you—though it's funny she didn't ask me about business properties at the time."

I was more baffled than ever. Had Allegra been planning to invite me up all along? Was I really destined to open this restaurant, one way or another?

Joanna was looking at me curiously as well, but I just shook my head.

"Well, anyway," the realtor said when I didn't answer, "I never was able to find anything to suit her, and since I didn't hear any more from her afterward, I assumed that she either found something through another company or made alternate plans. Are you sure you didn't know about any of this?"

"Quite sure."

"How strange." But she seemed philosophical; perhaps it was something she saw all too frequently in her business. Yet as much as I tried to explain it to myself over the next few days, I couldn't find an explanation that covered all the facts. Allegra wouldn't just rent me a house without telling me about it, and while she might have lied about me, I couldn't think what else she would have used the place for.

WHEN RICHARD PHONED LATE Wednesday night, I tried to figure a subtle way of asking if he knew anything about Allegra's intentions with regard to me, but he seemed clueless. As did Abby and Joanna, when I posed the question more directly.

I didn't feel capable of bringing up the issue with Tom.

As for Ronan, we had other issues entirely to discuss. I had not seen him once in the five days since he had fled my party, and it must have seemed as if I were deliberately avoiding him. In truth, I was just getting home to late to be of use to anyone, but I was determined to set the record straight. So on Thursday after work, I stopped by the garage, but he had already gone home for the evening. I then drove past the garish blue house he claimed was his, but there was no car in the drive, and no lights on inside. He must have been out somewhere, but where I couldn't think. I suddenly realized that I had never really thought of Ronan having a life outside the garage and my back porch, and I suddenly wondered what he did when he wasn't working or spending time with me.

But I never did have a chance to ask him, because when he materialized around my shore later that evening, I was so relieved to see him that all thoughts of extracurricular activities went straight out of my head. Especially since he looked oddly subdued as he rounded the point. No, worse: glum and dispirited. His step lacked its usual bounce, his eyes their usual light; even his dark hair seemed somehow lank and dull. I felt a surge of guilt fill me.

"Ronan," I exclaimed, when he was in hailing distance. "I am so sorry! I never meant for you to feel outcast, and I only wish there had been a chance to come after you, only . . ."

His face lit up fractionally and he paused, one foot on my back stairs. It was later than he usually appeared, and already the sun was beginning to sink, washing the sky a subtle pink. And backlit against the salmon clouds, he appeared almost magical, like a figure straight out of legend. A rush of happiness filled me at the sight. So why, then, did I seem to keep forgetting he was around when he wasn't immediately present?

"You would have come for me?" he asked, his rolling voice oddly plaintive.

"I *wanted* to come for you," I insisted, "but I couldn't exactly leave my own party. Not right then, when everyone was . . . But that's not important. What *is* important is that you never feel inferior around my friends. These people don't care how you look or how you dress, not at the heart of it. What matters is that you are my friend. And I wanted you to get to know more people on this island, so you would still have friends when I went away. Only . . ."

He didn't let me finish. Instead, his face contorted in a sudden panic. "You're going *away*?" It almost came out as a yip.

"No, that's what I wanted to tell you," I said, laying a brief had on his arm. As usual, the contact was electric, as if he carried a faint current under his skin, and I concentrated on breathing for several seconds. "I made a decision the other night. I'm staying on Seal Island. I'm opening a restaurant."

But far from lauding my ambitions, Ronan seemed fixated on my words from before. "You were going to leave?"

"This was only supposed to be a vacation for me," I said. "I was planning to leave in September."

"But you're not any more?" he said, his voice still containing sharp slivers of anxiety.

"No, I'm not. Honestly, Ronan. It's . . . I don't know. Like a revelation. Like fate. Like I was always meant to be here."

"Yes," he almost breathed, and smiled.

"And I swear you'll find other friends than me," I continued. "You'll be a part of this community before you know it." But I had a feeling he was no longer listening to me.

There was a moment of silence as he stared down at his feet, resting on the slowly silvering wood of my stairs, and then he looked back up at me again and his entire face was transformed. His eyes had regained their liquid sparkle, his mouth its mobility, and even his hair seemed to have acquired an added shine and bounce. His mouth gaped wide in a grin.

"Do you have any salmon dip?" he said.

27

IT CONTINUED TO BE a busy week. The police called on Thursday to say that they had no leads on the case. Save for substituting mine for Allegra's, they had found the same set of fingerprints at my place as they had the last time, and none of them showed up in any databases. And while they tried to out a more politic spin on it, I got the message clearly. They were a small department, with limited resources, and besides which nothing had been stolen and no one had been injured. Case closed.

I wondered why it didn't bother me more.

Richard came by with his photographer on Friday, and the photo shoot with Ragnarok went far better than I had expected. I admit that I was a bit nervous about seeing Richard, though, no longer certain what I thought about him in the light of the wholesale changes overtaking my life, and I was glad the photographer was around to mitigate things.

The photographer was older than Richard—in his mid-forties, I suspected—and was an obvious ex-hippie by the name of Jeff. He had long, sandy-brown hair and a beard, sported Birkenstocks and cargo pants, and carried easily a thousand dollars of camera equipment around his neck. He seemed pleased when Ragnarok, after a tiny bit of persuasion involving (of course) fish, humped up onto shore and began mugging for the camera like a true professional.

In fact, Jeff had more problems posing me than he did the seal. "Relax!" became his mantra for the afternoon, as he poked and prodded at my stiff limbs.

Richard seemed equally enchanted by Ragnarok's sudden transformation from elusive creature to seasoned performer, but he didn't let it distract him from his duties. In work mode, he was a consummate professional, asking intelligent questions that left me all too aware of the vast gaps in my knowledge about seals. This had two effects. First, it made me resolve to study up on seal lore as soon as possible. Second, it made me see Richard in a completely different light. All the times he had talked about his work, he had jokingly deprecated himself as an editor fit only for small-time papers, but even I could tell he was much more. The job competition must have been fierce in his field, the plum assignments too few and far between, but it still must have been soul-killing that he had never found a place where he could truly shine.

I think the knowledge that he could have been so much greater, and yet still managed to carve out a decent life for himself where he was, made me respect him all the more. Some men would have turned bitter; Richard had just found a way to accept it. And in the course of this revelation, I found that I had stopped nervously avoiding his gaze and was instead studying him openly, like some creature I had only just discovered. And for the first time, I was able to be objective.

Richard was a handsome man, and nice, and good, but while I respected him for accepting what he had, I also found a part of myself feeling vaguely scornful that he had never pushed hard enough for his dream. I was about to start a restaurant—a prospect that scared and excited me all at once. It could be a colossal mistake and I could fail miserably, but at least I was risking something. And it startled me, how good it felt *not* to accept the easy answer, the safe way out. Change terrified me, but this time I was embracing my fear, trying to rise above it. Like Tom, I was trying to make more of myself than my little island allowed me.

But more than that, it was the fact that I was staying on Seal Island that really changed everything. In the past, with New York as my safety valve, if things went too fast, got too intense, I could always retreat to my former life; it gave me an easy out. But now that that path was closed to me, that Seal Island would encompass of all my days, I had to be more honest with myself. And the fact that I had even wanted an out with Richard was telling. I had, I realized, spent the early part of the summer trying to convince myself that my reluctance to get involved with him had less to do with Richard than with me: with my fear of commitments in general. But now my eyes were open. It wasn't commitments I was scared of. Well, okay, be honest; they still scared me senseless. But I had proved myself capable of embracing them when they felt right. And Richard . . .

Richard had never felt completely right. But because he was interested and available, I had tried to convince myself that something was better than nothing. Only it wasn't. The wrong something was infinitely worse than the right nothing, and the truth of the matter was that I didn't love Richard. I liked and respected him, but the magic—whatever indefinable spark there was that lifted a relationship from the mundane into the transcendent—was missing. Richard didn't send shivers through me like Tom; he didn't pull me out of myself and into a timeless realm like Ronan. He was a lovely man who made me feel warm and comfortable inside, whose company I valued and whose friendship I craved, but that was all. And somehow I owed him the truth.

But how?

These thoughts ran like a looped tape at the back of my mind until my panic began returning, spiked by the sight of Jeff finally packing away his equipment. Ragnarok, full of fish, was bottling in the water just off shore, looking pitiful—in the vain hope that someone would feed him some more.

"Cecil?" Richard prompted. "You were a million miles away. Anything you want to add before Jeff leaves?"

"No. I . . ." My mind was a blank. "Just show me the article before you run it, in case I think of anything I want to add at the last moment."

"But of course," he said, with convincing horror, as if such a worry should never have crossed my mind.

Jeff shook my hand and drove away in a very old, and very battered, VW van—proving that it was all too easy to judge people solely on their appearances. Especially when Richard told me that Jeff had been a very successful bonds-trader in New York before he had packed it all in.

I stared after the retreating VW with renewed respect.

Talk of Jeff eased our awkwardness for a while. Then, in a moment of silence, I became aware that I was utterly alone with Richard on my shoreline; even Ragnarok had departed. And I flushed, wondering how on earth I was going to tell him there would never be anything between us but friendship.

I waffled my way around the issue, but it was Richard himself who saved me, saying, "This is not working out between us, is it?"

I looked up, startled. Instead of gazing at me with his

usual hopeful expression, Richard's eyes were full of a sort of resigned acceptance. It was enough to make me gather up the shards of my courage and say, "No. I'm sorry." I took a deep breath and kept going, not wanting to sound condescending but not knowing how else to put it but bluntly. "You're a wonderful guy, Richard—and a damn fine interviewer—but . . ."

His gaze sharpened. "It's Tom, isn't it?"

I shook my head. "No. Tom and I are just friends." That was true, wasn't it? "It's not anything in particular, Richard; it's just me." The usual excuses cluttered up my head: *I'm not ready; I'm going through a big change right now; I can't handle anything else.* And they were all true, in a way, but they were also all lies. Worse, they offered him hope for the future, and that was the one thing I couldn't do; it wasn't fair to either of us. "You deserve the best, Richard," I told him honestly. "Far better than me. And I wish I could fall in love with you; it would probably be the best thing in the world for me. But I do care a great deal about you, and value you as a friend. And I am not just saying that. *Can* we still be friends, despite everything? Because that would mean a lot to me."

He regarded me in silence for a moment, as if weighing my sincerity, then nodded. In truth, I had a feeling he was a little relieved himself. Suddenly, impulsive, I took his hand, and blurted, "Richard, if it makes any difference . . . I don't think Abby was ever quite as relaxed about this relationship as she let on. I think seeing you with someone else . . . Well, if any of that feeling still remains, she might not be so quick to reject you this time."

He looked down at my hand held in his, and a faint smile twitched his lips. "You think?"

"Well, it's only a suspicion, but . . ." I found myself grinning. "Yeah, I do. Just . . . Don't push her. Abby's . . . Well, you know."

"That I do," he said, somewhat ruefully. He released my hand. I was about to turn away when he said, "Cecil. . . ."

"What?"

"Just for the record, I don't think Tom's as indifferent as he paints himself, either."

The world seemed to hang suspended for a moment, then my heart thudded into painful motion once again. "No, I think he made himself rather clear on that point," I said tightly.

There was another moment of silence, then I felt Richard's finger under my chin, raising my head up. I stared up, startled, into his eyes, which danced with a sudden mischief.

"Come on, Cecil. What do you say we both take a chance?"

"But . . . I . . ." *What if it all goes horribly wrong?* I wanted to say.

"I dare you," he added.

"That's blackmail!" I exclaimed.

"Actually, it's called life," he countered reasonably. "You take chances. You and I took a chance. It didn't work. But that doesn't mean I still can't buy you dinner."

"What?"

"Tonight, as promised. I owe you."

"For what?"

"Giving me a story, of course," he said with a grin.

I smiled back. "Very well. But here's a trade I will make you. A year from now, I'll treat you to dinner at *my* restaurant. Deal?"

"Deal," he said. "I can't wait."

Oddly enough, neither could I.

THREE DAYS LATER, I took the big plunge and made an offer on the Bay Street storefront. I had gone to see Harry Cameron the first thing Monday, and he had helped me structure my offer based on my severance and Allegra's legacy, and advised me on small business loans. He was enormously helpful, although his first question was: "Does this mean you're planning to sell The Gull to Abby, then?"

Again I wished they weren't at odds, but for once I saw the wisdom of his objections. "No, not yet," I assured him. "I have no idea if I'm going to be able to make a go of this, so there's no point throwing away a guaranteed source of income. I've explained this to Abby, and she understands."

In fact, Abby had said, "I still don't know if I'm going to have to move within the year or not, so . . . Yeah, let's just see how it goes. Remember, I already told you I trust you. And in the meantime, I think I have a good lead on some help for the store. I'd like you to meet her tomorrow."

Which I did. Caitlyn was twenty-four and, like Abby, a single mother. Her recent divorce had left her without means, and I think Abby saw herself in Allegra's role, ministering to the next generation. For though Caitlyn lacked experience, she had a drive and determination we thought might suit us. When we offered her the job, she hugged us both with tears in her eyes and said, "You won't regret this, I promise."

I knew we wouldn't. Just as Allegra had with Abby eleven years earlier, we had won her loyalty.

After that, I went back to Harry's, and together we went over to the bank to begin the paperwork for the mortgage. Something was quivering inside me as we walked through the bank doors, and I was terrified all over again that I was making the biggest mistake of my life. Sure, my friends liked my cooking, but what right had I going up against the professionals with what had merely been a hobby? Who was I kidding?

But Harry's steady hand on my elbow was bracing, and at least if I failed, it would be in a small pond I could always slink back to New York in a year or two with my tail between my legs and lick my wounds in some small box of an apartment, miles from the beauty of the sea and its creatures.

Or I could stay and damn well *make* it work, even if it took the last bit of energy I had!

I straightened my spine and marched into the bank manager's office with Harry at my side.

I had always been terrified at the idea of purchasing something this large and permanent, but the whole process went so smoothly that I began to wonder, as I had said to Ronan, if it hadn't been destined, after all. Maybe Allegra was watching from beyond the grave, smoothing my way. Maybe she had intended this all along.

Or maybe, in small towns, things simply weren't filled with the litigious cantankerousness of larger cities.

In any case, the only complication we encountered wasn't even a true complication at all, but just another odd mystery surrounding Allegra's life. We were checking my bank balances to make sure that everything added up when we discovered a two hundred dollar deficit in the account. I hadn't been paying all that much attention to details in the past few weeks, which was why I had missed it. But under the intent scrutiny of a mortgage review, it came easily to light. Two hundred dollars that should have been in my account were missing. Not a vast sum, but quite definitely gone.

We traced the mystery back, the bank manager tapping industriously at the keys of his computer. "I don't understand," he muttered. "It seems to be an electronic transfer, but how it remained authorized when I transferred Allegra's accounts over to you . . ." He tapped some more. "Well, it's definitely pulling electronically, and automatically, every month. The money is going into an account at First Fidelity Bank in Ellsworth. Were you aware that your aunt had an auxiliary account?"

Both Harry and I shook our heads.

"Hmm." More tapping. "I'll check into it, but I suspect that what happened was, when you authorized me to transfer any electronic monthly withdrawals such as power and phone from the old account to the new, this one just slipped along. And I am sorry. I'll get back to you as soon as I've checked it out thoroughly."

I told Tom of the mystery when he came over Saturday night, bearing lobsters and champagne to celebrate my mortgage being approved, and he seemed as baffled as Harry.

"That *is* bizarre," he said, his brows pinched in a frown. "Did you determine what it was?"

"Yes. Allegra had set up an alternate account. She opened it in October, and had been feeding two hundred a month into it ever since, completely automatically. Of course that still doesn't explain the almost eighty thousand she pulled out over the winter, which wasn't in that account, either. But what's really odd is that the account wasn't just sitting there. It had an ATM card attached to it, and there have been regular withdrawals. Not in any set pattern, either, but exactly in the way you'd expect if someone had been living off it."

"And did these withdrawals stop with Allegra's death?" Tom asked, hitting upon the very question that had so stumped the bank manager and me.

"No," I said. "That's the oddest part. The withdrawals went on right past her death; the last was two days ago. And, no, I haven't found the card," I added, to forestall his next question.

"So what did you do?"

"Froze the account, of course. Reclaimed the money and stopped the withdrawals."

Tom raised an eyebrow. "Well, maybe this will draw our mystery mooch out of the woodwork."

"Yes, that was our hope, as well," I said. "But . . ."

"What?"

"Nothing. It's just odd," I said. "So many mysteries."

"Well, you'll have to let me know what happens."

"I will." I stared down into my champagne glass for a moment, then took a sip. An awkward silence descended as the lobsters boiled merrily on the stove, but I suddenly couldn't think of a single thing to say. In part because I was intensely aware of Tom's presence across the table, and in part because Richard's words kept haunting me. *I don't think Tom's as indifferent as he paints himself*. And: *It's called life. You take chances.*

I suddenly found myself wanting to take a chance in a way I never had before, but the habits of a lifetime die hard. The space seemed unbridgeable, as did this new tension sizzling between us. So I let the old habits take over and pretended that nothing was happening, and after a while I almost came to believe it. We made it through lobsters and salad, and berries and ice cream, in almost our normal fashion.

In many ways, I had all but forgotten that he was Thomas Moreland, and he seemed to have almost forgotten that I was a fan. To me, he was just Tom Moneghan—with all the contradictions that implied. An unpretentious man who genuinely relished the simple pleasures, yet who nonetheless lived in a comparative mansion, and gifted me with expensive bottles of Dom Perignon as casually as if it were Frexinet. And I was comfortable with him—so comfortable that at the end of the meal, I found myself curling casually up on the sofa next to him, twin glasses of brandy in our hands as we watched the moon rise over the water.

Tom alone seemed unafraid of the left-hand couch, with its underlying legacy of death, so we sat there, side by side, a companionable silence between us. I had flung open all three sets of French doors to the warm evening breeze. There was enough of a wind that the mosquitoes weren't a bother, and the moonlight streaked a silver path across the bay. It was a lovely evening, filled with perfume of salt and pine, and something else indefinably Maine. Replete with champagne and lobster, I found myself leaning into Tom's shoulder as inevitably as breathing.

That was the moment when everything changed, when the peaceful air became fraught with tension again, so thick and heady I could almost taste it. His head half-turned, and in the dim light of the room, he stared down at me with eyes as dark and fathomless as the ocean. Time seemed to slow, and I think I stopped breathing.

It's called life. You take chances, Richard's phantom voice whispered in my ear.

And so I did. I put down my brandy glass and I kissed Thomas Moreland.

Tom Moneghan.

Whatever. What did it matter? His face was so close to my own, I barely needed to bridge any distance at all. His mouth was warm and soft, still tasting faintly of lobster and brandy, then hard and demanding, and I still couldn't catch my breath. And then his hands came to my shoulders, gripped . . . and pushed me away, hard.

I fell back against the couch, blinking, disoriented.

Tom's eyes were shuttered again, inscrutable. He scrubbed a hand across his face, over his hair as he leaped to his feet.

"No," he said, his voice so rough as to be almost a stranger's. "Cecil, I . . . This isn't right. It's . . . No."

"No?" I managed, my own voice a croak. "No what?"

"Just no," he said. He seemed to be back in control of himself; his voice had a hard, angry edge. "We're friends, Cecil. That's all we can be. That's all we *are*, really. You're just letting your feelings about Thomas Moreland blind you. He's the one you want, and I'm not him. I'm not even who you think I am."

"No," I protested, still feeling numb. "I'm not. I . . ."

"You're young, Cecil," he said harshly. "What do you know of the world? This can't happen again. This *won't* happen again. I don't want it to happen again." He was pacing the rug, but here he turned to me. "Do you understand?"

I nodded woodenly.

"I'm sorry. I don't mean to hurt you. It's just that I . . . I should leave. I'm sorry."

And he did, just like that, vanishing out the open French doors and down the side steps of my deck.

I sat there in the suddenly cold breeze off the water, expecting him to return, but instead I only heard the angry roar of his truck engine as it started up, saw the sweep of headlights across my front window, and then he was gone. And I sat there, shivering as if someone had dumped a load of ice water over my head, staring down at the damp shards of Tom's brandy glass, which lay shattered on my rug, the liquor pooling out around it like blood.

28

I SPENT SUNDAY MORNING in a haze, wondering what I had done wrong, what signs I had failed to read correctly. That moment I had kissed Tom had felt so right, so natural, what had gone awry? Maybe it was just another instance of my usual pattern, picking the ones who were safe or inappropriate, only why did it hurt so much now? My mind kept playing the moment over and over, like an endless loop of tape—sometimes analyzing, sometimes torturing, like poking at a wound to see if it had healed.

Even Ragnarok must have sensed something wrong, for he appeared earlier than usual, humping up onto the rock ledge beside me where I sat, staring disconsolately out over the waves. And, for once, he didn't bark immediately and imperiously for fish, but instead butted his head into my side until I petted him and stroked him. *Then* he wanted fish.

It served as enough of a distraction that I didn't notice the truck bouncing into my driveway until Tom came around the side of the house, stopping about ten feet from me and my seal.

Ragnarok startled visibly, but Tom and I just stared at each other, a silence stretching out between us. His dark eyes were hooded again, and I couldn't begin to read them. Was this an apology in the making? Was he coming to tell me how sorry he was, how he had been awake all night realizing what a dreadful mistake he had made?

My heart stuttered into painful motion as he said, still from ten feet away, "Cecil, I'm sorry." I don't think I could have spoke then even had my life depended on it, but then he added, "I was inexcusably rude to you last night. I know I shouldn't have run out like I did, but . . ."

My burgeoning fantasy deflated like a pin-pricked balloon, and I heard the rest of his speech out with a dull, heavy lethargy.

"I've never been very good at confrontation, and you just scared me. What happened last night . . . Well, I'm sorry if I led you on in any way, made you think I wanted anything other than I did, but . . ." He laughed faintly. "How corny does this sound? Only it's true: I value my friendship with you too much to risk it. I mean, you're an undeniably beautiful woman, and I had a moment of temporary madness, but . . . You and I?" He shook his head ruefully. "It won't work in the long run, that I guarantee you. I'm not cut out for relationships; I'll only end up hurting you. And don't say you're willing to risk it," he added, forestalling my words, "because I am not. I . . ."

He sighed deeply and came to sit beside me then, leaning across to rub Ragnarok's head. The seal's eyes half-lidded in satisfaction, and he rested his head heavily on my thigh as he succumbed to Tom's caresses. I couldn't say I blamed him. My own arm tingled where Tom's shoulder bushed it as he leaned across me to pet Ragnarok. How could he be oblivious to this? Only it seemed he was, for after a moment he sat up straighter and looked over at me, Ragnarok apparently forgotten.

"I don't have many true friends in my life, Cecil," he concluded. "And you have become one. And I'm not going to let anything ruin that."

Another silence, and then Ragnarok—missing his scratching—barked imperiously. I forced a smile. "So this isn't one of those 'let's just be friends' lines, before you disappear forever?"

"Not even remotely," he said, with convincing passion. "I'm not going anywhere, Cecil. For one, your seal won't let me."

That much was true. Ragnarok had crawled half across my lap to butt at Tom. But I still couldn't resist phoning Richard later than afternoon, and saying, "Well, I hope your risk goes better than mine."

"What do you mean?" he asked.

"Tom," I said. "I think you were wrong."

At his prompting, I related the bare bones of the tale, and after he sighed deeply and said, "I'm sorry, Cecil. And, frankly, a bit surprised. I am usually not that bad at reading people. I could have sworn . . . But then, Tom always prided himself on being a bit of an enigma."

"Mmmm," I said. "But don't think this lets you off your side of the bargain. How's your campaign going?"

There was long silence from the other end of the phone.

"Well, don't think I'm letting you off this easily," I added. "Get moving!"

He laughed. "Yes, ma'am," he said, and shortly after we hung up. But I still found myself feeling at a bit of loose ends all day, not quite sure what to do with myself. I tried reading, but no book seemed capable of holding my attention. Then,

on the theory that nothing cure heartbreak better than a
fresh-baked batch of chocolate chip cookies I turned my
hand to cooking—with about as much success. I got the proportions of all the ingredients wrong, forgot the baking soda,
and ended up burning the damned things to boot.

So, there I was, my door and widows all flung open to
clear the smoke out of my house, when my last visitor of the
day arrived. My week had, once again, been busy enough
that my evenings with Ronan had been severely curtailed.
This was, I realized—as he appeared on my back porch,
looking rather uncertain as to his reception—only the second time I had seen him since the fiasco of my party.

"Ronan!" I exclaimed, feeling my mood lighten palpably
at the sight of him. "It's good to see you again. Come in. I'm
glad you came by."

He stepped though the centermost of the French doors as
tentatively as he always entered my house, as if it might
somehow trap him. And when he got closer, I couldn't help
noticing that there was something different about him: a
hungrier look to the hollows in his cheeks, a tightening of
strain around his eyes. Even his opening grin seemed to lack
something in wattage as he approached.

"Ronan, what is it?" I asked, concerned. "Is everything all
right?"

He shrugged vaguely. "It's just . . ." He seemed reluctant
to complete the sentence. "Well, money's been tight, lately."

"I'm sorry," I said, not liking the tension in his usually
fluid frame. "Can't you get Louis to pay you more?"

"Louis?" he said, looking almost startled. "Louis isn't paying me at all. It's . . . What do you call it? An app . . . app . . ."

"Apprenticeship?" I supplied. "It's a training position
only?"

Ronan nodded. His voice seemed slightly bitter as he
added, "For at least a year."

"But what have you been living off?" I asked, horrified.

"I had . . . some money," he said.

Whatever savings he had brought from home, I thought, now likely close to gone. "Do you want me to talk to Louis?" I said.

He flushed—an ugly, embarrassed red. "I can handle it," he replied tightly, and I felt a sudden shame sweep me. What business was it of mine? And why did I seem to have these moments of treating Ronan like a half-wit child I needed to protect? He was a full-grown man, and amply capable of taking care of himself. And just because he had grown up in a backwater didn't mean he was in any way deficient.

So, "I'm sorry, Ronan," I stammered. "I didn't mean . . . You're right; it's none of my business. I just don't like to see friends in trouble. Is there anything at all I can do to help? I mean . . . When was the last time you've eaten?"

"Two days ago," he admitted sheepishly.

I felt a wave of anger sweep me: at Louis and at the world. At Ronan for letting things get this far. I swallowed it.

"As you can tell," I said instead, sweeping a hand around the house, which still smelled faintly of smoke, "I'm not much up to cooking anything new today. It's been . . . an interesting day. But if the remains of the seafood stew I froze a while back will do, you are more than welcome to stay."

He seemed to debate for a moment, clearly torn between pride and need.

"Please," I added. "It's the least I can do to help."

That seemed to decide him, and he smiled faintly, inclining his head. "In which case . . . Thanks." And he seemed to relax, advancing farther into the room, though still picking his steps carefully like a dog.

I gestured him to a seat. "Wine?" I said. "Or something harder?"

He perched on the right-hand sofa, instinctually or by

design avoiding the left-hand couch with its underpinning of blood. He cocked his head. "Scotch?"

I poured us each a glass, handed him his, then glanced over at the clock. "Don't get up," I added. "I'm just going to go defrost the stew. I'll be right back."

When I returned, he had settled more deeply into the couch, one jean-clad leg crossed over the other, surveying the urn on my mantel.

"That's one of the only things that didn't get broken," I said, resuming my seat. "What with all the craziness of the past few weeks, I don't remember if I told you about my break-in."

He looked briefly disconcerted. "You might have. You were not hurt, then?"

"No, I was not hurt. But Tom put in an alarm system anyway."

"So the house now . . . goes off?"

I smiled at his phrasing. "In a sense."

He looked thoughtful. "That is good for you. If you remember to turn it on."

"Actually, the problem is not so much remembering to turn it on as remembering to turn it *off*. I'm driving the alarm company nuts; I've accidentally set it off five times already. Then they call up and I have to explain. And then we fight about my code word, which they perpetually think I'm mispronouncing, and we spend another fifteen minutes sorting that out. Quite the laugh-riot."

"Why?" he asked curiously. "What is your code?"

I clearly wasn't used to the nuances of owning an alarm system. I probably wasn't supposed to be relaying my password, but there was no way to get out of this without seeming rude. Besides, he didn't have my punch codes, and there was no way he could disguise his voice as mine. Still . . . "I don't think I'm really supposed to tell you that," I said.

He grinned. "Probably not. But I promise not to tell a

soul, and you have gotten me curious. What could they possibly think you were mispronouncing?"

To hell with it. "Selkie," I said, and he started visibly. "They always think I mean 'silky.'"

"And what made you pick *that* as a code word?"

I shrugged. "It was Tom's idea; my mind had gone blank at the time. Just goes to show I should never listen to fishermen. Or writers."

Something of my bitterness must have shown on my face, because Ronan turned toward me then, asking somewhat intensely, "What's the matter? Does this have anything to do with . . . how did you describe it? Your interesting day?"

His dark eyes shone with an unexpected compassion, drawing me in. All his attention was focused on me, and I almost felt I could fall into his regard as I would into a warm, dark pool. There was safety there, in his eyes. I don't know how I knew that, but there was. And I found myself pouring out the whole story in more detail than I had to Richard.

I told Ronan everything: my hopes and my humiliation. My hurt. "And maybe it only hurts because, for the first time in my life, I feel I am actually ready for something," I confessed. "I'm tired of fear. I'm tired of running. I'm finally ready to embrace something, but . . . What? Why are you smiling?" I asked.

Because he was, his mouth curved in a wide, fond grin, his bold nose mere inches from mine. And suddenly I found I couldn't breathe again. All my attention seemed focused on those dark eyes so close to mine; the dark head bowed close. It was just like last night . . . only it wasn't. All the magnetism Ronan seemed capable of exerting was now focused on me like a laser, making every inch of my skin tingle. Inevitable? Hell, this was way beyond inevitable. I didn't even have any words for this.

"Has it ever occurred to you," he continued, "that you were simply trying to embrace the wrong thing?"

I don't know how I managed to draw breath, let alone speak, but my voice certainly came out choked and strangled. "You? But I thought . . ."

He laughed then, low in his throat, an almost triumphant sound. "I've always been here, Cecil," he said. "Here and waiting. We're meant to be together. Can't you feel that? Don't you know it, in your bones?"

I no longer knew what I knew any more. All I was aware of was a compulsion more powerful than any I have ever experienced, drawing my head still closer to his. And if Tom's kisses had blotted out reality a bit, Ronan's annihilated it.

I had never in my life experienced anything like the sensation I did as Ronan's lips closed over mine. His kiss was masterful and demanding, his mouth both warm and hard, soft and glacial, his tongue stroking into me with a keen inevitability. And he was correct. If this wasn't right, I didn't know what was. I felt the rightness pouring out of him like a tide, drawing me under. Rightness and confidence, and . . .

Was this what drowning victims felt, I wondered, this tidal power? Whirlpools and undertow, and sinking amidst the waving weeds?

When he finally released me and I surfaced, it was with the same breathlessness as if I had drowned in truth.

I made one last stab at escape. "But what about dinner? Aren't you hungry?"

"To hell with dinner," he replied, his voice gratifyingly husky. "Do you know how long I have been waiting for this?"

All I could do was shake my head.

"My entire life," he said simply, and I knew—with a

shock—that it was no less than the truth. Then he smiled faintly and added, "And there's only one thing I'm hungry for now."

Once again, his lips captured mine with a searing intensity. There was a scent to him up close, of wind and sea and wild things. My hands went up to tangle in his hair. It was as thick and sleek as Ragnarok's coat, but longer, warmer. My heart was pounding uncontrollably.

Why hadn't I thought of Ronan this way before? Why hadn't I seen this coming?

I was not exactly a virgin physically, but I might well have been. I had only been eighteen when my parents had died and I had started closing myself off to caring. There had been a few vague fumblings before that—of the distinctly adolescent variety—and I had met one boy in college that I was starting to get serious about. But then the accident happened, and I started excising people out of my life. In the past ten years, there had been . . . nothing. A cold, sterile—and very safe—nothing.

And that was only physically. Mentally, I was as virginal as they came. Meaning I was now very far out of my depth, indeed.

I shivered, but maybe that was only because Ronan's lips slipped from my lips to my ear, and then to the line of my jaw, trailing a line of fire down my neck. His hands went to the buttons of my blouse, fumbled for a second, then ripped.

Buttons popped and clattered to the floor like knucklebones from a mystic's hand.

The sun was setting beyond the windows, the sky flaring crimson, as my blouse fell open, the cool evening breeze caressing bare skin. Goosebumps rose, and I felt my nipples tighten almost painfully in response.

Ronan made a wordless sound somewhere back in his

throat and dipped his head, kissing across my collarbones and lingering in the hollow of my throat, his hands cupping my breasts, thumbs stroking through the thin cotton of my bra until I thought I would die from that alone.

"Ronan," I managed, my voice thick with need, and when he showed no sign of coping with the bra, reached between us and undid the clasp myself, pushing both bra and shirt from my shoulders, baring myself to his gaze.

Bold, and not like me, but I couldn't help myself. He was doing something unholy to my insides.

His dark eyes gleamed, then he toppled me back onto the couch, following me down. His lean body pressed against me, his erection hard and hot against my thigh through his jeans, he took first one breast and then the other into his mouth, nipping and sucking and teasing.

My mind swirled with sensation. It was like he had to touch and devour every inch of me, making me his. Almost involuntarily, my arms tightened around him, pulling him closer, my hand slipping up under the back of his shirt, encountering the silky heat of bare skin.

I stroked upward, startled to suddenly feel a thick knot of scar under my fingers. I must have made a questioning sound, for Ronan raised his head slightly, then helped me divest him of his shirt.

His body was even leaner than Tom's, and smoother. His skin was a fine-grained gold even where the sun shouldn't have touched it, and dusted only with the faintest trace of fine dark hair. Under it, muscles rippled and flowed like water. I ran my fingers across it, discovering upon closer inspection the tiny, pink-prick scars like barnacles on a rock, small patches of grazing like sandpaper over skin.

And then I found the ridged scar my fingers had located earlier. It started at his left flank, curved around his side, and terminated midway up his back. And unlike the fine lines and almost delicate tracery of his other scars, this was coarser, deeper, more twisted. Once, it must have been very painful.

The life of a working man, I thought, almost awed. Life had marked him in a way it never would myself or my city colleagues, living soft behind desks. He had earned his scars. I, pale and unmarked, felt a novice before him—in more ways than one.

I ran a hand across it, about to ask him what had happened, only then he leaned close and kissed me once more, and I forgot all about it as the tide of sensation closed over me again. Ronan's passion ignited an answering spark in me, rousing a wild, animalistic side I hadn't even known I possessed. I dug my fingers into his back, my nails denting his skin, as his mouth sampled every inch of my body. And, I, too, bit and devoured whatever bit of him I could reach.

His skin tasted like salt, like the sea, and when he almost roughly pushed my jeans and underwear from my hips and lowered his mouth between my legs, I screamed and came right then.

But he wasn't done with me; not by a long-shot. When he finally separated from me long enough to strip his jeans and underwear off, he was magnificently, rampantly erect, his penis surging from a silky mat of dark hair. I drew in a breath. I wanted him inside me so badly it hurt.

"Condom?" I whispered, wondering how I managed to get out the word.

He stared at me blankly, and I cursed. What to do now? I was almost blind with need—especially since his hand had just drifted down between my legs, teasing and stroking. I arched against him, shuddering, as I came again, but it didn't even begin to fill the void.

"Disease?" I said, even more desperately.

Another blank look.

Damn it, this was hardly the time to have this discussion. "You?" I persisted. "No dread diseases or anything?"

Comprehension dawned in his eyes, and he shook his head.

It was damned irresponsible, I knew that. You were supposed to get tests and things, doctor-approved proof. But this was Ronan, for whom Seal Island was the big city, and cocktails with me a night on the town. And something in his intensity led me to believe that this wasn't something he did a great deal, either. I'd been on the pill for a while now for medical reasons, and still was. I trusted him. I had to trust him. I couldn't wait any longer. There would be plenty of time to broach the subject more responsibly later.

When he surged inside me, I cried out and came again.

Fortunately, he was made of hardier stuff. And while the narrow couch was hardly suited for such exertions as we were subjecting it to, the thought of moving was incomprehensible. So I just wrapped my legs around his back and let him take me for the ride of my life, while our dinner defrosted on merrily, unnoticed.

AFTER—HIM CLAD ONLY in boxers, and me in a robe—I persuaded him at last to eat. We made it about halfway through that meal before he carted me off again—to the bedroom, this time. And there, with more space to maneuver, our coupling was more acrobatic. And later still, more languid.

By this point, deep night had fallen, and we were drowsing in each other's arms amidst the tangled sheets. The only light in the room was the moonlight, pouring in through the wide bay window, spilling silver light across the bed. And my hands, idly stoking across his skin, once again discovered the knotted path of his scar.

I glanced up at him as I touched it, but his eyes were closed, his face languid and satisfied. Without the usual fire of his personality illuminating it, his countenance was oddly plainer, the proud curve of his Roman nose more pronounced.

"What?" he said sleepily, not opening his eyes as my fingers stilled.

You look different, I wanted to say. Instead I ventured, "What happened?" And rubbed my fingers again over the ridges of scar. I was expecting some tale of line and tackle, or whatever it was that fishermen used, back when he was a fisherman's son.

"Outboard motor," he mumbled. "Got a bit too close."

"You fell overboard?"

He shifted, and I looked up. His eyes were open now, glittering, no trace of languidness remaining. He was still hard to read, but after a moment I realized he was laughing at me.

"Swimming," he said. "I was younger then; more reckless. Didn't gauge distances as well."

"And you have no problem with distances now?"

"Not precisely. Some distances I have an objection to," he said, and closed the one between us, pulling me under yet again.

WHEN I FINALLY SLEPT, I dreamed of swimming. Naked and lithe, my body weaved among the deep rocks and weeds, feeling the textures of the currents against my skin. And while I know that, traditionally, dreams are supposed to equate sex with flying, maybe it was rhythmic crash of waves outside the window, slipping like a whisper into my subconscious, that transformed it. But whatever the case, there was an undeniable sensuality to the dream, for I seemed to be aware with senses beyond my own of the richness and complexity of the undersea world. Beams of sun filtered down like fairy columns through the skin of the sea, and silvery shoals of fish flashed and darted in the light. And with a bright, flashing joy, so sharp it was almost painful, I reveled in the speed, the freedom, the splendor of streaking through the endless waves.

I woke with a smile on my lips, feeling happier than I ever had in my life.

29

"I SLEPT WITH HIM!" I said to Abby three days later, as I drove us to Orono to visit the workshop of the potter Martha had guided me to. But my mind wasn't exactly on place settings that morning.

The Monday following my first night with Ronan, I received word that the storefront owners had counter-offered, but it was a reasonable one, so on Harry's advice I accepted. The deed was done. The Bay Street property was mine, pending the completion of the paperwork, title searches, and inspections, and my life would sink or swim on its success. But that was far from my top priority these days.

Abby was equally distracted, and I didn't think it was because of Richard. She had left Caitlyn in charge of the store, which was a big move for her. I suspected she hadn't been away from The Gull during high season for more than a week in her life, and not at all since Allegra had died. But my news was enough to divert her.

"You did what? With who?" she asked, turning incredulously to regard me. "Tom?"

"No, Ronan," I replied, suddenly remembering Tom for the first time since Sunday. How could I have forgotten about him so quickly? But then, I suppose, love could do that to you.

Well, maybe not love, I admitted. But lust.

Definitely lust.

I flushed hotly, suddenly relieved that I was driving and thus had a reason to keep my eyes fastened firmly to the road.

"Ronan?" she exclaimed. "I must say, that is the last thing I expected!"

"Me, too," I confessed. It still seemed unreal to me.

"So how was it?"

I flushed again. Abby was probably my best friend in the world, but how could I tell her this? I would sound like some green girl. Granted my experience wasn't all that vast, but "a revelation" was not an answer I could give. Though part of me did suspect that most people didn't get this sort of feeling once in their lives let alone five times in one night. Then, of course, three times the night after, and four times again the night after that . . .

God help me, the man was magic; there was no other explanation. Magical to touch, and magical to look at. Our connection was so intense that simply being out of his presence was like waking from a dream.

"That good, eh?" Abby grinned. "Wow. All right, then, girl, you know your duties. Dish!"

"I . . . Hey, isn't that our turn?"

"I think so. Are you trying to duck the subject?"

"No," I said, as I took the turn. "I've just never really discussed this sort of thing before."

She grinned. "For lack of girlfriends to discuss it with, or for lack of boyfriends to do it with?"

"Both?" I admitted, embarrassed.

"Well, you don't have to give me a blow-by-blow, but apart from the sex, which I assume is amazing"—I blushed again—"what is it like to be with a mechanic-in-training? What do the two of you talk about?"

"Talk?" I said blankly, and she laughed. But she was right. I hadn't noticed its lack until now, yet there hadn't been much talk over the past few evenings. Some nights, we didn't even make it all the way through dinner first.

"Oh, hell," Abby said, correctly interpreting my expression. "Don't sweat it. You have years in which to talk. Just enjoy what you have for now; it's more than most of us are getting. Though I must admit that Richard has been a bit more attentive of late. And perhaps . . . Well, perhaps I was a little hasty before in sending him away so quickly."

"Really?" I exclaimed. "Hooray!"

Abby shot me a sharp look. "Are you somehow responsible for this development, then? Richard said the two of you had come to a mutual agreement, but I wasn't aware I was part of it."

"You weren't, exactly," I admitted. "But I may have dropped a word in his ear that you were quite as indifferent as you pretended. Was I wrong? I mean, I only want you to be happy, Abby."

She was silent for a moment, and then grinned. "I guess that's what I get for interfering in your life. No, I don't expect you did do wrong—though I'm not quite ready to make the leap yet. But I am happy. And you?"

Someday, I was going to learn how to control this blushing thing. "Yeah, I'm doing great." I had a sudden memory of Ronan, stark naked and magnificently aroused, chasing me out onto the rock ledges of my shore in the thick darkness last night, long after the moon had set. Under the star-flecked sky, he had pulled me down on top of him, and I had ridden him to completion while the waves absorbed our cries . . .

Abby cleared her throat. "Uh, Cecil . . ."

"What?"

"You just drove past the pottery place."

ONCE IN THE STORE and faced with actual choices, my concentration returned and I was able to turn my full attention to patterns and glazes. There was a whole line featuring the coppery glaze I had admired at her house that evening. My choice, which had once seemed so simple, was now rendered complex.

With Abby serving as my moral support, I poked around and eventually decided to go with a whole line featuring the coppery glaze, but with undertones of black, brown, maroon, purple, blue and green. I could mix and match them creatively at settings, and each plate itself shaded from light in the center to darker around the edges.

Then, that decision made, I began the task of seriously dickering with the potter about bulk prices and the option of selling his wares through The Gull. It was an idea I had discussed with Abby previously—that whatever local pottery and other accoutrements I got for the restaurant we could also sell through the shop. My restaurant would, in a sense, be a local showcace as well as an eatery: restaurant and gallery combined. For this, Abby's years of expertise in wholesale were vital, and I introduced her to the potter as my partner and let her do most of the dickering until we had arrived at a mutually satisfactory deal. By spring, I would have an entire load of my chosen dishware for the restaurant, and a further consignment to carry at The Gull.

But when we got back into the car, I noticed Abby casting me the occasional querying glance as I started up the engine. After a few minutes on the road, she turned to me and said, "Partner? It makes it sound better, of course, but knowing you, you have something else up your sleeve. So what is it? You've already said you're not selling me The Gull for now, and I appreciate your reasoning, but I also don't think you've missed the fact that The Gull is a small shop and we're not going to have room to carry the full range of products you are proposing. So, what gives?"

"Wise as always." I grinned. "Okay, then. When I was buying the storefront, I learned from one of the realtors that Carolyn was thinking of selling her gallery. And that Len wants to expand the photo shop and was thinking taking over Carolyn's space in turn. Which means. . . ."

"An empty store front next to The Gull. Your proposal?"

"You buy the storefront and remodel it, join it to The Gull. Sell my restaurant-related wares. In return, I make you a full partner. Fifty percent of everything. What do you say?"

Abby looked stunned. "This is a big decision. Buying and remodeling a store in a year when I may have to buy a house and move as well. And what if your new line doesn't take off?"

"I know it's risky, which is why you don't have to make a decision right away. Carolyn hasn't even put the gallery up yet, so in a way it's all theoretical. But I think it is going to happen, and I think it is going to work. And I'd do it myself, only I can't afford two properties in a year. And since you were offering to buy The Gull, anyway . . ."

"True," she said, then went silent for a while. I watched the trees scrolling past my window, the ribbon of macadam vanishing beneath my tires, and contemplated our future. A year from now, where would we be? Right now, it seemed impossibly distant.

"All right, I'll do it," Abby said, startling me. When I stared at her, she added, "You said I had time to decide. Well, I've taken all the time I need. I'll call the realtor tomorrow, and have her notify me the minute Len's place is on the market."

The relief that poured through me left me almost limp in its wake. "You won't regret it!"

"You sound just like Allegra; she always used to say that when she was trying to persuade people to do something particularly risky. But she was never wrong, and nor, I suspect, will you be. To partners."

"To partners," I said, and a warm feeling went through me. Harry could bloody well lump it.

We got back to Seal Island a little before five, and I dropped Abby off in front of The Gull. "Still standing," she said. "Thank God. Go home to Ronan; celebrate in style. I'll talk to you tomorrow, and this time try to get some genuine details out of you. Deal?"

"You can try," I said. And, "Deal."

I drove home in a sudden sizzle of sexual anticipation—only it was not Ronan waiting on my back porch when I arrived but Tom, with another cooler of mackerel at his feet. Ragnarok was halfway up the beach, barking imperiously at him.

"You see? I told you we wouldn't have to wait long, you greedy bastard. Here she is," Tom told the seal as I rolled my car to a stop at the side of the house and got out. "Good day?" he asked. "Did you get what you wanted?"

I nodded. "Pretty much. I've still got some of the last load of fish left in the fridge, though. Shall we use that up first?"

He rose in silence, and I could sense the continued restraint between us that had been there since our dinner last week. How was I going to break the news to him about Ronan? Admittedly, he had pretty much left me to my own devices when he shut the door to anything but friendship between us, but if I had expected that my involvement with Ronan would negate my feeling for Tom, seeing him now put an end to that delusion. And that confused me more than ever. I was sleeping with Ronan. So how come, with Tom before me—all prickly demeanor and dark hooded eyes—I could barely remember what Ronan looked like? How come I still found myself wanting Tom? That wasn't the way this was supposed to work.

But maybe time, like everything else, would heal this particular wound.

In silence, we dealt with the fish, then carried a bucket out for Ragnarok. The sun was still shining strongly, the seal's fur drying to a silvery grey. I went down to stroke him. He barked.

"Let it warm up a little, first," I told him. "You know you don't like it too cold."

He looked grumpy, so I played with him a little more while Tom waited higher up the shore, a darkly looming presence. When I finally went up to join him, he was sitting on the back steps. I folded myself down beside him.

"There's something I should say to you, Cecil," he began, his eyes fixed on the distant horizon.

"No, me first. I want you to hear this from me before the rumor mill gets going."

"What?"

"I'm seeing Ronan," I said.

There was a moment of silence, then, "Your neighbor?" he said. "You mean seeing us in . . ."

"Dating, yes."

Another silence, then he turned to me, his expression caught somewhere between bitterness and triumph. "So, I was right then. We are just meant to be friends. Although good friends still, right?"

"The best," I said.

"And you are happy?"

"Yes, I'm happy," I answered, suddenly wondering if it was the truth. Otherwise, why did I suddenly feel as if my heart was breaking all over again?

"I'm glad," he said simply. "Now, shall we feed the seal?"

We rose. Ragnarok, who had been lurking in the shallows, surged back up onto shore. Once the fish were distributed to everyone's satisfaction, Tom departed. But he was back three days later, then four days after that. And this second time, after the feeding was over, Tom sat down on the rocks, his long legs drawn up to his chest. He rested his chin on his knees and peered out at Ragnarok, who was bottled off the shore, regarding him in turn.

"Seals love music, you know," he said. "Have you ever tried playing to Ragnarok?"

"Playing what?" I said.

He turned his head and looked up at me. "I'll show you. Are you free for dinner tonight?"

"I don't know," I said. "I'll ask Ronan." Then abruptly paused, remembering Ronan had no phone, and that I had no real way to contact him. What sort of relationship was it when a man just showed up on my doorstep and swept me into bed several nights in succession? Though, on the flip side, there were compensations . . .

My face must have gone dreamy, for Tom said, almost sharply, "Well, check. And call me back if you can. If not tonight, then some other night?"

"Of course," I said. "I promise. But I'll call you regardless. Okay?"

"All right," he said, and departed. As his truck rumbled out to the drive, I turned to Ragnarok, but the seal had vanished as well.

Lacking any other options, I was going to have to go in search of Ronan myself. It was late enough that I wasn't sure if he'd be at work or at home, but home seemed the easiest place to start my search, as it was closer. So I chose the route by which he usually sought me out, wending my way down along the shore.

The tide wasn't too high, and the ledges made easy footing. I passed four clearings, then turned the corner into another small cove where a seal was lying beached on the ledges. For a moment I thought it was Ragnarok, but when it turned at the sound of my footsteps, I saw that it was larger by far—over six feet—with a curving, equine profile. Its hide was dark, spotted with white, and its nostrils drooped in a wide, lugubrious W.

I froze. I couldn't tell if it was the seal that had been watching me, but it was definitely a grey, and larger and more muscular that Ragnarok could ever be. It humped towards me aggressively, as if blocking my path, then seemed to reconsider, sliding off the rock to vanish into the sea.

My breath started up again and I walked up into the clearing that contained Ronan's virulently blue dwelling. There was no car in the drive, no lights on. Silence seeped from the boards of the house.

Superstitiously, I looked back over my shoulder, but the big seal had gone, not even a horse-like head bobbing on the waves. I marched up to Ronan's back door and knocked.

It *was* an ugly house, I thought as I waited; not one true redeeming factor. Quite apart from the color, the structure was squat and vaguely out of proportion. There was no deck, no wide windows onto the view. No acknowledgement whatsoever of the vista that bordered the back side of the house. Instead, what windows existed were small and dingy, set high into the walls. I had to stand on tiptoe and peer through one when there was no answer in response to my knock.

It was hard to see inside, but the interior of the house seemed even less inviting than the outside—if such a thing were possible. The floor looked to be carpeted with what had once been shag, now matted down with age. The furniture looked functional and mismatched. I felt vaguely depressed. No wonder Ronan had taken to showing up on my doorstep, had never invited me around to his place. He was probably ashamed of it—all his meager savings could afford. If I could provide him with beauty and more luxurious surroundings, then what could be wrong with that?

I knocked again, more loudly, and called his name, but clearly he wasn't home. Work, then. I would try him at work.

I turned back to the shore and thought I saw a flash of movement—a head disappearing beneath the water as I turned—but perhaps that was only my imagination.

I trooped back to my house and fetched my car, driving out to the garage. Ronan was indeed there, with Louis at his side, both intent on something under the hood of a car. There seemed to be some sort of instruction going on. I could hear both their voices, muffled by the bonnet: Louis' thick Maine drawl, and Ronan's rough, rolling brogue, like waves over rocks.

I almost hated to disturb them.

When I knocked on the wall next to the open garage door, both of their heads popped up from the engine like seals disturbed from their rest. Still absorbed in his work, Ronan's face was alight with concentration, and his grin only increased in wattage as he saw me. I smiled back.

"I'm sorry to interrupt," I said, mostly to Louis. "But do you mind if I steal your assistant for a moment?"

"Be my guest," Louis drawled cheerfully. "And if you're the reason this lad's been so cheerful and eager for the past few days, then you're even more welcome to a few moments of his time."

I flushed slightly as Ronan loped over, wiping his hands on a rag he pulled from his back pocket. We paused for a moment in front of each other. It was the first time we had been forced to deal with out relationship in public, and it was more awkward than I had anticipated. Then he solved the dilemma by leaning over to kiss me briefly on the lips.

A wash of happiness seized me as his eyes met mine.

"What is it, Cecilia?" he asked. He alone refused to use my nickname.

I felt suddenly sheepish. "I was hoping you wouldn't mind that . . . Well, Tom invited me over for dinner tonight. Would you mind if I went?"

His expression dimmed visibly. "Tom?" he said, and I suddenly remembered spilling out my woes about Tom to him on the sofa, that first night we got together. I flushed slightly.

"We're just friends, Ronan," I said. "I picked you. I'm dating you."

"Are you sure?" He looked so vulnerable all of a sudden that I couldn't resist running a hand along his cheek and leaning in to kiss him again. I *had* made the right choice.

"I'm sure," I said. "But just because we're together doesn't mean I still can't see my friends. Right?"

"Right," he said. Then, "Just dinner?"

"Just dinner. I shouldn't be home much past eleven, I promise. I'll see you later?"

He nodded, and with another kiss I departed, leaving him to his work.

30

TOM SEEMED DISPROPORTIONATELY PLEASED when I called to tell him of my decision. "As for dinner," he added, "I have a bunch of crabmeat that Larry's wife gave me this morning. Is there anything we can do with that?"

"Absolutely! Crab cakes," I said, my brain ticking into overdrive as I began tossing ideas for ingredients about. I hadn't been quite happy with the batch I had made for Abby, and this would be a good opportunity to perfect the recipe.

". . . okay with it?" Tom was asking.

"Excuse me?" I said, bumping back down to earth.

I could hear the grin in his voice. "Nothing. I'll see you soon?"

"Yes. But how do I get through your gate?"

"Oh." He sounded embarrassed. "There's an intercom. Kind of hidden in the bushes, but you can't miss it if you know what you're looking for. When will you be over?"

"In about half an hour."

"Why so long?"

"Shopping," I said, and hung up.

Thirty-two minutes later, I pulled up before the imposing sweep of Tom's gates with two laden grocery bags on the seat beside me; I'd have to buy a car in addition to everything else, I realized. Something with a four-wheel drive, to get me though the winters.

I located the intercom, and pressed the button.

"Cecil?" Tom's voice issued, tinny, from the speaker.

"In the flesh," I agreed, and the gates slid silently open. As I drove inside, they whispered shut behind me.

Thomas Moreland, I thought again, wonderingly. *Good lord.*

Tom was waiting in the door as I pulled up the drive. He had clearly just showered, and was wearing his usual off-duty uniform of white T-shirt and jeans. His feet were bare, his hair still damply curling. Behind him, his house loomed imposingly, an odd contrast to his casual attire.

"Come in," he said, padding up to my car and reaching in through the open window to retrieve the bags of groceries. "Good heavens, did you buy out Gantry's?"

"Not quite, but close," I said, getting out and following him into the house. "As I said, we're having crab cakes. That is . . . if that's all right with you?"

"Brilliant. Do you have a recipe?"

"Nope," I said cheerfully. "I'm making it up as I go. How do you feel about being a guinea-pig?"

He turned briefly to survey me. "Rather good if you're at the helm," he said, and led the way into the kitchen.

He unloaded the bags and got out the crabmeat—fisherman's surplus, in an oversized tub—while I surveyed the room. For a man living alone who claimed no particular culinary skills, he was supremely well-supplied with pots and pans and mixing bowls—all of very high quality. The last time I had been in his kitchen, I had been too mortified to pay full attention, but now I was more impressed than ever.

Legacy of his wife, perhaps?

To cover my sudden awkwardness, I asked, "Spices? Measuring spoons?"

He pointed to a cabinet and a drawer, adding, "Feel free to poke around for anything you want. Can I get you some wine?" And when I agreed, he added, "Red or white?"

"White," I said instantly, thinking of my cooking, then realized that would do for drink as well. As he went off in search of a bottle, I poked happily through his drawers and cupboards. When he returned, it was with another vintage even I recognized as expensive. I paused in my examination of the utensil drawer. "Don't tell me you have a wine cellar?"

"A rather extensive one," he admitted, sounding embarrassed again. "Do you want to see it?"

"What sort of question is that?" I said, and followed him to the basement.

We toured the wine cellar—which really was quite impressive—then returned to the kitchen, establishing a companionable rhythm as I cooked. I had decided on a slightly spicy side dish of yellow squash, pattipans and sweet peppers garnished with a hint of sharp cheddar to go with the crab cakes, and a mesclun salad with a light citrus vinaigrette, and had him chopping vegetables as I mixed and tasted and measured and raided his spice rack.

At some point, I was aware that he had put on music in the background—something mellow and classical. I sipped my wine and watched the sunset flooding the sky with orange outside the windows as the ocean went deep and enigmatic.

We chatted in a desultory sort of way as we worked, but our long stretches of silence were not constrained. Rather, it was a comfortable hush, underscored by music and the whisper of waves against the rocks. A chef must have designed Tom's kitchen, and Tom himself was the ideal assistant. He even chopped like a pro, asking me for instruction rather than just assuming, producing neat, even pieces.

"Want a job?" I asked him at one point as he emptied a load of perfectly sliced squash into my pan. I was still amazed at how we managed to work like a single entity, as if he were an extension of myself rather than some other with whom I was compelled to share a space. I wondered how Ronan was at chopping squash.

"Tempting," Tom said. "And as I already seem to have one job too many . . . Why not add another?"

"Excellent. But who says you have too many jobs?" I asked, realizing it was high time I got comfortable addressing his other profession.

"My publisher. They keep trying to get me to give up my lobstering and concentrate all my time on writing."

"And what do you tell them?"

He grinned mischievously, looking for all the world like an overgrown boy. "That's the advantage to being the 800-pound gorilla; I tell them to go get stuffed—in politer words, of course." He went abruptly serious. "Lobstering keeps me sane, keeps me in touch with what is real. Though I suppose it is a bit hypocritical of me to say that, since I don't need it for my living the way the rest of my compatriots do. I make more in a month from writing than most of them do in a year of lobstering, which in many ways I find completely humiliating. But fame is an odd thing. It's all too easy to believe in your celebrity and start feeling you are in some way superior to your fellow man just because the thing you do to ease your own loneliness and relieve the pressure inside your head seems to please other people as much as it saves you. In many ways, my fellow lobstermen, who have to struggle to find ways to survive in a dying market, are far better people than I will ever be, and I admire them for that. I never set out to be a writer. I'm glad it happened, but it wasn't intended. And I don't ever want to let myself forget who I really am, at the base of it. Which is probably a longer explanation than you wanted, but so be it."

"Not at all," I said, fascinated by the insight into my former hero's mind. "But if lobstering is such a noble profession, why did you ever leave? Why escape to Boston, to law school? Why become an A.D.A. rather than just embracing family tradition?"

He gave a little snort of rueful laughter. "You don't ask the easy questions, do you?" He was silent for a moment. "I am tempted to say it's because I was young and callow, but that's not the answer either. And in some ways, going off about the noble working man and then rising above them makes me about as hypocritical as the British imperialists. And I admit, for many lobstermen, their lives are very far from noble. They are often poor, uneducated, sacrificing schooling for the boats and the necessity of making a living off a sea that is becoming increasingly overfished as the commercial demands for lobster increase. They are often alcoholics; some are domestically violent. But at the same time, many of them are just doing the best they can with a poor hand, and those are my friends and I admire them for it. But as for myself . . . I guess it wasn't as much the lobstering I repudiated as the lack of education and vision. I grew up reading books and hearing stories—the legacy of a Scottish father. I always knew there as a wider world out there. And there are those of us who, for whatever reason, always want to experience what lies on the other side of the fence. I might have spent my life in search of newer and greater fences if I hadn't been scared back into the familiar by an act of random violence."

He smiled faintly. "So, there's another contradiction for

you. I claim that lobstering keeps me in touch with what is real, but at the same time, it also protects me from reality. From a far more terrifying reality. I've worked in the D.A.'s office. I've seen the darkest sides of urban poverty and affliction. Comparatively, Seal Island is a safe haven. I ran away. So what about you?"

"I think," I said, in a small voice, "that I've been running away my entire life."

"And Ronan?" he said. "Is that running away or facing reality?"

I gave an awkward laugh. "You don't ask the easy questions either, do you?" Like him, I was silent for a moment, wondering if I was trying to determine the truth or merely discover a new way of lying.

"I don't know," I said at last, to all of it. "But I think that's what I'm trying to discover. And maybe that's the first part of the battle."

He smiled—the first unstrained expression I'd seen from him all evening. "Then perhaps there's hope."

"For me?"

"For all of us. Be careful; don't burn the squash."

I hastily plucked the pan from the heat, serious topics thankfully shelved as I attended to the last minute preparation of our meal.

While I searched for plates and dished out the meal like a restauranteur—paying as much attention to presentation as quantity—Tom set up the outdoor table. His deck was narrower than mine, but deeper, and commanded a more impressive view. His coastline was more rugged, the rocks more jagged, the fading trails of the sunset illuminating an endless sky that arched over a limitless sweep of open ocean.

The deck was raised in such a way that, from the table,

you could see neither grass nor rocks but merely water, as if you sat on the prow of a ship. Tom had set out flatware and cloth napkins, candles enclosed in hurricane glass. Our bottle of wine, was chilling in a silver bucket. The night was cool but not cold, and my meal looked flawless when I set it before us.

Cecil Hargrave, having dinner with Thomas Moreland. Who would have believed it? Except it was more than that. It was Thomas Moreland and Tom Moneghan, and even that indefinable combination of the two that was somehow greater than both their parts.

Tom raised a glass of wine to me and we clinked glasses. "To successful ventures," he said, and I repeated the toast back to him. Then he took a bite of his food. "Successful, indeed. Cecil, this is amazing! If this is going to represent the quality of your fare, you're going to have to reserve me a permanent table."

"And start rumors that famous authors are known to be seen at my place. Just think of the publicity!"

"You're going to blow my cover," he said glumly, and took another bite. "Carefully maintained; rigorously preserved. But for this . . ." He glanced up at me and smiled. "Fine. Just so long as you organize the autograph lines."

I laughed. "No autographs allowed, I promise. I protect my clientele. But still . . ." I frowned slightly and took another bite. "It's not perfect yet. The canned crab I get in New York is so bland, I have to over-flavor it. But this is sweeter; it needs a lighter touch than I gave it. And the squash . . . I think I should do it as more of a risotto than a straight vegetable dish if I'm still planning to serve it with the crab cakes. It needs a binder."

He was staring at me. "It seems perfect to me."

"You're not its author," I said. "I suppose it is somewhat like the plot of a novel. You don't send anything out into the world until you are happy with it."

"Or my editor is," he temporized. "Which I suppose amounts to the same thing." He raised his glass again. "To perfectionism."

"To perfectionism," I echoed, and reflected how different his reactions were to Ronan's. Ronan wouldn't have bothered with candles and place settings; Ronan would have wolfed down my meal with a swift efficiency, his gratitude expressed in the speed by which it disappeared. But, as I was beginning to understand, comparisons were odious—and there was something inherently refreshing about Ronan's pragmatic approach to life. With Tom, everything would be measured and weighed; compared. Whereas with Ronan, it either was or wasn't. Which didn't mean he was simplistic. He was simply more direct. Ronan had a way of getting down to the roots of life without getting too distracted by the furls and flowers along the way. He examined things for import, and weighted them accordingly.

Suddenly I felt better about his functional home. It probably didn't depress him in the way it did me. It gave him a roof above his head and a place to sleep, and why worry about more when he spent so little time in it as it was—and even less so now? Other things were more important. And the fact that I entered actively into that equation made me feel more privileged than ever.

Ronan wouldn't, like Tom, lean idly back in his chair when his dinner was finished and continue sipping his wine, lingering over the remains. Ronan, always full of an unresolved energy, would peer at me across the table with mischief sparkling in his night-dark eyes and make some suggestion in that magnificent voice of his that would have my knees turning to water beneath the table, then would cart me off make good on his suggestion until even his boundless energy and inventiveness were tapped . . .

"Cecil?" Tom said. I looked up. "The meal couldn't have

been that bad if you were drifting. Let's clear the table, and then I'll show you what I promised. Okay?"

We cleared the table, and then Tom vanished for a while. He returned, carrying something in a bag, and led me off the deck to the ledges at the back of the house.

"Mind your footing," he said, taking my elbow. "It gets treacherous here."

Indeed, in the growing chill of the evening, the previously sun-baked rocks were slick with moisture that coated them in a thin, slippery film. Full dark had fallen, and the moon sat low over the water, its gibbous curves casting a silver streak across the waves, frosting the peaks of Tom's curls. We rounded a slight curve in the shore, which hid the muted lights of his house behind it, and he handed me up onto one of the low boulders that had scattered higher up the beach.

"Sit," he said, "and observe. I come out here a lot when I'm feeling unhappy or blocked." He unfolded the bag from under his arm—which turned out not to be a bag at all, but rather a set of bagpipes. He shot me an oblique glance. "Did I mention the bit about being a Scotsman's son? My dad taught me this trick, and I've always been thankful for it."

Then, tucking the pipes beneath his arm, he pumped them up in a cacophony of odd, bleating moans and began to play.

He played beautifully, the haunting melodies rising over the water, seeming to carry for miles in the crystalline air. It was this, I realized, that I had heard on occasion from Allegra's back deck—not a phantom piper but Tom Moneghan, practicing an art his father had taught him, releasing whatever loneliness and frustration he felt into the night. And what better instrument to express it but the pipes, which seemed to sob not only a kind of grief into the air, but also a redemption.

I listened in rapture, too caught up in the music to even be

awed by yet another example of Tom's proficiency. But
when I looked over at him, pacing slowly up and down before my rock, he just shook his head faintly, as if to say: *Not
yet; there's more.*

And he was right; there was more to this than just a music
that seemed inherently suited to its wild setting. For as he
played, edging into a livelier air, a head popped up just off
the shore, followed by another, and then another. I didn't
know if any of them were Ragnarok; it was had to tell with
the heads all backlit by silvery moonlight. But before long
there were easily thirty seals arrayed before us, from the
pert, spaniel-like profiles of the harbor seals to the more
lugubrious droop of the greys.

The latter seemed particularly fascinated. Or perhaps I
should say approving, because I caught a glitter in one of the
largest grey's eyes: an almost preternatural intelligence. And
once, I thought he nodded in slow, dignified approval—
tribute to an ancient art still unforgotten. But maybe it was
just a trick of the moonlight and the tears that briefly blurred
my vision for this glimpse of inestimable beauty Tom had
gifted me with.

Finally, he stopped playing. The pipes whined into silence, and after a frozen moment, the heads bobbed away as
well, scattering into the dark waters. The greys were the last
to go, slow and standing on their dignity.

"This is one of the few times I see the greys so close to
shore," Tom said, in a voice that blended almost seamlessly
with the night. I was going to tell him about the grey on
Ronan's shore, but then he distracted me by saying,
"Sometimes, I have the odd feeling they are applauding me
for carrying on an ancient tradition. The greys always seem
to have an elder statesmen dignity to them that doesn't
quite hold with the modern ways. But as long as there are

Moneghans on this island, there will be people to pipe to the seals. I was teaching my son, before . . ."

His voice trailed off, and I didn't have the slightest desire to interfere. I could hear the raw edge of grief in his words, still unhealed. So I just let the silence stretch out until his voice was his own again.

"Well, then," he said. "Worth the show?"

"Absolutely," I said fervently. "And thank you. I wouldn't have missed this for the world."

31

It ended up being closer to midnight by the time I got
home. Unwilling to lose the magic of the evening so quickly,
we had lingered late over brandies, talking about I don't
know what, and I had forgotten my promise to Ronan until
the drive back.

I had half-expected him to be waiting for me when I returned—or find another shadowy figure fleeing across my
lawn—but my house was silent and deserted, and he was
probably long since asleep. So instead I did what I had done
every night before Ronan had showed up in my life and put
myself quietly to bed.

I woke about an hour later with the alarm screeching in
my ears, every nerve tingling with a wash of pure adrena-
line. A part of me wanted to burrow deeper under the covers
and hide, but a stronger part urged investigation. I wanted to
find out for once and for all who or what kept invading my
privacy—and put an end to it. Still, the thought of facing

some unknown intruder in no more than my nightgown was not to be tolerated.

Bathrobe first, then: the initial line of defense. I slid from beneath the covers, any noise I might have made masked beneath the whooping alarm, and retrieved my heavy terrycloth robe from behind the bathroom door, belting it tightly around my waist. Then, grabbing the toilet brush and a can of Lysol—the nearest I could find to weapons in my haste—I darted to my bedroom door and flung it open.

Ronan was standing in the center of my living room, hands over ears, his eyes even wider in frozen fear than mine seemed to be. Cursing, I dropped my impromptu weapons and ran for the control pad. Was that the phone, shrilling madly under the alarm?

I fumbled for the buttons, punching in my code.

The alarm stuttered into silence. It was the phone, indeed.

When I turned to dash for it, I nearly collided with Ronan, who had come up close behind me, as if seeking comfort from my presence. I pushed past him, intercepting the phone.

"No, it's okay," I explained to the much-abused alarm company. "It was my boyfriend this time." The word felt odd in my mouth. I glanced over at Ronan, who was still looking stunned. "Apparently he forgot I had an alarm. Yes, I'm sorry; I'll be sure to remind him. Yes; selkie. No, with an 'e.' And an 'ie' at the end. That's right. Thanks."

I hung up the phone and sighed, turning to Ronan.

"Sorry?" he offered, more subdued than I had seen him to date.

"You should be. Why did you try to break in?"

He looked puzzled. "To see you. You said that you would see me later. I didn't think you'd lock me out."

I sighed. "I'm sorry, Ronan. I came home late, and figured you'd be long asleep by this time. And just because we are dating doesn't mean we have to spend every evening together . . ."

"It doesn't?" he said, and I couldn't tell if he was disappointed or teasing me. "Don't you want me to stay? If I'm not here, I can't do this . . ."

"I . . ."

"Or this . . ."

"Ronan!"

"Or even this . . ."

"I . . . mmmm . . . Oh, hell!" I said. "Stay as long as you like. Only just don't stop!"

THAT NIGHT, I DREAMED I was sitting in my living room, only it wasn't quite my living room. The smaller area rugs were gone; the bare floor under both couches was unstained. An ideal living room, then, untouched by violence. The mantels were bare of both urns and vases, and cheerful fires burned in the grates of each fireplace. Outside the wide French doors it seemed to be deep fall edging into winter. The stand of deciduous trees by the water had shed most of their leaves, though a few still clung tenaciously, like small brown ghosts. A strong wind was blowing, clacking the almost-bare branches together, and the sea—cold grey under a low sky—was tossed with whitecaps. But inside it was warm and cozy, scented with woodsmoke, baked cinnamon, and hot chocolate.

I was sitting cross-legged on the lone large rug, with the guts of what must once have been a radio strewn out before me, intent on the pieces. And, with typical dream-logic, I was also curled up on the sofa, with my legs tucked up under me, and my hands wrapped around an oversized mug of hot chocolate, watching me work. A mug which, in fact, I recognized. I hadn't had a chance to use it yet, but I had noticed it often in the back of Allegra's cupboard, and had often thought it would be perfect for hot chocolate in the winter. And here I was, fulfilling that fantasy in my dreams. And another, I realized, for both the me-on-the-sofa and the me-on-the-rug had a plate of thick cinnamon toast beside us—likewise perfect for such an afternoon.

The me-on-the-rug reached down and took a bite of the toast, reveling in the warm crunch of the bread, the bright, sharp sweetness of the cinnamon topping which flooded my mouth. I laughed, and the me-on-the-couch smiled back.

Or maybe not quite me, I realized, for the me-on-the-sofa was older, gold hair starting to frost ever-so-faintly with silver, lines of life around mouth and eyes. Yet it was a face comfortable in its maturity, more beautiful than mine could ever be for the serenity it exuded.

Allegra, back from beyond the grave in dreams?

It must have been, for she smiled at me warmly and said, in a voice that was somewhat smokier and deeper than mine, "Are you happy now? Is this how you imagined it would be?"

"Yes," I told her, feeling an outpouring of joy in the moment flood me that I wanted to share so desperately with her, who had gifted this life to me.

Thank you, Allegra, I thought, *for giving me all this*. It was more than I had ever dreamed possible.

"Are you ever going to be able to get that radio back together?" she added.

The me-on-the-rug peered down at the scattered and glittering parts at my feet. A metaphor, I supposed—though for what I didn't know. "Maybe. Maybe not," I told her. "Does it matter?"

"I suppose not," she said, with the laugh, and the dream faded into trails of smoke and vanished . . .

FOUR DAYS LATER, I signed the last papers and closed on the storefront. And a week beyond that—once the last of my business loans had gone though, and despite the protestations of Ronan—I left for New York to get the rest of my stuff out of storage and start ordering some of the really nice, industrial kitchen equipment I had always wanted.

To my amazement, Tom offered to accompany me, claiming he had to visit his publisher. But if there was ever any editing business done, I never saw it, for he spent almost every waking minute with me.

We arrived in the city in the midst of an August heat wave: one hundred degrees and ninety-eight percent humidity. The heat was blasting off the pavements as we stepped out of the cab in front of his hotel. I instantly went limp, and even Tom looked a little wilted. There was no green in midtown, just an endless growth of concrete and steel that seemed intensely alien after weeks on Seal Island with its cool pines and birches. The air stank of fermenting garbage and urine instead of cut grass, pine, and salt.

"How could I have ever *lived* here?" I said as he guided me into the air-conditioned lobby of the Marriott Marquis. And if the atmosphere seemed inimical to me, I could never have pictured Ronan here, not in a million years.

But Tom just laughed. "It has its advantages," he said. Which he then proceeded to show me.

His publisher had gotten him corporate rates at a nearby hotel, but he had rented us a suite that, even with the discount, must have averaged $500 a night. I had my own king-sized room on the forty-five floor, with windows that overlooked the sweep of the Hudson and the docks, and our shared living room was bigger than the entirety of my former apartment. Tom's room commanded views of the Empire State Building and the rooftops of midtown. One night, we sipped wine on his bed with all the lights off, marveling at the twinkling, vital vista before us.

Throughout the entire process, Tom was a godsend—and a true friend. He helped me hire movers to empty out my storage space, and even pitched in to help, his T-shirt stained with sweat as he shifted furniture and boxes with the guys. He prowled the restaurant supply district with me for days on end, oblivious to the baking heat, negotiating deals and reductions with all the canny instincts of the former laywer.

To say I couldn't have done it without him would have been an understatement.

I got a wide double sink in stainless steel; a Viking stove. A vast, glass-fronted refrigerator, and a massive freezer. A cast-iron pot rack for the ceiling, and all the skillets and pans my heart desired. Whisks and spoons and spatulas galore.

Most men seemed to have a shopping tolerance of about three hours; Tom never got bored. If anyone faded by the end of the day, it was me. But every night, calling it research, he took me to one after another of the finest restaurants in New York—places I had only dreamed of, but never sampled. Jean-Georges, Le Cirque, Chanterelle, Le Bernardin, Auriolle, Lespinace, and that former home of Jean-Pierre, Le Coq Basque. I don't know who was opening the doors for him, because all his cards were in his own name. But perhaps money does speak, because we were never turned away. Dressed in Allegra's finest cast-offs and jewelry, I sampled dish after dish while Tom, elegantly clad in understated dark suits that must have cost a small fortune, ordered different dishes from me so I could sample as widely as possible.

Menu ideas escalated, and I began to believe I might be able to pull this restaurant thing off, after all.

It was an idyllic week, and odd, too, for how fast I seemed to forget Ronan in his absence. Tom and I talked incessantly, and we never ran out of topics of conversation, no matter how obscure or mundane. One night we spent hours on the minutia of seal biology, and the next we got into a huge discussion about the motivations of one of the characters in his second novel. At times during that latter conversation, I heard my words with a certain shock of horror. Who was I to tell Thomas Moreland what he had intended? But Tom didn't seem to take offense—even if I was not sure exactly who, if anyone, had won at the end.

The seal conversations were equally intriguing. Tom told me that in the late 1800s, Maine and Massachusetts had both offered a one dollar bounty on harbor seals to reduce their populations and help the fisheries because the seals were notorious for ripping through the fishermen's nets in search of food. By the early 1900s, the Maine harbor seal population had been nearly eliminated with no noticeable effect on the fishing industry.

"But that's horrible!" I said.

Tom just shrugged. "Humanity's standard response to a problem: kill it off. Whether it truly is the cause or not. Sometimes, I think it would be easier if we all were selkies. They don't tend to attack the innocent—at least not according to legend."

I arched an eyebrow. "Still, I'm sure even their justification sometimes follows a code incomprehensible to others. I mean, look at the legends. No matter how much wrong was done to one of their own, what good does drowning the children of the next generation do? There aren't blacks and whites when it comes to causality, Tom."

For the only time that week, I saw his face darken. "True enough—though perhaps it would be easier if there were. If evil deeds only came from evil people and not from ones who are only doing right as they see it, regardless of the consequences . . . Because no one understands better than I the desire to revenge a heinous act. But perhaps it is best that I was thwarted by fate in that one."

I could tell in an instant that, whatever private darkness he was contemplating, this was neither the time nor the place to pursue it. His face was tightly shuttered, lines drawn like canyons beside his mouth. So instead I said, "What happened to the seals?"

"Oh." He looked over at me, the light back in his eyes. "Maine wised up and lifted the bounty in 1905. Massachusetts, however, left it in place until 1962—another reason for us to resent them. But the seals made a comeback, and are still growing in number. I read somewhere that seal populations in our area were about six thousand in the early seventies. By the mid-eighties, they were close to fifteen thousand, and the numbers are probably even higher now. So I guess the message is that, ultimately, life will triumph."

But there was something still dubious about his gaze, as if he didn't believe his own words—at least not as applied to himself. Which saddened me. My wounds were deep, but Tom's ran deeper.

I hoped, someday, that he would begin to heal.

AND SO THE WEEK passed, and I arrived back on Seal Island feeling older but wiser, with a wealth of experience behind me and a delight at being back among the trees and the green. We got Tom's truck out of long-term parking and crossed onto the causeway at about five in the afternoon, with our luggage in the bed of Tom's truck behind us. And again, the sweep of the causeway seemed like a benediction.

I may not have been born here, but I knew I belonged. Finally, I belonged.

Ragnarok thought so, too—for after five minutes of sulking, he swarmed up onto shore, nearly tipping me over in his enthusiasm. Then, lest I think he was pining for me, he cocked his head and peered up at me with a reproachful look, as if to say: *Look how I have wasted away since you have been gone. Here I am, but a shadow of my former self.*

All one hundred-plus pounds of him, heavy and sleek with muscle.

I grinned and gave him fish, which Tom and I had stopped for on our way home. Then, when he was done, I installed myself on my back porch and waited for Ronan.

There was no doubt as to his welcome, either. How could have I almost have forgotten him over the past week? His shiny, dark hair; his lean, golden body; his boundless energy? He leaped on me almost as enthusiastically as Ragnarok, his presence overwhelming me with its usual power—or perhaps more so, given our time apart—and the ensuing wrestling match between us ended in a conclusion that was, for both of us, satisfying beyond belief.

Much, much later, snuggled with him among the rumpled bedsheets, my hand tracing the twisting course of his scar, I couldn't help an unshakeable feeling that all was right with the world again.

"You won't ever leave me again, will you?" he asked then, plaintively.

I leaned up on an elbow to look down at him. The sweat of our exertions, cooling on his body, had pooled in the hollow of his throat, and his eyes were dark and liquid. And, in that moment, leaving him seemed unthinkable.

"No, I won't, Ronan," I promised, impulsively.

"You swear?"

"I swear."

"Cross your heart and hope to die?"

I laughed at the childish words, laying one hand on his chest, right over the beating organ in question. "Cross my heart and hope to die," I repeated.

And he smiled, satisfied, and carried me down with him into sleep.

BUT MY REST WAS less than peaceful that night. Clearly reacting in some way to our separation and Ronan's almost child-like pleas, my sleeping mind cast up agonizing images. I was sitting on the ledge by the water, with the house a troubled, chaotic presence at my back, staring out at the waves with an almost palpable longing. No, worse—a sharp, biting sense of loss and desperation I hadn't felt since the night my family was ripped so cruelly from me. I stretched my fingers out to the waves. It was close enough to touch, and yet had never felt more distant. Tears spilled down my cheeks.

Behind me, the house almost throbbed with wrongness.

Again, with standard dream logic, the presence that seemed to haunt my waking hours now haunted my night: a dark, lugubrious seal head, floating on the waves. Only in my dream, it seemed to speak to me.

"WHAT HAVE YOU DONE?" it boomed, its voice echoing eerily in my head. "WHAT HAVE YOU *DONE*?"

I had no answer for it, but then the scene shifted, and I floated like a ghost above my living room. Like it had been on the night of my break-in, everything was in shambles—books scattered and furniture overturned, lights shattered on the floor. Only one thing was different and, seeing it, a shiver traced through me. Where once there was just a stain, now there was a body, sprawled limp in death—as I had probably been imagining it too many times. Limbs all disordered, face turned away, neck twisted under at an unnatural angle, golden hair staining crimson in the pool of spreading blood . . .

"It's over, all over," I wept, and woke sobbing.

32

I HAD ALL BUT forgotten my dream in the morning, and the next few weeks passed in a haze of industry. All the paperwork had finally gone through, and I had closed on the storefront. Joanna introduced me to her architect and, under her supervision, we were drawing up plans for the restaurant, laying out kitchen schemes and table arrangements. On the weekends, I would drive out to the crafts centers with Abby, seeking linens, flatware, glasses, tables and chairs. I visited Martha's studio and bought two pieces outright—including the one she had done of Allegra—and offered wall space for rotating gallery of unsold works. I cancelled the lease on my Honda, and Tom accompanied me to Ellsworth one weekend and helped me purchase a Subaru Outback to get me through the winter.

I was horrified at the rate I was flying through both my savings and the various business loans, but I was elated as well, to feel it all coming together.

I would dine occasionally with Tom or Abby or Richard or Joanna—small oases of sanity in the midst of the chaos— both as an excuse for me to try out new recipes, and to begin to introduce Ronan, one by one, to my friends. And while he still might not be good with crowds, he took to these meetings like a fish to water, despite his initial hesitations. All my friends loved him. Of course; how could they not? For when he set his mind to it, he was charm itself.

"It's amazing," Joanna said to me, after one of these dinners. "He's not really that good looking in repose, but then occasionally he turns and looks at you, and just *shines*. It's like there's no one else in the world but you. You are one lucky girl."

"I know," I said humbly. It was becoming my standard response these days. In fact, if I were a different sort of person, I might have even felt a bit jealous at how thoroughly my friends took to Ronan. It was like he magnetized them. Even Abby— whom I suspected was letting Richard in more closely by the day—would occasionally sit staring at Ronan as if hypnotized.

The only one, in fact, who didn't seem to succumb to Ronan's charms was Tom. The few times I made the mistake of putting them in the same room together, they treated each other with a guarded neutrality that, occasionally, edged into hostility. And it was for that reason, I told myself, that I resolved to keep them apart in future.

It had to be, right? Because if not, that would force me to examine my continued ambivalence in the face of these two men. For despite my facile promises to myself, my feelings toward Tom had not really diminished with time. When I was with Ronan, of course, it wasn't an issue. Ronan by himself, with his boundless energy and intensity, could blot out the world. But the moment I was not with him, thoughts of Tom began to creep back, like traitors in the night. And, along with them, my guilt.

Every rational thought said I should be with Ronan; that
was my fate. And yet . . . Why was I not getting over Tom?
Granted, when I was with Tom, I never forgot about Ronan
as completely as I forgot about Tom while I was with Ronan,
but I wasn't sure what that was a measure of, if anything.
And God forbid I should be in the same room with both of
them together! Then, I felt as if I was being pulled in seven-
teen directions at once.

It was just as well I had the excuse of their own antipathy
to keep them apart.

Still, thanks to the more successful of my small dinners,
I was feeling my way toward a proper menu for my restaurant, sampling reactions, discarding or keeping dishes
based on the opinions of my friends. And once a week, I entered into Jean-Pierre's tutelage and took over the cooking
at the Myrtle, learning the dynamics of preparing food for a
large crowd under his expert supervision. On those nights,
when I peeked out of the kitchen, I would always see either
Tom or Abby—and often both—in a position of honor in the
dining room, supporting me both with their presence and
their frequently overheard talk of my future restaurant.
Lately I had come to notice that, wherever Abby was,
Richard was not far off. Ostensibly, they both seemed to be
plotting out ways of making me a screaming success in my
new profession, but I suspected they were swiftly becoming
united in more than just this common purpose. And that, if
nothing else, gave me pleasure.

Of course, Abby had a stake in my future—much to
Harry's distress. She was, even now, busy buying Len's
store, making plans to expand The Gull. And Richard himself was not without involvement, either. His story on me
and Ragnarok, which had turned out even better than I had
hoped, was picked up by papers from Montreal to Connecti-
cut, and I became something of a local celebrity. Local news

and radio shows phoned wanting interviews, and I always made a point of mentioning both Richard's name and my future restaurant.

Ragnarok himself—at first spooked by the presence of so many people—soon became as much of a media whore as I, mugging shamelessly for the cameras and interviewers. Though he still would only let Tom and I touch him, and once Jessie—but only then because we made him.

As for Ronan and Ragnarok, they seemed to have an armed neutrality, but not a hostile one. In fact, there seemed an almost unspoken accord between these two as to which had what claims on my time, and neither ever seemed to encroach on the other's territory.

But mostly my days settled into sort of a comfortable routine. I would arrive home from the storefront, covered with sawdust and plaster from the remodeling, spend some quality time with my seal, then shower. At first, I had tried reversing the order of these two, unsure of how Ragnarok would adjust to the construction detritus which covered me, but lately the seal had become more physical in his affections and had recently discovered the apparently hilarious gag of dousing me with large quantities of seawater—which seemed to amuse both him and Tom, on the occasions that the latter joined us, and quickly put an end to the idea of showering first.

Then, right after my shower or sometimes during it, Ronan would appear, melting silently up from the shore path once Ragnarok had departed. I would cook us dinner—my restaurant, apparently, would be specializing in fish dishes thanks to Ronan's preferences—while he would skulk restlessly about the house, turning over items and peering into cupboards, waiting for me to return my full attention to him.

We still didn't talk extensively, and I had discovered he was hopeless in the kitchen. I had banished him from even such simple duties as chopping when he had once nearly sliced off a finger. But I was coming to appreciate our relationship for what it was. If I wanted conversation, I could always go to Tom or Abby or Richard. But there was an undeniable comfort in having Ronan's restless presence about my house, adding a new dimension to my life.

And the sex was as spectacular as ever.

I had learned that his restless energy kept him from needing much sleep. Most mornings he was up before me, and on those Sundays when he was missing from my bed, I could often find him down by the ledges, gazing out over the water—sometimes peacefully, and sometimes with an almost palpable longing. At which point I would sit down beside him, rub that smooth, well-muscled back, and entice him back inside for more of that magical passion which still had not faded from our relationship.

In fact, on such days, I often felt drugged, passing the day in a langorous haze, unable to move much beyond a crawl even when Ronan was not with me. And as the weeks wore on and we both grew more comfortable with each other, I would occasionally wake on a weekend to find him still in my bed, and that was beautiful, too. I had never considered myself an overly sexual person, but Ronan proved me wrong. The man was addictive.

And if, out of his presence, I occasionally questioned the viability of our relationship, one night alone with him would reel me back, craving more.

Labor Day—once to be my transition from Maine to New York—came and went without notice. Before long, the interior of the storefront almost looked like the restaurant I had envisioned. Soon, the equipment I had ordered from New York would arrive and we would be installing it. Then it was pretty much clean up and hiatus to spring, when the final touches would be put in before the summer opening. By that time, the tables and chairs I had commissioned from a local woodcarver should be ready, as should the hand-woven tablecloths. And the dishes and glassware.

It had proved to be more expensive than I had imagined to get all the pieces hand-made locally, and even Joanna had advised me to cut a few corners, but it was important for me to do it this way. Dating Ronan had made me more aware of the economics of the island and, whether the craftsmen had been born in Maine or merely transplanted, I wanted to do what I could to support them, to make this truly a Maine restaurant.

Of course, the irony that it was being run by a native New Yorker wasn't lost on me, but every day I spent on Seal Island, I felt Maine seeping more deeply into my blood. There *was* a sorcery to the place—profound and inescapable. Even Abby, who had received word last week that her house would be put up on the market after all, was not considering moving to the mainland, but was instead looking around for a new place on the island to rent.

Maybe it was something in the water, or in the fog that rolled in off the bay with increasing frequency as September deepened and the air grew colder.

"So, you made it," Tom said to me on one such night.

Despite Ronan's antipathy, we had established a pattern of semi-regular meals together that Ronan knew about well in advance, and that always ended by a certain hour. I still didn't like the feeling that I was catering to my boyfriend's paranoia by agreeing to this, but in other ways, it seemed the better part of valor. Because certain things in our relationship had surprised me. Like the fact that Ronan had no phone. Or no car.

"But how do you get around?" I had asked him, astonished, when I discovered this.

He had just shrugged. "Walk?"

The phone, in retrospect, seemed self-evident, given his chosen lack of contact with the world.

But not me; not any longer. Tom and I may have settled into a sort of friendship, but that didn't mean I valued his company any less, or that I was capable of feeling a week was complete without at least one night spent in that impressive mansion he called a home.

Tonight, in particular, was special—if only because of the fog, which had almost become an entity in itself. It was thick and heavy, wrapping fingers around Tom's house, clotting up against the glass until I had the feeling that the stretch of his walls was the entire extent of the world; that there was nothing at all beyond the swirling whiteness.

Focusing on Tom's question, I tried to keep my voice light as I answered, "What do you mean, I made it?"

He arched an eyebrow at me and took another lazy sip of his scotch. We had finished dinner about half an hour ago, and had retired to his living room. Tom was now stretched out on the sofa and I was curled near his head in a deep easy chair. The only light in the room was from the fire he had built in the hearth, and shadows flickered in and out of corners and tangled among the strands of mist that slid past the windowpanes. Flickered, too, among the planes of his face, making hard angles harder.

Most people softened in the firelight. Tom became stone: remote and untouchable. His eyes sank into unreadable pits; the lines of his nose and jaw could have cut like blades. And maybe that was why his voice seemed softer in comparison as he answered, "September, New York girl. It's almost done, and you're still here. You never went home."

"And why should I?" I said, feeling the ring of truth in my words. "This *is* home."

He smiled slightly, the expression warped by the firelight

into a sort of possessive triumph. "So it's caught you too. In-evitably it does everyone. Allegra's family spent every sum-mer at that house for generations; Allegra grew up along these shores. And she sacrificed half her life to remain here. But then again, at least that way, she didn't spend the other half of her life yearning for the thing she had cut off."

"What do you mean?"

"Maine." He shrugged. "I tried to escape. I built myself a life in Boston—a happy life. I loved my job, my family. . . ." His voice temporarily caught. "But even then, I missed these shores with a abiding ache. It gets in your blood, this place, until you can't ever live completely happily without it. But it can be a harsh mistress, too. In many ways, I think Allegra was one of the most profoundly lonely people I have ever en-countered. Oh, don't get me wrong; she was a strong woman, had a built a life for herself that did make her happy—mostly. But I think, down at the core of it, there was a long-ing to love and be loved that colored everything she did."

He turned fully towards me then, his eyes as dark and liq-uid in the firelight as Ragnarok's. As Ronan's. "And now it's caught you, too. Do you regret it?"

That was easy. "No. Not in the slightest."

"So you're happy?"

I considered that. For the first time in my life I had friends, a lover. I was taking a chance on my life, and it felt good. So what if nothing was quite perfect, or even quite as I had expected? Slowly, I was beginning to realize that per-fection didn't exist outside fairy stories. Life—real life—was messy, and never quite fit into the mold you cast for it. But there was a joy to that as well, that it still had the capac-ity to surprise you.

"Yes," I said finally, slowly—not really to convince my-self, but more just feeling out the concept. "Yes, I think I am."

"I'm glad," Tom said simply.

But there was still something so profoundly sad about his words that I couldn't help asking, "And you? Are you happy?"

He sighed deeply and transferred his gaze to the ceiling. For a long time, I thought he wasn't going to answer, but then he said, "I'm getting there. It's a slow process, but every day it gets a little better. Amazing and unbelievably, you start to heal. Whole days can go by now where I don't think about them at all."

I had assumed he was talking in generalities, and the use of the plural threw me.

"I used to feel guilty about those lapses," he continued, oblivious to my start; I had a feeling his eyes were fastened to a place many years and miles distant. "As if I were being unfaithful to their memory. But eventually I realized that life—my life—goes on. And that the last thing Laura would have wanted was for me to be eternally frozen, afraid to fall in love again because I knew only too well the incredible pain that comes when those you care about get ripped away."

A pang went through me; I, too, knew that feeling. But I kept quiet, sensing that something important was happening. That some strange combination of the scotch and firelight and mist was opening an unsuspected chink in his armor.

"But at some point," he added, "the wall has to come down. And life has to be lived again." He shot me an oblique glance. "I never told you any of this, did I?"

I shook my head wordlessly.

He laughed faintly, bitterly. "The keys to the kingdom. It's not a story I tell often, if at all. So where to begin?"

At the beginning? I thought, but still said nothing.

But somehow he must have sensed my thoughts, for he began: "I told you that I grew up on Seal Island, a fisherman's son. But what I didn't tell you about was the incredible chip

I bore on my shoulder because of that. Our school was divided between the more affluent children of the transplants and the poor fisherman's kids, like me. The Haves and the Have-nots. And I always wanted to be a Have, but there was no way I was ever going to be. At least, not given my background. Because I was always convinced they could smell the stink of the docks on me, as perhaps they could, since I projected them so strongly onto myself. So consequently I belonged to neither group, ostracized from one because I wanted to be part of it so badly, and from the other because I wanted so desperately to escape it.

"And maybe in a way that was good, since it turned me to my studies instead. *That* would be my ticket out—and having no real friends gave me plenty of time to pursue academics. I got the A's, and the high scores on the placement exams—which just isolated me further. But at that point, I no longer cared. I was getting away from it all. When I was accepted at Harvard, I couldn't shake the dust off my feet fast enough.

"But what I hadn't realized was that the chip was not only still there, but had grown. I arrived at college with quite a complex—the fisherman's son, still fighting for acceptance in a world that no longer judged quite so harshly. Or at least not by the same standards.

"I met Laura my sophomore year, in an English class. I had had a few abortive relationships before then, which I had always used my own self doubts to sabotage, but Laura was different; I knew that from the first minute she walked into the class. She was one of the Haves—that much was clear right away. But it was equally clear that she didn't really give a damn, that she judged people on their own merits rather than society's. And she must have seen something hopeful in me."

He laughed faintly. "To tell you the truth, she terrified me at first. She was this gorgeous, vivacious creature, with more life in her little finger than most people have in their entire bodies. I felt she was too far above me. In sheer defense, I started playing the fisherman's kid more than ever. And then one day she arrived at my dorm room, reeking of fish. I don't know how she did it, but it was really quite awful. She tossed back her hair, stared defiantly at me, and said, 'There. Now I stink of the docks even more than you do. So will you quit this ridiculous posing and have dinner with me?' We sat there in the restaurant with all the patrons staring at her, laughing and talking until the place closed and they threw us out." Tom's lips curved in a faint, reminiscent smile. "It was one of the best nights of my life, and taught me how foolish all my hang-ups had been.

"We were inseparable after that. She civilized me, smoothed down my rough edges, taught me how to enjoy life for what it was rather than what you expected it to be. Inevitably, I stayed in Boston and went on to law school at Harvard. We married right after I graduated, and I went on to become an A.D.A. Benjamin was born a year later, and Katie two years after that.

"We both had such high ideals; we were going to change the world. She was teaching the underprivileged, and I was going to make the world a safe and just place. And maybe it was a bit of an irony that we were living off Laura's family money rather than hunkering down in the trenches like the rest of the idealists, but we were happy. At first."

Tom sighed again, then flashed me a rueful grin. "How easy it would be to cast this story out of the cloth of high tragedy. The young couple, desperately in love, cast down in their prime. But this is real life, not fiction, and real life is a good deal more complex. For one thing, I found myself, amazingly, growing homesick for the very place I had struggled all my life to escape, and I think that is why I've always been attracted to the legends of the selkies. Not only because of the rumors that their blood flows in our family veins, but also because of the quiet desperation of their lives. I don't know if I've ever told you the full story of the selkies, but the most popular variation talks of the lonely fisherman who has always been kind to the seals. And one night, he is rewarded by a knock on his door, and there is a lovely woman, born from the sea. She is naked—black haired and black eyed—and with her she carries her sealskin, without which she cannot turn back into a seal. She trusts him with her skin and becomes his wife, and for a while there is love. But the woman is a seal at heart, and the call of the sea runs strong in her. She always yearns to return—subtle at first, then stronger as the years go on. And since the fisherman loves her, he hides her skin more carefully year after year so she won't find it and thus will be forced to stay. As for her, she becomes more and more obsessed, searching for it, for her way to return to the sea. And if she finds it, she dons it and slides into the waves, never to be seen again. But if she never finds it, if he destroys it, then she dies and her kind revenges her death."

Tom paused a moment, then added, "At times, I used to feel that I was that seal, and that Laura and my life in Boston had taken my skin. And every year, a little more, I wanted it back. Not that we weren't happy at first. Katie and Ben were miraculous, the center of my life. But I think they became a little too much the center of Laura's. She was a strong-willed woman. It was one of the things I loved most about her. But after a while she began to feel that she was curtailing her life and her ambitions for the kids. And my job, with its increasingly long hours, was keeping me away from home more frequently. But, God help me, I still believed in the system. I was still dedicated; I wouldn't give it up. I turned a blind eye to Laura's growing frustration. No matter what anyone tells you, having kids changes the dynamic of any relationship. They become the center rather than you, which, in some ways, is exactly how it should be.

"Still, Laura and I drifted apart. We stopped making love, stopped talking, started arguing. Maybe we had gotten married too young and life's inevitable changes were taking us in different directions. And maybe that's what makes it more tragic. If I had lost her at the height of perfection, I would have missed her profoundly, but I would never have had the awful guilt of not knowing what would have happened, if we could have patched things up, restored our relationship. We were trying. We had started building the house up here as a compromise and were talking about seeing a counselor. Then one night, when I was working late at the office on a case, a truck came out of nowhere and hit her car. She and Benjamin were killed on contact. Katie lived a week before dying of massive internal injuries."

The pain in his perfectly level voice was tearing me apart, but I had the sense that his previously stated theory was profoundly wrong. It hadn't been worse losing Laura after the problems; what was most untenable was losing something before it had lost its glow, before it had ceased to be the center of your universe. Like his kids. Because the whole time he had been talking about his wife's death, he had barely mentioned his kids—not because they meant less, but because they meant so much more.

Laura's death he could almost talk about; the death of his kids was still too terrible to contemplate, let alone relate.

My heart ached for him, but I knew that to reach out to him was the worst thing I could do. His pain was too raw for contact.

"They never did find the driver," he added. "Here I was,

the noble A.D.A., unable to bring anyone to justice. So I quit my job a month later and ran for home. And after a long, black period, I began to write, obsessively, to escape my own life and enter a world where good always triumphed over evil, where the bad guys never won. I had always sort of wanted to write when I was younger, had toyed with the idea—with Laura's support—but had never actually had the time to do it until her death. And look how it turned out."

He took another swig of his scotch and fell into a deep, unreachable gloom. The silence yawned around us, broken only by the fire's crackling, and the fog seemed to push aggressively against the glass as if seeking entry. As if seeking to pull us under like the sea, until we were never seen again.

Swamped in his misery, I had never felt so useless in my life. I didn't know how to help him. Then I did.

"I was in college," I said softly. "I had grown up in New York City. My parents were both teachers, not rich. But they believed in education, and were willing to sacrifice anything to make sure I got a good one. I attended a private high school, then went onto Wesleyan. I was a reasonably happy child: privileged, but not too privileged. I was aware of what I had and what I didn't, but I wasn't that obsessed with it. I had friends, the occasional boyfriend, parents who loved me. Oh, we had the inevitable problems and fights; what's childhood without it? And yes, I was an only child and so a bit spoiled. But on the whole I was secure."

My words had the desired effect. Tom's head had come up and he was listening. The fog shifted around us, restless. It wasn't a story I had ever told in its entirety, in full honesty, with no details left out. But I owed it to him, after the truth he had entrusted to me.

"I sometimes wonder if it wasn't a false security I was living in, a little bubble of dreamland in which nothing could possibly go wrong and nothing had any consequences. But all I know is that it was my selfishness that ended it."

It was harder than I thought to relate this, to try to force the words up past the clot in my throat. This was the part I had never admitted to anyone before, least of all myself, if I could help it. But he hadn't dressed up his tale for me, and I owed him the same. No explanations; no apologies. *Just the facts, ma'am.*

Just the truth.

Turned inward now, I barely noticed when he came up to kneel beside my chair and did what I had been patently unable to do: take my hand and physically offer his support. Nor was I really aware, except in a kind of superficial way, how hard I was gripping him, my nails digging half-moon circles into his flesh.

"It was Christmas break, freshman year. There was a storm coming and I was supposed to take the train home. But I selfishly wanted to bring my favorite study chair back home with me, so I convinced my parents to pick me up in the car. The storm blew up faster than anyone expected and they never arrived, all because of that stupid chair. The college dean had to tell me they lost control of their car on a patch of black ice, skidded off the road and into a ravine. Dead on impact, just like Laura."

Stark words; starker feelings. There was a pain in my hands, distracting me from the tears I refused to shed—had refused to shed since that night. I was too busy, struggling to survive, to finish college, with whatever small bit of money my parents had set aside. I didn't inherit much. Their apartment was a rental, my portion of their annuities minimal. And spring tuition loomed. I threw myself into a work-study program—all part of my attempts to be too busy to think—and used that as an excuse to excise anyone who mattered out of my life with the precision of a surgeon's scalpel. Then

I spent the next nine years never letting anyone close enough to care about their loss. Until another death had brought me Seal Island and slowly let me start living again.

Tom was gripping my hands painfully hard, his knuckles almost white. Unable to look at his face, I found myself fascinated by that joining of our flesh. His skin was taut and pale with tension, smeared lightly with blood where my nails had broken it.

Cecil Hargrave, who scarred everything she touched.

"It wasn't your fault," he said. "You know that, don't you? Whatever you may have believed, it wasn't your fault."

I muttered something incoherent, and then he held me as I wept, huddled on the floor in his lap as the fire died to embers behind us.

33

I WASN'T AWARE OF much as I wept, pouring out years of repressed grief and guilt. Still, a small part of me couldn't help noticing how strong and comforting Tom's arms were around me, how broad and solid his chest was under my cheek. A port in a storm, I thought, as I clung to him. His hands stroked my back, my hair. His deep voice murmured reassurances into my ear, soothing as the caress of waves on rock, though I couldn't have told you what he was saying.

But there was an odd moment when my tears finally began to dry and I shifted slightly in the circle of his arms, looking up at him. I had meant simply to offer thanks for his patience, but in the deep orange light of the dying fire, his face looked more like a creature of legend than ever, caught half out of time. The light was softer now, and slid through of the shining curves of his dark curls, spilled over cheeks and jaw and down the column of his throat, following the drying tracks of what must have been his tears. My breath caught in my throat, and I found myself just staring. His dark gaze met and locked with mine, and the lines of his mouth softened. For a moment, I thought he was going to close the small distance between us and kiss me, and the blood pounded wildly in my head.

Ronan was forgotten; all that remained was this moment that stretched between us, full and pregnant with promise. Frozen in its spell, neither of us moved, and on it stretched. And on, promise draining away into awkwardness . . .

I felt myself stiffen, pouring out apologies to fill the sudden, acute silence.

Tom just shrugged, his arms loosening around me. But reluctantly or in relief, I couldn't tell. "Wounds don't fully heal," he said, "until you begin to let the poisons out." There was a weight to his words that made me think that telling his story had been as important to him as telling mine had been to me.

And maybe that had been all there was between us: a gratitude built of need and mutual sharing. But it was enough. Because all my life I had been terrified of being judged and found wanting, of being blamed for the very act I had held myself responsible for all these years. But instead—and miraculously—Tom had absolved me. Which was more of a relief than I cared to contemplate.

Still, if he thought I had missed the tracks of his tears when he finally and, very practically, rose to fetch me a box of tissues after I snuffled my dripping nose across my sleeve, he was mistaken. And if I suspected that one or two had gone to his own use before he brought them to me, so much the better.

"Silly, isn't it?" he said eventually. "How the problems of fictional characters can seem so trifling in the face of real life crises?"

I blew my nose once more, loudly, then crumpled the tissue in my hand and looked up at him with interest, not just for the change in subject. I had finally grown accustomed to the idea that he was Thomas Moreland, but that didn't diminish my interest in his work.

"Why?" I asked, with perhaps a little too much bright-eyed enthusiasm. "Have you hit a snag in your next novel?"

"Inevitably. In every book, there's a point where the plot goes haring off on its own, and you have to figure out how to rein it back without destroying the story's integrity." He still seemed a bit embarrassed, but at least we were back on more neutral ground. "I can't decide what to do with it. What do you think?"

"I don't know. Follow your heart?" I said.

He stared at me with an odd intensity for a moment, a pale echo of that moment between us on the rug, as if contemplating how far to trust a rabid fan with his as-yet-unformed child. Then he said, somewhat tightly, "Sometimes, circumstances are such that following your heart could do more harm than good. And sometimes you just have to wait to see how a story will unfold, no matter how much some small part of you is certain that everything will turn out for the best."

"I suppose," I said. "But . . ." How far would he trust me with this? Still, he had trusted me with almost everything else, so why not leap boldly into this breach as well? "I could probably help more if I knew exactly what the problem was. What is this book about?"

He almost laughed. "Justice," he said, in a self-deprecating way. "What else?" Then, seeming to gather his resolve, he added, "It's probably easier just to show you." He smiled faintly. "And don't pretend you haven't been dying to see it anyway. There's one scene that's really worrying me. What if I gave you a draft copy tonight, and then you could tell me what you thought?"

"I'd love . . . I mean, I'd be happy to help," I said, trying vainly for a more professional tone. "Do you have an extra copy?"

"No, but I have my master. I'll give you that and print out another for myself tomorrow. Will that work?"

There was no sense hiding my excitement any longer. "Perfectly. And thanks! You're quite correct, of course; I *have* been dying to see it. Though I promise you, there will be no more obsequious fan-girl outbursts. I'm over all that now."

He smiled faintly. "Lo, how the mighty are fallen. I'll be right back, then."

He returned a few minutes later and placed a thick sheaf of papers in my hand. "There you go," he said. "The next Moreland. We'll see how many more of your illusions that will shatter."

"I very much doubt that." I clutched the book to my chest for a moment. "Thank you," I said. "For trusting me."

He just nodded. Outside the wide windows, the fog was lifting, revealing intermittent patches of star-strewn sky. My signal that reality was returning and that it was my time to depart?

"I'd better go," I said, "before the fog starts massing again. But thanks again for dinner. For . . . everything."

He smiled faintly. "I don't know why you keep thanking me for dinners since you persist in cooking them. Not that I'm complaining. Whatever you did with those little lamb things was divine. Will that be a staple at the restaurant?"

"Yeah, I think I've got that one perfected. And it's nice to have an appreciative audience. If it's not fish, Ronan couldn't be bothered."

Tom made some non-committal noise, and silence descended. After a moment, he led the way to the door and opened it. The fog was definitely lifting; it formed a web of expanding holes against the night, like a fishing net unfurled.

I paused on the threshold, one hand on his arm. When he looked down at me, I rose onto my toes and impulsively dropped a kiss on his cheek.

"You have no worries," I said, hoping that covered both reading his book and not betraying his secrets.

His mouth quirked. "I know."

I couldn't think of anything more to say to that, so I turned and walked to my car.

"Cecil?" he called

I turned, with one hand on the car door.

"Thank *you*," he said. And I had the feeling he wasn't talking about the book, either.

THE FOG CONTINUED TO lift as I drove home, my headlights eventually reflecting off nothing more than a faint mist, tiny droplets bleeding against my windscreen. By the time I reached my drive, the sweep of sky was almost fully visible, only faint, blowing curtains of mist still obscuring the trees. I pulled up to the house, acutely aware of the bulk of Tom's book beside me. I was both eager and apprehensive. What if it didn't live up to expectations? What if . . .

The porch lights flooded on as my car activated the motion detectors, illuminating columns of fog as tall and pale as attenuated ghosts. And a dark, motionless figure, equally lean but infinitely more solid, backlit against the lights . . .

My heart stuttered into a panicked beat. *Not again*. I thought. *Not now.*

When would I ever be *done* with this?

I forced myself to open my car door, and get out, but I still kept the vehicle between the figure and myself. "Ronan?" I said, as calmly as I could manage.

Maybe I was the only one to hear the faint quaver in my voice, because he stepped forward easily enough, and it was only when he entered the circle of my headlights that I could see his face.

Ronan, indeed.

I exhaled in a sudden relief that left me limp, but then I noticed that this was not the usual Ronan with his taut energy and mischievous smile. This Ronan's face was staid, composed. The proud arch of his nose, undiminished by the brightness of his smile, was hard and prominent.

Slowly I turned off my headlights and shut the car door, walked towards him.

"What's the matter, Ronan?"

He was silent for a long moment. Then, "Tom again?" he said.

I sighed. "Can we discuss this inside? It's cold out here."

It was even colder to my back as Ronan followed me inside in silence.

I shut the door and keyed on the alarm. "Coffee? Tea?" I asked, turning towards him.

Ronan shook his head.

"Right, then." I walked into the living room, uncaring if he followed.

He did.

I flopped down on the right-hand sofa, then patted the seat beside me. We both were still, instinctually, avoiding the left-hand couch.

"Sit," I said.

He complied.

I glanced over at him. There was no relief to the tightness of his mouth.

"What is it?" I said again.

"Why do you spend so much time over there?" he asked at last, almost plaintively.

"Ronan, I've already explained that. He's a friend."

"But you said you'd be back by eleven. It's almost one in the morning."

I felt a faint, sluggish stirring of guilt. It was true; I had broken the rules. To cover it up, I said, "I'm sorry. But things got a little . . . intense. I lost track of time."

His face closed still further. "Intense how?"

Okay, wrong word. I endeavored to explain. "We were just talking, Ronan. As friends. But he told me some stuff . . ." It wasn't my place to relay it. I had promised Tom; and, besides, they were his secrets to keep. "He just needed someone to listen," I finished lamely.

Ronan peered into my eyes, which were probably still bloodshot from weeping. "You don't need me anymore," he whispered. "You don't want me. I am not enough."

I thought of Richard—nice, kind, decent Richard—who had never made my heart beat even remotely fast. Tom, who . . . Well, best not to think about that. Then I looked over at Ronan, face long and slightly horse-like in repose, and yearned to see the smile back on his face, the light back in his eyes. I could feel the hurt and fear of abandonment radiating off him in palpable waves. Heaven only knew why he considered me so vital to his survival, but it conjured up an intense protectiveness in me.

And the realization that maybe no one got everything in their lives from just one person.

I looked at the hands that had touched me, the body I had caressed, the lips that brought a magic oblivion. The thick, dark hair, always so silky under my fingers that I wished for a whole pelt of it to wrap myself up in. Maybe Ronan and I ultimately wouldn't last, but if I had learned anything this night, it was that you couldn't hold yourself back from the future because of your past. It was worth at least a shot, for all that he had made me feel so far. For the fact that he had come closer than anyone but Tom to penetrating my walls.

And for the fact that it was only when I wasn't with him that I had any doubts. Here, in this room, with just the two of us, I felt even more enveloped than I had at Tom's, with the fog swathed about the house. There, I had at least been aware of the structure around us. Here, with Ronan, there was no more than just our two bodies and maybe a dim awareness of couch at the periphery.

"No," I said, with conviction. "I may go to Tom's, Ronan, but I always come back. To you."

I reached out and touched his arm, which was taut as Ragnarok's back when he was faced with too many strangers. I tried to soothe Ronan with the same touch I used on the seal. It struck me then that Ronan had always made the first move in any encounter—and that I had accepted that as my due. But maybe it was time to turn the tables a bit.

Swallowing down a residual nervousness that I might in some way be found wanting, I reached out and stroked that thick, silky hair; cupped that angular, almost dour face in both hands; kissed those unresponsive lips. I found that I enjoyed discovering his weaknesses, learning that he was just as vulnerable as Ragnarok, in his way.

But, damn the man, he was making me work for it tonight. I let my hands stray to his shirt, slowly unbuttoned it, ran my hands inside, across the smooth planes of his chest and down to the line of scar across his waist and back. He shuddered slightly; I could feel him warming. I leaned forwards, letting my hands dip lower, to his belt buckle, beyond, then fastened my lips to his once again.

He was thawing; no question. In fact, I began to sense he

was teasing me. There was a heat coming off his lips, and his heart was hammering. And no denying that other parts were perking up as well.

Fine, if that was the way he wanted to play it.

I continued to tease him with hands and lips until he growled and rolled me over, and pulled me under the restless tides of his desire.

THAT NIGHT I DREAMED again. I seemed to be having these dreams with more frequency of late. More so when Ronan and I had argued, and emotions were running high, but even on calmer nights, they still seemed to be present. Many of them centered on this house; sometimes Allegra was present. Other times, they had nothing to do with anything I knew. Sometimes they were just simple impressions: lying on a rock in the sun, basking and at peace. Swimming. Undersea scenes; clearly I was becoming as much a child of the sea as any true-born Mainer. Once something dark and turbulent: the sea in a storm. And once something that must have been my subconscious impression of Ronan's encounter with that outboard motor, all bright blood and pain. And sometimes just an inchoate longing, formless and powerful.

Tonight, though, was one of the more vivid, storied ones. And oddly, the ones I could make the least sense of. In this one, I seemed to be having a fight with Allegra. But an Allegra that looked thinner, gaunter, more wasted than she had in previous dreams. An Allegra with hollowed cheeks and shadowed eyes. Abby had mentioned how ill she had looked over the winter, so maybe it was just my mind filling in details, for clearly it was winter now outside the wide windows. There was a dusting of snow on the ground, on the rock ledges of the shore, barely visible in the gathering dusk.

But where last time the house had felt warm and comforting around me, now it felt close and constricting, claustrophobic, like too-tight clothing.

"Why aren't you happy?" she accused me. "I thought this was what you wanted."

"I am happy. And it is what I wanted," I found myself assuring her, almost desperately. "It's what I still want."

"So why do you keep leaving me?" It was so much like my argument with Ronan that I kept expecting her to mention Tom. I knew Ronan was threatened by Tom. How could he not be, when part of me was still in love with the man, had never stopped being in love with him? Nonetheless, I had made my choice, and I had chosen Ronan. It was a choice I intended to honor, but how to make that clear to him? Or to her, since she seemed to be my Ronan surrogate in this argument.

It was suddenly, desperately, important for me to explain; for her to understand. "It's not a question of leaving. I want to be with you; I want *this*. But I can't just abandon my old life, either. I need that, too, occasionally."

"But aren't I enough?" she said, pleading. Ronan's lines.

"It's not that simple. How would you feel if I asked you to stop breathing for me?"

"It's not the same," she said.

"It is! It's who I am. You know this. You've always known it. I can't change my nature for anyone—not even you, who has given me my dreams."

"Why not?" Almost whining.

"Because." A wave of desperation flooded me as I fought to batter back this wall of jealousy and need which threatened to wrap around me and drown me, like encroaching weeds. "Stop it, Allegra. You are smothering me."

And the dream swirled and faded around a bitter cry of denial: "Noooo . . ."

THE FOLLOWING MORNING, I woke alone. The bed still bore the warm imprint of Ronan's body, meaning he hadn't been gone that long. I peered out the window, but for once didn't see him out on the ledges. Instead, hearing a drift of voices from the front of the house, I padded, naked, to one of the windows of the solarium. There was Ronan on the lawn, bare-chested, in earnest conversation with a naked man, but speaking no language I had ever heard.

His companion was older than he by far. His hair was white, as was his beard, and his skin had the papery looseness associated with age. Still, his body was firmer than I would have expected, given the hair and the skin, retaining an impression of wiry resilience. His eyes, black as Ronan's, glittered with life.

I must have made some involuntary sound as I watched them, for I remembered that they both turned to me in surprise, their two heads rotating in unison. Their oddly fluid speech halted and they both stared at me. What was even stranger was that, instead of confronting them, I had simply turned and retreated to my bed, falling almost instantly asleep. So perhaps I only dreamed it, because I woke later to find Ronan still beside me. When I told him what I saw, he only smiled and said sleepily, in a tongue that bore the same fluidity if none of the oddness, "Silly girl. If I were to be found on the lawn with a naked person, it would certainly not be an old man." And proceeded to prove it.

THE DAY PASSED IN a delightful haze, and it wasn't until Monday, on my way to the storefront, that I found Tom's manuscript in a bundle on my car's front seat. I tamped down a surge of guilt and shock. The poor man must have thought I hated it when the truth was . . . What *was* the truth? That Ronan drove it clean out of my head? That one day of passion had made me forget I had the new Thomas Moreland—in manuscript, no less!—and that the author wanted my opinion on it? Whatever had I been *thinking?*

I picked it up the book and turned it over in my hands, frowning slightly, then righted it. Work was tailing off; I only needed half a day at the storefront. I would have time in the afternoon. And, sure enough, when I returned home, Ronan was still at work. With any luck, Tom would be, too. So I gathered up my courage, picked up the phone, crossed my fingers, and dialed.

Some kindly fate was smiling on me, because I got the answering machine.

"Tom," I said, trying not to babble. "It's me; Cecil. I . . . Shit, look, I don't hate your book. I mean, how can I, when I haven't even read it yet? Oh! Which is not to say that when I do read it, I will hate it. I mean, I'm sure I'm going to love it. When I read it. But . . . things came up, and I just didn't. . . . I mean, I just *haven't*. Read it. Yet." I drew a deep breath. "But I will. Soon. Now, in fact. You know, I'm hanging up the phone this very minute to go and read. So I'll, uh, call you later tonight. When I've finished. And I'm sorry if I made you nervous or anything; it wasn't intentional. Honest."

And I dropped the phone back into its cradle as if it had burned me.

Then I scooped up the manuscript, located my beach towel, and marched myself out onto the rocks to read.

I had, I think, developed some romantic idea of reading the latest Moreland manuscript with my seal at my feet—the luckiest girl in the universe. But life always has a way of sabotaging ideas, particularly the romantic ones. For one thing, it was well into October, and the sun no longer possessed the same power it had back in July; I was soon shivering in the faint breeze that blew off the water. And a manuscript, I discovered, was harder to manage than a book. The pages kept ruffling and threatening to blow away, and Ragnarok—who had come up to curl against my leg; the one part of the plan that *had* worked—thought it was a grand game expressly designed for his amusement and kept trying to eat it. The fourth time my seal lunged at me and grabbed the book, I gave up. I wrestled the pages back from him (this, too, he construed as a game), then retreated back to the house with my prize, which was now slightly damp and liberally covered in tooth marks.

Despite the well-gummed condition of the manuscript, I soon found myself as lost in it as I had been in all Tom's other work. The alien structure of the pages—initally distracting—soon vanished as I found myself caught up in the world, plunged into a bluff and wintery Boston that was steeped, as usual, in corruption. The hero was vintage Moreland: the overworked, underdog public prosecutor out for justice. The heroine was a strong-minded public defender with darkly blond hair. They battled in court, and fell in love off, as they both sought to uncover the truth behind the death of a homeless man that was far from the simple case it initially appeared.

Formula, perhaps, but he did it brilliantly, with genuine feeling for his characters and the world they inhabited: none of which were ever perfectly black and white. Like the author himself, I supposed. But, this time around, something about the book read . . . Well, not exactly flat; never flat, for a Moreland. But . . . paler, perhaps? Not that his characters were any less compelling. It was just that, having met their creator, I had begun to realize that even his most fully realized creations were merely fragments of Tom himself, shadows of their infinitely more complex maker.

Also, the more I read, the more I began to see the very process of creation in progress, and it awed me. His finished books were so tight, so polished, you couldn't see the joints, the seams where elements were stitched together. But here, in the rough, I became infinitely aware of the places where the narrative stumbled, began to comprehend the scaffolding on which it was born, and if anything my admiration for him increased. His effortless, soaring plots were underlain by a sweat and grit I had never truly comprehended.

I found myself reaching for a pen, scratching notes into the margins, trying to absorb his vision for the book. He had refused to tell me which was the problem scene, but I knew, almost instinctively, where the trouble lay. And while I didn't have a solution for it, maybe if I talked it out with him, explained why it didn't work, he would be able, once again, to work his magic.

When I reached the last page—which ended, frustratingly, in mid-chapter—I almost screamed. Then did, in earnest, as a dark figure swooped down and whispered, "Boo!" into one ear.

Manuscript pages flew like snow.

"Damn it, Ronan," I gasped. "Don't do that to me!"

He lolled back on the sofa, grinning smugly. Had I not flung the manuscript, I suspected he would have wrestled it from me, like Ragnarok.

"That good, huh?" he said, reaching down to pick up a page. He frowned at it.

Absurdly, protectively, I didn't want anyone to see Tom's unfinished work but me. But neither did I want to reawake Ronan's jealousy. So, "It has its moments," I said lightly, and plucked the page from his fingers. Kneeling down, I hastily gathered the rest into an untidy pile and swept them off to the side of the couch. Then, sitting back on my heels, I returned my attention to Ronan.

"You're back early. How did you get in?"

He pointed towards the French doors, which gaped widely.

"Oh." I glanced at the clock, then rose and peered out at the rocks, expecting to see Ragnarok clamoring for food. But the seal was nowhere to be seen, perhaps annoyed at the abrupt curtailment of our game earlier.

"I have to . . ." . . . *call Tom,* I was going to say, but then Ronan's arms slipped around my waist, his lips nuzzling the back of my neck, and I forgot all about it.

Again.

34

I FORGOT ABOUT IT until Tuesday night, so help me. Work on Seal Island seemed to be tailing off for everyone as the winter approached. I barely had half a days work to do at the storefront these days, and Louis had let Ronan off early on Tuesday afternoon, so I convinced him to accompany me to Ellsworth for some errands.

Sometimes I forgot what a sheltered life Ronan had led, but it lent him a delightful naïveté. To him, the quaint town of Ellsworth held all the bustling excitement of a big city, the shops the exotic splendor of a Far Eastern bazaar.

The days were growing shorter as October deepened, and already the light was slanting golden down Main Street as I led him to The Grasshopper Shop, where I wanted to look for a replacement vase for my mantel. Our progress was not exactly rapid because he had to stop at almost every window, his formidable nose pressed to the glass while his warm breath left clouds on the chilly panes. When we finally reached my target store I left him wandering the aisles while I searched, his deft fingers stroking and petting the merchandise. I found something I felt might suit me, and kept an eye on him while the clerk rang up my purchase.

Just as I was signing my slip, I heard a voice say incredulously, "Cecil?"

I turned to see Abby behind me, her wild hair almost tamed, dressed in far from her usual sweatshirt and jeans. I scrawled out the last of my signature, pushed the receipt across the counter, then reached out and hugged her. What with my ongoing—and Abby's incipient—renovations, I hadn't seen much of her lately, though we did try to talk on the phone at least once a week. Still, it was good to see her face again, vibrant and shining, and I realized how much I had missed her.

"What are you doing here?" she asked.

"I might ask the same of you."

She shrugged minutely and leaned closer. "Checking out the competition. Whenever I am in town, I always make sure to see what the Grasshopper is selling that I—am mean, we—should be. And vice-versa."

I raised an eyebrow. "And do you always wear your best dresses for such covert operations?"

To my amazement, she blushed a vivid scarlet. But before she could answer, the door to the shop tinkled open again and Richard walked in, followed by Jessie.

"There you are," he said. "I parked just down the . . . Oh, hello, Cecil."

He grinned at me over Abby's shoulder and dropped me a wink. I surveyed him. He was dressed rather nattily as well, in grey dress pants and a navy sweater. Dating garb, if I wasn't mistaken. I grinned back, broadly.

"Hello, Jessie. Hello, Richard—and by the way, congratulations. I heard that the Boston Globe liked your seal piece so much, they called to commission you for another on the fishing industry. I've been meaning to call and say how proud I am of you, but now I can do it in person. That's really wonderful."

His face lit up. "Thanks. But I was hoping to tell you myself. Who blabbed?"

"Small island," I said, enjoying the chance to turn the tables for once.

"Indeed. Though I suppose it's I who should be thanking you . . ."

"Or all of us thanking Allegra, for adopting Ragnarok in the first place," Abby inserted. Then she added, with another blush, "We were going out tonight to celebrate."

"As you should," I said, laughing.

She scowled at me. "Jess, why don't you show Richard that skirt you wanted? My partner and I need to confabulate for a moment."

"Sure, Mom. See you, Cecil." Jessie said, dragging Richard away.

Abby towed me in the opposite direction, behind a rack of dishes. "Stop laughing, Cecil!"

I couldn't help it. "So, you finally succumbed, did you?" I exclaimed, when I could no longer see Richard's blond head. "About damn time! How long has it been official?"

She flushed again, more faintly. "A few weeks. I've been wanting to tell you, but it's still new enough that I didn't want to jinx it. Besides, you're never home these days, anyway."

"I am, too!" I protested. "Every afternoon."

"Well, in which case, you never answer your damn phone."

She might have a point there, I realized, flushing faintly myself. The phone had rung several times this week while Ronan and I were . . . otherwise occupied. Now that I thought of it, I hadn't checked the answering machine in longer than I cared to think about. How stupid was that? What if there was an emergency with the storefront?

"Forgetting the phone for the moment," I said, which was exactly what I wanted to do, "how's it going? Dish, girl!"

Abby hesitated. Then, "Good," she said.

"Just good? That's it?"

Her blush flared again, and she grinned. "All right, damn you, great. Happy now?"

"Yes; blissfully. So, what happened to the 'lack of edge' and all?"

"Just a convenient excuse conjured by fear, if you haven't figured that one out already. I'm not good at trusting men after Brian, but Richard . . . He's a really nice guy, and Jessie likes him. He treats me well. And I'm finally beginning to believe I deserve that."

"Of course you do!" I said stoutly.

She laughed. "Yeah, well tell that to the subconscious. Besides . . . He doesn't always treat me with perfect decorum, if you know what I mean."

"Abby!"

"Yeah, and don't I feel a right fool?"

"What do you mean?"

"Well, c'mon; it's embarrassing. I spend half my life running from him, and then when you show up and reject him, I suddenly decide he's worth something and scoop him up? Please!"

"I very much doubt it's like that."

"Of course it's not!" she agreed indignantly, then grinned. "It's infinitely more fun. And, like I said, he does have a bit of an edge after all, buried under all that courtliness and good breeding."

"I'm delighted to hear it." And I was. It was lovely to see

Abby near-giddy with happiness. No one deserved it more.

"And you?" she said. "How's the studly Ronan?"

"He's fine." I peered about the shop for a moment, finally locating Ronan's dark head in the far corner. "He's just over there." Having a sneezing fit from having inhaled rather too deeply of one of the aromatic oils, I suspected.

"Listen," Abby said impulsively. "Do you two have any specific plans? I mean, do you want to join us for dinner tonight, maybe a movie after? I'm sure Richard and Jessie wouldn't mind."

"Are you sure? It's date night . . ."

"It's family night," she said firmly. "And you two are family, too. So are you in?"

"Of course!"

I went over to break the news to Ronan while Richard phoned ahead to the restaurant and Jessie pestered Abby into buying the skirt she had wanted. Abby completed her purchases while I collected my vase and introduced Ronan to Jessie, who was staring at him as if mesmerized. But then again, when Ronan turned on the charm, he was without peer.

"Right; ready?" Abby said gaily, turning away from the register.

In many ways, it was a lovely evening. Except that just when I thought I knew everything about this enigmatic man I was dating, he continued to surprise me—and sometimes not for the best. When we reached the restaurant, which fortunately was not crowded, we all piled around one of the round tables in the corner. Jessie, I noticed, had maneuvered herself next to Ronan, and was still staring at him with the same rapt fascination she regarded my seal. I suspected a crush, and stifled a smile behind my menu. Poor Jessie, I thought; I seemed to be forever stealing her men. Then I turned my attention to the menu. There were a baffling array of choices, and I turned my attention briefly to Ronan. We hadn't been out to a restaurant together before, I suddenly realized with a shock, and he might be a little overwhelmed by all the options.

He was more than overwhelmed. In fact, he was staring at his menu with something resembling panic on his face, his brow furrowed and his lips moving as he tried to sound out the words.

A bolt of pure shock went through me. To my shame, I found myself glancing across the table to Richard and Abby to make sure they hadn't noticed—they hadn't; both were absorbed in their own menus, as for the moment was Jessie—before I leaned over to Ronan.

"Can I help?" I whispered, tamping down a sudden, choking sense of betrayal.

Fortunately, Ronan didn't notice my reaction either, so caught up was he in his dilemma. "Does this say 'chicken?'" he asked softly, pointing. It did. I was about to nod when he added, "And what's vee-al?" He put the accent hard on the last syllable. "Is it fish? Where's the fish?"

His anguish at his confusion was beginning to infect his voice, so I glanced hastily at the seafood section, underlining a choice with my finger. "There's a grilled salmon that looks nice; comes with rice and green beans and a rhubarb compote. Want to try that?"

"Yes," he said. "Thanks." His dark, liquid eyes met mine, pathetically grateful for the help, and I tamped down another surge of guilt.

The rest of the meal went fine, Ronan covering admirably for his lack of knowledge, but I couldn't help chewing the whole thing over and over in my mind. I hated that it bothered me, but it did. It bothered me through dinner, and it bothered me later, as I stood in the movie line with my illiterate boyfriend. I mean, Ronan was still Ronan; nothing had changed but my perceptions. It shouldn't have mattered. But it did. Was I that much of a snob? Or was it just that I was so much a girl of letters? In many ways, books were my life; my lifeline. What could I possibly have in common with a man who couldn't even read? What sort of future did that conjure?

I had always envisioned myself ending up with someone more like Tom, who understood the magic of words. And it was only then I remembered that I had forgotten to call Tom, who must be convinced I despised his book, and I hated myself all the more.

"Are you okay?" Ronan whispered at one point, reaching over to take my hand—just as Richard had taken Abby's when he thought we weren't looking. But unlike Abby, my hand just lay cold and lifeless in Ronan's; I couldn't even bring myself to offer more than a half-hearted squeeze in return.

It *wasn't* okay, and I hated that it wasn't.

Ronan—so mesmerized by the movie that we actually had to remind him, several times, to stop talking so loudly during it—forgot all about the issue, but I could think of little else during the film and on the whole drive home. In fact, I gave myself a firm talking to, nodding at intervals to Ronan's spate of movie-related chatter to pretend that I was listening. Ronan wasn't dumb; occasional phrases that swam out of his analysis amply proved that. He just had a life that lacked certain opportunities. My God, you'd think he'd never even seen a *movie* before, given his level of enthusiasm! Not being able to read didn't make him any less of a valid person.

When we finally pulled into my drive, it was a black night, and I almost expected to see a figure materialize out of the shadows as my porch lights flooded on. But of course Ronan was in the car with me. My lawn was silent and still as I turned off the engine and walked to the house with him trailing behind. I unlocked the door and keyed my code into the alarm pad, then shut the door again behind us and rekeyed the system.

Then I stood there in the front hall, unmoving, Ronan a silent shadow behind me.

"I'm sorry," he said eventually. "It is that important?"

I slowly turned. He was staring at me, his eyes dark with hurt.

"What?" I said desperately, still pretending.

"That I can't read very well," he said. "I've learned—a bit. I can sound some things out if I need to. But . . . The type of life I had was never really conducive to such things. And there weren't really schools where I grew up. Well, not as you'd recognize them, anyway." And he offered a faint grin—the merest shadow of its usual brilliance.

Guilt washed over me anew, but before I could say anything, he added, "I want to learn, if it makes any difference. Will you help me?" His eyes pleaded with me, vulnerable and somehow scared.

Oh, God. What was I *doing*? How could I pass judgment on someone who was already so aware of his shortcomings? How much could I keep hurting the guy? He was just trying to fit into a world he hadn't been born into, and here I was only making it worse, drawing attention to all his shortcomings.

A wave of protectiveness for him washed over me, so strong it was almost palpable. Of course I would help him; he needed me. How hard could it be? I would get books out the library the next time it was open, and teach him. It was another thing we could share; another thing that would bind us more tightly together.

The thought almost seemed to come from outside me, and I started slightly. Was that what I wanted? So why was an insidious voice whispering, somewhere deep inside me, that he becoming too dependent on me? Was I really just his ticket into this other life he wanted? Because I couldn't help noticing that every time I showed signs of pulling away, he started panicking. Was he really that needy, that insecure? I wasn't that far from my own days of crippling self-doubt; I didn't know if I could handle being a crutch for somebody else.

Then he stepped closer and laid his hands on my shoulders, at first tentatively and then with more assurance as I didn't pull away, and brought his lips down to mine. He kissed me until I could no longer string half a thought together, let alone an entire argument.

And all was good again.

THAT NIGHT, EVEN MY dreams seemed to mirror my resolution. I sprawled, stomach-down, on the living room rug in a bright swathe of sunlight that spilled through the wide windows, my chin propped on my hands. Another body nudged up against mine, and a colorful picture book was laid wide between us. Peace and contentment permeated the scene, and I felt my eyes half-close in remembrance of earlier days, of lying warm and deliriously sun-baked on a rock with the waves lapping around me and a some cousin or other jostling companionably against me.

Only those had to be Allegra's memories, not mine—or, at least, my interpretation of Allegra's memories—for when my current companion poked me for my inattention and drew my focus back to the present, it was Allegra who sat beside me. Allegra, cross-legged, her face full, healthy, and alight with joy. She smiled at me, no longer the gaunt creature of my previous dreams, but simply an older echo of what I saw in the mirror every day. Her finger tapped the thick, black letters.

"Again," she said. "What does this say?"

Only maybe it was not Allegra, but me, because—as dreams do—the scene shifted faintly, and now it was recognizably myself cross-legged by a sprawled Ronan, his hair shining luxuriantly by my knee. I succumbed to the urge, running fingers through the dark, heavy pelt, as soft and thick as the fur coats I used to stroke surreptitiously on the subway when I was a kid.

He looked up, his eyes liquid and laughing.

"What does it say?" I insisted.

"What do I care?" he retorted, reaching up for me and pulling me down. I sprawled across him, his body taut, lean, and achingly familiar beneath me. He growled and rolled me over onto the book, the pages crumpling beneath us as he rose to cover me, his lips lowering to claim mine.

It's all going to be okay, now, I remember thinking, quite clearly. *It's all going to be okay.* And then the dream shivered and popped like a bubble.

35

I WOKE LATE THE next morning, still full of the same contentment. The bed was now empty beside me; Ronan was no doubt at work.

I stretched languidly and rose. If I remembered correctly, the library would be open today. I could get some books for Ronan. I showered and dressed in old jeans and an even older sweatshirt, then flung on my coat and headed into town.

The weather was getting noticeably colder now, the leaves almost all off the trees, and I felt a vague moment of disorientation. Fall was usually my favorite season; I loved the earthy smell in the air, the leaves deepening to the color of flame. So how had I missed it, this year? Except perhaps, I told myself, the season passed too fast this far north. For certainly now, there was no warm tint to the air. Bare branches clacked under a sky as hard and clear as blue ice, and what leaves still drifted down were brown and skeletal, crabbing about the tires of my car like spider husks.

I parked in front of the library, which was indeed open, and Mabel greeted me warmly. We chatted for a while, and then I lost myself among the shelves for a bit, sorting through picture books. One in particular caught my attention, something about the bold illustrations reminding of my dream. I wondered, if I opened it, if I would find the page Ronan and I had poured over, crumpled from our bodies.

I smiled faintly at the fantasy and opened the book, then suppressed a shudder at the sight of the thick crease down the center of a page that suddenly looked all too familiar.

Coincidence, I told myself firmly, and I slammed the book shut. I almost returned it to the shelf, but then some impulse made me tuck it among the pile I was checking out.

When I returned to the desk with my choices, Mabel smiled broadly. "Just like Allegra!" she exclaimed. "Did you find her manuscript, then? Or are you thinking of starting one of your own?"

I felt the same momentary disorientation that I had in the car, and stared at her blankly for a moment.

"Allegra's children's book?" she prompted me.

Memory came rushing back. That's right; Mabel had told me that Allegra had been taking out children's books last fall in preparation for writing a book of her own. I hadn't seen hide nor hair of a manuscript or even notes in the house, but then I hadn't looked. And it would serve as a good excuse as any to preserve Ronan's dignity now.

"Yes," I said, forcing a smile. I hated lying, but it seemed the path of least resistance. "I found some notes. I was hoping to finish what she started."

"Wonderful!" Mabel exclaimed. "You must be sure to let me see a copy of the manuscript when you are finished. That is, if you feel comfortable with that?"

"Yes," I said. "That is . . . Fine. Yeah, I'd be happy to have the feedback."

Mabel glowed. "Lovely. And, look, here you've picked Allegra's favorite! How did you know?" She held up the book with the crumpled page.

I shivered again. "I have no idea," I said.

I LEFT THE LIBRARY with my choices not long after, my morning's euphoria slowly eroding under the oddities of the day. The sky which had been so bright when I had driven to the library had now begun to go cold and grey, and a hard, sharp wind was blowing off the water.

When I returned to the house, I dumped the books on one of the hall tables and went out the doors on the back, huddled under the cold sky in my coat, watching the wind whip off the water and wondering why I felt I had forgotten something vital. But what? The restaurant was as complete as it would get for a while; Abby and Caitlyn had mostly shut up The Gull. So this would be my life for the next several months, staring out at the horizon as the days shortened and the waves grew winter-grey.

Fortunately, Ragnarok seemed to sense something of my continued disorientation, for he was more affectionate than he normally was that day, perhaps seeking to cheer. And for a while I did forget my troubles while I fussed over him. But even Ragnarok seemed needier than usual, nuzzling up under my arm with an affection that seemed more than just a ploy for fish, looking up at me out of large, liquid, vaguely mournful eyes that perversely reminded me of Ronan's.

What was it with me and wounded creatures? Or was it just that I was one myself?

I dropped my face into Ragnarok's neck and he actually snuffled my ear and licked my cheek, exhaling a breath rancid with fish into my face. I gasped, reflecting that there were disadvantages to a seal's affection. But still the two of us watched the water with an indefinable yearning until the sound of a truck pulling into the drive disturbed us, and Tom materialized around the corner.

We stared at each other for a long silent moment while Ragnarok wriggled beside me, seeking attention. But Tom ignored the seal, his face tightly shuttered, his walls as fortified as I had ever seen them. There was something almost formidable about his expression.

"You hate it, don't you?" he said eventually. "It's okay, you can tell me. I'm a big boy; I can handle it." But every tight line and angle seemed so say otherwise.

Tell him what? I thought, and then my eyes went wide and my hand flew to my mouth. His book! I had totally forgotten to call him about his book. Again.

I felt my face flood with color, and tears sprang to my eyes.

What was wrong with me? How could I possibly have forgotten?

I think even Tom realized my reaction was too extreme to be feigned, for his expression softened a bit and he said, "Cecil? Are you all right?"

Before I could answer, Ragnarok, irate at being ignored for so long, barked imperiously for attention, and Tom came over and knelt down beside him. Beside me. As he leaned over and rubbed the seal's back, he looked back up at me with half-tilted eyes and added, "Was it a little too much too fast between us? Should I not have told you what I did the night I gave you the book?"

The abrupt change of topic startled me for a moment. "No, not at all!" I insisted, when my mind caught up. "That was . . . intense, but in a good way. Honestly. Why?"

He shrugged faintly. "It's just that you haven't seemed quite yourself since then. I mean, I gave you my book, which is a huge big deal for me, and I did expect to hear from you the next day, and then I got this completely incoherent message, and then more silence. So what's a guy to think?"

"That I am horrible person and that I hated your book, neither of which are true. Or, at least, one of which isn't true. I did love your book, Tom, honestly I did, and I was so honored that you gave me a copy to read. And I *am* a horrible person, and now you'll probably never trust me again. Because I don't even have an excuse, except that . . . Maybe you're right; I haven't quite been myself lately. Ronan and I, we . . ."

'Distracted by love?" Tom said, clearly trying to sound cynical and not quite succeeding.

"No, not love," I said, more harshly than I intended, and Tom peered at me intently. I dropped my gaze. "It's just . . . Well, it's not important," I added. "But it's still no excuse for my behavior. I don't even know if there *is* an excuse for my behavior. But if there is, I offer it abjectly. Honestly I do." I gathered my courage and looked back up at him. As usual, I couldn't read his expression. "So is there any way I get another chance?"

He smile faintly and gave a strangled laugh. "You honestly didn't hate it?"

"Quite the opposite. I mean, there is that one scene where it stumbles a bit—and I know exactly which one you mean, too—but I know you can fix it. I think it's probably just a matter of figuring out Rob's motivations a bit better. Especially when he's trying to determine what he wants from Claudia. But . . ." Then, catching sight of Tom's expression, I made an effort to stem the tumbled flow. "Well, I wrote it all down in the margins, so you can see it. But I think Rob's one of your best heroes yet. I loved that part where his car broke down, and he was out on the streets late at night, and . . ."

Realizing I was babbling again, I trailed off and gazed at Tom somewhat sheepishly.

His lips were curved into half a smile. "So, you really didn't hate it." And, this time, it was not quite a question.

I rubbed Ragnarok's head. "No. Does this mean I get another chance, then? Am I redeemed?"

"Well, I always give everyone a second chance. But," he laughed again, faintly, and shook his finger at me, "you're on probation. So watch it." He tried to keep his voice light, but it was only then that I realized how much I had hurt him.

"I will; I promise. Do you want your manuscript now? It's right inside . . ."

"No, might as well wait. I didn't just come for that, anyway. I brought you more fish, though it'll probably be the last load for a while."

My pulse spiked. "Why?" Was I still being punished for my inattention?

For the first time, the full light of his smile was unleashed. But all he said was, "Because it's almost November, and time for the seals to migrate. By the end of the month, they'll pretty much all be gone until the following May."

Part of me must have sensed this; perhaps this was what accounted for my mood this morning. I found myself clutching at Ragnarok as if I could hold him to me through sheer force of will. "How long?"

"One week," he said. "Maybe two. But seals are creatures of habit, and Ragnarok left early last year, perhaps afraid of being left behind." His voice grew speculative. "I remember it distinctly, because Allegra was so upset about it. She was convinced she would never see Ragnarok again. As it happened, she was right—just for the wrong reasons."

Another silence descended, which Ragnarok filled with

insistent demands to be petted. Since he seemed to be growing hungry, Tom added, "I'll go get the fish."

He rose and retreated around the side of the house while I idly stroked the seal and gazed out over the waves. I could understand Allegra's sense of loss, magnified by the chill, October skies.

Then Tom was back and Ragnarok reclaimed my attention.

"So, how *are* you and Ronan?" Tom asked as he tried to prevent Ragnarok from diving headfirst into the bucket. "All still okay?"

I shrugged and tried to divert Ragnarok with a lone mackerel—only partly successfully. I suddenly didn't feel any more comfortable about sharing Ronan's secrets with Tom than I had about sharing Tom's with Ronan. So instead I said, "It's just . . . Well, maybe it's just the normal adjustment that any relationship must go through when you have to deal with the person as they are rather than how you imagined them to be. You know?"

"Not entirely. You willing to provide details?"

Not entirely. "It's . . . Look, it's really nothing," I said. "Just me, being silly. You know, you imagine Prince Charming on a white horse, then are surprised when he rides up on a bay. Everything's fine, really."

He didn't look convinced, but he let me take the out—almost. "So you're sure you're happy?" he persisted.

"Yes."

"Good. Then why don't you come inside now and tell me everything you loved about my book before I explode?"

I laughed. "Such restraint. But what about Ragnarok?"

He grinned and indicated the seal, who had taken advantage of our distraction to plant himself shoulder-deep in the bucket. Apparently he had finished the fish, for he was now industriously licking the bottom.

"Ragnarok!" I scolded.

The seal backed out of the bucket and looked up at me, his face a picture of wronged innocence.

"You scamp. Go," I ordered him, pointing at the waves. "And you." I indicated Tom. "You come with me, and I'll flatter you until your ears fall off!"

Tom and I passed a magical afternoon going through his book, talking out scenes until ideas escalated and caught fire, glowing like steel in a forge. I was not only forgiven, I was completely redeemed. And I had never felt so alive in my life.

What the hell, I remember thinking quite consciously at one point, *am I doing with illiterate Ronan when I've got* this *with Tom?*

And perhaps he felt it, too, for at one point he abruptly looked up at me and another of those long, tense moments stretched out between us. And I suddenly became aware of where we were.

We had started our confabulation on the couch, but lack of convenient space to spread out the manuscript had driven us to the bedroom where we both perched on the bed, the pages spread out between us. It wasn't much of a barrier. Thus a part of me wasn't surprised when Tom abruptly swept them out of the way and pulled me toward him. It felt inevitable as the tide.

Yet, at the same time, another part of me was stunned into incomprehension. Which was probably why I didn't even move as he closed the distance between us and lowered his lips to mine.

It must have been like kissing a china doll at first, I had so little control over my response. For a moment, I just sat there, numb and passive, as his arms wrapped me. It was only when I felt him stiffen, as if he would draw away, that my paralysis vanished.

I wrapped my arms fiercely around his back and opened my mouth to his, kissing him back with a will. With a sound that halfway between a growl and a groan, he toppled me backwards into the pillows, his body a welcome weight on top of mine. Madness; it was madness. But I no longer cared. My fingers dug into his back and I wrapped my legs around his hips, welcoming his fierce, needy assault of my mouth, giving back every inch as good as I got.

And that wasn't all. Before long, I became aware that he was rock-hard inside his jeans; that my hips, pressing hard against his erection, stroked a perilous rhythm all too close to where I desperately wanted him to be.

He shuddered slightly and pressed tighter. His hand slid up under my sweatshirt, gliding over the bare skin of my belly before rising up to cup a breast.

I gasped—and perhaps that was what brought us both to our senses.

He dropped me abruptly and sat up. He was breathing like a racehorse, sweat beading his hairline.

I doubt I was much better. I was shaking as if I were in the throes of withdrawal; I wondered if my pupils were really as huge and dilated as they felt.

"Wha . . . what was that?" I managed eventually.

"Madness," he said. "Sheer madness. And nothing that should ever have happened." But he did not sound completely convinced, and I was wondering if he was about to repeat it when suddenly there was a click of the front door opening, and Ronan's voice calling, "Hello?"

It hit us both like a bucket of cold water. I had forgotten that, with winter approaching, Louis rarely kept him around more than half a day.

"Hello," I called back, trying to keep my voice steady, my face flaming.

Tom was bent studiously over the bed, gathering up the pages of his novel in no particular order.

"Where are you?" Ronan called.

"Bedroom," I answered. Then, "Tom's here."

Still, by the time Ronan reached the bedroom door—in record time; he must have sprinted—Tom and I were a decorous distance apart, and I had my face back under control. The manuscript lay innocently between us again.

"Hello, Ronan," Tom said.

Ronan barely glanced at him, his dark eyes locked on mine.

"We were just going over his manuscript," I said, nodding at the pages.

"I'm sorry," Tom added, to both of us, or neither. "I should get going. Cecil, thanks for your input on the book. I really appreciate it. Ronan, sorry for interrupting, and thanks for the temporary loan of your girlfriend. She helped me solve a big problem."

It was amazing how inscrutable he looked. His voice was deep and even, his face baring not even a trace of the passion I had seen there, earlier. If I hadn't known better, I could have believed I'd imagined the whole incident.

Who knows? Maybe I had. Even Ronan seemed halfway convinced, his dark gaze flicking to Tom, acknowledging him with a nod.

Tom rose. I followed. "I'll walk you out," I said.

Ronan stiffened.

"No need," Tom said, casually. "I'll show myself out. I know the way." He gathered up his book. "Thanks again, Cecil."

And with that, he was gone, and Ronan and I stood silently side-by-side in the bedroom where we had made love only last night, listening to the sound of the front door shut behind Tom, the rumble of his engine as he started up his truck and drove away.

"Needs a new muffler," Ronan muttered, then turned to me. His eyes were wide and dark.

"It was nothing, Ronan," I said. "Just as Tom told you." It was the first time I had really lied to him, and guilt rose up to choke me. It wouldn't happen again, I vowed. I would find Tom tomorrow and resolve whatever remained unsaid between us. I couldn't hurt Ronan like this again.

And why is his well-being so all-fired important to me?

But it was.

And Tom? The only proof I had that there was anything between us but friendship was the ache of yearning between my legs. It still throbbed, like a void within me. But Ronan could obliterate that too, couldn't he?

"I went to the library today," I told him. "Brought you books. Shall we continue whatever reading lessons you started tonight?"

His face lit up. "You did?"

"I did," I confirmed, and stepped close to kiss him.

His arms tightened around me fiercely as his lips took mine, and the sensation was utterly different than with Tom. Better? Worse? I couldn't have said. It was just different, in all ways that such a thing could be different. I couldn't analyze it more than that—nor, at that moment, did I want to. A void still gaped within me, and I could think of only one way of filling it.

I dragged Ronan down onto the bed where Tom had had me before. I was using him, and I knew it, but I had ceased to care. "It's nice to have you home early," I said, by means of explanation, then wrestled him out of his jeans, shedding mine in turn. He was more than ready for me, which was good, because I don't know how much longer I could have waited.

I took him ruthlessly, both of us still half-clothed, and

rode him hard—as if the savage rhythm of our bodies could hammer Tom straight out of my mind.

And if a small part of me realized that I *still* had not resolved the condom issue, a larger passion hammered that straight out of my mind as well.

I COMPLETELY FORGOT MY resolution to clear things up with Tom, among other things, and five days later, after an hour spent shivering on the shore in my new down parka with a bucket of fish at my side, I realized that even the seals had gone.

Winter had truly arrived.

36

AS THE DAYS GREW still shorter, and the nights colder yet, the hours and days bled insidiously into one another, forming a kind of amalgam. I would cook or read, plan out menu layouts for the restaurant, while Ronan pored over his picture books or glued himself to the television that I had finally broken down and purchased. I had tried to get him hooked on Sesame Street, but he basically loved anything that was on, no matter how erudite or stupid. The whole concept seemed to fascinate him, and I often would find him as absorbed in a program on the History channel as he would be by the most asinine of sitcoms. But maybe he found tidbits of use in both. In fact, I suspect he did.

I didn't even notice it, at first, not consciously. All I was aware of was that, on the few rare occasions we got together with Abby and Richard, Joanna and Tom, or once even Harry and Martha, he seemed to have grown more comfortable with my friends. He interacted with them more naturally, didn't seem as crippled by shyness or intimidation—or whatever it was that had held him back before. And I was delighted, until I realized one day that he was leading Joanna in a conversation almost word for word from a program he had watched only the night before.

Still, if it helped him, who was I to complain about a bit of bad sitcom dialogue in a pinch?

What I could and did complain about was the day I came home from a large shopping expedition to find the TV in pieces on my floor and Ronan disconsolate at his inability both to put it back together and to figure out how it worked. Worse, he prodded me almost without mercy until I went out and bought him a new one.

But what I was most aware of is that it had, finally, given us something to talk about. I still found myself, occasionally and unloyally, comparing him unfavorably to Tom, but having a reliable topic of conversation eased things. Which was probably fortunate, since Tom and I had barely spoken since the incident in the bedroom. And if that wasn't proof Tom regretted the impulse and wanted nothing whatsoever to do with me romantically, then I don't know what was.

And if I still felt occasionally burdened by Ronan, who seemed to bind his life ever more firmly to mine as the days passed, then maybe that was just what a relationship was all about: accepting someone along with their faults, rather than expecting perfection.

There was one odd interval that did stand out in my mind, but maybe because it was the only real break in routine. One afternoon, when I had apparently forgotten to turn off the alarm before going out—thanks, most likely, to a Ronan-orchestrated distraction—I managed to set it off for the first time in months. When the alarm company called and I sheepishly explained it to them, I remember adding, "Well, I may be worse than the burglers, but at least I haven't set it off myself in a while."

"Well, at least a month," the girl who was currently manning the phones said cheerfully. "But then again, I suppose that wasn't you; that was your boyfriend. I remember because he had such a gorgeous voice. What nationality is he?"

"Scottish," I responded, feeling somewhat numb. "When did you say the alarm went off?"

She named the day. Calculating back, I realized it was the night when I was at Tom's, sharing confessions. "Why?" she added. "Is there a problem?" For the first time, she sounded concerned. "He had the right codes," she finished, almost defensively.

"Of course he did. It's no problem at all." Perhaps there was an innocent explanation for why Ronan should be breaking into my house when I was out. After all, I had told him I was going to be home by eleven that evening. And I had found him waiting outside when I got back after one. Perhaps he had just wanted to surprise me and then thought better of it, knowing how jumpy I was about break-ins.

When I confronted him about it, he looked embarrassed and admitted as much, confirming my theory.

"And you've had my codes for *how* long?" I asked.

He just smiled. "Honestly, Celia"—his new nickname for me—"I've been spending how many months with you, and you don't think I've figured out your codes yet?" Of course, I had told him 'selkie;' the other he had probably observed. But I don't know why the thought of Ronan suddenly having full access to my house made me shiver. I had consciously not given him either my code or keys before. But that was probably just a residual echo of my inherent fear of commitment—and ridiculous, anyway. Besides, a child could get through the catches on the French doors. It was easier this way.

Then Ronan sidetracked me and I forgot all about it. Which was probably also not surprising. I was starting to forget a lot of things lately that weren't directly involved in our lives. Abby hadn't been kidding about winter hibernation. As the days grew shorter and the nights grew colder, I began to feel that Ronan and I were building a warm cave around ourselves. Almost every night a fire blazed in one or both of our living room hearths—and they were lovely to make love in front of, too.

My dreams were growing more frequent, as well. No longer isolated incidents, they now came every night, and sometimes during the day when I dozed. Allegra was often there, her face sometimes open and happy, and at others gaunt and troubled, her cheeks and eyes hollow. One in particular I remember clearly, although it was no more than a snippet—and incomprehensible. It was only a few lines of dialogue, but surrounded by such a sense of dread and desperation that it took a few days to shake off the feelings it conjured.

"What have you done?" I shouted, in the dream. "Where is it?"

"I've burned it," she said. "And now maybe you will stop running away!"

"No!" I heard myself cry. And, broken, "I wasn't running away . . ."

I wondered what it meant, but there were always others to distract me. Sometimes I saw myself from the outside, too and, occasionally, Tom—the latter surrounded by a deep aura of suspicion and uncertainty. But more frequently, the dreams were just feelings: sometimes of peace and happiness, sea and water; sometimes a piercing, wrenching yearning. And sometimes a growing, unhappy dread that only Ronan could erase. Because every time I woke from one of these dreams, Ronan would be there, seemingly startled out of sleep as suddenly as me, ready to comfort with kisses and caresses.

And so life went on.

THANKSGIVING WOULD HAVE COME and gone without notice had Joanna not continued her yearly tradition of opening the Myrtle's dining room to all her friends and prevailing upon Jean-Pierre to forgo French cooking for the more traditional American. But being Jean-Pierre, he couldn't resist adding a few flourishes. We had a huge turkey infused with juniper and allspice, oyster stuffing, curried yams, cranberries, and a medley of winter vegetables. And, of course, pumpkin pie. And wine. Joanna opened the doors of her cellar and we partook of the bounty.

It was a lovely evening, free from tensions. Joanna and Tom were there; and Abby, Jessie, and Richard, who seemed more like a family than ever. Ronan and myself. And a handful of gallery owners and other local merchants I had met and liked over the fall and summer, even if I hadn't struck up full friendships with them yet. But as I sat there by Ronan's side, I genuinely felt part of a community. And I could tell, from the glowing expression on his face, that he did, too.

Which delighted me because of the apprehension that had seemed to dominate his preparations for the evening. We had spent the previous day oblivious to the wider world, but I could sense the tension shivering though him as I showered and started to dress.

"This shirt or this one?" he asked me at one point, clearly sublimating his anxieties about being accepted into his choice of clothing.

It was the least I could do to help. "That one," I said. "And don't worry, Ronan. Everyone's going to love you. How could they not?"

He grinned. "If you say so." And bent to kiss me.

"Isn't that the phone?" I said against his lips, thinking I heard a distant ring. But it must not have been, or else his kiss blotted out all else, because when we broke apart it was to silence—save for the wind, rustling along the side of the house.

And ultimately my predictions were correct; Ronan was a screaming success.

It was a magical evening, and I was only vaguely sad that this happiness had to be bought with Tom's absence. According to Abby, he had gone to spend Thanksgiving in Boston with Laura's family, as he had done every year since her death. Harry and Martha were off visiting their son and his family in North Carolina. So it was just us orphans, who somehow contrived not to feel like orphans at all.

So the days went on. And all my worries about how I was going to entertain myself over the long, dark winter vanished as the days continued to blend one into the other. I had decided to finally sort through the last of Allegra's possessions, and had managed to recruit Ronan without too much difficulty into my project. In fact, now that the lure of the television had begun to pale a bit, I suspected he was eager for something else to do. But still, not even I anticipated the enthusiasm with which he rooted through basements and attics and boxes with me. There were even days when I was otherwise engaged when I would see him burrowing into dusty corners and cabinets.

The only thing I missed during these days was Ragnarok—with a fierce, deep ache. My shore seemed so empty without his familiar head bottling off the rocks. So perhaps it was inevitable that I started dreaming of him, too. Maybe it was the only way to reach him.

So while my days were filled with the industry of cleaning, my nights were increasingly dominated by the sea. The other dreams continued, but these new ones joined the mix.

In fact, I wasn't even aware what was happening at first, the lead-in was so familiar. I had grown used to dreams of swimming, darting among the rocks and weeds, the currents sliding over my skin like silk. But then, one day, while chasing a shimmering shoal of fish, I bit down on one eagerly, feeling the sweet bright taste of blood in my mouth, and from then on I knew I had some of my dreams in seal-form.

Maybe that explained why, occasionally, I thought I caught glimpses of a lugubrious seal head bobbing on the waves, still watching—even though I knew all the seals had already gone.

One night, Abby and Tom—newly back from Boston, I supposed—showed up at my door and dragged me out to dinner at the Clamdigger, the only restaurant open year-round. "We were worried about you," Abby said at one point. "You never return our phone calls unless we reach you directly; your machine isn't even accepting messages any more. You're not becoming Allegra, are you?"

I laughed nervously. "I doubt it. Besides, it hasn't been all that long, anyway."

"Cecil," Tom said slowly, raising an eyebrow. "It's December 16th."

Two days from the anniversary of my parents' death; how could I have forgotten?

Though maybe, in retrospect, that was a blessing. This was probably the first year I had not dreaded Christmas coming, feared the first snowfall. But, now that I came to think of it, the snow had been falling without my notice for the past few days, clotting the ground and the trees with veils of white. But that was all part and parcel of the world Ronan and I kept striving to lock outside.

A cold, hard place, inimical to life . . .

Still, December *16th?* "Are you certain?" I asked, then

immediately felt foolish. Of course they knew the date. Which brought up another issue. What was I going to buy Ronan for Christmas?

"Are you okay?" Abby demanded.

"Fine." Then I looked at both their somber faces, and added, "Is this some sort of *intervention*?"

Tom smiled faintly. "We're just checking."

"Well, I'm fine," I said, firmly. "Honestly. Ronan and I have just been—well, I suppose your term for it is best, Abby—'in hibernation.' Nothing more than that. Why go out in this mess if you don't have to?" I indicated to the snow that I had been oblivious to mere moments before.

"As long as that's all it is," Abby said, with a frown.

"Yup, that's all."

Was I trying to convince myself or her?

Abby left to get back to Jessie, but Tom and I lingered over coffee.

"I've been meaning to ask you," I said. "How's the book?"

"I'm almost finished. And I incorporated all your suggestions, so thanks."

Still no mention of that day when he had kissed me—though seeing him again brought back all the old feelings, as strongly as if months hadn't passed in the interim. Instead, we discussed his story for a while, then he added, too casually, "So, do you want to read it when it's done?"

"What a question! Of course I do."

"And you won't take five weeks to get back to me like the time before?"

I flushed faintly. "Honestly, Tom; it was only five days. But I promise. I'll get back to you promptly if it's the last thing I do." *Even if it took every ounce of my concentration to remember.* "How was Boston?" I added, changing the subject.

His face grew quiet. "Hard."

"I'm sorry. It must be tough, constantly being reminded."

"It is, but that part gets a little easier every year. And I suspect that trend will only continue. No, what made the trip particularly difficult was that I finally told Laura's parents that this was the last Thanksgiving I would be spending with them. They didn't take it well. But just because they are still trapped in the past doesn't mean I have to be. So who knows?" He smiled faintly. "Next year I may actually join you at Joanna's. I've been thinking a lot since our conversation last month, and I've decided it's time for me to actively reclaim my own life, to stop dwelling in might-have-beens."

A jolt of pain that was almost physical went through me at his words. I seemed to be the catalyst for a lot of change on this island. First Abby, who had opened her life to Richard and now was happier than I had ever seen her. Then Tom, who would now rediscover his life and fall in love and leave. And I would be left with . . .

Nothing.

. . . with Ronan.

I forced a smile that I hoped was sincere. "That's wonderful, Tom. I'm glad. You deserve some happiness."

"And what about you, Cecil?" His eyes were oddly intense. "Are you happy? Truly? If you say you are, I'll go away and never bug you about it again, but you deserve the best as well."

I nearly wept; I didn't even know what the best was any more. *Was* I truly happy? But if this was what I got, then I suppose I had better be. Because otherwise I had sacrificed it all for nothing. But then, what was there not to be happy about? I had my beautiful house; my beautiful Ronan.

"Yes," I said. "I'm happy." And wondered again who I was trying to convince.

Shortly thereafter, Tom drove me home. "Remember, Cecil," he said at the door. "You still have friends out here, and they still care about you. So try not to be such a stranger."

Then he nodded silently to Ronan; who had padded up to meet me when he heard the sound of my key in the lock, and departed.

37

BUT I REMEMBERED HIS words, and Abby's, the next morning while Ronan was out rummaging through the garage, shifting the heavy boxes that I couldn't lift. I did miss my friends when I thought of them, and I promised myself I would be better. I would try harder. And the least I could do was check if my answering machine was broken, which it must have been if it hadn't been picking up messages.

I found it under a thin layer of dust. It wasn't broken. The tape was just full, the message-counter blinking twenty-five.

Twenty-five? How had I possibly managed to miss twenty-five messages?

Feeling flushed, I hunted for a pad of paper and a pen, then stood poised to transcribe.

November 15th, said the automated voice on the tape, and my heart began to pound. Surely there had to be some mistake . . .

"Hey, Cecil, it's Tom. I was just calling to say that I'm

leaving for Boston in six days, and was wondering if you wanted to grab dinner before I left. Or cook dinner. I'm hankering for some of those lamb things, and I figured practice makes perfect." He laughed. "Call me."

I stood with my pen poised motionless over the paper. No point in transcribing that one.

Beep. November 17th, my machine informed me. "Cecil, it's Tom again. I'm leaving on Tuesday. I just wanted to check in with you. Are you mad at me? Honestly, I don't give a damn about the book. Take as long as you want next time. And you don't have to cook me dinner; I was only kidding. Call me." *Beep.*

November 20th. "Cecil, it's Abby. The renovations on The Gull's annex are almost done, and look glorious! I knew you'd want a tour, so I'm just calling to set one up. Gimme a date, partner, and I'm all yours." *Beep.*

November 20th. "Cecil, Joanna here. Listen, could I presume for a moment and ask you a really obnoxious favor? Jean-Pierre is turning fucking diva on me *again,* pardon my French, and refuses to cook what he calls 'bland, uninspiring peasant food.' Gah! We have this fight every damn year, but I figured that with another chef on the island, maybe you could take over a few of his more apparently onerous duties. Or is this too much to ask? It's three days to Thanksgiving. I'm going to kill myself. Or him. Get back to me?" *Beep.*

November 21st. I was starting to hate the sound of that automated voice. So intrusive, so blandly accusing. "Cecil, it's Tom. Okay, so maybe you are mad at me. But we'll sort it out when I get back. I'm leaving in an hour, and I get back on the 27th. I'll call you then." *Beep.*

November 21st. "Hey, it's Abby. Joanna's in a tizzy, afraid she's offended you. She's apparently called you about seven times, and keeps hanging up on your machine when you won't answer, and since she couldn't get you, she's now decided to call me instead. Repeatedly. Do me a favor, will you, and get her off my back? Every year she loses it. I swear, some people should just be anesthetized for the holidays." *Beep*.

November 21st. "Cecil, Joanna again." Nervous laughter. "Look, forget I said anything. Apparently just the threat of your involvement was enough to catapult Jean-Pierre into action. So no worries. And sorry, again. Sometimes, I think I should just be anesthetized from Thanksgiving to New Years; it would make everything so much easier! And, contrary to appearances, I can't wait to see you and Ronan on Thursday." *Beep*.

I sank down on the couch, my pen slack against my pad, my body likewise limp. A puppet with my strings cut.

November 23rd. "Cecil, are you there? Cecil? Shit. It's Abby. Obviously. Listen, I was just wondering what you were planning to wear to Joanna's tonight. I mean, I'm sure you'll look gorgeous and all, but how formal are you going? I'm standing here dripping, trying to figure out what to wear. I know; I know. Too much information. But it's my first Thanksgiving with Richard and I just want to look good. But I don't want to look, you know, *overdone*. I'm panicking. Call me if you have a chance. Maybe it's me who needs the Valium rather than Joanna." *Beep*.

November 23rd. Tom, sounding tentative. "Cecil, are you there? Damn; I was hoping to catch you before left. You must already be at Joanna's by now. Sorry I missed you. But I just wanted to wish you a happy Thanksgiving. We'll talk when I'm back." *Beep*.

November 25th. Abby again. "I just realized that I had forgotten to ask you last night when you wanted The Gull tour. So call me. But that was fun, huh? Maybe too much fun. I haven't had a hangover like this since high school." Bubbly laughter. "Hope you're doing marginally better." *Beep*.

November 27th. Tom. "I'm back. But let me guess. You've

been abducted by aliens. I hope the Western Spiral Arm is nice. Please call me when you return." *Beep*.

Two artisans, calling me about various projects I had commissioned, reporting progress and delays.

Then back to the usual suspects.

Beep, beep, beep. An endless litany of dates and demands. "Cecil?" "Are you there?" "Are you okay?" "What's going on?" "Why aren't you answering?" "Call me." "Call me!"

Call me . . .

I dropped my head into my hands and almost missed the next message. No one I knew; not even calling for me. I shot upright and pressed rewind, scrolling back to the beginning of the message.

December 4th. "Allegra? It's Carol Patterson here, of Patterson Realty. I know that when I sold you that Seal Island property last year that you said it was a one-shot deal, but I was wondering if you wanted to expand your rental business a little. Because, if so, I have just the thing for you. It's not a large house, but it's on the water and perfect for a summer rental. And maybe by now you've figured just how much those things can net you. This place is on the island as well, not far from both your properties. So call me if you are interested."

The number was not a local one—probably Ellsworth or Bangor—but I scribbled madly, thinking: *What rental property?* And: Both *her properties?*

I barely listened to the rest of the tape—more artisans and tradesmen, interspersed with increasingly frantic messages from Tom and Abby. My mind was too busy spinning over the implications of Carol's message.

I looked down again at my notepad, the numbers hastily scrawled and heavily overscored, my pen absently and obsessively tracing the digits as I thought. Now it screamed up at me, big, bold and burning, as if it had been etched in acid.

I picked up the phone and dialed.

The line seemed to ring interminably, then a machine picked up. "Hello, you have reached Patterson Realty. I'm sorry we cannot answer your call right now. Our office hours from May to September are Monday through Saturday, 8 am–4 pm. And from October to April, we are in the office Monday through Wednesday, 11 am–3 pm. Please either call back during office hours, or leave your message after the tone, and we'll get back to you as soon as we can. Thank you very much, and we look forward to your business."

My mind went dead. Then I dropped the phone back onto the hook and scrambled for my purse. I fumbled out my checkbook, paged anxiously to the back of my deposit book. Yesterday was December 16th. It was the 17th today. I ran my finger across the calendar. December 17th was . . . Sunday. Oh, thank God! Tomorrow. I would only have to wait until tomorrow.

But because I had come to mistrust my memory, I quickly redialed the number, waited through the spiel again, then left a message.

"Carol, this is Cecil Hargrave, Allegra Gordon's niece. I'm calling about the Seal Island property you mentioned on the 4th. I'm sorry I've taken so long to get back to you, but I . . . Please do call me back, if you have a chance. I really need to talk to you. My number is . . ." What the hell *was* my number? Then memory kicked in, and I recited it and hung up.

Somehow, with a sick, nervous sensation, I knew that this was it; that Carol Patterson held the key that would unlock all the secrets that had plagued me for the last seven months. And I didn't know how I was going to make it all the way to tomorrow, but somehow I did—though I tossed and turned so much during the night that I was amazed Ronan didn't end up sleeping in one of the upstairs bedrooms.

I needn't have worried about forgetting; I was electrified.

I stared at the clock, willing the minutes and hours forward. But 11 A.M. came and went without a call. I then tried calling myself—several times, obsessively. When I finally got through to Patterson Realty a little past noon, I was informed that Carol was out on a call and wouldn't be back until sometime after 3. Could she call me then?

I was too numb to do anything but agree.

But twenty minutes later, I was feeling too restless to sit still. I called Abby, but there was no answer. I thought, for form's sake, about calling Joanna, but it wasn't really her I wanted to see. For that matter, it wasn't Abby I wanted to see, either.

I shrugged into my coat, went out, and found Ronan still rustling around in the garage. "I'm . . . uh . . . meeting Abby for lunch," I told him, and prayed she didn't call in the meantime, exposing my lie. "I'll be back in a bit. Will you be okay alone?"

"Fine," he responded, intent on his task and barely seeming to listen to me. So I got into my cold car—which almost didn't start. How long had it been since I'd driven it?—and drove to Tom's.

I could only hope he was home.

He was. "Cecil?" he said in surprise as I announced myself to his tinny intercom, and then the gate pulled back ponderously. I drove up the snowy drive to his house, which loomed even more imposingly from the snow, all hard lines and angles.

He had the front door open before I was even out of the car. He was dressed in a dark blue sweatshirt, black sweatpants, and fuzzy socks, and his breath steamed in the chill air.

"Cecil!" he exclaimed. "This is a surprise. But I'm glad you stopped by; I wanted to talk to you anyway, about something. Come in, come in." And as I complied and he caught a better look at my face, he added, sharply, "What's wrong?"

I felt suddenly overwhelmed—by everything. The house, his nearness, the cold . . . I couldn't even get a coherent word out.

But Tom handled it as competently as he handled everything. He put an arm around my shoulder and ushered me inside, sitting me down in his cavernous living room. "Can I get you something to drink?" he said. "Some hot tea?" He glanced at his watch. "Some lunch?"

He seemed, I noticed, suddenly nervous.

"Tea," I said. Maybe that would settle me. "I'm sorry to trouble you . . ."

"It's no trouble," he assured me. "I was just making some for myself. Look, there goes the kettle now." Indeed, a shrill whistling was echoing through the house. "I'll be back in a sec."

I must have zoned out in the time he was gone, for it seemed he was back in no time, thrusting a steaming mug into my hands.

"Thanks," I said. "I . . . I can't stay long. I have an important phone call coming at three, so I need to be home for that. But . . . I just needed to talk to someone."

"Well, you know you can always talk to me," he said. "So what's the matter? What is this phone call?"

I lowered my nose into the steam coming out of my mug; it was sharp and fragrant, clearing the cobwebs slightly from my mind. "You were right, Tom," I said, looking up. "I've really been out of it." My words came tumbling out in a rush, and he gazed at me in concern, his brows drawing together over his dark eyes.

"There were twenty-five messages on my answering machine," I continued. "*Twenty-five,* backed up from November 15th. That's almost a month. There was one from this realtor; she left it on December 4th. Tom, did you know anything about Allegra purchasing another piece of property? A rental property?"

"A rental property?" Tom repeated, incredulously. He shook his head. "The last thing Allegra would have wanted was to be a landlord. Why?"

"Because this woman who left the message, she said that Allegra had bought this place from her, that she now had another piece of land that might suit. Tom, she didn't even know Allegra was *dead*." I could hear my voice rising in hysteria, and took a deep, calming breath before Tom called out the authorities on me. "I left her a message last night, and talked to one of her colleagues this morning. She's supposed to call me back around 3. I . . . You don't know anything about this, do you?"

"Not a thing. What did you say her name was?"

"Carol something. Carol . . . Patterson, I think. Patterson Realty. Tom, it's . . . I don't know what is happening. What is happening to *me!*" And maybe that was the deepest fear of all. I hadn't been acting like myself for a long time—for longer than I cared to contemplate, really.

Tom was silent for a long moment—so long I feared he was going to call the authorities in earnest. Maybe I *was* going crazy. Otherwise, why did I have this feeling that I was standing on the edge of a long, dark abyss? Finally, "That makes two of us," he muttered.

That caught me off-guard. "What do you mean?"

"When's the last time you've looked at yourself, Cecil? I mean, really looked?"

"I don't know. It's not . . . What does that have to do with anything?"

"Everything, I suspect." He sighed deeply, seeming to debate with himself for a moment. Then he rose and held out a hand. "Come with me for a moment, will you?"

Puzzled, I compiled. He led me not into the guest quarters as I had expected, but into his wing. When he pushed open his bedroom door, I almost balked, but he led me through decisively, and on into his bathroom. He switched on the light.

I was more confused than ever. "What am I supposed to be seeing?" I said, looking around.

"You," he answered. He took my chin and turned it towards the large mirror that covered one wall. Yes, there was Tom reflected, dark hair tossled, chin shadowed with stubble, clearly not expecting visitors. And beside him stood . . . Someone I didn't even recognize. It was a girl, her face gaunt, her cheeks hollowed with strain—making her yellow-green eyes seem huge and intense. Or maybe it was just the fact that they were wide and brilliant with alarm that rendered them so bright. In contrast, her hair was dull and ragged, lifeless.

For a moment, I thought it was Allegra, come to life from some of my more disturbing dreams. But when I flinched, she flinched too, and then I realized it was me. How had I managed to lose this much weight and not notice it? My bones stuck out like a scarecrow's sticks. No wonder Tom and Abby had been worried.

"Oh, God," I said, and suddenly began to shake so violently I almost couldn't stand up. Tom pulled me tight against him, and I clung to him. "What's happening to me?"

"If I didn't know better," he said, "I'd think you were on drugs. You're not on drugs, are you?"

I shook my head, and he scooped me efficiently up in his arms, my head tucked beneath his chin. "Come on; let's get you warm before you shiver yourself to pieces," he said. He carried me back to the bedroom and sat me on the end of the bed, leaving only long enough to fetch a spare blanket from the closet, which he wrapped around my shoulders and held there until I finally stopped shaking.

"I feel like I'm on the verge of something, Tom," I said

eventually. "What happened to Allegra last winter . . . it's happening to me, too, isn't it? And I don't know why. The police seem more than happy to blame the house, but there's something more to it than that. I know there is. Something else that binds the two of us together besides our blood-ties. And I had this unshakeable feeling when I listened to Carol's message that this was going to be the clue that unlocked it all, that freed all the secrets. Do you think I'm crazy?"

He looked down at me—really looked, his gaze delving deep inside me—and I felt myself flush. "No, I don't think you're crazy," he said slowly, after a moment. "I know what I see, and what I see is not right. And I'll do whatever I can to help you get to the bottom of this."

The relief that swamped me was so profound that I almost started shaking again. "Thank you, Tom," was all I could say, humbly.

He smiled slightly, then deliberately lowered his head and kissed me.

It was not a demanding kiss; he wanted nothing from me. But it wasn't a kiss between friends, either. It was warm and giving, and sent electric shivers down my spine.

When he released me, I found myself asking, almost as I had before, "What was *that*? Madness again? Something that shouldn't be repeated?"

One corner of his mouth quirked up slightly in a rueful grin. "Far from it. I'm tired of running, Cecil. From you, from myself. Remember I said earlier that I wanted to talk to you? If you hadn't come by today, I was coming after you, to tell you this." He drew a deep breath, then shifted a hand to brush a trail of limp hair off my cheek. "I realized, several months back, very shortly after you first kissed me, in fact, that I had made a huge mistake. A vast mistake. I was so scared by the thought of caring again, of loving again, that I ran. And by the time I realized how stupid that was, you had already started seeing Ronan. So I told myself to trouble you, not to let my regrets and desires interfere with your happiness. Except," he smiled slightly, and touched my cheek, "you haven't exactly been happy, have you?"

I shook my head. "No, I haven't been happy for a while," I agreed, "although I didn't realize until now just how very unhappy I have been. Ronan is . . . Well, I don't know how to explain exactly what Ronan is, or what he does to me. I don't quite understand it, myself. But . . ." I managed a smile. "Maybe it was only biding time until you came to your senses."

Tom laughed and hugged me tightly. "I've been a great big idiot, haven't I?"

"Perhaps a bit . . ."

"But I love you, Cecil. I've loved you for a while, now. And although I have no reason to expect you to return the feeling . . ."

I pulled his head down to mine and kissed him, hoping that would express what I couldn't otherwise put into words. Because who was I to be the object of Thomas Moreland's affections, let alone Tom Moneghan's?

But he must have gotten the message, because he pushed the blanket from my shoulders and turned me toward him more fully, kissing me until I was breathless.

I was not, I found, the least bit cold any more. In fact, I was burning up. So it was almost a relief when he peeled off my sweater and long-sleeved T-shirt, unhooked my bra with expert hands. His mouth trailed fire down my neck and across my breasts. I slid my hands up under his sweatshirt, finding bare skin.

It was the work of moments to shed it.

His body was bigger than Ronan's; more muscular. But at

this point, I wouldn't have cared if it was grey and covered in lumps. This was Tom. How long had I waited for this?

A singing happiness—a *true* happiness—filled me as he toppled me back against the pillows, still kissing and caressing me as if he could not get enough of the taste and feel of my skin. How could I have gone without this for so many months, and not realized what I was missing? Admittedly, the sensation was in some ways paler than the heady absorption I felt with Ronan, but it was also more powerful, more real. Love versus lust. And in the long run, was there really any contest?

I locked my legs once more around his back and pulled him tighter against me—exactly the pose from which Ronan had interrupted us, all those many weeks ago. Except that we were now wearing fewer clothes. And this time, blessedly, there would be no interruption.

"Feel familiar?" he said into my ear, as if reading my thoughts, the ghost of a laugh in his voice.

"God, yes," I said, half-gasped, as his hand found my breast yet again. "And I remember this, too . . ."

He groaned against my neck as I instinctually found the hard bulge in his sweatpants and rocked against it. "Cecil, God, no! It's been so long, I'm going to embarrass us both if you don't stop that," he panted. "I nearly embarrassed us the last time, too . . ."

I couldn't help it; I had to laugh. And that, too, was a revelation. Ronan and I had never once laughed like this. It was wonderful, more intimate than a kiss.

"Tom . . ."

"Sssh," he said. He sat up slightly, and wrestled my jeans and underwear off my hips, until I lay naked to his gaze. It was more arousing than I could have envisioned. My heart pounded, and raw need pulsed from me.

If he didn't touch me soon, I was going to . . .

His hand stroked unerringly down my belly, making for the cleft between my legs. I moaned and quivered beneath his touch, arching up to meet his fingers, and spread my thighs wider.

He gave a strangled groan.

As did I, when a seeking finger slid deep inside me, his thumb teasing the bud of my clitoris. Unbearable tension gathered in my lower body, and my eyes drifted shut in pure ecstasy as he stroked me to a shuddering climax.

But still I wanted more, and when I opened my eyes again, I saw his face bent over me, his features still taut with concentration. He was still wearing his sweatpants, his erection straining boldly against the fabric.

"Tom . . ." I whispered.

"I know," he said. He stood, briefly, easing the waistband gingerly over his tumescence.

I had never, it seemed, seen an erection harder or more desperate than his. His penis jutted out at a rigid angle, practically purple with engorged blood. I reached toward him, fascinated, but he batted my hand away. "Not now, Cecil," he said, tightly. "Not if you want this to last any longer than about three seconds. This next part will be hard enough as it is."

I refrained from making the obvious comment, just said, "What part?"

He opened a drawer in one of the bedside tables and pulled out a small foil packet. He grinned faintly as he waved it at me. "Always the boy scout," he said. "Give me a minute here, okay?"

He sat down on the bed, his back to me, and after a moment of hard breathing, tore open the packet. I can't even say what it felt like, to see a man this close to losing control because of me. It was both heady and humbling. I desperately wanted to reach out, run a hand along his back, but I sensed this was not the time.

I also couldn't help wondering exactly how Ronan had managed to keep distracting me from this issue . . .

With another deep groan, Tom swiftly unrolled the condom onto himself, then sat and breathed some more. Finally he turned to me, still as painfully hard as before.

"I make no guarantees." he said, his voice thick.

"I don't care. Just . . ."

I pulled him onto me as words failed, and he buried himself to the hilt.

I gasped and clutched him, with a sudden sense of coming home.

Or coming, anyway.

He lasted longer than three seconds—but not by much. Just feeling him inside me triggered me, and that sent him over the edge. We shuddered and climaxed together.

AFTERWARD, WE JUST LAY there, sweaty skin to sweaty skin. Or rather, I just lay there, head pillowed on his chest, while his hands continued to stray idly over my body, stroking and tweaking my nipples, delving down between my legs.

Perhaps embarrassed by the speed of his release (something, I have to admit, that had me crowing in a certain inner triumph), he seemed to feel the need to hold up his end of the coital bargain—figuratively if not literally. And who was I to complain, since he brought me to three more climaxes—albeit slightly gentler and more muted ones—before I was finished.

After that, we drowsed and snuggled some more, and there was a poignant intimacy to that, as well. Eventually he said to me: "I'm sorry. I don't know about Ronan, but I'm not as young as I was, and things take a bit longer to come back then they used to. But don't worry; it will come back. And next time things will last longer, too, I promise."

I grinned, running a hand across his damp chest, and kissed him. "I'm not worried," I said. "I believe you. And I can't wait to put it to the test. But . . ." I gazed at the clock beside the bed. It was nearly 2:30. "It won't be now. I have to get back. Carol Patterson will be calling at 3:00, and I have to make sure I'm home to answer her call."

"You'll tell me what she said?" he asked, frowning faintly.

"Of course."

"And you'll tell Ronan about us?"

"Absolutely. In fact, given that, it's probably best if I come back and stay here for the night, don't you think?"

I meant it to sound flirtatious, but his frown deepened. "Do you think he'll try anything?"

I didn't know. He did seem disproportionately needy at times. How would he act if I suddenly threw him out? I felt a twinge of fear. At hurting him, or at his reaction?

"Shall I come with you?" Tom asked, concerned, sitting up and reaching for his sweats.

I halted him with a hand to his chest and laughed faintly. "I think that is just about the worst idea I have ever heard. No, I'll break up with Ronan myself, thank you. But I'll call you afterward, to let you know it is final. And if you don't hear from me in an hour," I joked, "come find me."

His eyes grew darker, more worried. "Cecil, are you sure?"

"Perfectly," I said. "I'll be fine. But thank you."

"For what?"

"Not for what you think," I said. "For putting everything in perspective, for making me realize I was not crazy. My mind feels clear for the first time in months, and that means more than I can tell you. Whatever happens, I feel like I can face it, now."

"I'm glad," he said simply, and kissed me.

* * *

WE ALMOST GOT DISTRACTED again, but ten minutes later I was back on the road. I *did* feel more clear-headed than I had in a long time. Though, admittedly, I was less than sure of my bold words to Tom. I had no idea how I was going to break the news to Ronan. What if he just sucked me under his particular Ronan-spell again? But fate saved me from having to worry. At least about that. For no sooner had I opened the door to the house than the phone shrilled loudly.

I snatched it up, idly noticing Ronan's dirty lunch dishes unwashed in the sink. A surge of resentment shot through me. Tom, I suspected, wouldn't expect me to clean up after him. How and why had I put up with this for so long?

"Hello?" I said, into the phone.

"Ms. Hargrave? It's Carol Patterson. I'm sorry that I've been out all day, but I understood that you wanted to talk to me?"

"Yes." And suddenly all the anxiety I had shed at Tom's surged back. I peered around, wondering where Ronan had got to.

"What can I do to help you?" she said. "I'm afraid the property I mentioned has already been sold . . ."

"No, that's not what I wanted. Listen . . ."

Hastily, and as coherently as I could, I told her about Allegra's death, the missing money from her accounts. How I was trying to solve a couple mysteries. "I hadn't even realized she had bought a property," I added. "Can I ask you: How much did she pay for it? And where is it located?"

"Goodness!" she said. "I'm so sorry to hear of her death; she was a lovely woman. But let me see what I can do to help. My records are just over . . . Ah, here it is. Right; now I remember. She paid a little over $75,000 for it"—close to the sum that was missing from her accounts—"and most of that was for the water view. The plot itself wasn't that large, and the house itself was kind of small. And painted a rather virulent blue, if I recall, though I'm sure she painted that over."

My knees suddenly felt weak; I had to sit or fall down. "I'm sorry. Did you say *blue*?" Where *had* Ronan gone?

"Yes, a rather unfortunate color for a house. Especially when there's so much of it. So you know the place?"

"I might," I hedged. "What was the address again?"

"122 Drewes Point Road."

Involuntarily, I glanced in the direction of the garage. I couldn't see it from this angle; I wondered if Ronan was still occupied there.

"Thank you," I said faintly, and hung up.

Then sat staring blankly at the walls of number 127 Drewes Point Road.

38

AFTER A FEW MOMENTS, I forced myself to move. I hadn't had time to take my coat off, yet, so I simply opened my front door and went out into the cold.

And cold it was, with a razor-edged bite to the air and low, grey sky that seemed to hover just above the roof of the house. A cold, grey, suddenly claustrophobic day.

It felt somehow unreal.

I walked to the garage. Ronan was still rooting industriously through boxes. What the hell was he looking for? The deed to the house Allegra had bought him?

I clutched my hands together to keep them from shaking, masking a surge of anger. Maybe there was still an innocent explanation for all this, but I didn't want to hear it. Not yet. First, I wanted to see what secrets that blue house contained. Then I would face him, with all my evidence in place. I shivered. How could he work without a coat when it was so damn cold? The sun was was already low in the sky, and a bitter wind was knifing through the clearing. Soon, true darkness would descend. True cold.

I had to move fast, before I lost my courage. Because some things were just not possible in the dark.

"Ronan," I said, trying to keep my voice as level as possible. "I'm going out for a bit again. I have to pick up some things at the store. I'll be back in an hour."

He looked up, vaguely puzzled, a dusty shock of thick, silky hair falling into his eyes. He brushed it absently away. Once, I might have been tempted to do it for him. But not now. Had he been using me all along?

"Again?" he said. I knew that face so well, pinched with a faint frown of bemusement. Or maybe something else—a strange intensity I couldn't fathom, a flaring of darkness in those liquid eyes. And where once it would have thrilled me, I now found it strangely sinister.

I shivered again, hoping he would blame my reaction on the cold.

"Yes, again," I confirmed. "Someone has to get the groceries." My voice came out sharper and harsher than I intended, and he peered at me.

I forced myself to gaze back at him, and the Ronan magic was absent this time, perhaps wiped clean by Tom's touch. What had I seen in this man, anyway, with his mismatched features and that harsh beak of a nose? I couldn't bring myself to touch him, let alone approach him.

But still, struggling for normalcy, I endeavored a smile. "See you in a bit, all right?"

His brows furrowed. And was that a flare of panic in his eyes? "Celia, are you okay?"

"Fine," I said brightly. "Never better." I'd tell him about Tom later; I couldn't handle it now. There were other things to discover first.

I fled before he could offer to accompany me.

It must have been the cold, because at first my hands were shaking so badly I couldn't get the key into the ignition. Then I took a deep breath and let the old walls slip back into place, felt myself cradled in a blissfully cool detachment. I started the engine, shifted into four-wheel drive, released the parking brake, and once again eased the car out onto the road.

126, 125, 124, 123 . . . 122. I suppose I had been hoping there was another blue house along the same stretch of road, but no. This was Ronan's place. Allegra's place. It hardly seemed worth the $75,000 . . .

Some impulse led me to pull the car up under the trees, half hidden beneath the low-hanging branches of the pines. The thin layer of snow on the ground had frozen under a hard cap of ice. It crunched loudly under my car tires, protesting. I turned off the engine, got out of the car, and shut the door, my nostrils filled with the sharp scent of cold, turned earth. And salt water.

Always, salt water.

Wrapping my arms round myself for warmth—or protection—I crunched across the snow to the front door. It had not, until this moment, occurred to me that it might be locked, but when I reached for the knob apprehensively, it turned easily under my hand.

And why not? What was there in this place worth stealing?

It was even grimmer on the inside than it was on the outside. The fading daylight trickled in through grimy windows, greyly illuminating a hopelessly outdated interior. To my left was an L-shaped nook of kitchen, the cabinets prefabricated in a cheap wood-grain, the floor laid with an ugly yellow and brown speckled linoleum, like curdled sewage. The appliances were a sour, avocado green. Before me was a hall, stepped down to a living room which was dark-paneled, with a brown plaid couch and chair set, a scarred coffee table, and a rather fine roll-top desk. The carpet was shag, probably once an orange-brown, but now matted and faded to a nondescript dun.

The door off to my right, now half-closed, must lead to the bedroom and bath.

I eased it open, the hinges creaking ominously in the silence.

The bedroom could have belonged to another house entirely. Its walls were white and clean, hung with the occasional framed print. The dresser, while old and slightly scarred, had clean, well-proportioned lines, and someone had clearly been refinishing it; one side still bore traces of old varnish and sanding. There was a massive and majestically curved sleigh-bed, covered with an elegant, if slightly faded, hand-sewn quilt—in the wedding ring pattern, if I wasn't mistaken.

Allegra's touch, I suspected; I recognized my former aunt's tastes by now.

The bathroom was more of a work in progress. The floor tile, while still a bit grimy, had been bleached as clean as many gallons of Clorox could get it. The walls themselves had been repapered with a cheerful pattern in whites, light blues, and a pale, sea-foam green. The wall tiles had been overpainted, a temporary solution that was already beginning to show cracks and peeling flakes of paint. The tub and sink had been re-enameled, and a plastic shower curtain stamped liberally with fish hung on the rod.

A private joke for Ronan?

I trailed back to the front hall, wondering where to begin. The house was freezing—hardly surprising, given that Ronan had been all but living with me for the past few months. But, though the silence roared in my ears, it didn't feel quite as stale and unused as I had expected. Someone, I thought, had been here—and recently. Though how I deduced that I couldn't have said.

A shiver traced up my spine and I started indiscriminately flinging open doors and cabinets.

The hall closet was empty save for a few, bent wires hangers, one old, dark, wool overcoat that smelled rather strongly of salt and fish, and a pair of knee-high rubber waders. A dusty box on one of the higher shelves contained no more than some old Christmas decorations: coiled strings of lights and a few broken ornaments.

The kitchen cabinets and cupboards were likewise mostly empty, save for a few dented aluminum pots, a chipped collection of Corelle-wear, a few utensils, and a drawer of assorted and mismatched flatware. There was a gallon of milk in the fridge, half-drunk but still fresh—as I discovered when I popped off the lid and took a tentative whiff. Emergency stores? Ronan couldn't get enough of the stuff, and was constantly guzzling through my supplies—and an open box of baking soda. A lone box of tea bags in a cupboard—Allegra's brand.

Nothing in the couch and chair cushions but crumbs and the inevitable handful of change. And as for the roll-top desk—also, I suspected, one of Allegra's additions—it dispensed no more than a few scraps of yellowed paper, though I pulled out every tiny drawer and rooted behind each one for hidden compartments.

The bedroom closet revealed another rod of bent and mismatched hangers, two of which held plaid flannel work shirts—Ronan's, I suspected. There were two musty wool blankets folded on a shelf, and a few old pillows. And, tucked into one corner of the closet floor, a pair of heavy work boots.

I reached for them and turned them over. It had been a long time since I had seen those prints near my greenhouse or on my front steps, but the treads struck a familiar chord. I could have sworn they were the same.

I dropped the boots and kicked them away. One skittered under the bed. When I peered after it, I found nothing else there. But under the mattress, between it and the box spring, were a few dirty, crumpled bills—mostly five and ones, with a scattering of tens and twenties mixed in. *Oh, Ronan*, I thought. *How clichéd.*

The small top drawers of the dresser were filled with an assortment of boxer shorts and socks; I stirred briefly among them, but saw nothing more. A few T-shirts and a pair of worn jeans in another drawer, and otherwise nothing else.

In the medicine cabinet of the bathroom was a tube of toothpaste, shaving cream, and an old razor. A lone, dusty toothbrush in a glass on the sink; a bar of soap and a bottle of shampoo in the shower.

Nothing, damn it. Nothing. How could this be?

The light was starting to go, fading to a muted pink below the clouds. I caught another glimpse of myself in the bathroom mirror. My hair was dusty, and there was smear of dirt across one cheekbone, another on my chin. My face still gaunt and skeletal, but my eyes were blazingly alive and angry. Determined.

I raised my chin and continued my search. On a whim, I returned to the bedroom, pulled out the top two drawers of the dresser and upended them onto the floor. Socks and boxers snowed out—along with a flash of black and blue, shiny and hard.

I flung the drawers away and fell to my knees, rooting through the underclothes in search of the elusive object. I must have missed it before, tucked back behind the piles . . .

But there it was; my fingers closed around the hard, flat edge of plastic.

I pulled it out, then sat slowly back on my heels, staring at my prize.

The light was almost gone; I could barely read the raised

letters on the card. But as I tilted it, holograms flashed, and the gold letters sprang into relief.

ATM, it said across the top. And *First Fidelity Bank.* And at the bottom, searing like fire, *Allegra Victoria Gordon.*

Now I knew, definitively, the connection between myself and Allegra—the one thing we had in common: Ronan.

Shadows massed thickly in the corners of the house. And at my back, a patch of darkness gathered itself and moved.

I screamed and whirled.

Slowly, a face materialized out of the gloom.

"What," Ronan said carefully, in his voice like the sea, "do you think you're doing?"

I COULDN'T MOVE; I couldn't speak. Ronan stepped forward and reached out, I thought to grab the card away. I flinched. Instead, he flipped on the overhead light.

Prosaic electrical illumination flooded the room, revealing the mess I had made. His socks and underwear, upended on the floor. Drawers flung about, the covers on the bed disarranged, the tilted mattress leaking money. A heavy work boot, stamped like an accusation in the center of the carpet. And me still in my coat, with Allegra's ATM card in my hand.

He made no move toward me; his face seemed merely puzzled.

Made bold by this, I stood and held out the card. "What," I unconsciously echoed him, "is this?"

He peered down at it, his expression barely changing, and I suddenly began to wonder if he was capable of affect at all. Capable of love.

"Allegra's card," he answered. "My card. My income. Which you cut off."

There was an emotion there now: anger. *My fault.*

"You killed her, didn't you?" I accused.

"No. I loved her," he cried, a sudden anguish showing on his face. "She was supposed to have been the one, but she destroyed everything! And then you arrived, looking so much like her, and I thought that maybe you were supposed to be the one, not her. Only you kept fighting me; it was never me you wanted. It was Tom, always Tom." He almost spat out the words. "No matter how hard I tried, I couldn't excise Tom."

I had, it seemed, solved one mystery, only to uncover a deeper one. What was going on?

He paused for a moment, then added, "Do you know how I knew you weren't out shopping? Tom called me."

"Tom? Oh, God. Did he tell you . . ."

"He didn't need to," Ronan said dully. "Your face says everything. You're leaving me for him."

"Yes. I'm sorry, Ronan. I . . ."

Why was I standing here being so calm with a man whom I still suspected had some hand in Allegra's death? Sure he had denied it, but . . . There was more going on here than I was aware of. I knew this guy—in a way. I had shared my house and bed with him, and once again the insidious magic of his presence was starting to work on me. I found myself wanting to trust him, to listen to him, but I knew I shouldn't. Couldn't.

I slammed my walls back up, and something seemed to snap in his eyes. "You think I killed Allegra?" he said bitterly. "Do you know how much I want her back? If only she had lived. If only she had not . . ."

"Not what?"

He sighed deeply, then locked his gaze with mine. "Perhaps I owe you an explanation," he said.

"Perhaps you do."

He turned, and walked from the room.

Not knowing what else to do, I tucked the card into my pocket and followed. He descended the two steps into the living room, turning on the few lights as he did so. Pale illumination seeped out over the carpet. "Sit," he said, indicating the brown plaid chair closest to the fireplace. There was a bucket of fire starters beside it, and a cradle of wood. He knelt and started to build up a blaze in the cold hearth.

Outside the small, high-set windows, the sky was almost fully dark, the glass reflecting the interior of the house, Ronan's industrious back. I curled in the chair he had indicated, listening to the crackle of matches and kindling. When the large logs had started to blaze, he rose and approached my chair.

"You look cold," he said. "Can I at least offer you some tea?"

When I nodded curtly, he retreated to the kitchen. I could hear him banging about as he filled a pot with water, set it on the stove. Then, wiping his hands, he returned to the living room, sinking down onto the sofa across from me.

There was another long silence.

"Well?" I said at last.

He seemed to consider this; his voice had gone quiet as the night. "It wasn't supposed to be this hard," he said. "Maybe that was my problem; that I listened too much to the legends. It was always easy, then. You just shed your skin and went on land. But this modern world is too harsh and cold. There's no room for magic anymore. No room for *us*."

"What are you talking about?" I said, but he wasn't listening to me.

"Jobs and money and proof of identity. No one can live outside the system anymore. I thought this was a small enough island; I thought that Allegra loved the seals enough to understand. But even she couldn't find a way to make me fit, to give me a life. To understand who I truly *was*. She had to go getting greedy, getting jealous of the sea, of all things. As if that had ever been enough for me. I told her and told her—I was the one who wanted out, who wanted the land. Grandfather warned me; he said she was too old, too needy. Too flawed. But she was my only chance, wasn't she? The only one who would—or *could*—believe me."

"Ronan . . ." I felt like I was drowning in his words, unable to ferret out the core of truth. All I knew was that there was something desperate in his voice, something broken.

"I just wanted a foothold," he said. "A way to reestablish the old communities. It was supposed to have worked. But then . . ." He fell into a brief, reflective silence, and in the sudden hush, I could hear the pot rattling on the stove as the water boiled over.

With an abrupt grimace, Ronan rose and retreated to the kitchen. More banging of the cabinets, and then he returned with two steaming mugs. He handed one to me, along with a spoon. The familiar scent of Allegra's beloved raspberry tea spiraled out—the only thing in this crazy room that made any sense.

He sat back across from me, burying his nose in the steam—a gesture I had seen too often in the past few months. I blew on the surface of my own tea, took a sip.

Oblivious to my confusion, he went on. "And then there was you. You never even realized, did you, though I never told you anything less than the truth. You never saw beneath the surface, either."

"Beneath the . . . Ronan, what in hell are you talking about?"

"That I'm a selkie," he said bitterly. "Just like your stupid codes on your stupid door. The truth was right in front of you all along, and you never saw. Why else do you think I don't read, don't drive, don't do any of the other things you damn humans seem to take so much for granted?"

My God, he's delusional! I thought. "So why not just put on your sealskin and swim away?" I countered, humoring him.

"Because," he said bitterly, "she burned it. Don't you understand? She burned it, and now I am trapped here. Trapped and suffering!"

"I don't have time for fairy stories, Ronan," I said, my voice harsh.

"It's not a fairy story." He looked at me directly then, and I almost flinched. His dark eyes were filled with a well of pain and a longing, bleeding off him in palpable waves. It couldn't be true, could it?

Of course not; there was no such thing as magic. But the heat of the fire and the familiar sound of his liquid, rolling vowels nonetheless cast a kind of spell, enfolding me in something that almost passed as warmth. A blanket of calm enfolded me. And the shivering chill—which had crept so deeply into my core that I didn't think it would ever melt—began to thaw. And maybe it was that alone that had me suddenly thinking in a whole new way.

I took another sip of my tea, memories of past dreams crashing over me. Swimming like a seal, the joy in the sea; the profound cry of loss at its lack. Allegra, teaching someone to read, laughing at a dismembered radio. Allegra—haggard, jealous, and desperate. Her voice: "I burned it."

It couldn't be true. *Could it?*

"Who burned your skin?" I asked, in almost a whisper, still unable to believe the words that were passing my lips. *Just humoring him,* I told myself. *Still humoring him.*

"Who else?" he said. "Allegra. She even showed me the ashes."

Kept in a black-and-red lacquer urn on her mantel. Oh my God.

It had to be a lie, but it explained so much. The dreams, the desperation. His love of fish. How he never seemed quite able to cope with the world. It even explained his wound. For what fisherman would start up a boat when there was a child in the water? But a seal? He would be invisible to them, only a creature.

It explained his obsessive searching of my house, hoping against hope that Allegra had been lying, that the ashes were something else entirely. And how he had come running to me not long after I had cut off his back card and his only access to money. His complete dependence.

He, literally, couldn't exist here without me. Without someone.

I took another deep slug of tea, feeling chilled again. Was that all the last five months had been about? Him needing a keeper?

Delusional, I thought again. But I was no longer sure if I was referring to myself or to him.

"Allegra should have been my perfect match," he said softly. "She loved the seals, and she was also so lonely. Nor was she adverse to a little magic in her life."

"So she knew?" I asked incredulously. *Humoring him.* "She knew what you were?"

He smiled, soft and reminiscent. "She watched me change, that first time, when I came to her. She knew all my secrets. And she helped me. Bought me a house, gave me money, helped me craft an identity. Taught me what it meant to be human. Come spring, she was going to take our relationship public. She never needed any . . . persuading."

"Persuading? What sort of persuading?"

"Just a little selkie survival trick," Ronan said. "We can speak to each other mind to mind. Sometimes, things just . . . bleed over."

"Bleed over?" I countered bitterly, thinking back to the past few months. To that feeling that I was encased in a warm and happy cocoon—one that never quite endured when Ronan was absent. "Like trying to convince someone that they are in love with you? That life with you is an endless perfection?"

"If need be. And it worked on you. Once."

"So was that all Allegra was to you? A means to an end? Nothing more than a rock for you to climb onto the land?"

"No! Allegra was different. Maybe it is impossible to be in my presence without a little leakage of my abilities, but I never had to influence her directly. Only *you* needed that." His voice was bitter. "You. Allegra loved me all on her own."

"So what happened? Some random burglar killed her and you had to latch onto her heir for survival—regardless of what that heir really wanted?"

"It wasn't like that! It was all supposed to be perfect. We would slowly take our relationship public, and when I moved in with her for good, the house she bought for me would go to future generations of my family, as a safe house on land. But then . . ."

The heat of the fire, the warmth of my jacket, the hot tea, were all contriving to make me sleepy. I shrugged out of the coat, which helped a bit, and kept my attention fastened on his words. *Humoring* . . .

"Then . . ." His voice was almost inaudible. "I hadn't realized how much I was going to miss the sea. Ironic, isn't it? All my life I yearned for land. And when I finally achieved it, all I wanted to do was to return home. Maybe not forever, but just for a bit. But Allegra had just lost Ragnarok, and she was terrified that she would lose me, too. So she hid my sealskin, and without that I couldn't change back. I started pleading with her to return it, but she wouldn't. And I think my demands only scared her more. I don't know if I was going to leave for good or not . . ."

"But you were considering it? I thought you said you loved her."

"I did," he said, somewhat desperately. "At least, I thought I did. But I do know that I needed her, and that should have been enough. Maybe it would have been, if she had trusted me; had given me a chance."

"But she didn't?"

"No. It was part of me," he cried, "and she destroyed it! She said she loved me, and yet she did this to me! How could she?"

He was weeping openly now.

I remembered Tom's words about Maine, a paler echo of Ronan's cry. And the dreams I had been having. Were the joy in the sea and the pain at its loss simply a vague echo of his feelings, bleeding over into me during sleep? If so, maybe I could understand his suffering. There were times, in the deepest parts of fall, when I, too, had felt it was a poor thing to be a human.

"I didn't mean to do it," he added, "but I was angry, hurting." He was staring at me through tear-blurred eyes. "I didn't mean to hurt her. I didn't even know what I was doing. I didn't believe her at first. How could I not have known? I would have felt it, wouldn't I, when she destroyed a part of myself like that? I started to tear her place apart, looking. But then she showed me . . ." His voice choked. "I went a little mad. I pushed her. She fell, hit her head on the mantel. She was bleeding. She wouldn't stop bleeding!"

Another dream: sitting out on the rocks, weeping, feeling the house a sinister, looming presence behind me. Or, more properly, him. It may have been an accident, but he killed her—destroyed her future as certainly as she destroyed his past.

I felt numb.

"The next thing I knew, Tom was banging at the door and I just fled. And there I was, trapped on the land, and I *couldn't get home*. Not ever. I'm stuck here forever, crippled, and I hate it. I hate it!"

His cheeks were wet.

"But I tried, Cecil; I tried. I used her money—the least she could have given me, after what she did—and tried to be content with this life I had always wanted, this life that was all I had left. I even thought you, looking like Allegra and with your name like a seal, would be my salvation. I tried to make it worth your while; I tried to make it good. But a part of you always fought me. Even when you didn't know it, you fought me!

"It was Tom, getting in the way again. And now you are leaving me for him, and I can't bring you back. I am going to be left with nothing again, and it *isn't fair!*"

The pain in his voice clawed at me. "I can help you," I said. "I'll reinstate you card, help you fix up the house . . ."

But he just shook his head. There was madness flaring from his eyes, and the room was spinning around me. His mania, sucking me under, or had he slipped something into my tea? I struggled to rise, but I had no control over my limbs. I flopped in the chair like a fish.

Ronan was staring at me. Maybe it was just the madness of delusion—his or mine—but I could see the animal in him, now. The seal staring out of his eyes.

A wild creature, untamed. Unaware of human morals. Of human decency.

My heart was hammering. Because Ronan was only partially right. I may have fought him, but I had also spent too much time under his spell to be completely free of him now. His misery was bleeding into me, shredding my soul with diamond claws. Through the roaring of blood in my ears, the sea sang to me, calling me home . . .

"This world doesn't look kindly on those they see as murderers," he said, his voice ragged, "even if they are only victims at first, just fighting back. I'm tired of trying to survive. Maybe if one of you had managed to end up pregnant, there would have been hope. But not now. Not any more. It hurts too much."

Pregnant? I thought with a shock. Had that been the goal, the reason for all the endless lovemaking? God help us all . . .

The pain was flowing out of him in palpable waves, and through its kaleidoscope eyes, I could sense that he could no longer see who I was—if I was myself or Allegra. I, too, felt the boundaries beginning to blur. Our looks, so similar. Our tastes, so alike. Our house, so much a part of us both. Our lover, shared between us . . .

It seemed inevitable.

"I'm going back," he said quietly. "To the only place I was ever happy. And you're coming with me, to see for yourself what you stole from me. The cycle is done."

"Ronan . . ."

His gaze bore down on me. Madness swirled.

I had lived as close to him as his skin for the past five months. How could I escape him now?

And he was right. I could feel the cry of the sea, singing through my blood. Salt calling out for salt, the cradle from which we all arose. I remembered the liquid freedom; the shimmering columns of light, the darting shoals of fish. The slow, waving curve of the watery weeds. It was where I belonged, and to which I must return.

Full circle.

Of course.

How simple.

I no longer resisted as he scooped me up in his arms. I would have walked beside him if I had the strength.

Together, we moved through the back door and across the lawn, out onto the rocks where the restless waves roared and summoned us home . . .

39

THE NIGHT WAS THICK and moonless, brutally chill. The part of me without my coat shivered deeply in Ronan's arms, but it was a remote sensation, barely acknowledged. A heavy fog lay over the water, obscuring both horizon and the farther reaches of the shore, enclosing us in a bubble like a fisherman's float. A puddle of yellow light, bleeding out of the house, weakly illuminated the slick, treacherous slopes of the rocks as Ronan slipped and slid his way down to the margin of the waves, bearing me to the sea.

The tide was almost fully out, exposing a scatting of seaweed- and barnacle-covered boulders, beds of jagged mussels gleaming blackly in the faint half-light. Farther out, there would be the waving beds of kelp, undulating before us like the curtain through which the magical kingdom lay. We would push through it to a land of deep rocks and shoals, gleaming schools of silvery fish darting around our sleek bodies. Weightless, fluid, free . . .

Home.

For an instant, I started to struggle in Ronan's grasp, but his arms tightened around me.

The waves wavered, then refocused.

His animal mind was twined with mine, as inseparable as our bodies when we made love. He knew every curve of me, every crevice . . .

But no. He had said I had fought him, so why couldn't I do so now? Remotely, a part of me knew this was wrong—even as a larger part reached out for the waves, yearning.

Needing.

No, my mind shrieked at me. *Stop. This is not right!*

But it was. It was home. We were going home.

After all those months, the skin was ours.

No! There is no skin. There's a jar of ashes on a mantel. Stop it, Ronan!

But there was a skin, soft as velvet, but thinner, more supple. Skin against skin.

Ours.

We stepped into the waves.

The water was fiercely cold; it bit at our feet, our calves, with teeth of ice.

Or maybe, still dry above the surface of the water, I was only imagining it.

Madness and delusion; revenge and self-destruction. I no longer knew where Ronan's thoughts ended and mine began. I didn't even know what his motives were. Had he fallen under the spell of his own ridiculous tales? For if he believed himself a seal, he couldn't return himself to the sea without his skin. And there was no skin, only ash in a jar. He would drown.

Or was this instead a murderer's act of self-preservation, dumping me to save his own skin, his own life, now that I knew his secrets?

NO! STOP IT. I COMMAND YOU!

My voice, or Ronan's?

Or another entirely, deeper and more commanding?

Alien . . .

We froze, looked out over the waves, the water lapping around our waist. Reality was wavering again. Was that a rock out there on the waves, or a head? A lugubrious, horse-faced head, with wide W-shaped nostrils and a thickly-whiskered lip?

NO MORE, RONAN. HAVEN'T YOU DONE ENOUGH ALREADY?

Our body stiffened with rebellion.

You were supposed to be gone!

I STAYED. TO WATCH YOU.

You've never trusted me. Never!

FOLLY OF YOUTH, HAVE YOU EVER GIVEN ME CAUSE TO? YOU'VE DEFIED US AT EVERY TURN. NO MORE, RONAN. YOU CAN COME HOME AND WEL-COME, BUT LEAVE HER BEHIND. SHE HAS NEVER HARMED US; IT GOES AGAINST OUR CODE.

Wild laughter. *I go against your code; I always have. And what makes you think I'm going to listen to you now when I never have before?*

But before the voice could answer, a pounding of foot-steps echoed from behind us. A figure came bursting through the curtain of mist, running towards us.

"Cecil? Cecil?"

Tom?

"Tom!"

Ronan's voice rose in wordless rage and his arms loos-ened, flinging me into the sea as he raced for the shore.

I landed with a frigid splash that drove all the breath from my body. And the rocks must have dropped off sharply from where Ronan had been standing, because there was nothing but black water under my feet as I tried to flail limbs that had gone abruptly numb from cold and shock.

I lost sight of Ronan and Tom as my head started to slip beneath the water, but I no longer craved the oblivion of the sea. I had already lost all feeling in my feet, and a radiant warmth—or pain—was starting to filter in towards my trunk.

Move, Cecil!

I struggled and beat against the waves, briefly thrusting my head above water in time to see Ronan, head down, launch himself into Tom.

The two went down together.

I managed to scream before I went under again.

"Cecil!" Tom rose and began to run for me, then slid from sight as Ronan tackled him yet again or I sank beneath the waves, I'm not sure which.

Suddenly, a large, black body bumped against me, raising me up. Or were those sinewy arms around my chest, sustaining me? I no longer knew. Shock, cold, and the drugs were sending the world sliding in and out of focus. But somehow there were rocks again under my feet, and I was flailing my way to shore to collapse, coughing and panting, across a boulder.

Cold air knifed through my wet clothes, and I was shaking.

Tom and Ronan were still down in the seaweed bed, their bodies sleek and dark and sinuous as they twisted about each other, fists flying, seeking dominance.

I coughed once more, then tried my voice. "Tom . . ."

No good; I could barely hear myself. I drew a painful breath and tried again.

"Tom!"

Two dark heads froze then raised at my cry, one tracking dark blood from a cut over one eye.

Tom . . .

I essayed a step. The world tilted and slipped sideways.

Canted at a crooked angle, the leaner figure flung itself towards me, but the taller, bloodier one, not far behind, launched into a flying tackle.

In treacle-slow motion, both figures went down . . .

There was a sharp crack, carrying across the damp rocks and through the blowing fog like a shotgun's report, then all went quiet.

I clutched at my rock. Framed crazily in my vision, Ronan lay on the rocks, a dark stain spreading out from beneath his head. And standing over him, half-crouched—panting so hard I could see it shaking his whole body—was Tom. He straightened with a slow, bone-deep weariness, still shaking, wiping the blood from his eyes.

Or maybe the one shaking was me. My teeth rattled in my head, and my arms could no longer maintain their grip on the rock.

Barnacles cut into my cheek as I slid down the wet stone, salt water burning in the wounds. Ronan came erect in my vision, Tom oddly prone. . . .

And then another figure was between us, bare, ropy calves rising from the rock before me like two pale trees. I glanced up the lean, wiry body to the shock of white hair on top, blowing in the breeze.

Something limp, dark, and hollow dangled from his hand. Something that might once have held the shape of a seal . . .

He and Tom faced each other over Ronan's body, a palpable tension flowing between them.

My vision blurred and faded. I was so weary; I just wanted to sleep.

No, Cecil. Don't let go now. Stick with it! Open your eyes! Now!

I didn't know whose voice was shrieking at me, but it was easier to obey than to sink into noisy oblivion. I wrenched my eyes back open.

Reality tilted and wavered.

No, not a man at all. A vast dark seal, nearly eight feet long, graying around head and muzzle—the very one who had been watching me, all these months. Head leaning down to poke at Ronan's limp body, rearing back in rage. As if to say:

WHO ARE YOU TO TOUCH MINE?

My eyes fluttered again, reality sliding away. I was shaking too badly to concentrate, but once, in the brief windows of consciousness when I fought to keep my eyes open, I thought I saw not one seal but two, reared up proudly and in challenge: the ancient patriarch and a younger buck, body sleek with muscles, dark eyes shining. And then, it seemed to me, the old seal bowed with an antique grace, acknowledging I knew not what. Kinship, defeat, peace . . .

But no, it was just Tom and that naked old man I had once seen on my front lawn, conversing with Ronan. Or had that been a dream, too?

And then there was nothing but a naked old man carrying a limp young body into the waves, pausing to pull a dark hood up over his head . . . The silky, dark head of his burden—Ronan's head—floated free and graceful for a moment before sinking beneath the waters. Then Tom's strong arms were around me, blood pouring blackly down his face, and his voice was saying, brokenly, "It's all right, Cecil. You're safe now. You're safe."

I blinked up at him; I could feel the blood pooling wetly under my cheek.

"What day?" I managed to croak.

Was he weeping? "Day?" he demanded. "You crazy, girl, it's December 18th."

Of course. Ten years past, on this very night, my parents

met their end in a dark horror of snow and metal, blood and glass. And now, ten years later, I had stared my own end in the face and come out the other side, if not healed then at least with that possibility shining before me.

And maybe yet another cycle had ended, another circle closed.

At the base of it, life was gift to be savored. And I intended to. Every minute.

I raised a hand, full of grand intentions. "Tom . . ." I began. And my consciousness blinked out like a light.

LATER, I LEARNED THAT I spent four days in the Blue Hill hospital as my body fought off fevers and the effects of severe hypothermia. All I remembered was flashes of sterile white, as disembodied and unreal as my dark visions on that shore as I lay there shaking. But now, as then, there was Tom, who never once left my side. And every time I thought it might just be easier to sink into the black oblivion that sang so seductively to me—a place of fish and waves and weed and liquid freedom—his voice was the one that drew me back.

Be, it seemed to whisper, and I accepted that.

And, gradually, my dreams of water faded, and the hospital sharpened around me.

I will never forget the day I opened my eyes, clear-headed for the first time in months, to see Tom bending over me, his hair limp and dirty, his face gaunt and heavily shadowed with beard. There was a smear of bruise across one cheek, a butterfly-bandaged cut on the opposite temple.

"Cecil?" he said, his voice ragged.

I nodded.

He gathered my weakly-fluttering hands in his, pressed them to his cheek, his heart.

It took several tries to get my voice to work.

"My hero," I finally croaked, with a throat that sounded like it been scoured raw by rocks.

"Cecil," he said, and his eyes were suddenly wet with tears. "I thought I had lost you forever."

I felt my lips beginning to curve in a smile. "I'm not that easy to get rid of," I rasped. "Especially since you promised me things to come. You know; more enduring things . . ." And he laughed through his tears.

They released me the following afternoon. I had sent Tom home that night to clean up and have a proper sleep, but he showed up the next day to collect me, freshly scrubbed and shaved, his collection of cuts and bruises the only indication of his ordeal. He lifted me from the hospital wheelchair they had insisted I use and placed me bodily into his truck. I had expected he would drive me back to my house, but instead we drove to his, the vast, iron gates that guarded his property drawing back silently on our approach. His scarred, ill-sprung—and, according to Ronan, ill-mufflered—truck bounced through and down his drive as the gates whispered shut behind us.

A thicker snow had fallen while I was in the hospital, and now his house rose like a cold and forbidding tor from the snowy ground, vaguely purple in the rising dusk. But it was bright with lights against the growing dark, and inside it was warm and toasty. He carried me across the threshold and into his living room, where a fire was smoldering on the hearth. He settled me on the sofa and tucked a blanket around my legs, then built up the flames.

I was surprised to see a large, and apparently very fresh-cut, Christmas tree off to the side of the fireplace, twinkling with colored lights and balls.

I glanced at him in surprise.

"Surprise," he said. "Happy Christmas Eve, Cecil."

I began to smile. "Do I get a present?"

My voice still sounded like it had been through a cheese grater, but maybe in a few days I could cross my fingers and call it sexy.

Tom folded himself down onto the floor beside me. He cocked his head, his lips slightly curved in a smile. "And what can Santa get you, little girl?"

"You," I said. "You promised. Didn't you?"

"I did. But are you sure?" he asked at last, in a voice almost as ragged as my own. "You've had a legend; I'm but a man. Will that be enough?"

I nodded silently, telling myself I was saving my voice, but really unable to speak. Then I added, "But Tom, I didn't have a legend. I only had a deluded man who believed too strongly in his own tales, and who, in the end, was only trying to save himself from a murder conviction."

Tom was silent for a long moment, the firelight flickering over his face, casting it into shadow. "That's what everyone else thinks. And that's the story that's going around the town. But . . ." Another pause. "You and I know better."

My voice was barely a whisper. "We do?"

He shivered slightly and rested his head against my arm. "How else do you explain what we saw on that beach?" he said at last, so softly I could barely hear the words.

His eyes were fastened resolutely on the flames.

"What did we see?" I countered. "I was woozy with drugs and cold." The doctors had found close to an overdose of sleeping tablets in my system, thanks to Ronan's tea. He could have been drugging me for months, and Allegra before me—all part of his delusion. That would explain my trance-like state, my dreams. "And you had a knock on the head. I would hardly call either of us reliable witnesses. What, exactly, did we see?"

He didn't answer. And maybe denial was the best. For

how else did I fit what I remembered into my view of the world: that old grey seal, at once both man and beast, bowing in respect to Tom's own selkie blood, acknowledging the kinship right of revenge? Drawing his skin up over his head before he descended into the sea? No, better to believe it all a fever dream, a crazy amalgam of drugs, hypothermia, and the seductive words of a charismatic madman.

"What I want to know," I said instead, "is how you found me in time."

Tom laughed faintly and looked back up at me. His eyes were shadowed by the flames, but I thought I was finally learning to read them.

"That was easy; Carol Patterson. I called your house when you didn't call me, as promised. I guess I was worried that Ronan might over-react. But Ronan answered the phone. He told me you had gone out. That didn't seem right, so I drove by your house. When neither of you were there, I raised holy hell with the phone company and started calling every Patterson from one end of Maine to the other until I found the one I wanted. I got the whole story out of her, and drove straight to the address she gave me. The rest you know."

I smiled and rested my shredded, scabbed cheek against his hair. "And I've never seen a more beautiful sight than you, flying through the mist to my rescue."

He laughed, and moved my head so he could to look at me. "I love you," he said. "You know that, don't you? If nothing else, I have learned during these past few months that my life is intolerable without you. Poor Ronan; I think he never actually realized what he had."

I reached out to stroke his cheek. "And you do?"

"Definitively."

"So . . . About that endurance?"

He grinned and pulled me closer. "Ready and waiting when you are, ma'am," he whispered, and—by God—he was.

I smiled and wrapped my arms around his neck, my lips parting under his. He was no Ronan, no creature of moonlight and magic. His mind did not seize mine and draw me under like a tide. The world did not vanish in a swimming, narcotic haze. But there was an enchantment to his kiss nonetheless, and perhaps an even more potent one.

Whatever his doubts, I suspected it would be more than enough.

40

SIX MONTHS LATER, TOM and I were cleaning out the last corners of Allegra's attic, preparing the house for its new tenants.

"Are you sure you are ready for this?" he asked, as he shifted boxes. "This is a big move."

"For you, too," I said. "Isn't the mantra of every writer to never move in with a rabid fan?"

He looked over at me and grinned. Or maybe grimaced. The cut on his head had long since healed, leaving a pale worm of scar. Likewise, in the right light, you could see the tracery of lines that would forever mark my left cheek. But both of us had felt more than our visible wounds heal over the past half-year. So it was with a calm acceptance that he was able to say, "Good heavens, you're right. What ever could I have been thinking?" And smacked himself in the head.

I laughed. I think it still bothered him that I knew his books almost better than he did, but we had worked that out.

And some other issues as well. And maybe no relationship was ever completely perfect, but I suspected that this was about as perfect as it was ever likely to get. And I was happy.

Absolutely happy. No justifications or excuses.

But all I said was, lightly, "Surely that's my line, for agreeing to marry a temperamental writer on the eve of my grand opening?"

"Ha," he replied. "You know it's going to go perfectly, if only because you've managed to get half the island addicted to your cooking before you've even opened."

"Well, it's not my fault that everyone wanted to come round to dinner once word got out that the famous author was no longer quite such a recluse as he used to be."

"Not to mention meeting his fiancée, who brought Allegra Gordon's killer to justice."

Ronan's body never had been found, but somehow that didn't seem to matter. Everyone just seemed to assume that it had washed up somewhere else—and if Tom and I suspected another truth, we never said a thing. It was one of the secrets that bound us.

But that was not the only thing that bound us. And on the day it became apparent that Tom and I no longer had need of two houses, I called Abby and said, "You still haven't found a place to live yet, have you?"

"No, why? Do you know of one?" She and Richard were still dating, but they hadn't yet made the commitment to co-habit. So who better to take Allegra's house, even if it did end up being for only a short while?

"Actually, I have just the thing."

Abby squealed. We had become almost inseparable as the final stages of stocking my restaurant-ware into the new annex of The Gull continued. The inside of the restaurant was all but complete, and I already had a full house booked for opening night.

"He asked you?" she exclaimed.

"He did, indeed. And I said yes. So do you want my house? Jessie will be delighted, because, in a sense, it comes with a seal."

Although, with the lure of a little fish and some guidance, Ragnarok—when he returned in the spring—had leaned where his new feeding place was. But he still could be found sunning on Allegra's ledges of an afternoon.

As for our shore, we had a new guest: a long-nosed grey who lurked off the rocks and would occasionally condescend to be tossed a fish. He seemed to be waiting for something, although we weren't quite sure what.

"You still haven't told me," Tom added, "just what you are planning to call your place."

"A girl's entitled to some surprises," I replied.

"I'll give you surprises," he said in a mock-growl and made as if to grab me. Only he stumbled over a loose floorboard in his attack. It flew up under his foot and smacked him in the chin, and he went reeling back.

I dropped the box I was carting and rushed over to administer kisses and sympathy, but instead I found my husband-to-be on his knees by the hole, peering down into an exposed niche below the floorboards.

"There's something in here," he said.

He inserted a long arm into the hole and fished around while I pried up a few more of the neighboring boards. And before long, we had dragged our prize up into the light.

It was a roll of blanket, about as long as Tom's arm, and surprisingly light. We looked at each other for a long moment, then with a quiet solemnity, unrolled it. Within was a sleek, dark skin, limp and velvety, save for a twisted swathe of scar along one side. There were holes for eyes and mouth, a long slit across the belly. And the unmistakable shape of flippers to either side.

I felt tears prickle my eyes. "She didn't burn it."

Tom shook his head. "I never suspected she did. Allegra would never have done that sort of harm. And in think, in a small, secret part of him, Ronan knew it as well. It was why he kept obsessively searching, every chance he got."

I ran tentative fingers over the skin, still not quite able to believe the proof before my eyes, then folded it back into the blanket.

Still . . . "You know what we have to do." I said.

Tom nodded. And later that afternoon, when the shadows stretched long over the ledges, we stood side by side on the rocks by his shore, waiting for the grizzled head that came every night about this time. Only this time, instead of a fish, we held in our arms the outstretched shape of Ronan's skin—well over six feet in length.

The selkie seemed to start, and then I could swear I saw the hint of a smile curl that lugubrious mouth. He swam toward the shore with silent dignity.

In concert, Tom and I knelt, extending the skin out over the water.

The seal stopped a foot from us, in a frozen tableau. Then, again—unmistakably—he bowed his thanks and swam up the remaining distance. Almost delicately, he seized the center of the skin in his jaws, sliding it off our arms with a toss of his head. His dark eyes held ours for a moment, then he turned and submerged, and the last we saw of him was the twin wakes of Ronan's skin before it and its bearer vanished beneath the waves forever.

Ronan had been right about one thing; there was little place in this world left for the selkies. Or, at least, on this corner of it. Maybe they would find another island—more remote and still traditional—that would keep the old customs alive. But something told me that Seal Island had seen the last of these particular seals forever.

* * *

A WEEK LATER, MY new husband and I stood in my empty restaurant, which was scrubbed and ready for its grand opening the next day. The walls were a pale terracotta, the floors a polished pine. The new tables and chairs gleamed richly, and atop the hand-woven cloths, the bronze-toned plates glowed like jewels. Martha's paintings hung on the walls, and in the place of honor on the far wall—the first thing you saw when you came in the door—was a bold creation of brown and green and yellow which I had first seen in Martha's studio the very week I had arrived in Maine.

Tom took my hand. "You've done beautifully. You must be proud."

"Yes," I said. "I am. Now, we've just got to make it work."

"We will," he said. "I have every faith."

"And, if not," I answered with a whimsical smile, "I've got a rich husband to support me."

His latest book, released just the previous week, had debuted at the top of the *New York Times* best-seller list.

"So, are you ready?" he asked.

"All but for one thing."

Still holding his hand in mine, I drew him out the door and locked it behind us. Then, as a final act, I tugged on the cord of the sheet that covered the hand-painted sign I had put in place the night before. The drapery tumbled down, and the sign shone forth, green and gold in the sun.

Allegra's.

It seemed a fitting tribute.

An Excerpt from . . .

The Challenge

SUSAN KEARNEY

"I'm concerned that there might be someone else on board besides you and me."

Kahn's amber eyes stared at her in puzzlement and his mouth frowned, then he checked his control screen. "We are alone. Why?"

"Someone is touching me."

"Ah, I was wondering when you would bring up that little matter."

That little matter?

He lifted a challenging eyebrow. "Your suit is touching you?"

"Well, it must be broken. It feels as if someone is kissing me and I don't appreciate being fondled. Can you fix it?"

"There's nothing to fix." He spoke with a sincerity she no longer believed.

"Make it stop. Come on, the joke is over."

"I assure you the suit is working perfectly."

She stared at him, flabbergasted. Either he was completely dense or the translator wasn't working properly. She was about to restate her problem when the sensation of two tongues simultaneously licking each of her nipples verified his candor. The man had only one mouth. He couldn't be creating the exquisite sensations that rocked her back on her heels. "What the hell is going on?"

"Your training has begun."

. . . on shelves now!

Windwalker
Natasha Mostert

Mason had said the murdered brother had the same coloring as his mother. So the boy with the fair hair and pale eyes must be Richard. And he had been his mother's favorite, and the artist had captured this moment in which she had placed her hand affectionately on her son's shoulder.

And therefore Adam must be the boy whose dark eyes had been following her ever since she entered the room. Such a very young face, with such a hard, obstinate mouth. An accident waiting to happen, Mason had said. She understood exactly what that meant—she knew all about bad seed.

She left the room, but at the doorway she turned back around. The painted faces looked out at her, and their eyes told her nothing.

Except for Adam's eyes. His eyes were burning.

. . . coming from Tor Romance
in April 2005

An Excerpt from . . .

Do You Believe?

Ann Lawrence

"I'll take my bag, please." She held out her hand. "I need to find my sister." She swept a hand out to encompass the street.

Vic pursed his lips. How could he delay her? Her skin was pale, her freckles like scattered gold dust on white silk. He took a grip of a budding lust.

"Just because your sister hasn't returned a few e-mails doesn't mean she's missing. Maybe she met the man of her dreams."

"Don't." She shook her head "Don't patronize me. I didn't fly over here because my sister failed to keep me informed of her social plans."

"Sorry, mate." He felt a compulsive desire to touch her. She had been his first thought when hunger had struck at dawn. And it hadn't been an English breakfast kind of hunger at that.

"Don't do it again," she said. "Now, good-bye."

"We were going to have tea."

"You can have tea. I want a cup of coffee. Black."

Her bum looked great as she stalked away.

"I have a coffee pot," he called.

She wheeled around and took a deep breath. "Mr. Drummond," she said. "If you can make a cup of coffee as well as you write about fornicating corpses, I'll follow you anywhere."

. . . coming from Tor Romance
in May 2005